A KILLER ROMANTIC COMEDY
GRACIE RUTH MITCHELL

To those who fear they will never truly be seen—your time is here, and your beauty is incandescent. Don't give your energy to the people who don't look for the real you.

CONTENT WARNING—
SPOILER WARNING

This book is a murder mystery, so it does contain a murder. It also deals with infertility.

CONTENTS

IN WHICH HEIDI IS NOT ABDUCTED

If you're looking for a good way to have a heart attack, I've got you covered. Wake up in a bed you don't recognize, in a room you don't recognize, with a blobbish figure hovering over you and shining a light directly into your bleary eyes.

There are several dignified ways to react to such a situation. You could sit up calmly and ask what's going on—effective and efficient. You could pretend to be asleep so that you can eavesdrop on the people in the room, thereby gleaning any helpful tidbits they might drop. You could ask the blob to *please for the love* redirect the spotlight that's blinding you so that you can use your eyes for their intended function.

All of these options are good.

Unfortunately, I do none of them.

I kick the blob instead.

It's instinct, not a well-reasoned decision, but the whole looming thing really freaks me out. I don't know if this is a kidnapping situation or an alien abduction (never say never), but I don't have time for any of that. My foot connects with something soft and squishy, and the figure doubles over with an *oomph*. This is followed by a clatter, and the light disappears.

After that, things become somewhat more clear.

"A doctor?" I say, blinking over at the man with a frown. He has on a white coat, and there's a stethoscope around his neck. "Oh, my goodness—I'm so sorry! Are you okay?"

"I'm fine," the man says, but he's still rubbing his belly where I kicked him.

I look around the room—note the sliding polyester curtain hanging from the ceiling, the IV stand, the pull-out couch—and then glance down at my left arm, where I see a neon bracelet and a needle sticking out of the back of my hand.

The hospital. I'm at the hospital, and he's the doctor.

Why am I at the hospital?

There's no hospital in Sunshine Springs. There's not one in Autumn Grove, either. You have to go all the way to Roberson, a fifteen-minute drive if you're finicky about speed limits— which I mostly am. So who brought me here?

"What's going on?" I say to the doctor. "What happened?"

But before the doctor can answer me, another person enters the room. Tall, scruffier than usual, his blond hair pulled into a stupid man bun.

I hate that bun. I fantasize about chopping it off. And only part of this animosity is due to my jealousy that my hair will never be that lovely or thick or golden.

Still, it's good to see a familiar face.

"What are you doing here?" I say, looking blankly at Soren. I watch him for a second, checking to make sure he's okay— we're in a hospital, after all—but he seems fine, no bumps or bruises. He just stands behind the doctor, his arms folded tightly over his chest.

I look back at the doctor. "Please tell me what's going on."

The doctor holds up his pen light, using it to point to my forehead. "You received a nasty blow. How does it feel?"

"I received—what?" I reach up automatically, wincing in pain when my fingers meet a large, gauze-covered lump on my forehead. "Ouch."

The doctor nods. "Can you tell me your name?"

I swallow. "Heidi Lucy."

He nods, scribbling on his clipboard. "And how old are you?"

"Uh," I say distractedly. I touch my head again, more gently this time, trying to get a feel for the pain.

"You're thirty-one," Soren says after a second of silence, his blue eyes widening on me. He looks at the doctor so abruptly he'll probably have a crick in his neck. "She's thirty-one." Then, turning back to me and rubbing one hand over his scruff, he says, "Do you not remember how old you are?"

"I remember how old I am," I say, frowning at him. "Why are you here?"

"I brought you," he says. "I found you unconscious on the floor of your shop."

He found me on the floor of the bookshop? When did that happen?

I take a deep breath, and then another, and another still. Next to my bed, the heart rate monitor begins beeping faster as my pulse spikes.

What exactly is going on here? There's a vague panic rising behind my sternum, an anxiety I can't place.

Something is wrong. I need to be somewhere else. Doing... something. There's somewhere I need to be.

Where do I need to be?

"And today's date?" the doctor says. He seems unperturbed, which is more than I can say for myself or Soren. Soren is pacing now, but his eyes never leave me; his jaw is tight, his

3

mouth compressed into a thin line. Meanwhile, my heart rate monitor continues to beep faster and faster.

"Miss Lucy," the doctor says in what I think is supposed to be a calming voice. "Take a deep breath, please."

I inhale automatically. None of us speak for several seconds, until Soren throws his hands up in the air.

"*Exhale*, Heidi," he says, abandoning his pacing. He crosses the room and reaches my bed in two long strides, where he reaches over and taps gently on my collarbone. "You're supposed to let the breath out."

I swat his hand away as my breath gusts out of me. Soren resumes his pacing, muttering something that sounds suspiciously like *Don't know how you've survived this long.*

"Miss Lucy," the doctor says again, still speaking gently. I think he's waiting for me to explode; that makes two of us. "Can you tell me the date, please?"

When I answer him, though, his brow furrows and his mouth turns down at the corners. He looks...concerned. Soren shoots him an equally worried look, which has me shifting in my bed.

"What's that?" I say, pointing to Soren's face. "That look. What is that look?" Then, to the doctor, I say, "Is something wrong? Is today not Wednesday?" Except no—that's not right. It's dark outside. Is it still Tuesday?

The doctor blinks at me owlishly. "Today," he says, "is not Wednesday. It is early Thursday morning"—he looks down at his watch—"at approximately twelve-fifteen a.m." He clears his throat, crossing his arms, clipboard still in hand. "You appear to be missing some time."

Maybe it's the head wound. Maybe I'm still regaining all my faculties. Whatever the reason, the doctor's meaning doesn't quite register at first.

"Time?" I say, looking blankly at him.

"Perhaps twenty-four hours," the doctor says. "You don't remember what day it is?"

Wordlessly, I shake my head.

He nods. "Then it seems that you've lost some of your memories."

"Some of my memories?" I say, and that stupid heart rate monitor starts beeping faster again. "What memories?"

And look. I am normally a calm, composed woman. But I am teetering on the edge of some sort of breakdown here. I can feel it in my calm, composed bones.

"We'll get to that in a moment," the doctor says. And his voice is still soothing, but he's moved closer to my bed now, and his eyes on me are more focused, more alert. "Tell me the last thing you remember, please."

"Uh," I say, racking my brain. My memories slide slowly past, a sluggish film playing back. "I went to bed. On Tuesday night," I clarify.

"At what time?"

I clear my throat. "It was...late-ish." *Please don't make me say it,* I beg him silently.

The doctor cocks an eyebrow, inviting me to go on. I look to Soren for help, but the only thing I find there is a crack in his stoic mask—the faintest twitch of his lips.

"She stays up late reading," Man Bun says. "You're probably looking at two or three in the morning."

I glare at him, but he just shrugs, looking unapologetic.

"That's about right," I say grudgingly. I resist the urge to touch my face, even though I can feel my cheeks burning.

I wish Soren didn't know that about me.

"Well," the doctor says, and I give my attention back to him. His frown is deeper than ever as he says, "It looks like we need to run some more tests."

It is roughly one million hours later that I finally get to go home.

Or three. Whatever.

Soren is being uncharacteristically gentle, and it's nearly as strange as waking up in the hospital in the first place. His hand hovers over my bandaged head as he helps me into the passenger seat of his car, and his murmured "Careful" is so low I almost don't hear it.

"Does it hurt?" he says once he gets in, buckling his seatbelt and looking at me.

"Yes," I admit. Even with the ibuprofen they gave me, there's a dull throb in my temple.

He starts the car and pulls out of our parking spot. "I'm sorry."

"Eh." I shrug. "I'm not worried about it." I've grown somewhat adept at sitting with my pain. An odd thing to say, maybe, but it's true. I taste it, touch it, find its textures and flavors and teach myself that no two hurts are the same, no two wounds will ever scar the same way—that some pain is sharp, some is bitter, some is sweet.

Maybe I collect my hurts like children collect spare change on the sidewalk. They don't look for it, but if they stumble upon it, they tuck it in their pocket and ferry it home.

Pain tells me that I'm alive; this pain will be no different.

"My grandmother would call that a goose egg," Soren says, pulling me from my wandering thoughts.

I poke the bump on my head gingerly; I might get a Harry Potter scar out of this. "More like an elephant egg," I mutter.

"Hmm," Soren says. He exhales loudly and shakes his head. "I have bad news for you about elephants and their egg-laying capabilities."

I turn to look out the window so he won't see my fleeting smile. "Yeah?"

"Yeah," he says. When he sighs, though, I look at him. His expression is stormy, his brows pulled low. His arm is draped lazily over the wheel, but the drumming of his fingers gives him away.

Something is wrong. That feeling returns, a nervous fluttering, a tremor in my veins.

"Soren—"

"What's going on, Heidi?" he says at the same time. "You really don't remember anything that happened today? Or yesterday, I guess, now that it's past midnight—whatever."

"I told you I don't." And it's bothering me. "I don't understand what happened."

"You called me," he says. He flicks the turn signal, a little *click-click, click-click, click-click* filling the space between us as he waits to turn out of the parking lot. "At...I don't know. Nine-thirty-ish, maybe."

"I called you?" I say. "That doesn't sound like something I would do." It's mostly true. Soren and I have a bit of an odd relationship. We're friends, I guess, but there's an awareness to our friendship that makes it nearly impossible to relax completely.

He snorts. "Well, you did. And you left a voicemail."

My eyebrows shoot up at this. "Did I?" I never leave voicemails.

But Soren nods, his eyes still trained on the passing cars. He hands me his phone. "Listen to it. It's...odd."

There's a strange note in his voice, something I can't place. I take the phone, swallowing my nervousness. It falls back down my throat and congeals in my gut.

"Passcode," I say, holding the phone out to him.

I expect him to take it and enter the code himself; I don't

expect him to answer immediately. But he does, without hesitation.

"One, zero, one, five," he says.

I start, tapping the numbers in quickly before I forget. "What's the significance?" I say. It's not his birthday.

"It's the date of my first novel," he says.

I look over at him, frowning. "Your first book was published at the end of May six years ago."

Silence. Pure silence, during which I realize what I've said.

"Sometimes, Miss Lucy," Soren murmurs finally, "I get the feeling that you're a bigger fan of mine than you let on."

I swallow. "It's because I remember you telling me, Man Bun. That's all."

His answering hum is musing, maybe even skeptical. "You seem to remember a lot of what I tell you."

"I remember a regular amount," I say, and I keep my eyes fixed firmly on the cars and stores that we're passing. Do I sound normal enough? Unaffected? "So...your first novel?" Because holy crap. Is there a Soren Mackenzie book I haven't read yet? How did I not know about this?

Keep it together. Never let him see you fangirl.

"The first one I ever wrote," he says with a nod. "Not the first one I published. It will probably never see the light of day. It was bad. I shopped it around; no one wanted it. But it was the first one I finished." He glances at me. "Now listen to the voicemail. Just...be prepared."

"Be prepared for what?" I say, but I'm already pulling up his missed calls. It's a good thing I'm not attached to that heart monitor anymore, because my pulse is galloping again, driven by that feeling I can't put my finger on—that feeling like there's somewhere I'm supposed to be.

I find the log of voicemails two seconds later and immediately spot mine, right at the top. With one trembling finger, I press the play button and hold the phone up to my ear.

And I don't know what I'm expecting to hear. I really don't. But whatever I'm expecting...it's not this.

"*Soren,*" my own voice says. It's low, worried, like I'm trying not to be overheard. "*I think I just learned a really scary secret, and now I don't know what to do, and I'm freaking out, so come to the bookshop as soon as possible. Please hurry.*" And on that ominous note, Voicemail Heidi hangs up.

I stare out the windshield for a moment, watching the street lamps whiz by as I try to process. Then I play the voicemail again—once, twice, three times. And by the time I've memorized the message, my mind is reeling.

Crap.

Crap.

Do I have a secret?

I'm not really a secret-keeper. I'll keep confidences, and there are things that I don't share because they're personal or painful, but I wouldn't call those *secrets.*

Has that changed? Is there something I'm supposed to know? Is that what this nagging feeling has been? I feel like the parents in *Home Alone* must have felt before they realized they left their kid behind.

Do I have a kid somewhere that I've forgotten about?

But no—of course not.

That's impossible.

Stupid. *Stupid Heidi.* I swallow the little stab of pain and blink forcefully.

Okay. Focus.

I turn in my seat to face Soren. "I left you this voicemail? I didn't text you or anything?"

Soren shakes his head and then gestures to the phone. "No texts. Go ahead and check."

9

"You're really going to let me poke around on your phone?" I say.

"Sure," he says with a shrug.

"Is your current manuscript on here?"

"Ah," he says, and the word sits awkwardly in between us. "Maybe? But it's trash."

"Oh, come on," I say. "I'm sure it's not—"

"It's trash," he says flatly. "Next subject, please."

"Someone is touchy," I say under my breath. "All right. So I left you this voicemail at..." I trail off, checking the timestamp. "Nine-thirty-eight in the evening. Okay. And then you came to the bookshop, where...?"

"Where you were lying on the floor, bleeding from that gash in your forehead," he says. "So I picked you up and rushed you to the hospital."

I shake my head. "Do you know how weird it is to not have any memories from yesterday?" I look at him again. "Did you see me during the day? Was I at work?"

"You were at the shop," he says with a nod. "I came at ten-thirty—"

"Ooh," I say, wincing. "That means you missed out on your spot."

"Carmina beat me to it, yes," he says, and I laugh at how surly he sounds.

Soren is one of the most faithful patrons of my little bookshop-slash-café, the Paper Patisserie. Almost every day he comes to write, and usually he shows up between nine-thirty and ten in the morning. If he shows up later than ten, his preferred seat has often been taken by Carmina Hildegarde, another regular and a real bear of a woman. She's eighty-something with a short fuse, a horrible temper, and thinly penciled eyebrows, and aside from her family, I'm not sure there's a single person in town who actually likes her. She and Soren have been in a less-than-silent war over seating arrangements for the past year.

"And I suppose you put up a fight," I say now, because Soren is picky about where he sits. He doesn't like people surrounding him, either; he glares at anyone who approaches and throws disgruntled looks around like confetti.

He huffs. "I just don't think she actually *needs* that spot."

"Of course she doesn't," I say with a snort. "And neither do you. It's a seat, Man Bun. You guys are just too petty and stubborn to concede."

"She's doing it to spite me—"

"Plus she doesn't stay for very long. She just eats breakfast. It wouldn't kill you to let her have it until she leaves."

"If I give that woman an inch, she'll take a mile—"

"And speaking of the shop, I do have to ask," I cut him off. "When's the last time you shaved?"

He rolls his eyes. "I'm not having this conversation with you."

"Because you're getting scruffy, and you look meaner when you're scruffy. You scare away my tourist customers."

"Not. Having. This. Conversation," he says pointedly.

"Fine." I fold my arms. It feels good to bicker with him; that's our normal, and *normal* is what I crave more than anything right now. "So I was at the shop yesterday. And everything seemed okay?"

"Everything seemed fine."

Well, that's not helpful. What happened to me yesterday? How did I get this bump on my head?

"Hey, do you have my phone?" I say when I realize it's not in my pockets. "Maybe I called or texted someone else."

"Oh, yeah," Soren says. "I do. Here." He digs in his pocket for a second and then passes me my phone.

"Thanks." I unlock it and check my text messages first, but

it looks like I only sent a few yesterday. One was to Gemma, asking her if she could come an hour early to help me restock. Another was a response to a text thread between me, Eric, and our mom. I open those messages, swallowing hard when I see the photos my mom has sent. She's getting ready to sell the house we grew up in, and I'm still not sure how I feel about it.

I scroll through the pictures, blinking rapidly. The living room is stripped bare, empty save for the spots of sun on the hardwood floor. The kitchen where Eric and I ate breakfast every morning is nothing more than four walls and a floor and the dying echoes of long-ago laughter. The bedroom where I once slept looms emptiest of all, bland and devoid of personality, a blank canvas for whoever will come next.

If I enlarged that photo and squinted, would I be able to see my ghost floating around in that space? Would I see her curled up asleep where the bed used to be? Would I find my childhood in the tracks she wore in the carpet, pacing as she waited for her first crush to call or her broken heart to heal?

And I find myself wondering, not for the first time, if there's a word for when a place that used to feel like home no longer seems familiar.

Time is sort of sad, isn't it?

Though Eric and I grew up in Boise, we both relocated to Sunshine Springs to go to the community college here. I decided to stay, and Eric, ever the wanderer, miraculously decided to stay with me—though I'm sure meeting Gemma had something to do with it. He started a job at an outdoor supply shop, working his way up, and now he helps run the place.

I sigh, rubbing my head absently as we pass the *Welcome to Sunshine Springs!* sign. Sunshine Springs is my home now, small and quaint but picturesque. We have bright blue skies and crisp air, farmland and then the Tetons framing the distant horizon, with vibrant yellow wildflowers springing up in patches along the roads. There's a farmers' market in the town square every weekend, with flower stands and baked goods and produce. Every year we have springs like the one we're having now, full of singing birds and watercolor days where the murky sky bleeds into the horizon and the air is scented with the warm, gritty smell of rain-soaked pavement. Even the winters here hold their own kind of beauty—a landscape layered in white and golden brown; still, frozen, crystalline nights.

This little town holds my life, including the people I love the most. My best friend, Gemma—my twin brother. My little shop and its staff.

My life is here, and for the most part, I'm content.

So what is this nagging feeling I can't place? What secret have I forgotten?

And why was Soren the person I called when I needed help?

🦋 2 🦋

FOUR YEARS AGO

IN WHICH HEIDI ACCIDENTALLY
COMMITS A CRIME

How many dogs is too many dogs?

If you had asked me that months ago, I would have thrown it out as a trick question. There's no such thing as *too many dogs*. The limit does not exist.

But that was before, in the past. And Past Heidi did not know what Current Heidi knows: that the limit very much does exist.

And it is seven.

Seven dogs is too many dogs.

For the most part, I believe in mind over matter. I can do anything I decide to do. And if some of these pups were smaller, it wouldn't be a problem. If I were walking Pomeranians or Dachshunds or Chihuahuas. But I'm not. I'm walking two Golden Retrievers, four Labradors in a spectrum of colors, and one large Poodle.

In fact, let's be more accurate: these dogs are walking me. Because *mind over matter* does not apply to instantaneous muscle growth, or to instantaneous dog-hypnosis skills.

My hands are turning red, rubbed raw by the plethora of

leashes removing layers of skin and cutting off my circulation. The Poodle is a complete hellion, an escape artist if I've ever seen one, and her pull is surprisingly strong as she attempts to run. I underestimated her—probably because of her ridiculous name, or maybe the stupid little poof of fur on top of her head— but I've seen the error of my ways. My leg muscles are now getting in a solid workout, and I'm walking with my body tilted backward at a weird angle to balance out the pull. I'm sure I look exactly how I feel: like a woman in over her head, on the verge of swearing off any and all future pets.

I can't feel my fingers.

When I began offering a dog-walking service a few months ago, I didn't think it would become too much. Dog walking doesn't look difficult. You put them on the leash, you walk them, you return them to their homes. Easy. Plus I was desperate for money, willing to scrape the bottom of any barrel if it meant I could eke out the final funds to start my bookshop. I hung fliers in the nicest neighborhoods in Sunshine Springs— all two of them, streets lined with giant houses and luxury townhomes—and before I knew it, business was zooming my way.

But I'm finally ready to admit that I bit off more than I can chew, what with the other part-time jobs I work on top of this one, and now here I am: being dragged down the sidewalk of a fancy street by two Golden Retrievers, four Labradors, and a Poodle from hell.

"Noodles," I snap at the Poodle. She's making a weird gurgling sound as she continues to pull on her leash. It could not be clearer that she's strangling herself. "Cut it out. You're going to get hurt." I am *thisclose* to turning around and taking her back to her cul-de-sac mansion.

Noodles ignores me, though, which is not surprising in the least. She always ignores me. The other dogs are decently well trained, but all it takes is one bad egg to rile the rest of them up.

Noodles is that egg.

My legs burn as the Poodle and her accomplices drag me up a hill that looks deceptively climbable. The incline can't be more than twenty degrees, but I feel like I'm walking up a freaking mountain. Despite the cool crispness of the spring morning, I am for sure rocking pit stains, and I think there's a pool of sweat in my belly button.

Can't check on that, of course, due to the leashes I'm clutching desperately with both hands.

My breath is coming in sharp, irregular bursts, tearing at my lungs and the back of my throat, but I muscle my way to the top of this stupid hill anyway. I'm trying to channel my inner warrior—someone I should not have to channel for a mere dog-walking job—but she seems to have fled along with the top layer of skin on my hands. I settle for channeling my inner survivor instead, the one who chants *Just one more step* over and over.

"Noodles," I say through gritted teeth. "If you do not cut that out this instant, I am going to turn you into Poodle stew. Stop *pulling—*"

But Noodles, it seems, is about as done with me as I am with her.

And though I will deny it until I'm blue in the face—which may very well be soon, the way things are going—it's almost a relief when her leash slips out of my sweaty, cramped, wildly grasping fingers.

For exactly one second, I allow myself to fantasize. I imagine that Noodles runs away, bolting as fast as her long legs will carry her until she's nothing but a black speck on the horizon, and I'll never have to see her and her head poof again.

Then I pop that fantasy bubble, wrangle my inner survivor, and kick my butt into gear.

"Noodles!" I shout, running after her. The rest of the dogs run with me, a swarming mass of legs and wagging tails and lolling tongues. It's chaos, pure chaos, but all I can do is keep running, because I need this money. "Noodles!" I yell again, trying not to trip over my own feet or any of the dogs. "Poodle stew, Noodles!"

Noodles, the bad egg that she is, does not listen. She just zooms away, down the hill she dragged me up, ears flapping in the wind.

And look. Running through a fancy neighborhood, screaming the word *Noodles* at the top of your lungs? I don't recommend it.

I go down the hill significantly faster than I went up it, my steps thundering along as the dogs strain against their leads. I fly past a woman who's tucking her briefcase into the passenger seat of her car, just as I'm halfway through a shouted tirade that involves the words *Poodle stew* and *minced meat*, so that's unfortunate. I wish I could stop to explain, but I don't have time. I don't stop for the scandalized-looking man taking his trash to the curb, either, or the guy with slick hair and a slick suit heading to his car. I am a sweaty, out-of-breath mess, sprinting through the most affluent neighborhood in town, screaming food-related threats at Noodles the Poodle. So I accept this moment for what it is: rock bottom.

Except rock bottom gets a little rockier when I trip over one of the Labradors.

The world tilts on its axis as I go skidding forward in slow motion, breaking my fall with my elbows, my palms, and pretty much everything in between. The scrape of pain is hot and jagged and sharp, and tears prick my eyes as I push myself into sitting position.

"No—wait—wait!" I say as the rest of the dogs scatter.

It's no good, of course. They abandon me there, every one

of them, and my last, desperate hope is that they'll at least go back to their homes so that I don't get in trouble for losing anyone's precious pooch.

Crap. Can you get sued for that kind of thing?

No time to ponder. I stumble to my feet, pushing a few strands of hair out of my face. Then I do a slow scan of my surroundings, looking for any of the dogs. I need to round up whoever I can.

But there's only one dog left near me: a large, black she-demon standing stock-still across the road in the front yard of a townhome I know for a fact does not belong to her.

"Noodles," I say as I begin to cross the street toward her. I'm holding my arms out at weird angles, as though that will somehow help the pain. It's only when I realize I'm limping that I look down and discover my knees are scraped up too. I shake my head, turning my gaze back to the Poodle.

Noodles looks at me. Cocks her head. Looks at me some more.

It's nuts, but I swear—I *swear*—this dog is daring me to come get her. She is taunting me right now.

"Noodles," I mutter, my eyes narrowing on her as I move closer.

And then I pick up my pace, because there's something about the curve of her tail and the arch of her back that I don't like.

And it happens slowly at first.

She doesn't break eye contact.

She doesn't turn away, either.

Nope. Noodles the Poodle looks me dead in the eye, pops a squat, and does her business—her *business* business—right there on the front lawn of the townhome that does not belong to her.

She drops those Poodle turds, and she stares at me *the whole time.*

I throw my hands up in exasperation. "Noodles!" I scream as I force myself into a stilted run. I can't imagine how deranged I must look, but honestly, I don't even care. I just want this to be over.

And then I might need to look into Witness Protection.

I run toward Noodles as fast as I can, and she shoots off across the lawn, her business completed. For a minute we play a bizarre game of tag in which I shout at her and she dodges my clumsy advances. I breathe a sigh of relief, though, when she darts up the path that leads to the porch.

This is it. I've finally got her cornered.

Except...

I frown. That can't be right.

The front door to this townhome is *open.* It's not gaping wide or anything, but it's definitely cracked.

Why is it open? Who leaves their door like that? Did someone break in?

The Poodle shares none of my concerns.

"No," I shout, my eyes widening. "No—don't you dare, Noodles—don't you—"

But it's no use.

Noodles runs right across the porch, through that open door, and into the townhome.

And following, hot on her heels and breathing like a winded rhinoceros, is me.

THE PLACE IS QUIET.

No, it's more than quiet. It's empty, even though there are sparse pieces of furniture, and it's that emptiness that eases my nerves at entering. The lights are off; there's no noise anywhere. There's a vacant feeling, too, like whoever lives here is in the process of moving out. It reminds me, bizarrely, of my old high school gymnasium. Of the way it would ring with the sound of cheering fans and bouncing basketballs and shouting coaches— only to be completely empty several hours later, lights off, so silent that my footsteps echoed and reverberated from wall to wall, bouncing off all the sleek surfaces, hunting in vain for a place to settle.

That's what this townhome feels like: an empty gymnasium, amplifying the sound of my solitary footsteps.

I shake my head. I need to stop thinking about weird things and find this stupid dog.

"Noodles!" I whisper-hiss, craning my neck to look all around. I don't see her, so I keep moving. "Where are you? Come here now. Noodles!"

I startle when I realize how I'm walking—a weird sort of half-crouching tiptoe that's neither stealthy nor energy efficient. I straighten up, smoothing my hands over my shirt and looking around once again, this time to make sure no one witnessed my idiocy.

No one. I'm good to go.

I'm sticking my head around the corner and into the kitchen—a fancy, largely metallic affair full of sleek surfaces— when my ears catch one very damning sound: a dog's bark, followed by a human shout.

And then more barking, and more shouting, and the little womp-womp sound I imagine my sinking heart is making.

Crap. Crap, crap, crap.

I scramble after the shouts and barks, bypassing the sparsely decorated living room and skidding down a long, wide hallway. At the end of the hallway is a wide-open door, and as I draw nearer, I hear a faint splashing noise from within, followed by a voice cursing.

I peek in, sticking my head over the threshold. It's a bedroom, huge but mostly empty except for a king bed and a chest of drawers. I don't see anyone.

But there's a light coming from a door on the other side of the room, and the sounds I've been hearing are echoing from within. I take a deep breath, trying to get it together.

I am a woman on a mission. I am strong. I can handle this. No Poodle is going to get the best of me. So I march across the bedroom, toward the second door, and step right inside—finding myself in what can only be the master bath.

It's tiled in pristine, gleaming white, with a large glass shower—ooh, double shower heads—and a claw-footed tub in the corner. But that's where my admiration ends.

Because there, sitting in the bathtub and staring at Noodles, is a hulking mass of a man pulled straight from a horror movie.

He's muscular. He's tan. He's probably totally hot, based on the aforementioned muscles.

But he's wearing a mask—white and papery with cutouts for his eyes, nose, and mouth.

And look. I like to keep my wits about me. But I am only human, and that is a *big* guy, and the mask thing is just...bizarre.

So I react like anyone would.

I let out some strange combination of a scream and a yelp, scrambling backward and clinging to the doorframe like it's a bodyguard. The man in the tub yelps in response, and for a second we just stare at each other.

"What the—who—get out!" he says. "Why would you come in?!"

Solid question. It seems briefly like he's going to stand up and chase me away; he starts to move. But then he must realize

21

he's not in a position to be running around, because he freezes. Even with the creepy mask, I can tell that the look he throws me is disgruntled. He sinks back into the tub.

"Take off the mask," I say, which doesn't even make sense. I have bigger worries than this guy's weirdo mask. But I have zero interest in slasher films or psycho creeps, and I will absolutely not put up with any of that nonsense. I can't die yet. I want to live to a ripe old age. I still have things to accomplish. I have *dreams*.

"Excuse me?" the man says. His voice rumbles low, threaded with annoyance and incredulity. The water ripples around him as he covers himself more thoroughly with his arms —not that I'm looking. "If you don't get out of my house immediately, I'm calling the police. This is breaking and entering. How did you get in? Is the dog yours?"

Crap. He's right. But something inside me relaxes the tiniest bit. If he were a killer, he wouldn't be threatening to call the police.

I swallow. "The front door was open," I say. Then I gesture to Noodles. "The dog bolted in. So...it's not really breaking and entering. Just entering. Technically."

This is bad. I am not a criminal, and I do not have time for jail.

The man swears. "That's the second time this week. The latch is broken."

"I know we don't know each other, and that I'm in your place without being invited," I say, trying to calm my racing heart, "but could you *please* take off the mask? It's really freaking me out. You look like the guy in that movie. *Friday the 13th*."

"Mmm," the man says, his voice musing now. "No. That one was a hockey mask."

I frown, thinking.

"Oh," he says, snapping his fingers. *"Texas Chainsaw Massacre."*

"Yes," I say with a nod. "That's it." Then I turn my gaze to the stupid black Poodle who's sniffing around the clawed feet of the bathtub. "Noodles," I say. "I am going to cut you up into tiny little pieces and then sauté you and feed you to your doggy friends if you do not come to me *this instant.*"

The man in the tub snorts. "Better listen to her, Noodles," he says, looking at the dog. "She seems sadistic."

"Sadistic?" I say, my jaw dropping. "I'm not—it isn't—" I break off, pointing to the mask still covering his face. "You're the one wearing a mask."

"It's a Korean sheet mask," he says defensively. "It's moisturizing. And hey—what I do in the privacy of my own bathroom is none of your business. I don't need to explain myself to you." Then he reaches up, peels the mask off, and points to the bathroom door. "Get out of my house, and take your dog with you."

For the first time, I can see what the man looks like—blond hair down to his shoulders, scruff a few shades darker, and the bluest eyes I've ever seen. I swallow. Blink. Clear my throat.

I've seen this man before.

Soren Mackenzie.

The Soren Mackenzie.

Crappity crappity crap.

"Noodles," I snap, forcing my gaze to the dog as I feel my cheeks heating. "Come *on.*"

Noodles just stares at me.

Taunting.

Like she *knows.*

She knows exactly how much trouble she's caused, and she's relishing it.

I squint my eyes until all I can see of the room is a series of fuzzy outlines, and then begin inching toward the Poodle, who's still standing at the foot of the tub. "I'm not looking," I say quickly to Soren Mackenzie. "I just need to get the dog."

"Fine," he says, his voice gruff. "Get it and get out." He pauses for a moment, then adds, "What happened to you?"

"Huh?" I say, my eyes popping open. "Oh," I say when I see him frowning at my scraped arms and knees. "Uh, I fell." It sounds better than *I fought the sidewalk, and the sidewalk won.*

His frown deepens as he eyes the scrapes and cuts. "Probably gonna get tetanus if you don't clean those out."

"That seems unlikely."

He ignores me, pointing instead to one of the cabinets. "There's a first aid kit under there"—he clears his throat—"if you want it."

"Uh, yeah," I say faintly. "Thanks."

What even is happening right now?

I am in *Soren Mackenzie's* townhome. Though I knew he was a local at one point—the town library always has an endcap display dedicated to him—I didn't know he'd moved back. But here he is.

He is *in the tub. NAKED.* And he just invited me to use his first aid kit.

I am talking to Soren Mackenzie and he said I could use his first aid kit and—

Ahem.

Fangirl Heidi is in control right now, and I'm not proud of her.

Get it together, Heidi, I tell myself firmly. *This is not your favorite author of all time. This is just a man in the bathtub, trying to moisturize without being judged. Get the dog, see yourself out, and pray that Soren Mackenzie forgets all about this.*

"Actually," I say, and I hate the way my voice is more breathless and high-pitched than before, "thanks for the first aid offer, but I'm just gonna go." I scurry over to Noodles, clip the leash to her collar, and then begin tugging her out of the bathroom behind me. "Uh, enjoy your naked."

Oops. Freudian slip.

"Your *bath*," I blurt. My correction is way louder than it needs to be, but I don't soften my voice as I go on. "Sorry. Your *bath*. Enjoy your *bath*."

I don't look at him. I just put all my weight into dragging the Poodle out of the bathroom.

"Hey," he calls from behind me when I've almost reached the door. His voice is gruff, reluctant, but he speaks again, and I turn to look at him. "While you're here." He rubs the back of his neck. "Do you know of any good cafés around here? Someplace not too loud that will let you sit there?"

I swallow. "I hear there's going to be a bookshop and café opening in the town square."

He cocks an eyebrow at me. "Soon?" he says.

My answering nod is firm. "Yes. Soon."

❧ 3 ❧
IN WHICH SOREN IS A
SCAREDY CAT

Do you think every man is terrified of the woman he
loves?

No?

Just me, then?

There are different kinds of scary in life. The boogeyman
under your bed as a kid—that's a sort of nebulous, intangible
fear that looms as large as a child's imagination. The fear of
failure as you grow older—that one is more tangible, the source
of a constant internal slideshow of worst-case scenarios.

But the fear of a woman? That one is in its own class.
Tangible and intangible, because she's both impossibly out of
reach and close enough that you can smell her perfume. Sour
and bittersweet, because while the thought of her rejection
ferments your insides, at the same time...if somebody is going to
destroy you eventually, you'd rather it be her than anyone else.

At first glance, Heidi Lucy isn't a scary woman.

On an average day, anyway. The first time we met, that day
four years ago when she burst into my bathroom chasing a dog,
I almost peed myself from how startled I was. She was red-

faced and sweaty and heaving for breath, and her light brown hair was coming out of its ponytail in little swirling tendrils around her face. I was annoyed at the intrusion and then, later, amused. But I didn't see her again until about a year after that when she opened Paper Patisserie, exactly where she said she would: facing the town square. And that was the day that my stubborn heart cracked, just a little.

It's been shattering for her ever since.

Not the sad, painful kind of shattering—it's more like the when a doctor rebreaks two bones that have healed improperly so that they can realign and become whole again.

She's smart, competent, hardworking—fiercely protective of her dreams and her tribe. She's endlessly fun to rile up with the most amazing (if not rare) laugh.

She makes things happen. She expects life to go her way, because she will bend the universe to her will.

I adore her.

And she has no idea.

My bandaged, fresh-from-the-hospital Heidi fights me all the way up the stairs when we reach Paper Patisserie and, above that, her little flat.

"You don't need to help me walk," she says, pushing my hand off her arm as I try to steady her. "What you need to do is go home and shave, because I don't want you showing up tomorrow morning looking like a mountain man."

I ignore this. "The doctor said you need to be woken up every few hours to make sure you're able to awaken normally. So you'll need to sleep on your couch, unless you want me in your bedroom—"

"Whoa, whoa," she cuts in. She turns to look at me over her shoulder. "That is not happening."

I smile serenely at her, enjoying the way her brows furrow. "Doctor's orders, Miss Lucy."

"Doctor's orders my *foot*, Man Bun. You're not staying at my place tonight."

I shrug much more casually than I feel. "That's fine." Then I pull out my phone. "I'll call your brother, in that case—"

"Don't—don't! Ugh," she says, stomping her foot. The time-worn stairs creak beneath us.

Eric would freak out. We both know it. He's a laid-back guy, easygoing and chill with a cocky smile, but his twin is his soft spot.

"Or Gemma?" I go on. "It's only"—I look at the time on my phone—"three-fifteen. She wouldn't mind coming over."

"Don't. You can stay," Heidi snaps, and I suppress my smile.

"If you insist."

I stand behind her as we climb the few remaining stairs, my hands hovering over her back in case she stumbles or falls. She's unsteady on her feet, but she makes it to the top without incident, even managing to throw me a few dirty looks as she goes.

She unlocks her door, and we step inside. She doesn't flick on the lights, instead dropping her keys onto the tiny table by the front door and then shuffling further into the dark living room.

I follow her, watching carefully. There's a slump to her shoulders I don't like. I hurry over to the couch and grab the fleece blanket that's bunched up there.

"Get some rest," I say quietly, gesturing to the sofa.

"I can't," she says, and she sounds exhausted. "I need to get cleaned off."

"Do it in the morning."

"I'm not going to be able to sleep with blood in my hair, Soren," she says.

That's fair. She's probably overwhelmed, and the head wound isn't helping.

"All right," I say, nodding. "Come on."

I cross the small room and step into the itty-bitty bathroom, turning on the lights. And it's funny, but I've always preferred Heidi's tiny little place to my larger one. I don't spend much time here, but I've been enough to know that it's homey in a way my townhome never was.

Really, I should have gotten someplace smaller. My town-home was an impulsive investment, luxurious and unnecessary, but I was loaded with income from my first bestseller and I needed a new place to live. What was supposed to be a triumphant return to my hometown ended up being a slinking, tail-between-my-legs retreat when book number two bombed big time.

I reach up, opening the cabinet above the toilet. It's the only cabinet in the little bathroom, so it takes me two seconds to find the spare towels. I grab a few of them and then stand back up, setting them on the closed toilet seat.

"Come on," I say to Heidi again, gesturing. She's standing right outside the door, watching me warily as she clutches the doorframe for support.

Taking her time.

That's fine. Heidi is like that. She'll come to you, not the other way around. So I take the time to wash my hands, even though I scrubbed them thoroughly at the hospital. Her soap smells like apples, and I massage it into my hands, trying not to remember the sight of her blood on my skin—one of the worst things I've ever seen.

Head wounds bleed a *lot*. I knew that, but I didn't really comprehend it until Heidi was the one unconscious in my arms, her skin too pale, her body limp.

I shudder, shutting the water off and drying my hands on my shirt. Then I turn to her.

"Do you want to call the police?" I say.

29

"No," she says immediately, shuddering. "No. I'm fine; everything is fine."

I nod slowly but don't protest. "All right. Can you stand in the shower and wash your hair by yourself?" I say. Judging by her white-knuckled fingers still gripping the doorframe, I know the answer, but I'll never convince her if she doesn't arrive at the conclusion herself first. So I wait, watching her.

"I—maybe. I don't—" She clears her throat. "You can't shower with me."

I nod. "That's fine. But if you sit in the tub, I can wash your hair under the faucet. We can drape a towel around your shoulders so you don't get your clothes wet." I turn to look at the little pedestal sink. "Or you can sit in a chair and tilt your head back into the sink."

She eyes the sink. "Like at the salon?"

"I guess," I say with a shrug. "I don't know. It's been a while since I got my hair cut." Years, actually.

"I can do that myself," she says, stepping into the bathroom.

I hold my tongue instead of arguing. She's a grown woman, stubborn but not stupid. I grab one of the two chairs at her kitchen table and carry it back to the bathroom. Then I say, "I'll be out here. Ask for help, please, if you need it."

Her cheeks turn red, but all she does is nod.

I skirt past her, closing the door behind me as I step back into the living room.

I force myself not to listen at the door, because there is a line, and that crosses it. I pace the room instead, my ears making up all sorts of little sounds that my brain tries to blow out of proportion. A little *clink* conjures the image of Heidi on the floor of her shop, bleeding—a mild *thump* has me imagining her slumping unconscious over the sink. I shake my head and make myself sit on the couch, my knee bouncing with anxious energy that has nowhere to go.

I pull out my phone, opening Google Docs on autopilot. I let my finger hover over my current work in progress for a second before tapping the screen, and a sick sense of dread washes over me. I force myself to scroll to the bottom anyway, where I find the cursor blinking at me like a neon light. I don't go back and read the thousand or so words I got in yesterday; I know it will make me more antsy. The blank space taunts me, laughing with gaping jaws as my nerves threaten to swallow me whole.

I fling my phone away and give in to the litany of excuses the situation offers.

I'm not going to be able to focus while I'm worrying about Heidi. It's stupid to try to concentrate on my imaginary world when I'm so concerned about the real one.

But it's fine. Heidi is fine. She's—

"Man Bun?" Heidi's voice calls.

I shoot off the couch like it's electrocuted me, and I've never crossed a room faster. "Yeah?" I say, speaking to the closed door.

"Uh, I can't—could you—can you help with something?"

She's not one to stammer or stutter, which tells me how uncomfortable she must be.

"Yeah," I say again, more softly this time. "I'm coming in."

I enter the bathroom to see Heidi seated in the chair, her head leaning back against the sink. I spot the trouble she's having immediately; her medium-length hair fills the sink enough that the water and suds don't drain as well, causing a layer of shampoo bubbles to remain. She probably can't get it rinsed.

"Can you help get the shampoo out?" she says, looking up at me but not quite meeting my eye.

I hum my assent, moving closer.

I feel the water; it's a little chilly, so I turn the knob until it's warmer. Then I lift her hair, heavy and wet, and run it under the faucet. I hold this little piece of her in my hands, and I savor it, because I'm not sure I'll ever get to do this again. Her shampoo smells like something tropical, and I inhale as much as I can without being a weirdo.

I rinse her hair until I can no longer pretend there's any soap left to wash out. Then I shut the water off, lifting her hair and wringing the excess water. I lean over her to grab the extra towel from on top of the toilet before wrapping it around her hair, and my hands work mindlessly as I dry it.

"Soren."

I freeze at the sound of my name. A sudden stillness falls thickly around us, and I clear my throat. "Yeah."

"What are you doing?" Her voice is hesitant, curious.

Crap. "Just—nothing. Helping. Sorry." I drop the towel and step away quickly.

"It's fine," she says after a second. "Thank you."

I nod without speaking, and then I back out of the room, closing the door.

By the time Heidi falls asleep on the couch thirty minutes later, my mind is spinning once more. I stretch out on the floor, but I don't expect I'll really be able to sleep. I keep listening to the sound of her breathing, deep and even, just to make sure she's fine. I do briefly consider trying to get in some words, but the thought has never been less appealing—and that's saying something. This entire book has been like pulling teeth, and with every word of praise I hear for my first novel, it gets worse.

My debut novel was a bestseller. My second was a flop. How am I supposed to follow that up? The only thing worse than people expecting great things is knowing that people *no longer* expect great things, because you've already proved them wrong.

I set my phone aside and then fold my arms across my

chest, letting my eyes flutter closed. I have an alarm set; I'll wake Heidi to check on her in two hours.

But my eyes open after a few seconds, against my will, and try as I might, I can't get them to close again.

I guess I'll spend this night memorizing the texture of the paint on Heidi's ceiling, and I'll try not to think about how badly I wish the two of us were staring at the paint on my ceiling instead.

❧

To absolutely nobody's surprise, Heidi does not take kindly to being woken up every two hours. She swats my hand away when I shake her awake at five-thirty, grumbling about my man bun; she does the same at seven-forty. My hair is one of her favorite things to gripe about, her go-to complaint, and this time I let it slide. I make sure the blinds are closed as tightly as possible, but it doesn't stop the muted sunlight from filtering in. By eight-thirty, she's up and moving around, despite my protests that she should rest and open the shop a bit later today.

"I have things to do. I can't rest," she says as she shuffles around the kitchen. Then she stops and gives me a critical look. "You should, though. You look like you got run over."

"Such a sweet woman," I mutter, rolling my eyes.

She shrugs as her lips twitch. "No one ever called me *sweet*."

That's true enough. "I'll go home in a bit."

"Shave before you come back," she says.

I don't make her a promise I know I'm not going to keep. I watch her lean down and open the refrigerator instead. She's dressed in her usual attire—jeans and a soft-looking t-shirt. Sometimes she wears denim shorts, and sometimes it's jeans that hit just above her ankles—cropped? Is that what those pants are called?—but it's almost always jeans of some sort.

It might be pathetic that I know this about her. But I'm observant; it's part of my nature. And...well, she's Heidi.

I do what I can to help as Heidi bustles around getting ready for the day, but she mostly swats me away whenever I approach. Surprisingly, not once does she tell me to leave; I was expecting it the second she woke up. When she's finally ready to go downstairs, she looks at me over her shoulder.

"Let's go," she says, and I nod.

We both make our way into the cramped stairwell, and Heidi locks the door behind her. I keep a close eye on her as we descend, but she seems fine.

The second we emerge from the stairwell, though, we come face-to-face with Gemma. It's clear she's just arrived; her keys are still in her hand, and she's halfway through pulling off her jacket.

"What happened to you?" she says immediately. She gestures to Heidi's forehead bandage, looking concerned.

"Oh, it's nothing. I bumped it," Heidi says.

"Are you okay?" Gemma says as she tucks her jacket under her arm.

"I'm fine," Heidi says, waving away the question.

I snort but don't say anything. She's playing it awfully cool for someone who has no memory of the past twenty-four hours.

Gemma shrugs. "Okay. So..." But she trails off as she seems to realize what's going on—that Heidi and I have both emerged from the stairwell, relatively early in the morning. Her dark eyes widen, and the three of us stand in silence, looking at each other, for probably five seconds.

"Ah," Gemma says finally, tucking a few strands of dark hair behind her ear. She looks back and forth between the two of us, and a smile unfurls on her face. She points first at Heidi, then at me, and then at Heidi again.

"Did you...?"

"No," Heidi says quickly.

"Are you—"

"*No*," Heidi says again.

"Because you know I've always thought—"

"Gemma," Heidi cuts her off, her voice loud, her eyes darting quickly to me and then away again.

"*Gemma!*" comes a squawking voice from the corner behind the counter.

"Shut up, Jojo," Gemma says to the parakeet, a small bird in vibrant shades of green and yellow. Jojo adjusts his wings in his cage, hopping along his bar.

"Can you feed him, Man Bun?" Heidi says as she moves away from me, heading in the direction of the back room. "I need to unload a few boxes before we start in the kitchen."

"Again?" Gemma says.

Heidi freezes in her tracks and then turns to look at Gemma, whose head tilts to the side.

"We did the shipment yesterday. Is there more?"

Heidi blinks once. Twice. Then, completely composed, she says, "Sorry, you're right. I forgot."

"Feed the bird, Man Bun," Gemma says. She hurries over to Heidi, her eyes sparkling. "I need to have a *chat* with Heidi."

I bet she does.

Gemma drags Heidi in the direction of the café half of the shop, and I round the checkout counter. I scoop some feed into the bowl in Jojo's cage, closing it and fastening the latch again. Jojo eyes me for a second and then squawks again:

"*Pockets of sunshine! Pockets of sunshine!*"

I snort, shaking my head.

A few months ago Heidi and Gemma made the mistake of

introducing Jojo to the world of audiobooks while they closed at the end of the day, and Jojo has displayed an expanded vocabulary ever since. I'm not sure what kind of books they were listening to—they won't tell me, which I find suspicious—but I'll figure it out. I pull out my phone and jot down this latest phrase before tucking it back in my pocket. Then I head to the closet behind the café counter and drag out the spot cleaner. It takes me a few moments at most to get the blood off the floor, and after that I put the spot cleaner away again.

"Heidi," I call as I head to the front door. "I'm leaving."

"See you later," she calls from somewhere over in the café, and with that, I head out into the sun.

4

IN WHICH HEIDI WITNESSES
A DEATH

Gemma is not satisfied with my explanation of why Soren stayed at my place last night.

"You said your head was fine," she says accusingly. "You said you bumped it."

"I did bump it, technically," I say as I get started on a giant batch of muffins.

"And you can't remember anything from yesterday?" she goes on, ignoring me.

"No," I admit. "And I haven't sat down to figure everything out yet. After Soren brought me home from the hospital, I just wanted to sleep."

Gemma sighs and leans back against the counter. "I was so sure something had finally happened."

"You're a hopeless romantic," I say, shaking my head.

"I absolutely am," she says with a smile. "And I refuse to be ashamed."

My answering smile is small, but it warms me. "Good. You shouldn't be." I hesitate, then add, "But nothing is going to happen with me and Soren. We don't have those feelings for each other."

"Speak for yourself," she says under her breath. Then she reaches up and pulls an apron off the hook on the wall. "I'll start the scones."

Gemma and I almost always bake the first batches of the day. I have another kitchen employee that comes a bit later when the café section opens, but I like doing this first round myself. It's relaxing, and starting my day with baked goods is always a plus.

I need a relaxing morning right about now. Because what the heck *happened* last night?

I don't only mean the mysterious head injury or the voicemail or the secret I apparently learned and then forgot. I mean Soren Mackenzie, rinsing my hair, toweling it dry more carefully than I've ever seen him do anything. Usually we're a mess of squabbling chaos, and we both seem to like it like that. Last night was...different.

He was so *gentle*. I can handle immature Soren and petty Soren and flippant Soren. But gentle Soren? He's a beast I'm unaccustomed to.

I let my mind wander wherever it wants as I mix batter, adding and stirring and folding until it's ready. And though I usually feel relaxed by the time I leave Gemma to get things in the oven, when I head back out to the main café area, there's still a sense of unease writhing inside.

Gentle Soren. My head wound. The voicemail. And, most concerning because of how it's making me feel, this nagging sense that there's something I need to be doing.

What is it? What am I forgetting?

It's driving me nuts.

My main kitchen employee shuffles past me as I'm rounding the café counter, and I nod to her.

"Hi," Mel says, sounding out of breath. "Sorry I'm late."

"You're fine," I say. "You're not late. Gemma's getting the muffins in the oven, and I think she started the scones."

"Perfect," Mel says. She pulls her long, graying hair into a ponytail. "I'll go fill the lemonade dispensers and then take over the baking." She pauses, looking at my forehead. "Are you okay?"

"I'm fine," I say, relieved that she's not asking for details. Mel is great. She's not even a trained baker; she's someone that Gemma recommended when we were starting out, a woman in her fifties, and we ended up becoming friends. People loved the muffins and scones she made. I wish I could afford to pay her more. Though she's never asked, and I've never said anything, I think she needs the money.

It only takes me a couple seconds to move to the other side of the shop. My bookshop-slash-café is a longish space, with the kitchen and café counter at one end and the bookshop counter at the other. With how much space the bookshelves take up, the dining area comprises only a couple tables and a few comfy armchairs, but my customers seem to like it fine. The front entrance is roughly in the middle, and the wall that faces the town square is lined with giant display windows. It's a perfect little place.

I knew it would be. I saved for years to be able to rent here. The building owner is some rich guy who has a home and some land in the rolling hills outside of town, but the monthly cost is fair, which I appreciate.

The appearance of my last employee through the front entrance brings with it a gust of air that *feels* like spring—it smells green, somehow, and crisp, and it makes me think of clear blue skies. Winter in Idaho lasts approximately forever, so I'm glad the snow has finally thawed. I live for the little peeks of green in the rich brown soil and the chirping of birds and unfurling of flower petals.

"Hi," I say to Calvin as he makes his way from the door to the bookshop sales counter on light feet. He waves at me and then gives his attention to the computer, where I assume he's clocking in.

"Don't know how to tell you this," he says a second later, bounding out from behind the counter and pointing at me, "but I feel like someone should." Then he jerks his chin up at my forehead. "You did something to your head."

"Ugh," Gemma says as she rounds the corner from behind a bookshelf. She wrinkles her nose at him. "You're disgustingly chipper this morning."

"I got my beauty sleep," he says, running one hand over his light brown hair.

Gemma snorts and points at him. "That face makes me think you missed a few hours."

"Children," I say in a flat voice. "Play nicely, please."

"Yes, Mother," they reply—like they always do. Bickering like children is how they communicate. As long as they get things done, I'm not too concerned. And really, it's part of our dynamic by now; Calvin is like our little brother, and we're the sisters he tolerates. I wish any of us were interested in him romantically, because he's a great guy, but sadly, none of us are. Maybe it's because he's younger by quite a few years. But I'm certainly not, Mel is old enough to be his mother, and Gemma has been dating my twin brother on and off for years.

I glance at my watch—it's time, which means no more speculating on intershop relationships. "Hey, Gemma," I call over my shoulder as I head to the storeroom. "Go ahead and flip the sign?"

"Done," she calls back a second later.

I push open the storeroom door, and it swings open and

then closed behind me, squeaking slightly on its hinges. The storeroom is muted and dusty with a light that buzzes when I flick it on. Still, it's one of my favorite places to be in the entire world. It's quiet, stacked with boxes and boxes of books—mostly extra stock of our best-selling sections. I know where everything is, and something about the way the walls gather around me feels comforting rather than claustrophobic.

I grab a pen and a spare piece of paper, and then I sit down on the brown carpet and take a few deep breaths. I need to organize my thoughts, which means I need to make a list.

I love lists. Like...so much.

I write *To-Do* at the top, and then I begin jotting things down.

-Figure out last night/yesterday

-Retrace steps?

I bite my lip, thinking, until another idea comes to me.

-Call security company for tapes!!!

-Sample a muffin and a scone. For Important Mental Health Reasons.

-Make sure Man Bun shaved/isn't disturbing the peace

-And then stop thinking about how he was acting last night

-Get a drink of water

Is it the most professional list in the world? No.

But will it keep me fed and hydrated? Yes.

Nodding, I look over my list with satisfaction. I can do most of these with no problems. So I take a deep breath, savor my last few seconds of peace and quiet, and stand up. Then I tuck my list into my pocket and head back out to the shop.

We've only just opened, so I have the rows to myself as I walk through the bookshelves, inhaling with a smile. There's nothing better than that smell—the smell of books and paper and little worlds tucked away between the pages. It smells even better in the secondhand aisle, where all the books have been donated and loved before.

I'm just in time to see Soren when I emerge from the mystery section, settling himself in his favorite leather armchair with a smug look of satisfaction on his face. And glaring at him by the door, clearly fresh from outside, is none other than Carmina Hildegarde.

She's dressed immaculately, as per usual. I don't understand how someone that old can still look so elegant. But she does; she always does. I think part of it is her facial expression— a haughty look that proclaims her to be better than everyone else around her. I heard she used to be a model back in the day, and I believe it. Her white hair is fluffy but smoothed into a fancy twist at the back of her head, and her sneering lips are a vibrant red. Her blouse and skirt, though simple, look expensive.

Soren, I can't help but notice, does not look elegant. His hair is in its typical bun, and he did not shave. I roll my eyes.

Carmina places her bony, wrinkled hands on her hips, her large purse dangling from one arm. Then she stomps over to Soren, so violently that for a second I worry she's going to snap her high heels. She doesn't, though; she reaches him fine and then stands there, glaring down at him, while he pretends not to notice her.

Because of course he does.

I sigh. "Carmina," I say, approaching the two of them before they come to blows. "Do you want to sit over here?" I say, gesturing to an empty table. "It gets great sunlight; you'll be nice and warm."

"No," Carmina snaps. She doesn't even look at me; she keeps her beady little eyes on Soren. "I want to sit here." She punctuates that last word with a stomp of her foot.

"Well, this seat's taken, unfortunately"—I glare at Soren

too, because he's being a child about this—"so come sit over here. Come on," I say, taking her gently by the elbow and leading her away from the hulking blond man bun occupying her favorite chair. I settle her gently at the table in the sun and then say, "Let me get you your muffin, and then I'll grab you a drink, okay?"

Carmina sniffs haughtily and sets her handbag on the table next to her. "Lemonade, please. And is there blueberry today?"

I nod. "Of course." We always make blueberry muffins and orange zest muffins.

She sniffs again. "That will do, I suppose."

I do my best not to roll my eyes at this. It's the same thing she gets every time; there's no need to be so uppity. But I force a smile and then hurry behind the counter, using the tongs to grab a blueberry muffin from out of the display case. I put it on one of our little white plates, and then I return to the impatient old woman.

"Here you go," I say, setting the plate in front of her with a little *clink*. "Give me a minute to get your drink, all right?"

She doesn't answer, and she doesn't thank me. She just begins unwrapping her muffing with spindly fingers.

Fine. It's fine. She's a paying customer; her money can be her thanks.

Because I am professional rather than petty, I don't make Carmina wait for her drink—even though it's more tempting than I'd ever admit out loud. I just fill a medium cup with lemonade and a bit of ice before going back to her table once more. I set the drink and a wrapped straw in front of her.

"Let someone know if you need anything else," I say. Then I leave her alone.

I smile with satisfaction as several more customers enter the shop. It's a popular breakfast spot, since we offer fresh muffins and scones as well as lemonade, hot chocolate, coffee, and several different kinds of herbal teas. My smile twists into a scowl, though, when I notice people purposefully avoiding the seat right next to Soren's.

"Man Bun," I say, approaching him, because this isn't the first time I've seen it happen.

He holds up one finger without looking up from his laptop. "No," he says.

"You're scaring away customers," I say.

His snort is little more than a puff of breath. "Don't be ridiculous. Of course I'm not."

"I told you to shave. You're a scruffy mess!" I say.

"And you're wearing two different shoes," he replies.

"I—what?" I look down at my feet, where sure enough, there are two different flats: one silver and shiny, the other matte black.

How did that happen? I changed from the silver to the black this morning before we came down; did I forget to change the other shoe?

"Did you notice that this morning, and you're only now saying something?" I say.

"I would have told you," he says with a roll of his eyes. "I only noticed when you were serving Carmina."

I clear my throat. "Well," I say. "We're not talking about me. We're talking about you. You look like a homeless man."

"If I don't get this novel turned in on time, I'll do more than *look* like a homeless man," he says darkly. "My publisher will drop me and then I'll go broke and I won't be able to make payments and I'll have to sleep on your couch, Miss Heidi" — he finally looks up at me—"and is that what you want?"

"What I want," I say stubbornly, "is for you to comb your hair, trim your beard, and stop glaring at everyone who comes within a six-foot radius."

"No."

My words come out through gritted teeth. "Since I acknowledge that I cannot legally make you shave or comb your hair"—he snorts again—"at least stop giving the other customers the stink eye. Especially Carmina."

"I need to establish my dominance so that she'll stop trying to steal my spot," he mutters, going back to his laptop.

"*Soren.*"

He sighs. "I'll try, but I can't make any promises." He glares in Carmina's direction and then says, more loudly, "I'm going to dropkick that woman all the way to Yellowstone."

"Shut up," I say. "Also." I take a step closer to him, lowering my voice. "I'm going to call the security company and have them send over the tapes for yesterday. So I can see what happened. But where exactly did you find me?"

When Soren looks up at me, his smart-aleck air is gone, replaced by the same serious version of him I got last night. He nods his head in the direction of the front entrance. "Face up a few feet from the door," he says, his eyes troubled. "I cleaned the blood off the floor before I left this morning, but I didn't check anywhere else yet. I figured it wouldn't be tampering with evidence or anything since you didn't want to call the police."

"Okay, thank you." I turn to go, but he reaches out and grabs my arm.

"Wait," he says.

I look down at his hand wrapped around my wrist, and he lets go quickly.

"Sorry," he says, running one hand over his head. "But I asked you yesterday, and I just realized you won't remember. I wanted to have my writing group here next week."

"I didn't know you have a writing group," I say, thinking. But try as I might, he's correct; I can't remember having this conversation yesterday.

"I don't—yet," he says. "I'm part of a few writer communities online, and those of us who are local decided we would try meeting up and see how it goes. This would be the first meeting."

"What did I say yesterday?" I don't think there should be any problem with it, but who knows what I said then.

Soren's shrug is casual as he turns back to his computer screen. "You said it was fine as long as there weren't too many of us."

"That's fine, then. I can't think of any problems," I admit. "Just don't stay past close, and don't be too loud." Then I sniff. "And one last thing—don't call me Miss Heidi. It's Miss Lucy to you."

His fingers cease their click-clacking as he turns his gaze on me, and I am absolutely not ready for the smile he shoots me. One part charming, one part gentle, warm amusement sparkling in his blue eyes. "No promises there either, Miss *Lucy.*"

And even though I've heard him call me that a million times...this is different. He caresses the word, turning my plain last name into something sensual. Then he gives his attention back to his computer screen, and I stomp away, taking deep breaths as though maybe that will stop my face from turning red.

That man is just—he's just—

Well. He's something, that's for sure.

I retreat behind the bakery display case, telling myself I'm not running away.

"How's it going?" I ask Mel, who's still shuffling around in her apron.

"Good," she says easily. "Just got another batch of muffins in." She glances over the counter at Soren and Carmina, her gaze darting back and forth between them. Then she looks at me. "Want me to bake some hot sauce into the next batch and give it to them?"

I laugh, something that makes Soren's head lift. He turns in his seat, looking at me. "Tempting," I say, pulling my eyes away from him.

"What's tempting—Soren or the hot sauce idea?" Mel says with a smile.

I roll my eyes. "The hot sauce."

"Because Gemma says you and Mr. Mackenzie came down from your flat together this morning—"

"How did she manage to tell you that already?" I say, outraged. "She's been up at the book counter."

"She told me when I first got here," Mel says with a wide smile.

Of course she did. I hope Gemma didn't say anything about my missing memories; I'm not sure what to tell people yet.

"Well, I'll keep the hot sauce offer in mind," I say. "We might need it."

Mel shrugs, still smiling, and she has the tact not to push about Soren. "I'll be ready," she says.

"I know who to call, then," I say, and I can't help returning her smile, even if I know I'll never put hot sauce in Carmina's food.

Soren's, on the other hand...

I'm not writing the idea off completely.

The display case I'm leaning against gives off a nice glow of warmth, and it would be nice if I could linger here for a while, but I can't. So I straighten up and then say, "Okay, I'm heading back over to the books. Let me know if you need help with anything."

Mel nods. "Will do," she says. "I should be fine, though—"

But she breaks off when a strange sound drifts over from

47

the tables, a horrible, eerie gasping noise that sends shivers down my spine.

Where's it coming from?

I round the counter, my head jerking this way and that as I search for the source of the sound, until my eyes land—on Carmina Hildegarde.

I'm not the only one who hears it; there are only three or four people eating here, but every one of them glances at the old woman. Several look away again, only to turn back when Carmina makes that same noise again.

"Carmina?" I say as I rush over to her. "Carmina? Carmina!" I kneel down beside her chair, looking up at her. "What's wrong?"

She doubles over, her bony arms wrapped around her middle.

"Carmina," I say again. "Talk to me."

And for a few eternal seconds, her bulging eyes just stare at me.

"Find—" she rasps then, a desperate, scary sound. "Pick—"

"Pick?" I repeat. "Pick what? What should I pick?" My words are rushed, half-coherent at best. But when Carmina's eyes lock on mine, I know her next words are meant for me.

"Lock..." she says, and her voice is thinner now. "Lock..."

"Pick? Lock? Pick a lock?" I say wildly, as though the answer to this question can stop the life from leaving her eyes, can stop the little trickle of blood that's dribbling out of the corner of her lips. I'm dimly aware of growing chaos in the background, but I keep my eyes on Carmina. "Pick what lock, Carmina? *What lock?*" Then, speaking over my shoulder, I yell, "Somebody call an ambulance!"

"I just did," comes Soren's voice from directly behind me, hoarse and stilted.

I look up, and he bends over into my field of vision.

"Murdered..." Carmina says now, pulling my attention back to her. I have to lean closer to hear. "Murdered..." But her voice fades away as her head drops to the table with an awful, sickening finality. I reach over and grab her wrist, knocking her purse off the table. I ignore the shower of contents that fall, searching desperately for a pulse instead.

Nothing.

There's nothing beneath that thin, papery skin.

She's dead.

The shop erupts into chaos.

5

IN WHICH SOREN REGRETS
THE DEATH OF HIS NEMESIS

There is a dead woman at that table.
That table, right there—right in front of me, where Heidi is kneeling.

That woman is dead.

Carmina Hildegarde is dead.

Stop saying 'dead,' my brain snaps at itself. But I can't help it; the word is reverberating through my skull, bouncing off of one wall and then the other.

There's one other word zooming around in there, too: *murder.*

That's what Carmina said, right? Did I hear correctly? She said she was murdered. I'm almost positive. It made the hair on the back of my neck stand up.

I scratch my scalp, feeling suddenly itchy—the kind of sticky grossness that you get after you've been on a long run in the humidity. But scratching does nothing; the sensation persists, and I have a feeling it's psychological.

Dead.

I exhale shakily, looking at the scene around us. Everyone

who was in the bookshop is now gathered around Heidi and Carmina—eight, nine, maybe ten people. Some of them have their phones out; others are gawking. All of them are buzzing, talking to each other and to themselves and who knows what else; I only register one person leaving, the faint glint of glasses and a flash of brown. I wish the rest of them would follow.

We need to get them out of here. And when will help arrive?

Some distant part of my brain—the writer bit, if I had to guess—notes how strange it is, how odd, that your mind seems to stop working in situations like this. You accept people dying in books and movies and games. But seeing it happen right in front of you? The human brain isn't so quick to believe that.

My thoughts are somehow racing and moving sluggishly at the same time; going so quickly, perhaps, that I can't catch any of them and I'm left with empty hands. I know I called the ambulance, but to be completely honest, I don't remember what I told them. I think I just stammered something about Carmina and the bookshop and then hung up automatically. Should I have stayed on the line? Should I call them back and make sure I gave them the address? I'm not sure I did. I'm not even sure I explained the situation properly.

Murder.

"Carmina," Heidi says. She's still kneeling next to Carmina's chair. "Come on. Carmina." She shakes the woman by the shoulder, but it's no use. I can tell that even from here. I think Heidi can too, because she finally sits back on her heels and sighs. She rubs her temples before her chin comes up. She scans the group gathered around her until she finds Mel, the woman who works in the kitchen.

"Get everyone out," she says, her voice faint. "We're shutting down for the day. Get everyone out of here."

Mel nods, a sharp, decisive motion, before spreading her

arms wide. "Everyone out, please," she says, shepherding people to the door. "We're closing shop."

I ignore the bustling throng, stepping closer to Heidi instead, until I'm near enough that I can rest my hands on her shoulders. I give them a squeeze—hope that's not creepy—and lean down so she can hear me. "Come on," I say to her in a low voice. "Let's get up, okay?"

Heidi doesn't answer; she doesn't move. She doesn't even look at me. So I stand there, waiting for her, trying to wrap my brain around what's happening.

Dead.

Murder.

It's only a few seconds later that Heidi gets to her feet. I resist the urge to help her, because I'm not sure she'd appreciate that. I hover obnoxiously instead, trying to look casual while also being ready to catch her if she stumbles. She might not think she needs help, and maybe she doesn't, but she has a nasty head wound. Better safe than sorry.

She makes it to her feet fine, but when she turns toward me, her eyes are blank. I can see what's going on in her mind plain as day; there may as well be a big sign on her forehead that reads DOES NOT COMPUTE. She's still staring sightlessly, her eyes wide, confusion and disbelief etched in every line of her face.

She's processing.

Dead.

I shake the word out of my head.

"Sit," I tell Heidi. I need to focus on her right now. Not on Carmina or my jumbled thoughts. I can freak out later if I need to. So I steer her gently with one hand to her lower back, giving Carmina—no, Carmina's *body*—a wide berth as I lead her to a different table. I pull out the chair, and Heidi sinks into it, that same dazed look still on her face.

In the distance, sirens sound. I sigh, moving back to Carmina's body. Wordlessly, I crouch down, picking up the contents of her purse. Calvin appears out of nowhere and bends down to help me, and together the two of us get all of her stuff back in the purse—the most cliché bunch of old lady junk I've ever seen, mints and hard candies and medicine bottles and packets of tissues. Nothing about the contents of her bag suggests that she was any different from the other old women out there; nothing displays her sour personality or haughty demeanor.

Shouldn't something about her bag tell us that? Shouldn't we be able to see those traits—something vindictive in the clasp of her wallet, something arrogant in the flavor of her mints? Or are all humans really the same when it comes down to the contents of their purses, the contents of their minds and their hearts?

Are we all, at our cores and in our purses, the kind of people who could die at a café table, here one day and gone the next?

"Shut up," I mutter to my brain, rubbing my head. My thoughts are spiraling again, running circles and playing games and bumping repeatedly into the wall they can't seem to get past: that *a woman just died right in front of me.*

Dead.

I drag myself over to the table where Heidi is sitting and collapse in the seat across from her. She doesn't look good—tense, drawn, pale. I'm not sure I look any better. I can hear someone crying—Gemma, maybe—and Mel's soothing, motherly voice over her. Calvin is pacing by the door, and none of his usual lightheartedness shows on his face. He just looks solemn and anxious.

When Heidi fixes her eyes on me, though, I sit up straighter. It's instinct.

"Should I cover her body with something?" she says, her

teeth digging into her bottom lip. Her gaze darts to Carmina, still slumped over the table, and then back to me.

"It's probably a good idea," I say heavily. I hold one hand out when she starts to stand. "I'll do it," I say, scooting my chair back with a loud scrape. "Just—rest, please."

She doesn't fight me on this; she nods, looking tired. "There are some tablecloths in the storage closet off the kitchen," she says.

I dig through the contents of the closet with frantic hands; when I hold them out in front of me, they're shaking. I keep looking anyway, and thirty seconds later I locate two folded tablecloths. They're plastic, the disposable kind used for kids' parties, but they'll do. One of them is bright green with a pattern of confetti and party hats—completely inappropriate for covering a dead body—and the other is a plain sky blue.

The blue will have to do. Still, I offer a silent apology to Carmina as I return to the tables and drape the cheap plastic over her body. I didn't like her, and I never apologized to her when she was alive, but it sort of feels like I should.

It sort of feels like I should have let her sit in the stupid armchair.

It's a relief when the police and the EMTs arrive. They burst through the door just as I'm settling back into the chair across from Heidi, and I know I'm not the only person who's glad to see them.

"Get comfortable," I mutter to Heidi, watching as they wheel a stretcher in. "I think we're going to be here for quite a while."

Somewhere, from the other side of the shop, the parakeet squawks.

It's the longest morning of my life.

They take Carmina away immediately, thank goodness, but the number of people we end up having to talk to is staggering —apparently in my phone call I mentioned Carmina's claim that she was murdered, although I have no memory of that. No one is very happy that we put a tablecloth over the body or picked up the contents of Carmina's purse; if I'd been thinking with even half my brain I would have realized we shouldn't have touched anything. I apologize multiple times, but all I get are disgruntled looks.

Random people show up every so often—Eric storms past the crime scene tape about an hour after the police come, shouting for Heidi. I can't fault him for rushing over. I'm an only child, but if I heard that someone died in my theoretical sister's theoretical shop, I'd book it over there too.

"What are you doing here?" Heidi says when Eric barges past the officer trying to keep him outside. Her eyes are wide, her hands on her hips.

"Gemma texted me," Eric says as he reaches her. He and Gemma are dating, though I don't know how long that's been going on. He grabs Heidi by the shoulders and holds her at arm's length, looking her over. "Are you okay? What happened to your head? Did someone hit you?"

Heidi throws a *look* at Gemma, but her gaze softens when she sees her best friend—Gemma looks a little worse for wear. She's sitting on the floor, her knees pulled up to her chest, her back against a bookshelf. Her nose is red, and her eye makeup has stained her tear-tracks dark gray.

"I'm fine," Heidi says with a sigh. Then she gestures to the table where I'm seated. "Sit down if you're going to be here. Don't hover."

Eric's jaw twitches, but he nods. The set of his mouth is the same as the set of Heidi's when she's not happy about something—that reluctant turn of her lips that says she's going along with something but she's not convinced. Eric is a good six inches taller than her, but they look undeniably similar; they have the same hair color, and the same fine features that make Heidi look deceptively delicate serve to make Eric look prettier than most men.

Heidi points to my table once again. "Sit," she repeats.

Eric doesn't listen to her immediately; he moves to Gemma first, crouching down next to her and reaching for her hand. He says something I can't hear, then gestures to the table. She shakes her head; he nods, kisses her on the forehead, and then comes to settle himself in the seat across from me.

"Hey," he says, still looking tense. He can't seem to decide where to rest his gaze; it jumps back and forth between Heidi and Gemma before he finally faces forward.

I give him a nod. "Hey," I say.

"You're here most days, right?" he says, and his eyes on me are more discerning than I would expect from someone who flits through life seemingly carefree.

"I am, yeah," I say.

"Good," he says. "You watching out for my girlfriend?"

I blink at him. "Not...really?"

He grunts. "Fair. What about my sister?"

"I would if she'd let me," I say, frowning at Heidi, who's now bustling around anxiously and watching the police do their thing.

Eric snorts, leaning back in his seat and relaxing a bit. "That sounds about right."

I'm not sure if he knows how I feel about Heidi, but as protective as he is, I've never seen him pull that card when it comes to the men in her life—although thankfully there aren't very many of those.

He glances around. "So what happened here exactly? And

what happened to Heidi's head?"

"You're gonna have to ask her about her head," I say slowly. "But over there"—I point to the table where Carmina sat—"one of her customers just...died."

Dead.

Murder.

Eric shudders, a look of distaste crossing his face. He folds his arms over his chest. "She just..."

"Died, yeah," I say with a nod. "Sort of slumped over."

"Wow," Eric says. He glances at Carmina's table. "That's horrible."

"It was," I admit. "It was pretty—"

But I break off when the building owner enters, the bell over the door jingling in a way that's much too merry. I've only seen the man once, but I recognize the dyed black hair and the waxy tanned skin and the custom suit. He's got to be pushing eighty, but he clearly spends an exorbitant amount of money to appear younger, and—though I feel bad thinking it—it's cringe-worthy almost to the point of patheticness.

"Whoa," Eric whispers, his eyes widening. "He's so...old."

That is...accurate.

"Mr. Mills," Heidi says, hurrying over to him. She keeps her head held high, but there's a tremor in her voice when she goes on, "I am so, so sorry."

Mr. Mills raises one eyebrow, a motion that hardly registers on his suspiciously wrinkle-free forehead, and a little smile flits across his stretched, puffy lips. "It is unfortunate, but I hardly think you're at fault, young lady."

My shoulders slump in relief. At least he's not going to blame her.

He strides over to one of the policemen, passing him a business card that he's seemingly conjured from nowhere. "Roger Mills," he says. "I'm the building owner."

He stays just long enough to speak to several people; they pass him around, though I can't hear everything they talk about. He seems oblivious to the rest of us staring at him, Gemma and Heidi with wide eyes and Mel with distrust. He leaves thirty minutes later with no problems, and I watch him go with envy, rubbing my growling stomach.

By the time the police finally clear out, my insides are devouring themselves.

I look around at the bunch of us. Heidi is sitting and staring off into the distance, looking preoccupied and deeply troubled. Eric has moved to sit next to Gemma, his arm around her, his hand playing absently with her hair; in a move that perfectly defines their relationship, every now and then she reaches up and swats him away, and despite the solemnity of the situation, he just grins. Mel is slumped next to them; Calvin is in the chair I usually sit in, and I'm at my own table. No one is sitting where Carmina sat, and no one is speaking.

"Who wants a muffin?" I say, standing up. "I'll pay," I add, looking at Heidi.

She nods tiredly and stands up. Mel and Gemma begin to protest, but she shushes them. "I need to be doing something."

She follows me behind the counter and heads straight to a wall cabinet, opening it and standing on her tiptoes as she rummages around. She can reach the bottom shelf of the cabinet fine, but her fingers fall short of the top.

"What do you need?" I say, stepping up behind her.

She points, her back still to me. "There's a display platter back there somewhere," she says.

I nod, reaching up. Her hand falls out of the way, but I have to take a step closer to get to the top shelf. My breath catches in my throat as my body brushes against hers, and I force myself not to freeze or draw attention to it. I don't want to make things awkward. So I continue feeling around on the top shelf until my hand finds some sort of scalloped edge. I grab it gratefully, pulling it down and then stepping back to put some space between us.

My heart has hummingbird wings, and my ears feel hot.

Heidi turns to face me.

"Here," I say, holding the platter out to her. It basically looks like a pie pan with a stand attached. "For the muffins?"

"Mm-hmm," she says, taking it.

"Are you okay?" I ask, looking more closely at her. My hummingbird heart beats its wings more rapidly. "You look flushed."

She clears her throat. "I'm fine. Just a little warm." She lifts the hair off her neck with her free hand, and I turn away to hide my smile.

"Let's get some sustenance," I say, sliding open the door of the display case.

"The police are getting the security tapes," she says under her breath as she begins pulling muffins out. "I won't be able to watch it until they're done with it. I wanted to see the footage from yesterday, but..." She trails off, sounding frustrated.

"We'll get it back," I tell her. "And in the meantime we can keep trying to figure things out on our own."

She shoots me a skeptical look. Her cheeks aren't as pink anymore, sadly. "And how are we going to do that?"

"I don't know," I say. "I just wanted to reassure you."

She turns her attention back to the display case, but I catch a hint of a smile. "Nice of you." Then her smile fades, and she begins pulling muffins and scones out with renewed vigor, looking troubled once more.

"Hey," I say, and I hate the way my voice softens with her, the way I turn all mushy and gentle, because I know how transparent I must be. "It will be okay. All right?"

"Yeah," she says. "It's just..." She takes a deep, unsteady breath, and then she looks at me. "What if I knew, Soren?"

I frown.

"What if I knew Carmina was going to die?" she clarifies. "She said she was murdered. What if I somehow found out she was going to be murdered, and that's the secret I knew?"

I stare at her, dumbstruck. I didn't even think of that, but...

"That's unlikely," I say.

"But possible," she says.

I don't want to say it. I want to lie. Anything to remove that little frown from her lips. And yet...

"But possible," I agree, my voice heavy.

"And what if I could have stopped it?" she goes on. Her words are spilling out in a rush now, and it's clear that this is what's been bothering her. "What if I could have stopped it, but I didn't because I forgot?"

"Stop," I say firmly. "Don't do this. Okay?" I take the platter gently out of her grasp and set it on the counter. I debate only for a second before I give in to the urge to touch her; I take her face in my hands, my thumbs tracing absently over her cheekbones. "Whatever you knew or didn't know, this wasn't your fault. Okay?"

And she looks perfect like this—her lips parted, her eyes wide, her cheeks turning pink once more.

Shut up, I snap at myself. *This is not the time.*

"You're going to catch flies with that mouth," I murmur, placing one finger under her chin.

Her jaw snaps shut, and I remove my other hand from her face, because she couldn't look any more shocked if she tried.

"Come on," I say, nodding to the platter of muffins. "We'll figure everything out later, okay? Let's eat first. Get some rest."

And from the other end of the shop, Jojo squawks once again. "*Secret realities!*" he crows. "*Secret realities!*"

60

❧ 6 ❧

IN WHICH HEIDI REMAINS
VERY PROFESSIONAL

I don't know what's going on, or what to think, or what to do, and it's freaking me out.

I manage to keep the panic at a low-grade simmer, partially because I absolutely will not let myself fall apart in front of my staff—or the landlord, or the police. It doesn't matter if twenty people die in my café; I don't have time for meltdowns, especially when I'm in charge. I need to keep it *together,* dangit, because I am a professional. And professionals don't have meltdowns during the work day.

They handle their business. They maintain control of the situation with an air of confidence and competence.

Then they go home, down a pint of Rocky Road, and cry in the bathtub.

But I don't feel confident. I don't feel competent. All I feel is the storm brewing somewhere behind my sternum, an electricity-charged cloud of anxiety and concern, along with a healthy dose of mind-numbing confusion.

Because what. Is. Happening.

My brain is being overloaded with data and stimuli, and

what I need is to go sit in a quiet room, by myself, and *process.* Until I'm able to do that, I can't let myself think about any of this. Not Carmina, or my missing memories, or the nagging voice that tells me I might have known she was going to die. And I definitely can't think about Soren on top of all of that, or how *weird* he's being, or how it makes me feel strange inside.

I cannot handle any of that right now. I know my limits. So we are living firmly in denial until everyone leaves and I can lose my mind in the peace and quiet of my own home.

Soren and I distribute muffins to the group, and I eat mine without paying a lick of attention. In fact, I almost take a bite with the liner still on; I only realize at the last moment when I feel the paper brush against my lip. I definitely couldn't tell you if I had blueberry or orange zest.

It doesn't matter anyway. All the aftertaste sours when the topic of conversation turns, inevitably, to Carmina.

"So..." Eric says, looking around at us. He's got three muffin liners scattered in front of him. "What the heck happened, exactly?"

"We told you what happened," Gemma says with a glance at him. "She just—" She gestures to the empty table where Carmina was sitting, swallowing hard. When she speaks again, her voice is shaky. "She *died.*"

"We should replace that table," Mel says in a flat voice.

"It's on my list of things to do tomorrow," I reply. Then I look back to Gemma, who's still looking at my brother...who's helping himself to a fourth muffin.

I roll my eyes. "Save some for everyone else," I tell him.

Eric blinks at me. He says something I don't understand, a convoluted garble of muffin-hindered noise, and then he gestures to the platter.

"No, we can't," Gemma says—I look at her, because of *course* she understood him—and she rolls her eyes at him too. She thumbs over her shoulder at the empty display case. "This was the last of them. Are *you* going to bake more?"

Eric grumbles something unintelligible, but he sits back in his chair, folding his arms over his chest.

"Do you have the number of the wholesaler we used for these?" I say to her, tapping the tabletop.

"Yeah," she says with a nod, running one hand through her long, dark hair. "I know I saved it. I can find it."

"Don't worry about it today," I say, and she nods again.

We sit in silence for a minute, until Calvin speaks up for the first time. "Um," he says, sounding nervous. He shifts, crossing his legs in the seat Soren and Carmina always fight over.

Or...*fought* over.

"So...what did she say, exactly?" Calvin goes on. He twists his hands together. "Carmina. Because it sounded like she said she was murdered. Right? Did I hear that wrong?"

Mel glances at me; when I don't say anything, she looks over at Calvin.

"No," she says. "You heard right."

I clasp my hands tightly, fighting the urge to fidget. All this anxious, unsettled energy is still brewing within me, and I swallow down my panic.

"But the police will take care of it," she goes on in a no-nonsense voice. "Don't worry about that."

I can't tell if her words are intended for Calvin or for me.

"Yeah," Calvin says, and he still sounds unsure. "But still. Murder is, like, a big deal."

He's right. Murder is a very big deal. A huge deal.

I force myself to take deep breaths, in through my nose, out through my mouth.

Did I know Carmina Hildegarde was going to die? Did I

know something was going to happen to her? Could I have stopped this?

In through your nose, out through your mouth. I squeeze my hands into fists, letting my fingernails dig into my palms. I squeeze tighter, intensifying the sensation. The sharp, lightning-bolt sting of my nails grounds me.

You are alive, I tell myself. *You feel pain, which means you are not defeated.*

I am alive, which means there is still hope.

I can handle this.

"All right," Soren says, and I look quickly at him. He's been quiet so far, listening and observing, but now his eyes are on me, narrowed with concern. "Let's close shop for the day. We should all go rest."

"Agreed," Mel and Gemma say at the same time, and I'm surprised to see that they're looking at me too. The two of them stand up in unison, their chairs scraping against the cheerful checkered tile.

"Come on," Mel says, making a shooing motion toward the door.

"Everyone out," Gemma says.

"But—" Eric says, breaking off when Gemma strides over to him, throws her arm around his shoulder, and clamps one hand over his mouth.

He looks down at her with outrage, but she just smiles serenely at him.

"Don't you have a job?" she says.

His shoulders slump as he mumbles something behind her hand.

She nods. "That's what I thought. You—hey. Hey!" she says as Eric grabs her hand and pulls it away from his mouth with ease. She struggles against his grip, but he doesn't let go; he glares down at her.

Gemma puts her hand on her hip. "Oh, bite me," she says, still trying to free herself.

"Maybe I will," he says, cocking one eyebrow at her, and I wrinkle my nose in disgust. Then he removes her arm from around him and moves over to me. He leans down, gives me a quick kiss on the forehead, and turns away again, heading for the door. Just as he's about to exit, he looks over his shoulder and speaks to Soren. "Keep an eye on my sister," he says.

"Hey," Calvin says before I can protest. "Eric. Do you not like me? Why are you saying that to him?"

Eric snorts, looking Calvin over. "How old are you?" he says, not unkindly.

My youngest employee flushes a dull pink. "Twenty-three," he mutters.

Eric nods. "When you grow up big and strong, you can take care of my sister too," he says with a smirk.

I roll my eyes—something I do with Eric more than with anyone else in my life. "Get out," I say, pointing to the door.

"I'm going, I'm going," my brother says, still smirking. He glances at Gemma, and his smile softens. "I'll call you later." The bell over the door jingles as he pushes it open, and then he's gone.

"You too, gents," Mel says to Soren and Calvin. "We'll take care of everything here, don't you worry."

Calvin trudges toward the door, sulking. As soon as he's left, Gemma turns to me, putting her hands on her hips.

"You need to go upstairs and run a bubble bath," she says. She eyes me critically. "You look like you're about to lose it. Mel?"

Mel nods, her gaze sympathetic on me. "I'll get the ice cream. What flavor?"

"Rocky Road," Soren says as he gathers his things. "Häagen-Dazs."

Mel blinks at him and then looks at me. "Is that right?"

"Yes," I say, and my eyes inexplicably well with tears.

This is stupid. I shouldn't be crying. I don't need to cry.

Why am I crying?

I just have really great friends, and someone died right in front of me, and I can't remember anything that happened yesterday.

Also—I look down—I'm still wearing mismatched shoes, like an idiot. Why didn't I change them as soon as Soren pointed them out?

"I can't," I say, sniffing desperately so that no snot leaks out of my runny nose. I don't want Soren to see me like that. It's not cute. I angle my body away from him and go on, "I need to get everything sorted here."

"I'll close," Gemma says firmly. "I'll put something on the record player and get things figured out, and it will take me two minutes. You go upstairs. Now." She points toward the back corner of the bookshop, where the stairs are located. "Go."

More tears cloud my eyes. "But—"

I break off, jumping as I feel Soren's hands settle on my shoulders from behind. Don't ask me how I know it's him; I just do.

"Come on," he says, his voice low in my ear. "Let's go, honey."

My eyes flare wider, and I jerk my head to the side to look at Gemma and Mel.

Honey? Gemma mouths, her eyebrows raised, and Mel looks like she's about to cackle with glee.

Soren gives me a gentle nudge, and I stumble forward, walking mechanically past the front entrance, through the bookshelves, and to the back stairs, his hands still urging me forward while my brain moves decidedly in circles.

Honey?

He called me *honey*, right? Everyone heard that?

"Hey," I say, stopping abruptly in my tracks as I'm about to climb the steps. I turn around and face Soren, who looks surprised by my sudden motion.

"Yeah," he says. His hands are hovering awkwardly over my shoulders, no longer touching me, but he doesn't seem embarrassed. He just waits for me to speak, his eyes expectant.

"What did you call me?" I say, and my voice sounds unnaturally loud in the tiny, enclosed space of the stairwell. I soften my voice so I don't feel like I'm yelling. "Just now?"

Soren blinks at me, and for the briefest second, I swear I see a flash of surprise. But it vanishes as quickly as it appeared, and then he says, "What do you mean?"

I study his face closely, thrown into exaggerated shadow by the yellow light directly overhead. His expression is unruffled, though.

"*Honey*," I say, swallowing. "You called me *honey*."

He cocks one brow at me. "Did I?" he says.

"Yes." My voice is surer now. "You did. I heard you."

"Hmm." He takes one slow step closer. "I don't call my friends *honey*. Do you?"

"Wait," I say before I can stop myself. "Do you have someone you call *honey*? Are you—do you have a girlfriend?"

I've never actually asked him this question. It never even occurred to me. He's at my bookshop every day. When would he be with a woman?

"It's fine if you do, obviously," I say quickly. "It's actually none of my business. I just—was surprised." Crap. I sound flustered.

I'm always easily flustered with him, and I hate it. But he's my favorite author, and he's stupidly handsome, and he pushes my buttons in such a distracting way—

"I didn't say I have a girlfriend," he says, pulling me back to

67

our conversation. He gives me a little smile. "I don't. But you don't need to worry about my love life right now." He points up the stairs. "Go rest. Take care of yourself."

I arch one brow at him. "According to Eric, *you're* supposed to take care of me." My brother is a grand total of twenty-one minutes older than me, and he thinks he can pull the overprotective card.

Although...I swallow, my cheeks heating slightly. What would that even look like, Soren taking care of me?

Soren hums. "Are you gonna let me take care of you?"

I blink, surprised. "No." I'm a grown woman. I'll take care of myself.

He nods. "I didn't think so. Do it yourself, then. Take a bath. Watch a movie. Cry. Scream. Stare at the wall. Whatever you need to do."

"Yeah," I say faintly. "I'll do that." I back up slowly, and I can't quite stop myself from staring at him, cataloging the features I've seen a million times before.

Has his hair always had that many shades of gold?

I blink a few times, shaking my head. I'm being stupid. "Okay," I say. I thumb awkwardly over my shoulder. "I'm going."

He smiles, nods, and then disappears back into the rows of bookshelves.

It's only when I'm neck-deep in a coconut-scented bubble bath that I realize he never answered my original question.

࿇

WHEN I EMERGE FROM MY BATH A SOLID TWO HOURS later—don't judge, and don't ask how pruney my fingers and toes are—it's to find Mel and Gemma sitting on my couch, booing as they chuck popcorn at my TV.

"Are you gonna pick that up?" I say, watching as kernel after kernel bounces off the little screen. I'm glad they're making use of it; I rarely use my actual TV to watch anything. I've been thinking about getting rid of it, in fact, because I mostly use my laptop.

"Of course, sweetie. But I do have to point out," Mel says, "she started it." She jerks her thumb at Gemma. "I got swept along against my will."

Gemma reaches over and nudges Mel in the arm. "What do you mean, against your will—we were both talking about how much we hate him. Besides, I bet you haven't felt this young in years."

Mel laughs, and I glance at the screen more closely.

"Hate who?" But it only takes me a second to recognize *A Walk to Remember*. "Oh," I say with a nod. "The bully popular friend?"

"The bully popular friend," Gemma repeats, and she nods too. "He's the worst. But enough about this." She scrambles for the remote and turns the TV off, looking at me. "Let's talk about you."

The look she and Mel pin me with has me suddenly fidgeting, picking at my short, bitten-down fingernails.

"Are you okay?" Gemma says, tilting her head as she eyes me carefully.

When I hesitate, Mel jumps in.

"Do you not want to talk about it?" she says.

"I..." I think for a second, poking and prodding at my emotions. "I think I don't know how to talk about it right now," I say honestly. I don't have words yet for the things I'm feeling or the things that have happened.

"That's valid," Gemma says, and Mel nods. Gemma's voice softens as she goes on, "We're here if you change your mind. You know that?"

"I know," I say, my voice cracking. "I'll let you know."

"Moving on, then," Gemma says, clapping her hands. Her expression changes, and the look on her face worries me—her eyes are gleaming, and a smile is unfurling over her lips.

"Moving on how?" I say slowly.

"We have something to discuss," Gemma says.

Mel nods. "We do. So let's get down to business. Our question is very simple: Did Soren call you *honey,* or did he not?"

"Because we both heard *honey,*" Gemma adds, and Mel nods.

I sigh, slouching over to the couch and then slumping down next to them. "I don't know," I say. "He didn't exactly deny it, but he also sort of made it sound like he didn't?"

"Hmm," Mel says slowly.

"Tricky man," Gemma says, though this seems to delight her rather than anything else. "He's so into you."

I snort, letting my head drop back against the couch. "No, he's not. He's Soren Mackenzie. We exist on two different planes of being."

"Yeah, he's Soren Mackenzie, but he's also a human being," Gemma says, exasperated. "And you are a hot slice of sexy pie—"

I burst out laughing, and it honestly feels amazing. For a moment, I'm able to forget everything that's happened in the past twenty-four hours—Carmina's death, my missing memories, the gash on my head.

"Okay, sexy pie. If we're going to have this conversation," I say, "we're going to cover *all* aspects." I give her a meaningful look so she knows what's coming.

But Mel jumps in and beats me to it. "Yes," she says, turning her body sideways on the couch to face Gemma. "Let's talk about your hunk of a boyfriend, and how long you've been dating, and when he's going to propose."

But here's the thing about Gemma. At first she seems like someone who would spill all her secrets with no hesitation. She's a talker. It's one of the things I love most about her, because I'm the opposite, and we complement each other well.

But there are things it's almost impossible to get her to talk about, and my brother is one of them. An *Emma* situation, maybe—if she loved him less she could talk about it more. They met when we were in college, began dating several months later, and have had an on-again-off-again relationship ever since.

"Or," Gemma says brightly, "instead of talking about Eric, we could talk about literally anything else. If we decide to get married, it will happen when we're good and ready."

I grin, and so does Mel.

"Are you guys staying over tonight?" I say, standing up. "I've got a couple camping sleeping pads."

"Pass," Gemma says, wrinkling her nose, and she stands up too. "I love you, but I don't sleep on the floor when it can be avoided."

I shrug. "That's fine. Mel?"

"You flatterer," she says with a smile. "It's sweet of you to pretend you don't know that sleeping on the floor would kill my back."

Gemma takes me by the shoulders and peers into my face, inspecting with a critical expression. "Did the bath help, at least? Are you doing better now?"

"I'll be fine," I say with a sigh.

Mel's eyes narrow. "'I'll be fine' is not the same as 'I'm fine,'" she says.

I laugh. "I truly will. It's fine. I'm fine. Go home," I say, waving toward the door. "I'm going to go to bed. That will help."

"All right," Gemma says, but she doesn't sound convinced.

She lets her arms drop and then begins gathering her things, slipping her purse over her shoulder and draping her jacket over her arm.

"The ice cream is in the freezer," Mel says as she begins picking kernels of popcorn up from around the TV. Gemma stoops down to help her, and I watch them with a little smile.

"Thank you," I say. I try to convey my sincerity in those two little syllables, and I hope they can tell I mean it—that I'm grateful for the way they take care of me and look out for me. "Really."

"You would do the same for us," Mel says, waving my thanks away.

"Yeah," Gemma says. "And we love you."

"Drive safe," I say as they head to the door, mostly to stop things from getting too mushy. I'm not great at mush.

"We will!" Gemma says brightly, and Mel gives me a little wave.

Then they're gone, their footsteps disappearing as they descend the steps, and I'm left alone once more.

❦ 7 ❦

IN WHICH HEIDI REMAINS SIGNIFICANTLY LESS PROFESSIONAL

I trudge to my little bedroom, flopping face-first onto the bed. The space is mostly done in shades of white and cream, something I originally did because it was so small, but I ended up liking how calming it was. The decor is pretty minimal—a few plants, a white dresser, and a simple wall hanging—but I don't need a lot, and I don't need fancy.

After a few seconds of struggling to breathe due to the face full of pillow I've got, I roll over and then sit up. I dress quickly in my pajamas, hanging my robe on the clothes rack that's set up in the corner. Then I flick the overhead light off, set my alarm clock, and crawl under the covers.

I'm about to drift off to sleep when I hear a distant squawk.

"Jojo," I groan, pulling a pillow over my face.

Another squawk.

I don't think he ever got his dinner in all the hubbub.

For a moment I debate with myself, running groggily through my options. But no matter how I look at things, Jojo does need to eat. He won't die if I don't feed him, but...I would feel bad.

Is it possible he possesses an as-of-yet unseen skill set that would allow him to get his own food? Could something like that have developed in him?

It seems unlikely.

"Fine," I say. I unplug my phone, drag myself out of bed—my nice, warm, comfortable bed—and grumble my way out to the living room, sliding on the slippers that are by the front door.

Then I grumble all the way down the stairs, emerging from the stairwell with a scowl on my face. I round the counter, and when I come face-to-face with Jojo in his cage, he has the nerve to squawk at me and do that cute little head tilt he does.

"Stupid bird," I say, even as I fill his food scoop up to the very top to make sure he gets enough to eat.

Once I've fed Jojo, I stand there in the dark for a few seconds.

I've always liked the shop at night. Don't ask me why; I don't know. People like to watch their loved ones sleeping—the chubby cheeks of their children, the slow breath of their lover—so maybe the shop at night is my version of that. I trail through the aisles, admire the swimming shadows, press a kiss to the forehead of my greatest achievement before tucking it in to rest.

I make my way slowly past the shelves, letting my fingers trail over the spines of the books as I walk. The used section is my favorite, so full of personality and lives already lived. Then I emerge from the stacks and find myself face-to-face with what I think was my destination all along: the café, and Carmina's table, and the ghost of everything that happened here this morning.

I look around briefly and then sit on the floor, close to where Gemma sat and cried earlier, my back against the bookshelf.

The lamp light pouring in through the display windows

blankets the tile in a yellow-orange glow; back in the kitchen, the refrigerator hums. All too clearly I can see Carmina, just as she was—slumped over at the table, skin pale, contents of her purse scattered everywhere. But my mind tries to superimpose another figure on the scene as well—me, unconscious, face up in front of the door, like Soren said.

What happened to me here?

I eye the entrance, my gaze lingering on the waist-high shelf next to the door. If I were hit over the head by someone, there might not be anything. But if I were pushed from behind...

I stand up so abruptly that my head spins for a second, and I bend over, putting my hands on my knees and waiting for the head rush to calm down. Then I hurry over to the shelf by the door, pulling my phone out.

What if my wound came from falling forward and hitting this shelf?

I shine my phone's flashlight on the top edge of the shelf, leaning down so I can see better. It's dark wood, but blood should be visible, shouldn't it? I trail my light down the edge, further, further, until—

"Bingo," I whisper.

There, on the corner of the shelf nearest the door, is a faint red smudge.

Blood. *My* blood, probably.

Crap. What do I do? Can I clean it up? Yes, right?

I don't want it here. I want it gone. I want everything in this café clean and spotless.

Except—what if it's not mine? What if it has something to do with whoever gave me this gash?

"No," I say to myself. "It's reckless to assume. Let's leave it for now and figure it out tomorrow."

But now that I've noticed it, I can't see anything else; that little smudge of blood is a neon sign, pulling my attention, making me feel dirty and itchy, and the panic that was rising in me earlier threatens once more.

"Okay," I say, talking to myself once again, because I guess that's a thing I do now. "I'll do a quick clean. Just a sweep." The police are done here. It should be fine.

I think that will help me feel better. Of course, what I would *really* love to do is douse this entire building in industrial cleaner or maybe hand sanitizer, but that feels unrealistic. It would take forever for the Roomba to do its job, too. A sweep will have to do for tonight.

So I grab the broom from the kitchen storage closet and then get to work. First, though, I put a record on the record player—it's Gemma's, but we keep it here so we can listen to music while we're opening and closing. I nod to the beat for a second and tell myself I'm listening because I like the music, not because I'm scared of the silence. Then I'm off, sweeping like I've never swept before.

I am an avenging angel tonight, clutching desperately as I hunt for a level of clean that will keep the panic at bay. A little voice in my head that sounds an awful lot like Soren whispers *That's not how it works*, but I ignore this.

Sweeping carpet isn't as effective as vacuuming, but I do my best anyway. When I reach the café section where the carpet turns into cheerful tile, I pick up the speed. I move tables. I move chairs. I even move the armchair that Soren always sits in.

And the entire time, I swallow my tears, forcing myself not to let them fall. Crying is not productive; it's not going to help me accomplish anything. So I'm not going to let those tears out.

I'm mostly successful.

I keep sweeping, moving everything in my way. It's not until I move the other armchair—the one next to the display windows—that I find anything of interest, not that I'm searching.

"What's that?" I mutter, my eyes taking in the trash. I set the broom aside, balancing it against the wall, before bending over to pick it up.

At first I think it's random junk, and some of it is—an old receipt, it looks like—but when I look closer, I see that there's an envelope, too, and an attached sticky note.

My heart stutters a little bit when I read the spiky, black handwriting on the sticky: *You'll not get a penny more out of me, you old hag. I'll make you regret this.*

I read it again, and then another time, and then once more still. And with each pass of my eyes, my racing thoughts become increasingly tangled, and the darkness around me seems to grow darker.

Old hag?

I can feel my pulse thundering in my veins, which is stupid; I'm sitting here looking at an envelope. But my heart doesn't seem to care; it beats faster and faster, a caged animal trying to escape from behind my ribs.

I hesitate for only a beat before I grab the corner of the sticky note. Part of me wants to drop this stuff back on the floor and pretend I never found it, because there's an ominous feeling to this moment—an inevitability that makes me wonder if the entire universe has propelled me toward this time and this place just so that I can pick up this envelope.

The other part of me, the louder part, just wants to know what the heck is going on in my innocent little café.

I sell books and baked goods and delicious warm drinks. There is no place for the rest of this nonsense in my life, and I want to pluck it out by the roots.

So I peel the sticky note off with one shaking hand.

There, beneath the note and scrawled in the same spiky handwriting, are two letters: *C. H.*

"Carmina Hildegarde," I whisper.

It has to be. Right?

I crane my neck around, looking at the table where Carmina was sitting. It's maybe two arms' length away; how did this stuff get all the way over here?

But my mind answers this question before I'm even done asking it, replaying the crowd of people gathered around and the rush of everyone leaving. It would have been easy for someone to accidentally kick this envelope when people started milling around. It absolutely could have skittered away under the chair.

I swallow, staring down at the envelope. There's only one thing left to do: open it. And I bet I know what's inside, judging by the note on the front and the shape of the contents.

I open the unsealed flap of the envelope with shaking fingers. Weirdly, bizarrely, my brain conjures up the image of little Charlie Bucket, opening his Wonka bar to see if he got a golden ticket—that's how I peek at the contents of the envelope. Slowly, hesitantly, wanting to both hasten and prolong the moment of discovery.

It would be nice if I could get a chocolate factory out of this whole ordeal.

But no golden ticket peeks out at me; no invitation with my name flutters down from the sky. When I open that envelope, all I see is a wad of cold, hard cash.

So much cash.

Crap.

My eyes widen as I thumb through the stack; a precursory look tells me they're all twenties. I slow down and then start over, and even though I'm no mathematician, it only takes me a couple seconds to realize this has to be many hundreds of dollars, if not more.

I glance around nervously at the empty shop; somehow I feel like the IRS is going to pop out from behind the bookshelves at any second. They'll know that I was in the same vicinity as this much cash, and I'll get in massive trouble for just existing here.

Crap. Crap, crap, crap. What do I do?

I'm pulling up his contact before I'm even fully aware of it, pressing the *call* button despite all the logic telling me not to.

Somehow it feels like he's part of this with me. Maybe it's because he's the one I called the other night, even though I don't remember it. Or maybe it's because there's something about him I trust—an air of competence and calm that ground me.

He answers after six rings.

"Soren!" I whisper, clutching the phone with one still-shaking hand. "Soren!"

There's a muffled sort of grunting sound on the other end, then a second of silence, and then a groggy voice.

"Mmm? Hello?" he says. It could not be clearer that I am waking him out of a dead sleep.

"Soren!" I whisper again, looking down at the envelope in my hand. "I just found—"

"Heidi?" he says, cutting me off, his voice still bleary.

Hearing his voice saying my name triggers a memory, and it takes me a second to realize what I'm thinking of.

"Oh," I say, more to myself than to him as I recall the feeling of his hands on my shoulders, propelling me gently through the bookshop. "You didn't call me *honey* today at all. You just called me Heidi. Heidi, honey. Heidi, honey." They sound relatively similar, especially when you're speaking quietly. That makes sense.

I swallow down my strange stab of disappointment.

"Heidi?" Soren says again. "Is that you? Hang on—what time is it?"

"Yes, it's me. And it's...late," I say with a wince. "Sorry."

"Why are you whispering?" he says. "Are you okay?"

"I'm—oh," I say, looking around. He's right; why am I whispering? I don't need to be. It's just me here. "Sorry," I say, clearing my throat. "Yes. It's me. And I'm fine. But I found something super sketchy, Soren, and I think Carmina might have been blackmailing someone."

"What? Hang on," Soren mutters. "Just—hang on. Give me a second."

"Yeah," I say breathlessly. "That's fine."

I listen to the sound of rustling, and in the background I hear a faint *click*; turning a lamp on, maybe. Then he returns.

"Okay," he says. "Start from the beginning, please."

"Right," I say, and I begin to pace. "So. I came downstairs to feed Jojo, and then I wanted to clean everything, so I started sweeping, and then—"

"In the middle of the night?" he says, his voice flat. "You wanted to sweep the floor right this very second?"

"I needed to *clean*, Soren," I snap as some of that panic bubbles up like a fizzy drink in the back of my throat. "I watched someone die today. Please let me entertain the illusion that cleaning the shop will give me a measure of control over my life."

"Fine," he says, though it's more of a grunt. "Fine. Go on."

"So I was sweeping, right?"

"Apparently."

"And I wanted to get under the chairs and tables—"

"Sure, why not?"

"Shut up," I say. "So then I moved the other armchair, the one that's over by the windows—"

"Naturally."

"And there was this envelope underneath."

"Okay. What envelope?" He sounds more awake now.

"It's just a standard white envelope," I say, looking at it clasped in my hand. "Totally normal. But there's a sticky note attached that has a message on it. 'You'll not get a penny more out of me, you old hag. I'll make you regret this,'" I read. "That's what the note says."

"'You'll not get a penny more...'" Soren says slowly.

"'Out of me, you old hag,'" I finish with a nod. "'I'll make you regret this.' Yeah. That's what it says."

"And inside the envelope?"

I cock one eyebrow. "What do you think?"

"Not...is it money?" he says, and his voice is incredulous. I don't blame him. It's hard to believe.

"Yep," I say. "A bunch of it. Cash."

"How much?"

"Give me a sec." I sandwich the phone uncomfortably between my shoulder and my cheek and then do a quick count. "One thousand," I say.

"Denomination?"

"Twenties."

"Okay," he says, and his voice is musing as he goes on, "okay. Got it. But what makes you think this has anything to do with Carmina?"

"Oh," I say. "Her initials are on the envelope. Sorry, I forgot that part."

"Her initials are written on the envelope? Or are they on the sticky note?"

"They're on the envelope, but the sticky note is stuck *to* the envelope."

"Hang on," Soren says. "I'm going to video chat. This is confusing."

"What?" I squawk, sounding like Jojo. "Don't video chat me!" Doesn't he know I need time to prepare mentally for any and all video correspondence? I need to check and make sure I don't look stupid. I need to make sure this lighting doesn't give me a double chin. I need to take some deep breaths and remind myself that people do video calls every day, all over the world, and they manage fine.

But it's too late; my phone is ringing once more, my startled expression staring back at me as my video connects.

"Soren," I groan as I answer, and his image pops up. "You can't just—just—"

But I break off, swallowing. Then I lick my lips.

Why is my mouth suddenly dry?

Soren is shirtless, and he looks like he's in bed, like I thought; there's what looks like a pillow propped up behind him. His hair is loose, mussed but perfectly golden, and for a moment I flash back to that day we met for the first time—when I burst in on him in the bathtub. This isn't a high definition video; things are a little pixelated. But even so...

"Unnecessarily hot," I mutter.

Don't ogle the pretty man, Heidi.

"Why are you shirtless?" I say with a sigh. I think it's best if I address the most pressing issues first.

"Hang on," he says. "What did you say?"

"I said 'Why are you shirtless—'"

"No," he cuts me off, and a strange expression crosses his face, one I'm not sure I've seen before. It's a smirk, the kind my brother used to give every girl he met before Gemma came into his life—self-assured, bordering on cocky, and undeniably flirtatious.

Why is he smirking at me? And why do I *like* it? Because I do. But I don't like cocky men.

And yet as that smirk grows even more prominent, my stomach flips.

"Before that," he goes on, completely oblivious to my internal dilemma. "What did you say before that? Did you call me *hot*?"

Time to lie through my freaking teeth.

"No," I say. "I said—" I break off, casting around desperately for phrases that rhyme with *unnecessarily hot*. All I can come up with are *a mercenary snot* and *a messy fairly lot*, both of which are less than helpful.

"You did. You said I was hot," he says, and even through the video chat I can see his eyes sparkling. For some reason, this makes him inordinately happy.

"Fine," I say, stomping my foot. "Yes. That's what I said." I refuse to let myself be embarrassed about this. I have too many other things to worry about. "Physical attraction is a perfectly normal occurrence, Soren. There's nothing strange about it."

"Sure," he says comfortably, running one hand through his long hair. "I just didn't realize you felt that way about *me*."

"I don't," I say. "It was a momentary thing."

"That's too bad," he murmurs, and my stupid stomach flips again.

"Anyway," I say.

"Wait," he says. His voice is more normal now, and that smirk melts away into something that looks like concern. His eyes narrow. "Were you crying?"

My jaw drops. "How could you possibly know that?"

He points at me through the screen. "Your eyes are red."

I squint at my picture in the corner of the screen. "I don't think they are."

He shrugs, which only serves to draw my attention back to his stupid muscles. "They look red to me. Why were you crying?"

The tears prick at my eyes again. "It's nothing. It's stupid. I'm just overwhelmed. And kind of freaked out, I guess. By Carmina and the voicemail I left you." I swallow down the guilt that rises like bile in my throat. "I keep thinking that maybe I knew she was going to die, and I could have done something to help."

"You can't blame yourself for this," he says.

"I know," I say with a sigh. "I know that. I still feel bad."

"And crying isn't stupid," he goes on. "It's healthy. You're allowed to cry."

I don't tell him the truth: that I'm done crying. That crying has never done anything for me; it's never fixed my body, and it's never made me feel better.

So I took all of those tears and channeled them into productivity instead.

Soren clears his throat, probably because I've been silent for too long. "Well, show me the envelope," he says.

Yes. The envelope. Good.

"Here," I say, holding it up. "The initials, see? And then the sticky note was right here" —I place the sticky note back where it was— "and then the cash is inside."

"Hmm," Soren says.

It's a low, gravelly sound, and for a brief second I imagine pressing my finger to his Adam's apple when he hums like that; would I feel the vibrations?

"Heidi?" he says, and I startle.

Crap. I'm being weird.

"Yeah?" I say in my best non-weird voice.

"You still with me?"

I'm a little *too* with him. But "Yes" is all I say.

"Well, we can't do anything about this tonight, and you need to sleep. So let's talk tomorrow, okay?" he says.

Part of me wants to argue, because I find some sort of perverse joy in pushing back with Soren. But I know he's right.

"Okay," I say, and my voice sounds heavy. "Talk to you tomorrow, then."

He murmurs a goodbye, and I force myself to end the call first, so I'm not tempted to linger.

Before I put the chair back and head to my flat, I snap a few quick photos of the envelope. Then I put the broom away and trudge back upstairs.

My pillowcase is damp by the time I finally fall asleep.

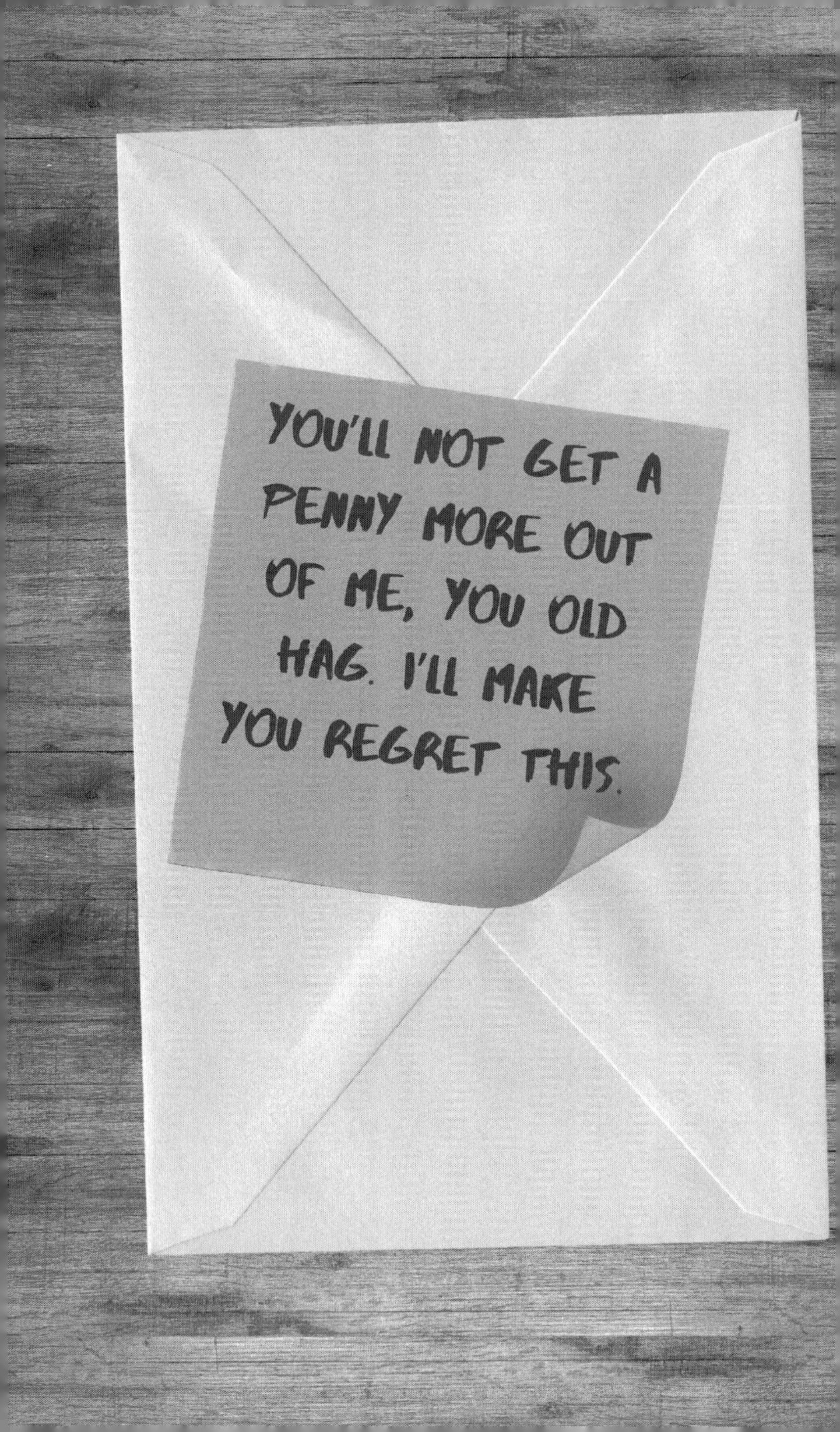
YOU'LL NOT GET A PENNY MORE OUT OF ME, YOU OLD HAG. I'LL MAKE YOU REGRET THIS.

8

IN WHICH SOREN MAKES A
DECISION

Video chatting with a pajama-clad Heidi in the middle of the night doesn't do great things for my dreams after I fall back asleep. Or, rather, it does too many great things—when I wake up the next day, my bed feels larger and colder and emptier than normal. I sigh, sitting up and looking around the bedroom.

I thought putting more furniture in here would make it feel less lonely, but it didn't. It just makes the loneliness feel claustrophobic instead of vast and echoing.

I need to move. I need to *downsize*. I don't love this neighborhood anyway. It has an old money feeling to it that makes me feel like all the neighbors are judging me. Part of that sensation might be in my head, but part of it is real. I'll be the first to admit that when I'm buried in a manuscript, I turn into a bit of a slob. I'm sure a hulking man with long hair and ketchup-stained sweatpants taking his trash out to the curb is not what my neighbors want to see all the time. I don't need to live someplace where everything is so stately, anyway. I'm not a stately guy. I'm pretty simple.

I would like my publishers not to drop me, and I would like to date my favorite bookshop owner, and I would like to not run through all my savings.

I get out of bed and hop in the shower, ignoring the truth trying to worm its way between the folds of my brain: that a different apartment or house or neighborhood is never going to help me accomplish any of those things, and it definitely won't alleviate the loneliness.

But like Heidi did last night, cleaning in the middle of the night in order to exert some control over her life, I'll probably do the same by trying to move.

At first while I'm in the shower, I rush through washing my hair and my body, so that I can get to the bookstore earlier—until it dawns on me that Carmina Hildegarde is no longer around to steal my spot. When I feel the tiniest spark of relief at that, I'm so revolted with myself that I almost vomit.

By the time I get to Paper Patisserie an hour later, I'm feeling distinctly wrong-footed.

"Hi," I mouth to Heidi when I spot her, a cardboard box in her arms as she emerges from the bookshelves and heads in the direction of the kitchen.

"Oh, hi," she says. She changes course, heading to my chair instead.

My chair that I'm not ever going to have to fight Carmina for again. I rub my stomach, that faint swell of nausea rising once more.

I take a moment to look Heidi over as she approaches. She's wearing her hair in a ponytail today, fresh-faced and natural with a yellow t-shirt and slouchy jeans. I peer more intently at her as she stops in front of me.

You'd never know she was struggling so much yesterday. She looks fine—a serious expression, maybe, and the bandage on her forehead makes her look tough, but there are no red eyes or red nose or tear tracks. I don't even see her fidgeting with that nervous energy she gets sometimes.

I'll have to see how she does when she's not holding a box with both hands.

"I'm glad you're here," she says, stepping closer. Then she crouches down next to my armchair, setting the box on the ground beside her.

It's the same way she crouched next to Carmina's chair at the table yesterday. I banish that image from my mind, though I know it will return to haunt me again anyway.

"I have the envelope," she whispers. "It's upstairs."

"Can I look at it?" I say.

She nods, standing up. "I can slip away for a second." Then she uses her foot to push her cardboard box closer to the armchair so that it's out of the way.

I stand too, turning and placing my laptop and notebook in my chair. I hesitate, though, and then change my mind, grabbing my things and tucking them under my arm.

For most of the year, I wouldn't worry much about someone stealing my things. This is Sunshine Springs; I know at least half the residents personally, and I recognize the other half by sight. But during the summer, our little town turns into something of a tourist hub, partly from people making pit stops on their way north to bigger places like Jackson Hole or Yellowstone. We also get tourists visiting the natural hot springs we're named for. I'm sure someday someone will build a resort or something around those springs, but for now they're a hidden gem, located a little way outside of town and toward the Teton Valley.

It's the tourists I don't fully trust with my laptop. So my things will come with me.

I follow Heidi as she weaves through the bookshelves,

nodding at Calvin when we pass the sales counter and then eyeing Jojo. I'm always interested to hear what that bird has to say, but today he's silent, hopping around on his bar and rustling his feathers. Heidi and I are silent too, making our way up the narrow stairs until we reach her door. A few seconds later, it's unlocked.

"Here," she says as she opens the door. She moves immediately to her little kitchen table. She picks up the envelope that's lying there and then turns and hands it to me.

She was right; it's a completely normal-looking envelope, except for the sticky note attached. I read the threatening words a few times, noting the handwriting especially; I'm certainly no expert, but it looks like a man's writing to me.

"Do you think a man wrote this, or a woman?" I say, still looking at the jagged letters.

"I get male vibes," Heidi says immediately, and I nod. "Me too."

"Not that vibes are necessarily anything to go on," she adds.

"No," I say quickly. "They're not."

"But still." She bites her lip—which I do *not* stare at, because I am mostly a gentleman—and goes on, "I don't know what to do with it. Do you think I should turn it in to the police? That seems like something they'd want."

I nod again. "I think that would be best. I don't know what happened to Carmina, but if this came from her purse, it would probably be relevant. You said it was underneath that other armchair?"

"Yes," she says. "And it's not far from the table where Carmina—" She breaks off, clearing her throat. "Where her stuff spilled. I think it's hers, and it probably got kicked by an errant foot or something and slid under there."

That seems the most likely to me too. Her initials on the

front of the envelope and the *old hag* reference seem like decent indicators. Heck, I think *I* might have called her that before.

"Okay," Heidi says with a sigh. "I need to get back downstairs."

"Yeah," I say, handing her the envelope. "Let's go. Thanks for letting me take a look."

When we get back downstairs, Heidi retrieves her box, but I stand staring at my armchair. Someone has taken my seat—a tourist with a fanny pack and a Yellowstone t-shirt.

My little stab of irritation feels an awful lot like penance.

TWO POLICE OFFICERS SHOW UP MIDDAY. THEY'RE SO mismatched that it would be funny, were it not for the looks on their faces. They're both men, one tall and thin with red hair, one short and fat with blond.

But their expressions are far too serious for someplace as cheerful as the bookshop. Sure, it's a little cramped in here, but the sun pours through the front windows, and the walls are a buttery yellow, and—if I were the kind of man to use such words—I would call the checkered floor of the café *adorable*. And while I am a firm believer in the power of the written word for anyone and everyone, policemen included...I don't think they're here to find a summer read.

Did Heidi call them to come take the envelope? I figured she would run it over to the station later. Maybe she called them instead.

She appears from nowhere, bustling over to them. They're standing in the entrance, looking around; I feel an inexplicable twinge of foreboding when their eyes fall on me.

"Hi," Heidi says, tucking a few strands of hair behind her

ear. She's nervous now, fidgety in little ways that she tries to conceal, and there's no box in her hands to hide behind.

I can only tell these things because I've been studying her for years, like a borderline stalker.

"What can I do for you?" she says to the policemen. "Are you here to shop?"

I blink in surprise; I guess she didn't call them. Why are they here, then?

"We're not here to shop, no," the tall one says, his voice clipped, businesslike. "Is there someplace we could have a private word?"

"Of course," Heidi says with a nod. "This way, please."

Despite the situation, I'm weirdly proud of her, the way she's maintaining her composure. She disappears into the bookshelves with her head held high, the policemen following her—an odd group of ducklings after their mother.

Can I follow them without looking suspicious?

Crap. No. I can't. Besides, as much as I hate to admit it...it's none of my business what they talk to her about. So I stare at my laptop instead, the cursor blinking at the bottom of my last paragraph.

Maybe I'll get my new writing group to take a look at some of this. I'm so far in my head with this manuscript, so deeply and embarrassingly insecure, that I have no idea if this idea is even worth writing, or if I should chuck it and start something new.

Ugh. No. I can't start something new; I'm on a deadline.

So I guess I'll workshop it, as much as I don't want to. I've been chatting a bit with the group ever since we decided to meet a few days from now, and they're cool. There's not too many of them, either, which is a big plus. Just another guy and a girl.

Ideally, no one would be subjected to my first draft. But I

need help. I'm man enough to admit that, even if my problems don't feel fixable. Because I know—I *know,* dang it—that the issue is not with my writing, or at least it doesn't start with my writing. My problem is all mental.

I'm stuck in my head, second guessing every word I write, and it's making everything come out stilted and ridiculous. I'm terrified that I've peaked already, terrified that this book will bomb like the last one did, terrified that for the rest of my life I'll be known as S. Mackenzie, the one-hit wonder.

I shake my head vigorously, pulling myself back to my work. I need to focus. But only half of my brain is able to pay attention to the words I'm trying to write; the other half is on Heidi and the policemen. They've been back there for probably ten minutes now.

"Gemma," I whisper when she walks past, heading for the café counter.

Gemma turns to me, looking surprised. "Yeah," she says. "What's up?"

I beckon her closer. "What are they talking about with Heidi? Did you hear anything?" I say when she's standing right in front of me.

"No," she says, and I'm relieved to see an anxious look on her face, too; it's nice to know I'm not crazy for being nervous. "She just took them into the back room." She fiddles with her jewelry, twisting one of her silver rings around and around on her finger. Then, biting her lip, she adds, "You don't think anything's wrong, do you?"

"I don't know," I say, and my frustration is evident in my voice. I shouldn't be this on edge. Of course the police would want to talk to the business owner after something like yesterday. I just can't get rid of this boulder that seems to have settled on my gut.

"What about you?" Gemma says. "Have you ever written about anything like this? Murder and police and stuff?"

I blink at her. "My books are literary fiction."

"I don't know what that means," she says, flipping her hair over her shoulder. "I read fantasy and romance. No offense," she adds belatedly.

I don't let her see my smile. "None taken." I'm well aware that my books aren't for everyone.

Still, there's an ugly little voice in my head that whispers, *If you wrote a better literary novel, she would like it. Yours isn't good enough.*

"So, that's a no on the murder and police stuff in your books?" she says.

"Correct," I say, nodding. "Mine don't have any of that."

"And is that a literary fiction thing, or a you thing?" Gemma says, and she actually looks interested in my answer.

"A me thing," I say. "There are lots of literary novels that have crimes in them." I shrug. "It's just not something I've done."

"Huh," she says. "I learned something new today."

I smile at her. "I guess you did."

Then she nods to the café counter. "Well, I'm gonna go talk to Mel so we can speculate wildly about why the police are here," she says. "Later, Man Bun."

"Heidi is the only one who gets to call me that," I say with narrowed eyes.

"Nope," she says, popping the *p*. "Sorry. It's public domain." And then she's off, waltzing around the café counter and back into the kitchen, and I'm left shaking my head.

I write a total of two hundred words while I'm waiting for Heidi to come back, and it's like pulling teeth. I force myself not to jump out of my seat when she reappears, leading the policemen to the door. I also force myself not to stare at her, not to examine her facial expression for any clues as to how she's feeling.

She'll tell me if she wants to.

The foreboding in my gut intensifies, however, when instead of leaving, the policemen swerve toward me. Heidi looks surprised.

"Are you Soren Mackenzie?" the short one says.

I clear my throat. "Yes," I say.

Why am I so nervous? He's just asking my name. It's not like I'm lying to him. Still, with the way my heart is racing, I would absolutely fail a polygraph right now.

"Could we have a word?" the tall one says.

I want to say no. I want to tell him to leave me alone. But that doesn't feel like the smart option, so I nod. I set my computer aside and stand, and the tall one gestures for me to follow him.

Maybe they want to get my statement again.

My gait is stiff, my arms swinging awkwardly at my sides as I trail through the shelves, emerging by the bookshop sales counter and then passing into the storeroom in the back. It's cluttered enough that the three of us have to squeeze, shuffling around and finding our footing between the stacks of boxes.

"What can I help you with?" I say, forcing myself to breathe normally.

"You were present yesterday during the death of Mrs. Carmina Hildegarde, is that correct?"

"Yes," I say.

"You should know that that death is being treated as suspicious, due to the claim of the deceased that she was murdered," the tall one says. "We contacted a number of eyewitnesses yesterday, based on Miss Lucy's account of everyone who was present at the time of the death. It appears that there was some contention between you and the deceased that you didn't mention at the time of your statement yesterday; is that correct?"

His voice isn't hostile, but it's not friendly, either. It's businesslike bordering on curt, and the look on his face is the same. His partner's expression is no better.

"We—we argued sometimes, yes," I say.

The short one nods. "Want to tell us more about that?" It's not a question.

Crap. *Crap.*

"I'm sorry," I say stupidly. "I don't understand what's going on right now. Am I a suspect?"

"Let's not put labels on things yet," the tall one says. "We just want to talk."

I almost snort. I'm a suspect here. I'm totally a suspect. What the heck is happening right now?

"Carmina and I fought over the same chair," I say, and I can hear the dazed note in my voice. "That's it. That's all."

The short one nods, flipping through a notepad that seems to have materialized out of thin air. "We have a report here that you were heard threatening violence to the deceased."

"I—what?" I say, bewildered.

"Mmm," the short one says. "'I swear I'm going to dropkick that woman all the way to Yellowstone,' according to my report."

Holy crap. I *did* say that. I said that yesterday.

Why did I say that? And who snitched on me?

"Look," I say. I reign in my panic, forcing my voice to remain calm and innocent. "Carmina and I didn't get along. And I did say that. But I didn't *kill* her. Good grief." I blink. "I have trouble killing off *characters,* much less a real human being."

When they stare at me blankly, I clarify. "I'm a writer."

"Ah," they both say, nodding. Then the short one pulls the pen out of his pocket. "And do you often write about inflicting violence on others?" he says, looking intently at me.

"What—no!" I say. "No! I'm saying I *don't* do that! I write about—about—I don't know. People, and relationships, and the dynamics of dysfunctional families, and society, and what it means to be human!"

It sounds lame even to me. But no one ever said I was high concept.

This is going very poorly.

"Well, Mr. Mackenzie, we're going to ask that you stick around for a while, okay?"

Good grief. They're doing that thing where they ask me not to leave town. This is so bad.

"I didn't kill anyone!" I burst out, throwing my hands in the air.

All they do is nod.

"We'll be in touch," the short one says.

I wave my understanding, feeling suddenly exhausted and weak, like there are weights tied around my bones. I bet if you dropped me in a river, I'd sink right to the bottom.

Don't be needlessly morbid, I tell my brain.

I watch as Tall and Thin follows Short and Fat out of the storeroom, and I breathe a sigh of relief.

Heidi bursts in thirty seconds later.

"What happened?" she says, out of breath.

"Pretty sure I'm a suspect," I say dully.

"I think I might be too."

"I threatened to dropkick Carmina all the way to Yellowstone."

Heidi looks at me disapprovingly, and then she sighs. "I served her her food and drink," she says.

I frown. "What does that have to do with anything?"

Heidi shrugs. "I got the feeling it was a potential poison thing."

My answering sigh is loud in the cramped space. "Did you give them the envelope?"

"I did, yeah. I told them about the blood I found last night, too. Before I called," she says, playing absently with the end of her ponytail where it falls over her shoulder. Then she looks at me. "I think it might have been mine, but they said they'd have someone come and collect a sample." She sighs. "I need to figure out what happened to her. I keep feeling like I'm missing something, and I *know* it's whatever secret I forgot. I *know* it. And I can't shake the feeling that it has something to do with Carmina."

"Okay," I say slowly, thinking.

"And now with the police asking me these questions," she goes on, "I can't sit here and do nothing. I'm not going to get in trouble for something I didn't do. I don't have time for that. I need to figure out what happened."

I watch her for a moment, the faraway look in her eyes, the tension around her mouth, her slightly-too-pale face. And it hits me then, so powerfully that I almost lose my breath.

I'm going to date this woman.

I watched someone die yesterday, and now the police are looking at me with suspicious eyes. I'm stumbling my way through a manuscript that still feels totally foreign to me, and I'm tense most of the time.

But even with all of that going on, I can't think of anything I would rather do at this very moment than kiss Heidi Lucy on the lips.

Maybe it's a weird time to be thinking about all this, but I can't help it. Life is short. I'm not going to waste any more of it.

So when she turns her big hazel eyes on me and asks the question I've been waiting for, I only have one response.

"Will you help me?" she says.

I nod, squaring my shoulders. "Absolutely."

❧ 9 ❧

IN WHICH HEIDI AND SOREN
GET MUCH, MUCH CLOSER

My laundry seems to have multiplied. I sit on my couch, trying to get a good amount of folding in before Soren gets here. I'm not a messy person, and I'm not a slob. How do I have so many clothes that are all dirty at the same time?

Be more productive, a little voice whispers in my mind. *Earn your keep.* I try to push it away, try to ignore it like my therapist taught me all those years ago, but I can still feel the words embedding themselves, needling under my skin. I shake my head, squeezing my eyes shut and opening them again. Then I resume my folding.

After the policemen collected the blood sample and then left yesterday, Soren and I agreed to meet this morning at ten-thirty to make a plan and figure out details. If we're going to look into what happened to Carmina, we need to strategize.

"'Find, pick, lock,'" I mutter to myself as I fold mindlessly. "That's definitely what she said." But how on earth am I supposed to know what lock she wants me to pick? She was very much mistaken if she thought picking *any* kind of lock was part of my skill set.

I'll talk to Soren, and we'll figure it out. It's not how I would normally spend my Saturday, but Carmina's last words are propelling me just as much as my desire to learn what memories I've lost. She looked right at me and said those things; how can I not take them seriously? So we'll figure out everything we can today; Mel and Gemma can handle the shop fine.

Speaking of my best friend...

I hold up the t-shirt I've just reached, snorting with laughter. It feels good, and I test the smile on my face, pushing it further until it's stretched unnaturally wide. I look like a maniac, I'm sure, but I read once that the action of smiling can improve your mood. So I keep it there, forcing it to stay, while I look at the shirt.

After devouring Soren's first book—and immediately preordering the second—I kept telling Gemma about it. I tried to get her to read it multiple times. I begged. I pleaded. But she never would. Instead she started teasing me about being such a fangirl, and on the day Soren's second book released, she presented me with this t-shirt: bright, vivid pink, adorned with block letters that read *I WANT TO MARRY S. MACKENZIE.*

It's not something I would ever make or choose for myself, but...well, I'd be lying if I said I don't wear it to sleep sometimes when my other pajamas are in the wash. I cringe at myself in the mirror, but I wear it.

I fold the shirt quickly and then lift a pair of pants off the top of my stack, placing the shirt underneath so that it's not visible. Then I sigh.

I'm tired. I'm so tired. I slept horribly last night.

That, combined with the trauma of the last few days and

the still-healing lump on my head, might be enough for me to justify a nap later this afternoon. Just a little one, maybe?

I hurry through three more shirts before I hear a knock on my door.

I jump up, grabbing the pile of unfolded clothing and rushing to my bedroom. I dump it all on the bed—which I'm positive I will regret later when I'm ready to sleep—and then hurry out, closing the door behind me so Soren won't get a peek at my mess.

"Hi," I say when I open my front door, stepping back to let Soren in. Then I blink at him. "You trimmed your beard," I say, surprised.

"I did," he says, rubbing his hand over his shorter facial hair. "Do I look handsome?"

"I—what?" I heard him. I heard him fine. But maybe if I pretend I didn't, I won't have to answer.

He takes a step further inside, a little smile tugging at the corner of his lips. "I asked if I look handsome."

Well. So much for that.

I clear my throat. "That's random." I press my hand to my chest, frowning absently—why can I hear my heartbeat whooshing in my ears?—and then say, "You look fine. Normal." I clear my throat again, more aggressively this time, like a motorcycle revving its engine. "Normal fine." It's a lie; he looks neither normal nor fine. He just looks *good*. His plain blue t-shirt is tight enough that I can see muscle definition, but not so tight that he looks obnoxious, and his jeans hug his thighs perfectly.

Soren hums, nodding slowly as he cocks one eyebrow. "I look...normal fine?"

"Yes," I say, because at this point I have no choice but to embrace my made-up phrase. I smooth my hands over my own loose t-shirt. "Normal fine."

"That's an interesting term," he says, still looking down at me with that little smile. My pulse hasn't slowed; it's still trying to jump out of my veins, and the look he's giving me isn't helping. His gaze is brimming with a quiet amusement, and it makes his eyes sparkle. "But a bit of a downgrade. You said *unnecessarily hot* last time. Can't I at least have *handsome* today?"

"You may not," I say primly. "Try again tomorrow." Then I turn my back on him and move to the couch, resisting the urge to fan my face. "Sit," I say, pointing. I hurry before him and grab my stack of folded laundry, moving it to the floor, and Soren settles on the couch—a large, beautiful man on my squashy, cramped, dingy, pinkish-gray sofa.

He's really too big for this apartment. I'm a fan of minimalism in my living space, which does help keep things tidy, and the exposed brick gives it an air of urbanity. But when it comes down to it, this flat is still itty bitty.

"Okay," I say without preamble, ignoring how much he stands out in this place. "Based on the events of yesterday, we both seem to have come under suspicion for Carmina's death." I sit on the couch next to him, pulling my legs up.

Soren nods but doesn't speak.

"You didn't kill her, did you?" I say, glancing over at him. "Because we're friends, but I'm not going to help you cover anything up."

Now he rolls his eyes. "Your opinion of me is awfully low today."

I do my best to hide the twitching of my lips. Soren would never kill anyone; he's a big guy, but he has a gentle soul.

"What if you killed her?" he says now. "I've heard you threatening violence on a certain Poodle."

My jaw drops. "Oh, no," I whisper as my eyes widen on him. "Do you think—"

"What?" he cuts me off, laughing. "No. Of course I don't. I was joking, Heidi. Sorry—it was a bad joke. No. You wouldn't do that."

"In that case," I say, breathing a little more easily. "I'm not going to sit around and wait for the police to decide that we're somehow guilty. I want to figure out what happened here and get this whole thing behind me."

I don't mention my other reasons for wanting to solve this puzzle. It might help my memories return, for one. It's an unfounded assumption at best. But I can't shake the feeling that Carmina had something to do with the cryptic phone call I made to Soren the other night. I can feel it in my bones.

And I can't help thinking that when Carmina directed her last words at me, she was basically begging me to help her find justice.

"Do you not trust the police to do their job properly?" Soren says.

"It's not that," I say. "I have no idea if they'll do a good job. I'm just hesitant to sit around twiddling my thumbs when there's a possibility that I could be doing something to speed the process along."

"I would like to go on record and state that this could be a bad idea."

"Nah," I say, waving his concern away. "It will be fine." I can't do nothing. I just...can't.

"All right," Soren says with a sigh. "Let's pick a starting place, then."

"I think we should visit the son first," I say.

"Carmina's son?"

"Yes. All we have to go on right now is the envelope of money and her last words—something about picking a lock. We can ask him about both of those."

Soren frowns. "Do you know him?"

"Vaguely. You might have seen him too; he came in with her sometimes. He's introduced himself. But we could tell him about the envelope and ask if he knows anything about it. Maybe he knows of anyone who had issues with her."

"It feels wrong to speak ill of the dead," Soren says slowly, "but I imagine a lot of people had issues with her."

"Me too," I say, my voice grudging.

"We don't know where the son lives, though," Soren says.

"I think he and his wife lived with Carmina," I say, thinking. "Or the other way around; she lived with them. We'd still have to figure that out, though—"

"Oh, I know *her* address," Soren cuts me off. "Are you sure they lived together?"

I don't know why his use of the past tense hits me when I've been using it too, but it does; I stumble over my next words.

"Pretty sure," I say. Then, looking at him, I blurt out the nonsensical thought that's running through my mind. "Death is kind of weird, isn't it?"

"Mmm," Soren says, a thoughtful expression on his face. He leans back, settling further into my little sofa. I can objectively admit that he is the most attractive person who ever sits there. "How so?"

"It's just—life is such a big thing," I say. I stare at my hands. "*Living* is such an all-consuming thing. And yet people die so quickly, so easily. One second you're here, and the next second you're gone. It really can happen that fast. Things can change that fast." I swallow, looking more intently at my hands, idly examining my fingernails. "My mom is selling the house we grew up in, me and her and Eric. She sent me pictures of the empty rooms, and whenever I think about it, I keep wondering how someplace that was so full can suddenly seem so empty."

I don't know where all this is coming from, and I feel stupid for saying it. At the same time, though...I've let loose the thoughts that have been swirling around, and somehow it feels easier to breathe now that I have. Isn't it strange, how speaking your thoughts can feel like removing a thorn from tender skin? You feel better when you get it out.

I risk a glance at Soren again, and my heart stutters; his eyes, vivid and blue, are darting over my face, and he's wearing an expression I can't quite place. My little sofa doesn't allow for much space between us; his side is pressed up against mine, radiating the kind of warmth you want to curl up in.

Silence falls, laced suddenly with awareness. It's not a scary silence or a damning silence; it's a tentative, blooming thing, like the flowers that are starting to peek through the rich soil outside—alive, full of possibility.

What is Soren going to do with the piece of my mind I've given him? Laugh? Scoff? Shrug it off? Embrace it? And why is he the one I say these things to, anyway? Why him? Why not any of my other friends, or Eric?

But the answer to that comes, unbidden, in a flash of realization: because Soren is the person who has never once looked at me with judgment.

We argue and bicker, but there's a level of play to it that stops things from ever becoming truly contentious. Even with all of our quarreling, he never judges me.

"It is kind of weird, now that you mention it," he says with a nod, and the anxious fist that was clenched around my insides loosens a bit. Then, hesitantly, he reaches up and brushes my hair away from my face, his eyes lingering on my bandaged forehead. The skim of his fingers over my skin sends a strange thrill through me, a current of electricity that's both foreign and familiar. "How does it feel?"

"So good," I breathe without thinking.

His hand freezes on my forehead; his eyes flare wider, and a muscle twitches in his jaw. The hand that's on the armrest clenches tighter until his knuckles are white.

Hot. It's hot in here. It's really, really warm in here, especially where our sides are pressed together.

"It's fine," I say, trying to keep my voice strong and firm. I clear my throat. "That's what I meant. It's good. It doesn't hurt too much."

He hesitates for a beat and then nods, looking away from me. His hand drops from my face, rubbing over his newly trimmed scruff instead. Then he crosses his legs and rests one ankle on his knee, a manly stance that's...weirdly attractive?

I shake my head, tearing my gaze away. What is wrong with me today? Why am I like this? It's Soren. Yes, he's handsome, and yes, he has the most beautiful hair I've ever seen, and yes, he smells good—a sharp, peppery scent—but still.

That's no reason for me to lose my mind.

"Yeah," I say, tucking my hair behind my ear despite the fact that he just did it for me. "Anyway." I hunt desperately for words, seizing gratefully upon a question when it pops into my mind. "Uh, how do you know Carmina's address?"

"I saw her ID when I was picking up the stuff that fell out of her purse," he says with a shrug.

Good. This is good. A shrug is very natural, very easy, very casual—all good things.

"And you're positive you remember what it said?"

"Yeah, I remember," he says. "It was over in Maplewood."

Maplewood—one of the two sprawling neighborhoods where I did my ill-advised dog-walking stint.

"A townhome or a house?"

"I don't know," he says with another shrug.

"All right," I say. "We can try that."

Despite all the shrugging and the return to normalcy, it still feels warm in here to me, and I'm still unnaturally aware of

Soren's body pressed close to mine. I stand up, which takes a bit since I'm wedged in there pretty good, and then try to walk as casually as possible to the refrigerator. I open the freezer and rummage around for a minute, doing absolutely nothing productive, welcoming the icy breath on my skin.

I do not press my single-serving frozen dinner to my cheeks like I want to, because I would have no explanation for that. I just waft the air toward me a few more times before closing the freezer and turning back around. Then I say, "So how about..."

But I trail off when I register what it is I'm seeing, my mouth still hanging open unflatteringly.

It's Soren, standing next to the couch, and he's holding something in his hands.

Something...pink.

Something with black lettering.

Something suspiciously...t-shirt-like.

Yes, I realize with a stab of horror. That is my fangirl t-shirt dangling from Soren's pinched fingers. The ridiculous one that Gemma made for me.

The one that says *I WANT TO MARRY S. MACKENZIE* in big, bold letters.

Because within five minutes of me blurting out that his hand feels amazing on my skin, of course something like this would happen. How did he even find that shirt? I buried it.

My gaze travels from the shirt to Soren's face, my heart thumping a little too quickly, heat flooding my body. Forget pressing my freezer meal to my cheeks; I'm going to dump the tray of ice cubes down my shirt.

I shut the freezer and move back to the couch like I'm in some sort of trance, my eyes wide, my steps shuffling. Soren is staring at the t-shirt with furrowed brows and narrowed eyes, and he's opening his mouth like he's about to speak, and this is not good. This is not good at *all*.

Would it be the end of the world if he knew I was his number one fan? No. But telling him that feels as personal as telling someone you have feelings for them. It's basically confessing that I'm halfway in love with his mind. Plus, how would I even explain that I don't *really* want to marry him—it was a stupid joke my best friend thought was hilarious?

I'm not ready for that conversation.

So I do the first thing I can think of.

And look. It's not a smart move. It's certainly not the most rational move.

But I am a desperate woman.

So just like when I kicked the doctor in the gut at the hospital...I launch myself at Soren, purely on instinct.

I know—I *know*. It's stupid. But all I can think of is that I have to get that t-shirt out of his hands, and I have to distract him. And for some reason my tired, humiliated, overheated brain takes this input and translates it as *Must jump on Soren*.

So to Soren I go, in one flying leap, like an awkward baseball player trying to reach home plate. I crash into him, my *oomph* mixing with his startled yelp as we both go down, tumbling to the ground in a chaotic heap of limbs and swear words.

"What the—hey," he says from his position beneath me. I blink my eyes open, terrified to move even an inch because our bodies are twisted and tangled in such a way that I really don't know what I'm touching right now. It puts me in mind of those lotion ads, where it's a close-up shot of a bunch of skin, and I always find myself wondering what body part I'm looking at— except now I'm worried about what I might be in *contact* with.

I'm a woman on a mission, though, and I will not let this horrifically executed move be for nothing. So I raise my head up—it seems to be resting somewhere over Soren's right shoulder—except Soren moves at the same time, rolling his body slightly sideways.

And it is at that precise moment, at approximately ten-forty in the morning on the floor of my living room, that Soren Mackenzie and I have our very first kiss—against our wills and certainly against all logic.

Because my mouth has slammed into his with *way* too much force as we both move simultaneously, our faces colliding. We're nothing but lips and chins and smooshed noses. I watch as his eyes all but pop out of his head in shock, the mirror of mine doing the same thing. For one terrible second, we're still and silent, staring bug-eyed at each other—

Until we jerk apart at the same time, yelping loudly into the awkward quiet that permeates the air around us.

I push myself desperately down Soren's body, heading toward his feet until my face is somewhere closer to his pecs.

We just kissed we just kissed we just—the t-shirt! I lift myself to my elbows so that I can get a better look around—

There. Pink t-shirt at three o'clock, still grasped loosely in Soren's hand. I snatch at it, catching him off guard and retrieving it with no problems. Then I fling it wildly away, launching it blindly behind me. I hear it land softly a good distance away, and then...silence.

Silence, except for the sounds of my labored breathing mingled with Soren's.

Slowly, carefully, I bring my eyes back to the man I'm currently squashing. My gaze finds that right pectoral first, then travels up, up, neck, beard, nose...until I meet the stormy, confused stare of a man who has *questions*.

"Hi," I say breathlessly, because I have no idea how I'm going to explain this.

"Hi," he grunts. There's a pause, then he says, "Want to get off me?"

But he doesn't wait for me to move. Instead he grips my upper arms firmly in a surprising display of strength and *lifts* me, separating our upper bodies and then dropping me flat on my face right next to him so that I'm pretty much eating carpet.

I guess I deserve that.

I'm not mad about it, either. Maybe I could stay here for a while—like maybe forever—so I don't have to make eye contact with anyone ever again, least of all Soren.

I hear him move next to me, shifting away, and I stay exactly as I am until I finally have to come up for air. I push myself into a sitting position, pulling my knees up and hugging them.

"So..." Soren says from beside me. "That shirt...?"

Crap. What do I say? *What do I say?*

My best friend thinks I'm secretly in love with you?

No. Embarrassing.

My best friend snuck it in my laundry as a prank?

No. Weird prank; weirder best friend.

Crap, crap, crap.

Finally I sigh. "It was a joke gift from Gemma, okay? It's hard to explain. Don't read into it."

"But—"

"No."

"I—"

"Drop it." Then I look at him, exasperated. "And how did you even see that? I specifically buried it in the pile of clothes. Were you digging through my folded laundry?"

"Of course not," he says, looking affronted. "I was bending over to tie my shoe and I saw my last name poking out of the stack. But you—" He smooths his hand over his hair. "You tackled me."

"Sorry," I say with a wince. "It was sort of a survival instinct thing."

"You should try some different survival instincts," he grunts.

He's probably not wrong. Those same survival instincts are screaming at me now that it's dangerous to ignore what just happened—that I need to make sure we're good, despite the fact that our lips have now touched. I'm not willing to risk my friendship with Soren just so that I can avoid discussing uncomfortable subjects.

"Uh," I say into the silence, my eyes fixed with unnecessary focus on my left thumb nail. "So...are we good?"

"About what?" he says, and in my peripheral vision I can see him turn his head to look at me. "Are you talking about how your face smashed into mine?"

"It was an accident," I say, fanning my cheeks with one insufficient hand. "But yes."

"We're good," he says. He gets to his feet, holding his hand out to pull me up. I take it, my palm sliding warmly into his, and he gives me a little tug. I stumble to my feet, my body colliding with his. My free hand flies to his chest as I steady myself, and he leans down, bringing his face closer to mine until I can count his eyelashes, smell the sharp scent of his aftershave, map the shape of his lips.

"We're good," he repeats, his voice low, his eyes fixed on me. "If you and I ever kiss"—he moves until his mouth is no more than a hair's breadth away from my ear—"and I do believe we will," he adds, making my heart stop midbeat. "There will be nothing accidental about it."

My jaw drops unflatteringly, and it's still hanging wide open when Soren straightens back up. He tucks one finger under my chin and shuts my mouth, his eyes brimming with amusement once again.

"I—you—what?" I say. It's more of a splutter, actually, and once again—it's not flattering. But really, how am I supposed to keep my composure when he's walking around saying things like *that*?

"What?" he says, cocking his head as he looks down at me. His eyes flit to my lips so briefly I almost miss it. "Have you never thought about kissing me?"

"You can't just *ask* people that!" I say, stomping my foot. "No! Of course not. Of course I've never thought about it."

"Mmm," he hums. He doesn't seem at all fazed by this; his eyes are still sparkling. He folds his arms across his chest. "And you don't think you might like kissing me?"

"I—I don't—I've never thought about it," I say. The words are more feeble than they should be.

He nods, still looking at me. Then he takes one step closer. He uncrosses his arms, lifting one slowly. I watch that moving hand in complete and utter shock, frozen, my eyes wide, my heart thundering out of control.

And it's no more than the touch of his finger, feather-light, skimming my temple and then tucking my hair behind my ear. But I shudder all the same—doing my very best to look completely shudder-free.

"Do you like that?" he says hoarsely. It's not a cocky question, or a taunt, or a stupid pickup line. It's simply a question he wants to know the answer to.

"I—I don't know," I say honestly. I need more than a map to navigate all the emotions and thoughts and reactions happening in my body and my brain right now.

"That's fair," he says. "What about this, then: How does it make you feel?"

I clear my throat, trying to dislodge my heart and send it back down to my chest cavity where it belongs. "Warm," I admit in a whisper. "And...jittery."

"And," he says, stepping closer once more. He's still moving impossibly slowly, giving me time to object, time to push him away as his arms wrap around me, pulling my body into his. "What about this?" he says. "Do you like this?"

His scruff is scratchy against my temple; his body is too warm, too close. And yet...

"Yes," I say again, even more quietly this time.

Why am I telling him this?

All I know is I can't lie right now. I don't have it in me to lie —not when he's being this vulnerable. I don't know what this development means, but I can't do that to him.

I feel him nod; his arms release me and then take gentle hold of my shoulders, nudging me backward so that there's space between us once more. "Then I think," he says, "you might enjoy kissing me someday." He hesitates for a second before pinning me with those impossibly blue eyes. "*I* would certainly enjoy kissing *you*."

Somewhere in the depths of my scrambled, confused mind, one thought worms its way to the surface: *this is so like Soren.* It's so like him to spring this on me out of the blue, and yet to do it so gently that somehow I'm not overwhelmed.

"I don't know what's happening," I say. My filter is gone; the survival instinct that had me jumping on Soren now seems to be sending my thoughts directly to my mouth with no censoring in between.

"Nothing has to happen yet," he says after a second. "Or ever. If you don't want it to."

I don't answer that, because I don't know what I want or what he's proposing. "Are you gonna be weird about this?" I say instead.

He gives me a little half-smile. "No," he says, letting his hands fall away from my shoulders. "I won't be weird."

I swallow the sudden anxiety that rises up within me. "Are

you still going to be my friend who pushes all my buttons and comes to the shop every day?"

He gives me another smile, but this one looks sadder, somehow. "I'll be whatever you need me to be, honey." Then he nods at my front door, taking a step back. "Come on," he says, like he didn't just drop that term of endearment. "Let's go visit Carmina Hildegarde's son."

❧ 10 ❧

IN WHICH SOREN AND HEIDI MEET THE NOT-NOTICEABLY-GRIEVING FAMILY

Maplewood is the subdivision that borders mine, and it's just as ostentatious.

The town square where Heidi's shop is located is roughly at the center of Sunshine Springs. It's the social hub, the place where people gather, especially during the months when the farmer's market is going on. The community college, meanwhile, is in one corner of town, and the Maplewood and Lafayette subdivisions are in the opposite corner.

Considering the scant population—something like twelve thousand including students—the housing situation here is surprisingly diverse. We have large homes and small homes and townhomes and apartments, although admittedly that last one is mostly located around the college. I think there's even a dormitory on campus.

The car is totally silent as Heidi and I drive away from Paper Patisserie, past some of those small homes and medium-sized homes and a few patchwork squares of farmland. It takes all my self-control to keep my eyes on the road instead of glancing over at her every five seconds, but I really don't want to freak her out. She's jittery, and I don't need to make it worse. I've introduced the possibility of her and I; that's enough for now. All I can do is wait and see if she warms up to the idea.

And I can't believe I'm saying this, but...I think she might.

It will take some time—I've always known that—but I'm in no rush. I can wait as long as I need to for her. I've been sustaining myself on her rare smiles and her nagging all this time. A while longer won't hurt me. And if she decides she's not interested...well, I'll have to find a way to be okay with that, I guess. I don't know how I would do it, but I'm sure I could figure it out.

Probably.

"So how do we want to do this?" I say when I finally can't take the silence any longer. "Do you want to take the lead?" I'm still not convinced this is a good idea, but I know that Heidi will do what she wants on her own if I refuse to help. I'd rather be with her than know she's off by herself.

"Yeah," she says with a nod that registers in the corner of my vision. "I can do that."

I try not to make my relief obvious, but I can't help the way my shoulders relax and my hands loosen on the steering wheel. She's not acting like anything is wrong.

She's not acting like we accidentally kissed less than an hour ago.

Don't think about it, I tell myself firmly. *Don't think about it, don't remember it, don't imagine it—*

Ha. Fat chance. That moment will be burned into my memory for the rest of my life. It will linger on the surface of my mind until it eventually seeps into the cracks and folds and becomes a fundamental part of who I am.

A simple, accidental, less-than-romantic kiss has done all that to me. What would it be like to kiss her for real?

My hands tighten on the steering wheel once more, and I

force myself to take a deep, steadying breath. "What are you going to say?" I ask. Then I frown. "And what's this guy's name?"

"His name is Phil."

"Phil," I say, trying not to picture the satyr from *Hercules*.

"Yeah," she says with a nod. "Phil. Like the little goat guy in *Hercules*. The Danny DeVito character."

I rub one hand over my scruff, hiding my smile. "All right. And how are you going to approach him?"

"I'm going to feel it out, to be honest," she says with a sigh. "I'll see how he's doing. Even if Carmina was unpleasant, he's still her son. My parents were divorced, and I didn't see my dad much, but when he died I was still devastated."

"How old were you?" I say. I knew her dad had passed, and I knew her parents had divorced, but she's never mentioned details.

"I was little when they divorced; three, I think," she says, running her hand through her hair. "And then he died when I was six."

I nod but don't say anything, and after a few seconds of silence, she says, "Aren't you going to ask how he died?"

"It felt rude to pry," I say.

I look over in time to catch her smile.

"I don't mind," she says. "He was killed by a drunk driver."

"I'm sorry," I say. "That sucks. Do you remember him much?"

"No," she says, and her smile has faded into something sadder. "Not really. What I remember is good, though."

I nod, my mind turning to my own family. "My dad is one of those gruff, emotionally constipated types," I say. "He wanted me to be a lawyer."

"Is he a lawyer?" Heidi says. "And your mom stays home, right? Am I remembering that correctly?"

GRACIE RUTH MITCHELL

"Yeah," I say as a little bubble of happiness floats in my chest. I like that she remembers what I tell her. "You remembered right. And yes, my dad is a lawyer." A lawyer who thinks man buns, face masks, and writing books are all for pansies.

AKA, my father thinks I am a pansy. I gave up trying to please him a long time ago, when I realized it wasn't possible. No matter what I do, he'll find something to criticize.

May as well do what makes me happy. If he wants to be part of my life someday, he knows where to find me.

The streets of Maplewood are winding and lined with trees, with cheerful flowers beginning to bloom in neatly curated beds. We pass a clubhouse with a fenced-in pool and a tennis court, and across from that is a pond. The subdivision branches in two shortly after that, and after consulting the GPS on my phone, I take the left fork. A few hundred yards later it becomes clear that this branch is where the townhomes are located; the absence of any single-family homes makes me think that those would be found if we had turned right.

"I think I would really dislike living here," Heidi says, her voice musing as we continue to wind our way through the neighborhood. "The landscaping is pretty, but the buildings are so close together."

She's not wrong; the cookie cutter duplexes are squeezed into cramped lots, and you could easily throw a stone out the window of one duplex and shatter the window of the next.

We wind around a few more curves before my phone announces that our destination is on the left, and I slow down, pulling up in front of the duplex and then parking. I don't want to block anyone's driveway; if the residents here are anything like in my neighborhood, they're picky about that kind of thing.

"This is it?" Heidi says, peering out the window and looking at the duplex we're in front of.

"Looks like it," I say. "That one, I think." I point to the unit on the left.

"I walked a dog that lived down there," Heidi says, pointing down the street. "A Schnauzer named Lady Madonna."

"Mmm," I say, my lips twitching as I unbuckle. "And what was the Poodle's name?"

"Noodles," she says, and her eyes narrow. "With her stupid little head poof and her constant escape attempts and her snooty owner—"

"Speak for yourself," I say with a snort. "If that Poodle hadn't run into my townhome, you and I probably wouldn't have met. You would have no one in your life with a man bun, and you would be devastated."

"Well, that's true," she says. My stomach flips at her little smile. "Come on. Let's go."

The weather is perfect today, sunny and warm with a cool breeze that makes the world dance. It makes me forget for a second that we're here to ask a man about his mother's death; all I want to do is lie down on the pavement with Heidi next to me and soak up the sun.

She doesn't seem to share my feelings; she more or less marches up the driveway, her hair swinging behind her, and I lengthen my stride to keep up. When I look over at her, her face is set in a mask of determination.

She's in the mood to get stuff *done*.

I hide my smile and shove my hands in my pockets. This is one of Heidi's main settings: Productive Heidi.

I watch as she lifts one hand to knock on the front door, as enraptured as I am curious. But she hesitates for only the briefest of seconds before delivering three firm raps, the sound carrying.

There are so many times this woman seems fearless. It makes me want to pull her close to my chest when I see those rare flashes of vulnerability. I would happily run around behind her for the rest of my life, following her as she changes the world, providing her a safe place to retreat when she needs to rest.

I shake my head, giving my cheek a few firm pats. Now is not the time to get mushy.

But my focus is pulled to the task at hand a few seconds later, when the door swings open, revealing a petite woman with dark hair and a hesitant smile, beautiful but not in the prime of her youth.

"Hi," she says, looking back and forth between Heidi and me.

"Hi," Heidi says quickly. "Is Phil home? We were wondering if we could talk to him for a moment." Heidi can clearly read this woman's wariness as well as I can; she keeps her voice light and cheerful, her expression open.

It works; the woman visibly relaxes as she nods. "Of course; I'm his wife. Just a minute, please."

She leaves the door gaping as she turns and begins to retreat into the townhome, calling up the stairs that are barely visible from where we stand. "Phil, you have guests!"

A few seconds later a man appears as his wife disappears; he swings the door wider and steps forward to meet us.

"Hello," he says, looking as wary as his wife.

"Phil?" Heidi says, moving closer and holding out her hand. "I'm not sure if you remember me," she says. "I'm—"

"Oh," he cuts her off, looking faintly surprised. "You're the bookstore lady."

"I am," Heidi says with a nod. "I'm Heidi from Paper Patisserie." She's still holding her hand out for him to shake, but he doesn't take it.

"Where my mom died," he says instead, looking at Heidi with renewed interest.

I try to hide my shock, but I think my eyebrows still twitch. He doesn't seem brokenhearted. He doesn't even seem sad. I'm well aware that everyone grieves in their own way, but...how many people could speak so casually about such a recent death?

And he's still not shaking her hand. Why isn't he shaking her hand?

She lets her hand fall back to her side, somehow making the movement look natural instead of awkward. "I was wondering if we could chat with you for a minute," she says now, and although you'd never notice it if you didn't know her, I can see the questions in her eyes. "This is Soren," she adds, gesturing to me. "He was also present at the time of—of your mother's passing."

"We're sorry for your loss," I say automatically. Then I cringe. It's fine, I guess, but it just feels so cliché. Besides, this man hardly looks like he's in mourning.

"Thanks," he says, his eyes darting back and forth between us. "Uh, sure. If it really is a minute. I've got to run in a bit. I work from home, but I've got a few meetings." He glances down at his wristwatch, a shiny, expensive-looking piece.

In fact, everything about him is flashy. He looks remarkably like Carmina—the same haughty features more roughly hewn on him. And I never thought I would have anything good to say about the woman, but looking at her son, I can't help my comparison. Where Carmina gave off the appearance of high class, her son gives off a distinct feeling of sleaziness; he's in his late forties, maybe, with his dark hair slicked back. His fitted suit doesn't quite hide a paunch, and his cufflinks are somehow too shiny.

He looks like he's compensating for something, like a man who's deeply insecure and is trying to hide it by piling on all the bells and whistles. It's the opposite of how Carmina behaved; she acted like she *knew* she was better than everyone else, like she was so confident that she didn't even feel the need to prove it. The people around her were beneath her notice.

But Phil Hildegarde seems to me like a man who's desperately concerned with what other people think of him.

I shake my head, barely stopping myself from rolling my eyes. I'm being ridiculous, jumping to conclusions left and right based on flash judgments. This is the problem with being an author; your mind dissects everything and everyone as though you're going to be writing about them, because writing is how you understand the world. You turn regular people into characters and regular events into plot twists.

I wonder if his friends call him Phildegarde.

"We'll make it quick," Heidi promises, clearly not burdened by the same thought processes as I am.

"Come in, then," Phildegarde says. He steps back and opens the door wider, gesturing for us to enter.

Heidi gives me a quick look, one of worry and hesitation, and I nod. Her expression relaxes.

I guess going inside wasn't in Heidi's original plan, but I think it should be fine. I follow her as she crosses the threshold, maybe standing closer than I need to, but...well, we're in unknown territory.

We trail down the hall after Phil, and although Heidi's gaze is trained on the man, mine is darting all over the place, taking in everything I can see.

There's a dining room to the left, one of those fancy affairs that looks like it only gets used on special occasions, with a small chandelier and a shiny patterned tablecloth.

The tablecloth I draped over Phil's deceased mother was made of cheap plastic. The juxtaposition of the two somehow strikes me as horribly sad, although for the life of me I can't put my finger on why, and I don't let myself dwell on it. It's the sort of thing that could drag my mood all the way down for no reason at all. So I force my attention elsewhere.

The table's centerpiece is a gaudy basket of flowers—not natural but overworked, somehow, with heavy colors and weird metallic things throughout. There's even a hutch against the wall that has fine China displayed.

I turn and look at the wall of photos we're passing, resisting the urge to slow down and take in the details of each. They're mostly Phil and the woman who opened the door—his wife, he said—with only one photo depicting anyone else. It looks like a family photo; I recognize a much younger Carmina, realizing with a start that I never once in my life saw her smile. I was always too busy arguing with her. But she's smiling in the picture, her eyes on the man next to her, and both of them have their arms draped around the young boy in front of them. It must be Phil, when he was a young teenager, still gangly and awkward-looking.

How weird, to see such a happy expression on Carmina Hildegarde's face. She's undeniably beautiful.

I tamp down on the little zing of guilt that hits me somewhere in the gut.

You can't change how you treated her now, I remind myself, feeling suddenly heavy. *Just do better in the future. Treat everyone like they could be murdered tomorrow.*

Words to live by. I don't know if the thought makes me want to laugh sardonically or retreat into the waiting sadness that lurks, sometimes, at the edge of my consciousness.

There are just so many heavy things in the world, and my brain is so overactive. My thoughts often feel so nebulous, slippery, expanding and shifting in ways I can't pin down. I think about everything, dissecting life's nuances, holding up the light and the dark and trying to keep them balanced. I can drown in the darkness or fly in the light, but I'm most functional when my feet are firmly on solid ground, somewhere in between the two.

"Please, sit," Phil says, pulling me out of my random thoughts as we reach what seems to be the family room. There's a large sectional, a fancy upholstered chair, and a giant flat screen, muted but displaying some sort of golfing thing.

I guess I just don't understand the purpose of golf.

Phil gestures to the sectional, and Heidi and I sit. It's uncomfortable, firm and cold, and I don't shift away when the side of Heidi's body presses into mine. I want her close. I always want her close, of course, but especially when we're in the home of a stranger, sitting on this weirdly stiff couch.

"So," Phil says as he settles himself in the upholstered chair, manspreading like it's his God-given right. "What can I help you with?"

And he sounds so *conversational*—there's absolutely nothing about him or about this home that says someone just died. I don't get it.

"Well," Heidi says. "I was cleaning the café the other night, and I found some stuff that had fallen out of your mother's purse." She glances at me quickly before going on. "It was an envelope of cash, and there was a note attached that made it seem like—" She breaks off, and I know exactly why; she's trying to figure out the most tactful way to accuse Phil's recently deceased mother of blackmail. "It seems someone felt they were being extorted for money," she finally says. "Now I may have been reading the situation incorrectly, of course, and you know your mother best. But I wanted to make you aware of the situation—"

"An envelope of cash?" Phil cuts her off. "Do you still have it?"

Heidi blinks at him. "No," she says after a tiny pause. "I gave it to the police."

Phil's shoulders slump. "Oh," he says. Then, straightening once more, he adds, "Good. That's good." One tiny piece of his slicked-back hair comes loose, slowly falling over his forehead. He sighs. "My mother was not an easy woman to live with."

"How so?" Heidi says, keeping her voice calm and only vaguely interested.

"She was just difficult," he says. "She was a model, you know, back in the day. Internationally known, very successful. But it gave her a high opinion of herself. Even so..." He shakes his head, looking troubled. "I don't know who she would be extorting, or why. She was a bit of a loner."

"And you don't know of any troubles she was having?" Heidi says gently. "The police seem to think foul play may have been involved." I have to give her credit; she's coming here asking questions she frankly has no right to ask, and she's delivering them in such a way that she doesn't come off as prying or rude.

"No," Phil says, shaking his head once again. "I really don't. Like I said, she could be difficult, but she kept mostly to herself." Then he looks at his watch, that greasy little strand over his forehead flopping. "I'm sorry to be rude, but I really do need to run. If that's everything...?"

"Of course," Heidi says quickly, standing up. "We'll let you get on with your day. I'm so sorry to intrude like this. I just wanted to make you aware."

"Not a problem," he says, and he stands too. "I appreciate it."

"Can I give you my number?" Heidi says. "In case you think of anything?"

"Sure," Phil says. He reaches in his pocket and pulls out a crumpled piece of paper after rummaging around for a moment. Then he grabs a pen and passes them both to Heidi, who scribbles her number and then passes the paper back.

Phil tucks it in his pocket. "Elsie?" he calls.

A few seconds later, the petite woman who opened the door for us hurries into the room. "Yes," she says.

"Could you see them out?" Phil says. "I need to grab my briefcase from upstairs."

"Sure," the woman—Elsie, I guess—says. She gives us a little smile and gestures down the hall to where we came in.

I stand up, following closely behind Heidi as we return to the front door. Phil bounds up the stairs with more energy than I'd expect from someone who's trying so hard to seem dignified.

Elsie watches him for a second, and when she turns back to Heidi and me, I'm surprised to see that her expression has shifted into something more determined. "Look," she says in a low voice. "I'll tell you what my husband won't: his mother was more than difficult. She was an incredibly demanding woman."

Heidi and I look at each other, our surprised faces mirrors of each other.

"What do you mean?" Heidi says, looking back at Elsie.

Elsie glances back at the stairs, then beckons for us to follow her. She opens the front door and steps out onto the porch, and once again Heidi and I follow.

"My husband can be very blind," she says when she's pulled the door closed. "But his mother was an awful woman. I'm sorry to say that," she adds. "And I know I should be more sensitive, given that she just passed. But..." She trails off, shaking her head and looking frustrated. "She had problems with *everyone*. She interfered in our marriage, although I suppose that's not out of the norm for a mother-in-law. But she had a spat with the neighbor too, filed a complaint—she picked fights left and right." She takes a deep breath. "We wanted to live with her to help take care of her," she explains. "She was getting so old. But...she didn't make it easy."

"She had problems with the neighbor?" Heidi says, frowning.

"Mr. Foster, yes. Something about his dog," Elsie says, gesturing at the other unit of the duplex and looking tired. "She really didn't like animals."

"Mmm," Heidi hums sympathetically. "Thank you for letting us know."

Elsie nods, giving us a tight smile. "Sure. Have a good day."

It's a clear dismissal, and Heidi and I nod too. "You as well," Heidi says, and with that, Elsie opens the door and disappears, closing it with a gentle thud.

We're silent on our way to the car, both of us moving quickly. We were in that townhome for all of five minutes, but my brain feels full to the brim.

"So," I say once we've reached the car. I lean against it, letting the heat seep through my shirt to warm my back. Then I look over at Heidi. "You wanted to 'make him aware,' huh? Are you sure you're not just nosy?"

"Oh, shut up," she says, and I smile. "I can't very well tell him that the police are giving me funny looks and I need to clear my name. Besides, I *did* want to make him aware."

I raise one eyebrow at her.

"And then I wanted to see how he reacted," she admits, throwing her hands up in the air. "Because yes, fine, I'm being nosy. But am I being unreasonable?" she goes on. "Is it unreasonable to want to figure out why someone died right in front of me, in my café?"

"No," I say. "It's not unreasonable." I hesitate. "I'm not sure it's a good idea, but it's not unreasonable."

Heidi sighs, looking down at the grass. She's fidgeting again, wringing her hands. "I just think—I don't know. Maybe I'm way off. But I think if I look into what happened to Carmina a little more, I might be able to figure out what happened to me, too."

Heidi is a smart woman, and I trust her instincts. If she thinks investigating Carmina might help with her memories, I'll support her.

"Plus...I don't know," she says, looking uneasy. "Every now and then I get flashes of Carmina's last words, and it feels like she's asking me for help."

I nod. "Well, what do you think about Phil and Elsie?" I say, watching as the breeze plays with her hair. "Do you think they know something? Or do you think they killed her?"

She sighs again. "I don't know. On one hand it feels absolutely ridiculous to be throwing around words like *murder*. And with them, my gut says no, based on how much I love my own parents, I guess; it's hard to imagine someone killing their own mother. But...Carmina said *murder* first," she says, looking over at me. "And the police seem to think it's possible. So that makes me wonder."

It makes me wonder too.

"And—oh!" She breaks off as she slaps one palm against her leg. "I didn't get to ask about what Carmina said. *Lock* and *pick*."

"We can come back if we need to," I say, thinking. I keep my voice low as I go on. "I will say...Phil does not act like someone whose mother just died."

"No," Heidi agrees. "He was very weird. Did you get that vibe?"

"A little bit," I say. "He seemed totally normal. That was what was weird to me. Elsie, too."

"Yes," she says. "Exactly." Then she looks over at me. "Do you think anyone ever calls him Phildegarde?"

I smile.

❈ 11 ❈

FROM THE LIFE OF CARMINA
HILDEGARDE

AUGUST 5

C armina Hildegarde sat in her room, on her bed, and listened to her son and his wife argue.

People seemed to think that since she was old, Carmina's faculties weren't fully intact. But she was as sharp as she'd always been, and her hearing was just as good. So the angry tirades, the complaints, the grumbling about her presence in the house—she heard them all.

"She's *your* mother—you need to help me clean up this mess!" Elsie's voice was low, barely audible, but Carmina could understand fine. She pictured her daughter-in-law gesturing to the messy kitchen counter with one petite, fine-boned hand. Then she imagined her son wrinkling his nose at the mess of dirty dishes she'd left in the sink after an afternoon of cooking and baking.

"You know I don't have time to do a bunch of cleaning," his voice replied, more loudly than Elsie's had been. "I have three calls I need to make and a report to finalize before the weekend."

"Fine," Elsie snapped, and for the tiniest moment, Carmina

felt sorry for the girl. "Fine. Go do your work. I'll clean it all up."

Carmina considered going down to help. But, she thought as she stretched, she was so very tired.

Perhaps she would jot down some thoughts in her journal and then lie down for a little nap instead.

12

IN WHICH HEIDI SAMPLES
SALTED CARAMEL

The sun is shining, the breeze is cool, and Carmina Hildegarde's son and daughter-in-law are very odd. These three things I know with absolute certainty.

Why don't Phil and Elsie Hildegarde seem at all sad about Carmina's passing?

Soren and I are still standing by his car, talking in low voices, and it's a struggle not to look back over my shoulder at the townhome every two seconds. My skin is prickling like someone's watching us, and I have no idea if I'm imagining things. I pull my hair up off my neck, using the hair tie around my wrist to wrangle it into a ponytail. Then I rub the back of my neck a few times, trying to get rid of that creeping sensation. My brain is running rampant with visions of people peeking at us from behind their curtains.

I glance at Soren, but his blue eyes are fixed on where my hand is massaging my neck, and my mind jumps back to what he said before we came here.

He thinks we might kiss in the future.

And judging by how he's looking at me—and how suddenly warm it makes me feel—I can maybe see why he thinks that.

I'm not saying it's going to happen. I can't imagine myself actually kissing Soren. He's my favorite author. My feelings for him are those of a major (closeted) fangirl: unconditional support with zero expectations of reciprocation.

And yet...

I also have to admit that over the past few years, I've come to know the real Soren, too. Not the author S. Mackenzie, but the *man*. The snarky, playful one who looks like a caveman half the time and refuses to change—but the one who also washed my hair with impossibly gentle hands, who agreed to help me investigate Carmina with zero hesitation.

He's the one I called before I hit my head. And I didn't understand why until I was holding that envelope of cash in my hand the other night, pulling up his number before I even realized what I was doing.

With Soren I am safe.

With S. Mackenzie I'm a rabid fangirl who would buy his grocery list and frame it on my wall.

But with Soren the man...I'm just safe, and comfortable, and secure.

"Let's get going," Soren says, and I realize with a start that now I'm the one staring at him. His eyes aren't on my neck anymore—which I'm still rubbing absently—they're glancing at the townhomes around us and the empty street. "We shouldn't stand here in front of their house. Unless..." he says, trailing off.

"Unless what?" I say.

He nods discreetly behind me. "Do you think that's the neighbor Carmina was in a fight with? Mr. Foster?"

My eyebrows shoot up, but I resist the urge to whirl around. Instead I turn and rest my back against the car, right next to Soren, trying to look as natural as possible.

"Oh," I say, distracted momentarily. "That's nice and warm."

"Mmm," he says.

"Yes, I think that's him," I say as my eyes find the man coming out of the garage on the opposite end of the duplex. "He's got a big dog, look."

"Is that the dog you walked?"

"No," I say, shaking my head. "That one was further down the street." I take a deep breath, steeling myself. I'm not the sort of person to waste an opportunity when it pops up. "Let's go," I say.

"Let's—what?"

"Let's go," I repeat, and then I push myself off the car and paste a big smile on my face.

And look. I am a little torn. Part of me feels very deceptive, pretending that I'm not here to pry around and look into Carmina's death. But at the same time...my survival instincts are strong, and I don't think it's a good idea to shout about what we're doing.

I don't like deceiving people. But I think it's the safest move for now. So I waltz down the sidewalk toward Mr. Foster and his dog with a big old smile on my face, even though it feels unnatural.

"What a lovely dog," I call when I'm close enough for the man to hear. He's meandering back up his driveway, barely watching where he's going as he shuffles through his mail, the sun glinting off his bald head, a brown leather jacket hanging too loose on his frame.

He turns and looks at me, clearly surprised. "Oh," he says, and then he looks at his dog—a large German Shepherd that really is pretty. "Thank you." He squints back at me, and then his eyes jump to somewhere behind me, where I assume he's looking at Soren. "I don't believe we've met, Miss...?"

"We were here visiting with Phil and Elsie," I say, avoiding his question. I lower my voice, letting the smile drop a bit. "It was so horrible, what happened to Carmina. Did you know her well?"

Mr. Foster bristles, pushing his wire-framed glasses up his nose. "No," he says shortly, his gaze darting shiftily this way and that. "I didn't know her. Her packages came to my unit occasionally, and I brought them back over to her. Other than that, we never spoke."

Huh. If we believe what Elsie said, that means this man is lying. She said he and Carmina had an ongoing feud. That's...interesting.

Although to be fair, he seems about as pleasant as Carmina did. I wouldn't be surprised if they were having troubles.

But I nod. "Well, I'm sorry for the loss all the same." Then I wave at him. "Have a nice day!"

And with that I turn and head back to the car, meeting Soren partway. "Let's go," I mutter, grabbing his arm. "Act natural."

"I always act natural," he says as he walks with me. "You're the one who's smiling like a loon."

"I was trying to be pleasant," I say. Then I frown, looking over at him. "And hey—I smile sometimes."

"You do," he says with a nod. "Sometimes." He glances at me and then laughs at the look on my face. "I'm not saying it's a bad thing. Some people are more reserved. There's nothing wrong with not smiling as much. People wear their emotions differently. That's fine."

"Oh," I say. I open the passenger door and slide in, waiting for him to get behind the wheel. "It still seems like a bad thing," I go on when his door opens. "Should I smile more?"

"You should smile however much you want," he says. He

buckles and then starts the car. "No more, no less. Now," he says, pinning me with his gaze. "Where to, Miss Lucy?"

WE END UP BACK IN THE TOWN SQUARE, BUT NOT AT PAPER Patisserie.

It feels good to be out and about. When you live where you work, you don't get out as much, and it can be tough on your mental health. There's something to be said for looking up and seeing the sky instead of a ceiling.

"Here," Soren says, passing me an ice cream cone. I reach up and take it, shivering suddenly as his shadow blocks the sun. He sits a second later, though, pulling out the metal chair with a loud scraping noise against the stone pavement.

"Thank you," I say, eyeing my ice cream. Rocky road is my favorite, and Teddy's has the best waffle cones. It's a little ice cream parlor located directly across the town square from me, and it does a raging business with the tourists, especially in the summer. In a few weeks, once summer officially begins and people start taking family vacations, it will be impossible to find seating at any of the little tables out here. So I soak it in while I can, watching as Soren digs into his ice cream too.

"Is that a new flavor?" I say, taking a lick of mine. I nod at his cone, which is piled high with one gigantic scoop of something tannish-brownish. "Don't you usually eat strawberry?"

"I wanted to try the salted caramel," he says.

I stare at him for a second. This was a man who was made for the sun—it makes everything about him more beautiful. His hair goes from golden to multihued and shining, his tanned skin seems to glow, and the sunlight on his body casts shadows that bring his musculature into sharp relief.

"Did you know you have a bit of red in your beard?" I say, my gaze transfixed.

"I did," he says with a little nod. He takes a lick of his ice cream. "Mostly in the sun."

"Mm-hmm," I say. Then I blink hard, forcing myself to stop staring.

I'm being weird.

"So. Thoughts?" I say. I stare with determination at my ice cream as I speak, mostly so I won't stare at Soren instead.

"I like it," he says with a shrug that I see out of the corner of my eye. "It's not as good as strawberry, but it's worth finishing, definitely."

I snort. "I wasn't talking about the ice cream," I say, my lips tugging into a smile. "I meant Phil and Elsie and Mr. Foster and all that."

"Oh," he says with a bark of laughter. "Right. Uh, I think they're all sketchy."

"The neighbor had to be lying, right?" I say. "Didn't Elsie say he and Carmina were in some sort of feud about his dog?"

"Yep," Soren says, still paying attention to his ice cream.

"So either Elsie was lying, or Mr. Foster was lying," I say. I'm mostly thinking out loud at this point. "And to be honest, she didn't seem too torn up about her mother-in-law dying."

"Nope," Soren says. "She didn't."

I squeeze my eyes shut, racking my brain. I picture Elsie, and Phil, and then the neighbor. Do any of them seem familiar? Do I recognize any of them?

Oddly enough, Mr. Foster's face does ring a bell, but I can't for the life of me figure out why. He's a generic-looking man, I guess; there are probably a lot of people who look like him. And nothing in my memory stirs for Phil and Elsie; no flash of recognition tells me that maybe I'd seen or heard from any of them during my missing day.

I sigh, my eyes popping open. I take another lick of my ice cream as I comb through what I *do* remember.

"I'm trying to think about what I did on Tuesday," I say. "I know I stayed up late reading that night."

Soren nods. "And during the day?"

"I worked," I say slowly. "Gemma and I closed…" But the combination of thinking about Tuesday as well as Gemma pulls a new memory to the front, one I grasp eagerly. "My hair," I say, sitting up straighter. I look at Soren. "I made a hair appointment."

"Did you?" he says, looking surprised. Then he glances at my hair. "I don't notice any difference."

I roll my eyes. "I wouldn't expect you to. Men usually don't. Let me see." I pull my hair out of its ponytail, letting it fall around my face. Then I examine the ends, noticing where they fall. "It's shorter," I say, my pulse picking up. "And the ends are cleaner. I got it trimmed." I look back at Soren. "I made the appointment because I noticed I had a lot of split ends," I explain. "I must have gone on Wednesday!"

"We can check it out," Soren says with a shrug, looking at me. "It won't hurt to try."

"I agree," I say. "I'm not getting my hopes up, exactly, because whatever happened to me happened at night, but still. Maybe I said something at my appointment."

Soren nods. "Do you want to go over there today?" he says. He picks up my phone, which is sitting on the table in front of us, and presses the home button. "It's not too late," he says when the time flashes. "They probably close at five."

"Yeah," I say. "Let's finish our ice cream and then go."

He gives me another nod and continues eating.

"Are you sure that's okay, though?" I add. "Do you need to work at all today?"

"It's fine," he says with a shrug. "I did a thousand words this

morning. I don't know if I can handle any more right now. It's
slow going at the moment."

"Huh," I say slowly. "Is writing always like that? Or is it
usually easier?"

"Uh," he says, his eyes fixing suddenly on his ice cream
instead of looking at me. "It's not always this bad. I'm struggling
with this book."

"Are you?" I say, surprised. I wondered how it was going,
since he mentioned the other night that his current draft was
trash, but this is the first time he's said anything else.

"Yeah," he says, his voice heavy. "I'm in my head too much.
It's hard when you've written both a bestseller and then a
complete flop. I keep worrying that I'll never do anything better
than the bestseller while also worrying that people now expect
more flops."

"Oof," I say, and I wince. "I hadn't thought of that. That
sounds like a lot of pressure."

"It is," he says dryly. "And while some readers are compli-
mentary, some are not. People can get pretty mean about books
they don't like."

"Did your second book do okay? If you don't mind me
asking," I add. The second one is my favorite, personally, but to
each their own.

"Preorders were high, but the overall public opinion is that
the book is not good," he says. "And I'm contracted for three
books, which means I really *have* to write this one. I don't know
how I'm going to meet my deadline, especially because it's
going so poorly. But I'm meeting with a critique group on
Monday." He finally looks at me again. "Maybe some outside
feedback will help."

"I'm sure it will," I say. It's a stupid thing to say; how can I
be sure? I can't. But I want him to feel better.

We continue to eat in silence, listening to the sounds of the day—the chatter of people around us and the chirping of birds, the faint *whoosh* of the breeze. I find my eyes returning to Soren more and more as he eats. He seems more relaxed now that we're not talking about his writing anymore, which makes me happy.

I continue to watch him, trying not to smile, but finally I shake my head.

"You're getting ice cream all over your face," I say, passing him a napkin. I point at his chin. "It's in your beard."

"Oh," he says, and I'm surprised to see a pinkish tinge appear in his cheeks. He wipes his beard and then continues eating.

I laugh—it feels amazing to laugh—and then point at his mouth. "It's still getting everywhere."

Soren's lips twitch. "So critical. Get it off, then."

"You get it off," I say, tossing another napkin at him.

But he gives a little shake of his head and licks his ice cream cone again. "It doesn't bother me." His eyes sparkle as he looks at me, even while he continues to eat. "Feel free to get it yourself."

I bite back my smile. I know what he's doing. He's teasing me, needling me—maybe even flirting. It's not just him, either; my mind is teasing me, too. Because instead of imagining wiping his face with a napkin, a different image pops into my brain: leaning closer and *licking* the ice cream off his lips. My heart stutters at the thought, and—

"Yes," Soren says, pulling me out of my wildly inappropriate daydream. His voice is hoarse, and when my gaze meets his, my heart stutters again, this time accompanied by a strange flip-flop sensation in my stomach.

His eyes are *searing*. They're burning like the sun itself, so vividly blue, so full of raw hunger that I can barely breathe.

"What?" I whisper.

"Yes," he repeats. "Whatever you're thinking of right now —do it."

My eyebrows climb so high that the cut on my head gives a twinge of pain. "I don't know what you mean," I say, my voice breathless.

He leans closer. "Liar," he says. Then, with a challenge in his gaze, he repeats, "*Do it.*"

And I don't know what comes over me. I truly don't. I have no explanation, no excuse. I set my ice cream cone down on my napkin, place my hands on the sides of his face, and lean forward until we're so close that our noses are almost touching.

For a second I breathe him in—caramel breath, warm skin under my fingers, rough beard edging my palm.

Electric eyes, long lashes, and a heady, intoxicating warmth rising in my chest.

Then—for reasons known only to the Good Lord, I might add—I close the distance between us and lick the ice cream from his lips.

First from the corner of his mouth with the flick of my tongue; then from his lower lip with a slow sweep.

And then I gasp as he moves, quicker than I can process, his hand curling around the back of my neck as his lips slam into mine.

They move furiously, hungrily, and I gasp again, completely overwhelmed. I push frantically against his shoulders, and he backs away immediately, like my touch has electrocuted him; his breath is rapid, his eyes wide.

He stands up so suddenly his chair clatters backward, but he doesn't seem to notice. I barely do either; my mind is reeling, a cyclone of competing thoughts and words and feelings.

"I'm so sorry," Soren gasps, his gaze wild, darting this way and that like he's hunting for an exit. His ice cream cone is hanging limply from one hand, dripping in giant caramel globs onto the stone. "I'm so sorry. I shouldn't have done that. You weren't—you didn't—you didn't want that." He swallows. "I'm so, so sorry. I lost my head for a second." His eyes finally meet mine. "I'm gonna go. I need to go."

"I—okay—" I stutter, flustered by the kiss and even more so by his reaction.

"I'll talk to you later," he mutters. And then, without another word, he hurries away, practically running. I watch as he crosses the square and rounds my building, heading to the lot where his car is parked, and I'm left wondering what on *earth* just happened.

When I lick my lips, they taste like salted caramel.

13

IN WHICH SOREN MAKES A PROMISE

Heidi texts me while I'm driving home, and I read it once I've pulled into my driveway and parked.

Don't feel bad, the text says. *You stopped as soon as I told you to. Plus I was licking you. I'm not mad, and you didn't do anything wrong.*

I let my head drop forward onto the steering wheel, gripping it tightly and then letting my hands relax again. Her words ease some of the churning in my gut, but not all of it. I get out of the car and march myself inside, where I hop straight into an ice-cold shower.

I stand under the cascade for a long, long time. I stand there until my hair is drenched and there's water in my eyes and the message is drilled firmly into my mind: *You cannot kiss women who do not want to be kissed.*

I know that. Of course I know that. I've always known that.

I just...snapped. I could feel her tongue tracing my lips with a boldness I never expected, and I guess it made me bold, too.

"All right," I say under my breath, finally turning the water warmer. "No more boldness. Let her make the first move, or at least ask permission before you do anything else. Don't assume you're picking up the right signals." It's all I can do. Strangely enough, I'm not even embarrassed; I just feel bad.

I wash quickly, probably not giving my hair the attention it requires before shutting the water off again. Then I climb out of the shower and dry off, looking around my bathroom. The clawfoot tub is still in the corner, and I can imagine exactly where that big black Poodle was sniffing around all those years ago. I shake my head and then head out to the bedroom to get changed. Usually I would do something with my hair—dry it, or at least throw it up into a bun—but right now I leave it. I'm too preoccupied to worry about that. I flop down onto my bed instead, staring at the ceiling as I feel my wet hair slowly turn my pillow damp.

What is this going to do to our relationship? I know Heidi said she wasn't mad, but what if she was lying? Are things going to be weird?

I alternate between looking at my phone and then at the ceiling, going back and forth and back and forth. Should I call her? Should I not? Since when have I been this bad at interacting with women? Since when have I been this clueless?

When my phone rings a few moments later, I'm so startled that I jump and drop it right on my face.

"Ow," I groan, rubbing my nose. When I pick the phone up and see that it's Heidi, however, I sit upright, my throbbing nose forgotten.

I stare at her name on the screen for a few seconds before I finally have the courage to answer.

"Hi," I say, the greeting heavy on my tongue.

"Look, Soren, I'm not mad, okay?" Her voice comes in a burst of sound, her words spilling into the silence. "I'm not mad."

"Maybe you should be," I say, rubbing my hand down my face. "I'm so sorry, Heidi. I have no excuse. I'm so, so—"

"Stop apologizing," she says, and I'm surprised to hear that she sounds...frustrated. Irritable. "I'm the one who was licking you. *I* should apologize. I don't know what came over me." She sighs, a staticky rush.

"Yeah," I say, my heart thudding. "But I liked it." My voice cracks at the admission, my cheeks heating. "That's the difference. I liked it; I wanted it. You didn't. So...I'm sorry. And"—I swallow, forcing myself to go on—"I understand if you don't want to see me anymore. I can write somewhere else if you need me to. For a while or forever, your call. Just let me know."

There's silence for a few beats, and then Heidi speaks. "What do you mean, you'll write somewhere else?"

I hold back the sigh that's trying to escape, my heart sinking in my chest. I don't want to go anywhere but Paper Patisserie. I want to see her every day. But she might need space. "I mean I can work from home if you want," I say. "Or there are a few other cafés in town. If you feel weird or uncomfortable or—"

"Stop it," she snaps, cutting me off. "Just—stop it. You didn't do anything wrong, and I don't feel weird or uncomfortable, and I don't want you to write anywhere else but at my shop, okay?" I can hear her breathing, heavy and loud. "You're mine, all right? Don't go to a different café."

My heart stops beating altogether. She's talking so quickly, so heatedly, that I'm not even sure she realizes what she's said, but I've registered every word.

"Promise me," she says now, her voice demanding. "Unless you personally and specifically want to go somewhere else, stay at Paper Patisserie."

My eyes widen further, my jaw dropping slightly. "You sound...angry," I say. "Why are you snapping at me?" I hesitate, thinking hard. Heidi is not someone who's overly in touch with her emotions. She keeps up walls. I could see her reacting like this if she was suddenly bombarded with a bunch of feelings she doesn't understand or know what to do with. Maybe that's what's happening here.

So, gently, I say, "Does it bother you that much, the thought of me going somewhere else?"

"Yes," she says, her voice smaller now. The fight seems to have drained out of her. "I don't like it, okay? So if you want to go somewhere else, that's fine; I'll support whatever you decide. But don't go on my account. Please."

There's a fire burning deep within my chest, something warm and all-consuming. It rises higher as she speaks, until it threatens to overtake me.

"I'll stay," I manage to get out, speaking past the inexplicable lump in my throat. "I want to stay. I won't go anywhere else."

There's a pause, and then Heidi says, "You promise?"

A tiny smile tries to form on my lips. "I promise, honey."

"Okay, good," she says with a sigh of relief.

"And I won't kiss you again unless you ask me to, all right?" I say. "Does that sound good?"

"Yes," she says in that same small voice. "And what about —" She clears her throat. "What about me? Should I not kiss you either?"

"Uh," I say. There's heat creeping into my cheeks and my ears; I reach up and grab a chunk of my wet hair, pressing it to my skin to cool down. "Is that something you want to do?"

"I don't know," she says musingly. "I haven't given it a lot of thought."

"Well, you can do whatever you want to me," I say. "Hug me, kiss me, tackle me. Free reign. All right?"

Silence, and then one word. "Soren."

"Hmm."

"You like me." It's not a question.

"Yes," I say, because there's no point in playing things close to the chest anymore. "I like you. But I also understand that you might not feel the same way."

"I don't—I don't know how I feel," she says, her voice cracking.

I'm not surprised. "That's fine too," I say. "What I said still stands. I won't kiss you unless you ask me to, and you can do whatever you want with me. Figure things out at your own pace. I'll be here, and I won't make any assumptions about your intentions. Okay?"

"And you won't go to anyone else's café?" she says.

My smile blossoms freely this time. "No," I say. "Only yours."

❦

I don't see Heidi at all on Sunday. We don't speak, either.

This is actually normal for us. Paper Patisserie is closed on Sundays, and Heidi and I don't do a lot of purposeless "hanging out," just the two of us. If we're together it's because we have something we're doing, somewhere we're going, or it's because there are other people there besides us.

Today, though, it feels weird not to talk to her. Our conversation from yesterday is still ringing in my ears, still making my heart pound in my chest.

I didn't imagine that, did I? Did yesterday actually happen? Was it all a very strange dream?

I touch my lower lip with my thumb, dragging it lightly against my skin.

No. Yesterday definitely happened. Heidi licked my lips, and then I attacked her.

I cringe, leaning against my kitchen counter and staring blankly at my refrigerator as I remember the way I lost my mind completely. I would love for that part to have been a dream.

I pull out my phone and check the call log, before I can convince myself I'm being ridiculous. I want to see one more time, for myself, the proof that we really did talk on the phone yesterday—that she really did say those things.

I don't want you to write anywhere else but at my shop, okay? You're mine, all right? Don't go to a different café.

She called me *hers.*

And I know—I *know*—that she was just saying things. I think her thoughts and feelings were coming faster than she could process them, and she was spitting out the first things that popped into her head.

But it doesn't change the fact that there appears to be some part of Heidi that feels very possessive over me.

I'm aware, too, that she reads my books, and that she likes them. I've seen little hints here and there. She knew when my first book was published; she knows the names of my books, even though I never mentioned them to her. Plus she has that t-shirt—the one she told me not to read into.

The one I definitely read into.

So I guess it's possible that she wants S. *Mackenzie* to write at her shop instead of somewhere else. Maybe she views me the same way she views Jojo—as the shop pet.

I snort, running my hand over my beard. I'm thinking too much.

I fling the refrigerator door open, grabbing my bottle of water. Then I head to the space that's technically labeled *dining room* on the floor plans, even though that's not how I use it. I have a little table in my kitchen; that's all I need. I put the treadmill and my weights here instead. When your job involves lots of sitting, it's important to get up and move every now and then.

I tie my hair in a tighter bun than usual so that it won't fall out, and then I hop on the treadmill. I do my best not to think about Heidi as I run, trying to give my brain a break from the agonizing and the wondering and the longing. I blast my workout playlist instead and think through my current work in progress, trying to figure out where to take it from here.

I have a plot. It's all mapped out. But I'm second guessing everything. Every character, every word, every turn of events. I look at my writing, and I'm convinced it sucks.

I finish up the day in a flurry of pacing and waiting and generally wasting time, and when night comes, I sleep horribly.

I arrive at Paper Patisserie thirty minutes after it opens the next morning.

"Hi," I say as I spot Gemma, who's on her way to the kitchen. I can hear Calvin chattering away from over by the book desk, though the shelves block my view of him. There's the usual clanging of pots and pans from the kitchen, the opening and closing of cupboards.

"Hi," Gemma says, giving me a little wave. The bracelets on her wrist jingle slightly.

I'm not an expert in women's fashion, but Gemma is usually fancier than Heidi; she seems to prefer fitted clothing and nicer shoes, where Heidi often dons t-shirts and jeans. Gemma wears a lot of jewelry, too; she looks nice, and she is beautiful, but it's not my style.

"How's it going?" I say, a reflexive question rather than genuine curiosity. My eyes are darting all over, looking around before I even notice what I'm doing. It takes me a second to realize I'm searching for Heidi; my gaze lingers on the book-shelves, waiting for her to appear.

"Going fine," Gemma says, looking amused. Then she jerks her chin toward the shelves. "She's in the back."

"Ah," I say, and I can feel my ears turning red. "Right." There's no point in denying anything; I'll give Heidi however much time she needs, but if I had my way, we'd be dating by this time tomorrow. I would love nothing more than to hold her hand in public and send her giant bouquets of flowers for everyone to see.

My lips curl as I smirk; she would absolutely hate that. I might have to try it.

"Oh," I say as Gemma resumes her path to the kitchen. "Sorry. But just letting someone know—I'm meeting a couple people here in"—I check my watch—"twenty minutes. We'll use one of the tables."

"Oh, Heidi said something about that," Gemma says, standing up straighter. "But I thought it was tonight. Book club?"

"Writing critique group," I correct her. "And no, they'll be here in a little bit. They're coming from Autumn Grove."

"How many people?" she says, turning to look at the tables. "Do you need to scoot two tables together?"

"I think three of us," I say. "We should all fit around one table."

I head over to the armchair next to the display windows— since she died I haven't been able to make myself sit in the chair Carmina and I always fought over, ironically enough—and collapse into it. I might be able to get in a few words before my writing group shows up. In fact, I have enough time to hammer out two hundred words, hate every one of them, and then delete them all.

In the end, I do about three hundred words. As predicted, I hate all of them. I don't delete them immediately, though, even if that's my first instinct. At some point I have to stop deleting things. My first draft might be rubbish, but you can't edit a blank page. I know this.

I know this. So why is my mind fighting so hard against my imperfections?

I sigh and shut my laptop, looking up in time to hear the little bell over the door jingle. Two people enter the shop, a man and a woman, both of them looking around curiously.

"Oh my goodness, look how cute it is!" the woman says, her head turning this way and that. She's wearing a short dress with what looks like a pattern of...porcupines, maybe? Or hedgehogs? Maybe very round cats? I shake my head; the pattern isn't important. Her chin-length hair is a shade of pastel pink, and even though she's barely stepped in the shop, she moves with the kind of energy that would leave me exhausted.

She tucks a few strands of pink hair behind her ear, and then she glances at her companion—a grumpy-looking man in a tweed blazer with elbow patches. "Isn't it cute?"

"I...guess?" he says slowly, his face wrinkling as he looks around too. Then he frowns at the woman. "What am I even saying?" he mutters. More clearly, he adds, "No. Buildings aren't cute. Stores aren't cute."

"Oh, sure they are," she says, waving this away. She doesn't seem at all put off by the expression on his face; if anything, her smile widens when she sees his frown. "Look at the checkered floor." She points to the floor of the café. "Look at the cozy bookshelves." She points to those too. "It's cute. It's all cute."

The man rolls his eyes, but I see the look he gives her when she bounds toward the bookshelves and starts thumbing down the row; it's nothing short of adoring.

Crap. Is that how I look at Heidi? Am I that obvious?

Probably.

Speaking of the woman I attacked with my mouth—she rounds the corner at that exact moment, looking hurried but in good spirits. She smiles at the newcomers, and into my mind pops her words from Saturday: *You're mine, all right?*

Don't think about that right now, I tell myself. *Don't think about any of that conversation.*

But it's not easy to pull my thoughts away from the things Heidi said to me—from how possessive she got, without even realizing it. Never in my life did I think I'd be attracted to something like that, but...

I shake my head, trying to dislodge those distractions as I watch the newcomers.

"Welcome!" Heidi says to them. "How's it going?"

"Good," the pink-haired woman says. "This place is so cute!"

Heidi smiles at her. "Thank you. I think so too. Anything I can help you find?"

"Shakespeare," the man says immediately, and the woman with pink hair rolls her eyes.

"So pretentious," she says under her breath.

"Do you sell special editions?" he says, ignoring her.

"A few," Heidi says, "but not many. You're welcome to look around."

"We're actually here for a writing group," Pink Hair says with a smile. Her Shakespeare-loving companion turns away from the bookshelves, looking at Heidi instead. He looks less than thrilled to be here, I notice; whether he dislikes writing groups or is just antisocial, I'm not sure yet.

I stand up, grabbing my bag and my laptop and moving them to one of the little round tables. I frown at the spot; now that my stuff is there, I'm not sure three of us will fit after all. But I'll figure that out in a minute; I approach Heidi and the newcomers by the door first.

"Hey," I say, nodding at them. "You said you're here for a writing group?"

The man with elbow patches looks me over, his eyes narrowing the longer he stares. Then he turns to the woman. "Is this the guy you're going to be meeting with every month?" he says, looking incredulous.

The woman with pink hair frowns at him. "I don't know," she says. "I don't even know his name yet." Then she turns to me. "Are you Soren?"

"Yep," I say, giving her an awkward little wave that I really could have done without. "Nice to meet you."

"Nice to meet you too. I'm—" But she breaks off as her companion claps his hand over her mouth.

"He looks like a male model," the guy with elbow patches says. "And he's huge. Were you going to go meet a random stranger in a random bookshop and hope for the best? Have you learned nothing?"

The woman pries the man's hand off of her mouth. "He's not *that* big," she says, sounding reasonable. Then she narrows her eyes at me, sizing me up. "Smaller than Gus."

"That's not saying much," the guy mutters. "Everyone is smaller than Gus."

"All right, fine," the woman with pink hair says. She puts her hands on her hips and pins me with a look. "Are you going to murder me?"

I blink, surprised. "Um. No," I say, scooting closer to Heidi.

"See?" the woman says, turning to her companion. "He's not going to murder me."

"Ah," the guy says, holding up one finger. "But that's what any murderer would say."

"Yeah, that's true," Heidi says with a nod. "Sorry," she adds to the woman with pink hair. "I know what it's like to have an overprotective man hovering around. But that really is what a murderer would say." She pauses, her gaze swinging to me, her eyes lighting up in a way that promises trouble. It's a rare expression for Heidi, but one that I love—even though it bodes ill for me. "I think you should probably make him prove he's a good citizen," she goes on. "A show of good faith."

"Mmm," the woman says, and she nods, looking serious. "That's a good idea."

"Hey," I say, giving Heidi a look of mingled protest and outrage. "What is this? What are you doing?"

"It's important to make our customers feel safe, Soren," she says. "So please answer the question we're all wondering: Will you or will you not submit to a full-body search?"

I'm pretty sure my eyes bulge out of my head. "I absolutely will *not*—"

But I fall silent as Heidi and the woman begin to laugh, while the man shoots me a look that's half disgruntled, half commiserating—like he deals with this kind of thing every day.

I give him a faint smile, but my attention really is focused on Heidi—on that laugh. She doesn't laugh very often, so I love to see it when it happens.

She and the pink-haired woman are still smiling when the woman holds out her hand. "I'm Juniper," she says.

"Heidi," Heidi says. "And you've been in touch with Soren, I guess?"

"Yes," Juniper says with a nod. "We connected through a local writing site. This is Aiden," she adds, gesturing to her companion. Her boyfriend, maybe? There's definitely *something* there; he seems perpetually grumpy, but there's no denying the way his eyes soften on Juniper. "He came along to make sure this wasn't a predator situation or anything."

"He's not a predator," Heidi says, smiling slightly. She glances at me, her smile fading into something a bit more uncertain. I frown, but the expression freezes on my face when she links her elbow through mine. "He's just a man."

Contact. She initiated contact. Our arms are touching.

It's happening.

Juniper—an odd name that strangely suits the pink-haired woman—smiles as she looks at the two of us, her eyes lingering especially on where Heidi's arm is linked through mine. "I see that now," she says. Then she looks back up at me. "How long did it take you to grow your hair out that long?" she says. She steps away from her companion—Aiden—and begins to circle me, studying my hair.

"Uh," I say, squirming under the scrutiny. "Quite a few years, I guess."

She tilts her head, her expression calculating. Then she turns to Aiden.

"Don't even ask," he says before she can say anything. "It's not happening. No offense," he adds, glancing at me.

I shrug. "None taken."

Juniper nods. "You guys seem like fun," she says, smiling once more. "We should double sometime. Aiden and I have no couple friends."

"I'm not sure we have any single friends, either," Aiden says after a second, his brow furrowing. He reaches for her hand and intertwines their fingers. "Do we?"

Juniper sighs. "No, not really. We're loners." Then she turns to us. "What do you think? Want to hang out with us?"

I clear my throat, gesturing back and forth between Heidi and me. "Uh, I don't know. We're not actually—"

"Oh," Juniper says. She claps her hand over her mouth. "You're not together. I'm so sorry. I misread the situation."

"It's fine," Heidi says, but her smile is slightly uncomfortable, and she pulls her arm out of mine. "Well, feel free to work anywhere you guys want," she says, gesturing to the shop. "We're not too busy at the moment, so you won't be disturbing anyone."

"Of course," Juniper says brightly. "Thank you so much." Then she tugs on Aiden's arm. "Let's go," she says, pointing to the table where my stuff is already laid out.

I follow them, glancing back at Heidi. What was all that? But she's already disappearing into the bookshelves.

14

IN WHICH HEIDI MAKES
A PLAN

"All right," I say, pointing at my reflection in the mirror. Despite my neat hair and perfectly normal outfit, there's a panicked gleam in my eye that I can't quite get rid of. "Sure, you said some embarrassing things yesterday. But he didn't care. He kissed you. He *likes* you. So there's no need to feel so humiliated. Just face him with your head held high."

He kissed me. Soren *kissed* me. And then he promised not to do it again, and I felt...something. Relieved, but also disappointed.

Why did I feel both of those things at the same time? It doesn't make sense. None of this makes sense. Soren is out of my league in every possible way. He's brilliant and attractive and successful, even if he doesn't see it. He's a man I never let myself think about romantically, because I knew it would never happen. It didn't even occur to me to have a crush on him; he's *Soren freaking Mackenzie.* People like me do not have crushes on people like him.

There's a little knock at the door, and I jump as the sound

echoes through the tiny bathroom of Paper Patisserie. "Hang on," I call, my voice weird and strangled. I smooth my hair down and then fling the door open—only to find Gemma on the other side, giving me a funny look.

"Oh, thank goodness," I say. I grab her arm, yank her into the bathroom, and then close the door again. "Gemma," I whisper. "*Help.*"

Gemma nods immediately, her expression turning deadly serious. "What do you need? Do you need money? Or is someone bothering you? Or—" Her eyes widen. "Are you sick again? Is it—"

"No, no, no," I say quickly. "It's nothing like that." Then I sigh.

I can't believe what I'm about to tell her. I can't believe what I'm about to admit.

"Something...happened on Saturday," I say.

Gemma raises one eyebrow at me, waiting.

"With Soren," I say.

My best friend's expression clears. "Ah," she says slowly. "Okay. Tell me."

"I don't know," I say, and I can hear the frustration leaking into my words. "We—he kissed me? Kind of? Just for a second. And then I sort of freaked out, and he said he wouldn't kiss me again unless I asked him to, and I'm pretty sure—" I break off, gulping in a deep breath. "I'm pretty sure I told him he was *mine*, like this was some shifter fated mates romance or something, and I have no idea what to do or what's going on."

"Okay, wow," Gemma says, looking stunned. She blinks a few times. "I have so many questions."

"Don't ask them," I say miserably. "I have no answers." I slump down, sitting on the closed toilet seat and resting my elbows on my knees.

"All right, all right," she says, and her voice is gentle now.

"This is fine, okay? Look." She crouches down next to me. "He kissed you? And it was on purpose—like he didn't just bump into you or anything?"

"No," I say, my cheeks heating as I remember the way his lips moved. "It was definitely a kiss."

"But it freaked you out."

"Kind of, yeah," I say. "I wasn't expecting it. And I wasn't really thinking straight. I—he was—we—" I break off. "I had just licked him."

Gemma blinks at me again. "You...licked him."

I nod. "On the *lips*," I wail, burying my face in my hands. "Because he had ice cream on his mouth and—and—"

But I cut off as Gemma begins to laugh. "Amazing," she says breathlessly. "That's incredible. Okay. All right." Then she tucks her dark hair behind her ear and looks up at me. "Heidi, you *like* him."

I swallow. "I think I might?"

"You do," Gemma insists. "You've liked him forever. It's just that you don't ever seek out romantic connection. You binge romance novels and call it good. And I understand why," she says, her words softer now. "I really do. You've always played things close to the chest, and I know you're wary of what your future might look like. I've never seen you date anyone. You've never even liked anyone in the time that I've known you, have you?"

"Not really," I admit. "I'm just..." I don't want to say the word, but I spit it out anyway. "I guess it's kind of scary to open up. I don't know the first thing about relationships. And I don't know what kind of future he wants."

"You're allowed to be scared," Gemma says. "But you're healthy now, and there's no use worrying about something that hasn't happened yet. All you can do is tell him the truth and see what happens."

"'Never let the fear of striking out keep you from playing the game,'" I say with a sigh. "Babe Ruth."

"Don't be stupid," Gemma says with a snort. "That was Hilary Duff's dad in that Cinderella movie."

I smile despite myself. "Silly me," I say. Then, with a sigh, I add, "I don't know how to do that."

"Start slow," Gemma suggests, tilting her head. "Do you like Soren? Not the author—the person. Do you like him?"

"I...yeah, I think so. Maybe," I say. "I'm not completely sure."

"I think you do," she says. "But take some time to figure it out. There's no rush. He's not the kind of guy to push you."

"He's not," I agree.

"And he kissed you," Gemma goes on, "but do you know if it was just a kiss, or if he has feelings for you?"

"He said he likes me, but that could mean so many different things," I say as my thoughts whirl. "Like maybe he thinks I'm cute and he'd like to kiss me some more, or maybe he wants to marry me tomorrow." Both thoughts are terrifying. "I really have no idea."

"Hmm," Gemma says, her eyes narrowing as she thinks. "Okay. Well, keep thinking about it. Spend some time with him and see how you feel."

"I will," I say, since I know I'm not going to be able to get him out of my brain anyway. I can't believe the things I said to him. Have I lost my mind?

I must have. There's no other explanation.

Gemma and I chat for a few more minutes—in the bathroom, because why not—before we go back out to the shop. Jojo squawks when we emerge, and Gemma shoots him a nasty look. She's not his biggest fan. To be fair, I don't think he's particularly fond of her either.

I loiter at the book counter for a bit, ringing up a few

customers and rearranging things needlessly. Then I head back to the kitchen to check on Mel, trying to look casual as I pass Soren and his writing group. Juniper, the woman with pink hair, has a notebook open in front of her, and she's nodding as Soren says something. Her boyfriend is leaning back in his chair, paying little attention to them; I don't think he's actually doing any writing. I think he came along to be with her. I don't let myself stare at any of them—Soren especially—even though I could sit and watch him write for hours and not get bored. This is work for him; he doesn't need distractions.

I thought it would be a good idea to touch him earlier; wrapping my arm around his felt natural. Nice, even. But I wasn't prepared for someone to assume that we were a couple. It's something I should have thought about.

I should have thought about everything.

A list. I need to make a list. Pronto.

I abandon my trajectory, doing an awkward turn in the middle of the café and then heading straight back to the storage room—my list-making haven. It feels a little different in here now, given the whole police interrogation from the other day, but I close the door behind me all the same.

"Paper," I mutter under my breath, glancing around. "Paper, paper—ah." I spot a notepad resting on top of a large cardboard box, a pen right next to it. "Excellent. Okay."

I start immediately, scrawling the letters *S. M.* across the top. Then I begin listing pros and cons, off the top of my head.

And yes. I know it's kind of crappy to make a pros and cons list about a person. But...that's kind of where I am right now, and I kind of need to figure my thoughts and feelings out. So I continue to write.

Pros:

-I might secretly love his hair

-He makes me smile

-His books are incredible
-He smells good
-I liked when he hugged me
-He makes me feel safe

I tap my pen against my lips for a second, rereading what I've got. I think that covers the heart of it—I feel safe and happy with him. So I move on.

Cons:

-I might secretly hate his hair?
-Because maybe I'm jealous of how pretty it is and also it's annoying that he's so attractive?
-He's kind of famous
-I don't know what kind of future we would have
-He's obnoxious
-

I frown as I stare at that little dash, waiting for me to fill in another con.

I can't think of one.

Why can't I think of one? Surely there are more cons than this. There have to be. Granted, the *I don't know what kind of future we would have* con is a pretty massive one, but...

I shake my head and flip the sheet over. Maybe first I should figure out how I already feel, and then I can move on to deciding if I want to pursue him or not. That's a more efficient use of my time and energy.

So how can I clarify my feelings for him? How can I tell if I like him?

Touch his arm, I scribble on the back of my first list. *See how you feel inside. Warm and tingly?*

I nod. This is good.

-Hug him. Do you feel excited, or do you feel like barfing?

-*Now hug a different man, not Eric. Calvin? See if you feel different or the same.*

-*Find an excuse to touch his hand*

-*Repeat with another man, again not Eric—again see if you feel the same way about both of them*

-*Take a really good look at him.* DO NOT GET CAUGHT STARING. *See if you really, truly find him attractive.*

I swallow, staring at the little paper, and then add one more thing:

-*Maybe kiss him?* DO NOT DO THIS UNLESS YOU'VE DONE THE OTHER ONES.

Okay. All right. This is okay. This is fine. I can do these things. I am a strong woman, and I am able to take charge of my emotions. Of course I am. Of course I am!

"Of course I am," I say, trying to pump myself up. I bounce back and forth on light feet like a boxer in the ring. I look like a loon. "Of course I can take charge of my emotions."

I've been handling my emotions my whole life. The only problem is, usually that means shoving them down and putting them away. I've never tried to take them out and explore them before. It sounds...messy.

I don't like messy.

I sigh, the sound loud in the muted room. "It's fine," I say. "Now stop talking to yourself and go do your job."

I rip the sheet of paper off the notepad and fold it neatly, shoving it into my pocket. I've just grabbed the door handle when I feel a push from the other side, and the door swings open. I jump back, stumbling over my feet and catching myself at the last minute.

"Whoa," Soren says quickly. His hand darts out and closes firmly around my wrist, steadying me. "You okay?"

"Yeah," I say, breathless.

He nods and lets his arm drop back to his side. "I was looking for you."

My heart stumbles a little, and purely on instinct I shut the response down. But I blink in surprise as I realize what's happening. I do it so naturally, completely without thinking; have I always been that way? Have I always closed myself off like that?

I frown, looking down at the large, masculine hand that was on my arm. My heart trips again as I reach out and grab it, bringing Soren's touch back to my wrist.

"Grab me again," I hear myself saying, my brows still furrowed.

"What?" Soren says, and though I'm not looking at his face, I can hear the curiosity in his voice.

I jerk my chin at the spot where his hand is now resting lightly on my arm. "Grab me. Like you did when you first opened the door."

This time he doesn't say anything; his fingers wrap snugly around my wrist, warm and firm and confident.

I touch my chest with my free hand, pressing it over my heart. The reactions I would normally stifle—this time I let them free, forcing myself to acknowledge them. I feel...warm. My face feels hot. And there's something behind my breast bone that's pleasantly squirmy, a kind of adrenaline rush that's both anxiety-inducing and exciting.

"Should I let go now?" Soren says, and I glance up at the sound of his voice, low and gravelly.

"Yes," I say, startling out of my thoughts. I pull my arm out of his grasp, and he lets it go with no fight. "Sorry."

"Don't apologize," he says, his voice lower still. "I told you you could do whatever you want with me."

My eyes dart over his face, checking his expression, but all I see is raw honesty—an open gaze, straight nose, perfect lips that are neither smiling nor frowning.

"Do you need a minute?" he says, his eyebrows quirking.

"No," I say quickly. "No. I'm good. What's up? You were looking for me?"

He nods. "I stepped away for a second because I had a thought. About Carmina."

I perk up at this. "Tell me."

"We should talk to the head of the HOA in her neighborhood. We were wondering about Mr. Foster, right? If Carmina filed complaints against him, they would be with the HOA representative," he says.

"That's true," I say, thinking. If we're looking for people who had grudges against the woman, that's a place to start. "I bet we could find out who that is online. Maplewood is an entire community thing, right? Like they probably have a website?" I pat around in my pockets before realizing I left my phone out behind the cash register.

"Definitely," Soren says with a nod. He's close enough that if I inhale deeply, I can smell that sharp, peppery scent—his bodywash, maybe? "Here." He holds out his phone. "Look it up. We can go over there later. I need to get back to my table."

I cock one eyebrow at him as I take the phone. "Letting me poke around again?" I say.

"I have nothing to hide from you," he says with a shrug.

From you.

I take those words, swallow them—and for the first time, I let myself think about how sweet they might taste if I were brave enough to savor them.

THE HEAD OF THE MAPLEWOOD HOMEOWNER'S association is one Stanley Riggs, whose address is not listed, but his phone number is. That makes sense, I guess. I wouldn't want my address on the internet either.

I wait for Soren's writing group to end, ringing up the small but steady trickle of customers and helping Mel at the bakery counter for a while. Even after I spot Juniper and Aiden leaving, I keep myself busy; I don't know if Soren has more he still needs to do now that they're gone. But he finds me several minutes later, restocking the flour and brown sugar. He leans against the doorframe of the pantry, his arms folded over his chest, and looks down at where I'm kneeling on the floor.

"Need help?" he says.

"Nah," I say, emptying the bag of brown sugar into the large canister. It comes out in clumps, that sweet molasses smell wafting past me. "I'm almost done."

"Did you find anything about the HOA?" he says.

"I did." I close the canister lid and then stand up, massaging my lower back. "His name is Stanley Riggs; there's a screenshot of his number on your phone." I pull his phone out of my pocket and pass it to him.

"No address?" he says.

"No." I wince as I try to knead the muscles in my back. "And I don't understand how I'm already having aches and pains at my age. I'm thirty-one. Isn't that still considered a woman's prime?"

"I wouldn't know," Soren says, his voice musing. His gaze drops to my torso. "I'd offer to give you a massage, but considering that I basically tackled you when you licked me..." His blue eyes flash as they return to mine. "Who knows what I might do if I actually got my hands on you."

Oh.

I gulp.

Oh dear.

"It's fine," I say in a voice that's weaker than I'd prefer. "It doesn't hurt too much. I probably slept funny."

"Mmm," he says. His eyes trail over me. "Well, let me know if you want me to knead some of those muscles," he says, flexing his hands. "And in the meantime—should we call this guy?"

"Do we want to call him or go visit him?" I say, glad for the distraction. I press my hands to my cheeks, trying to look casual.

"Let's call him first," Soren says. He steps further into the pantry and pulls the door closed behind him.

My breath catches in my throat, hitching somewhere around my clavicle and then disappearing entirely. This pantry is small, and with the two of us in here together, it feels even smaller.

"Okay," I say. "Let's call."

"I mean, do you think we need to go see him in person?" he says. He sounds totally normal now, which I do not appreciate. Didn't he say he likes me? How is he completely unaffected by the two of us being shoved in this tiny space?

"Not necessarily," I say absently, looking more closely at him. He seems to be breathing normally, and I can't tell any difference in his skin tone. I don't think he's flushed or blushing.

There are a few seconds of silence, and I start when Soren breaks them.

"What are you looking at?" he says. He speaks the words quietly, low, like he's asking me to tell him a secret.

And I don't have it in me to be coy; that's not who I am. I don't play games, even of the flirtatious variety. So I ask him one question.

"Do you really want to know?"

He turns his body to face me more fully, making the pantry

feel tinier than ever. The overhead light is doing incredible things for the color of his hair, and it casts long shadows over his features.

"Mm-hmm," he says in a low rumble. "I always want to know."

"You said you like me," I say.

"Mmm."

"But you seem totally fine being in here with me like this." I tilt my head as I look up at him.

To my surprise, though, he cocks one eyebrow at me. "Do I?" he says, his mouth crooking into an amused smile.

I nod shakily, because I don't entirely trust my speaking voice right now.

I'm waiting for him to respond, but he doesn't—not verbally, anyway. Instead he reaches for my hand, his movements slow, measured. Then he lifts my arm, placing my hand directly against his chest, right over his heart.

"Oh." The word slips out of me, barely a whisper, as my eyes widen. I press my palm more firmly into him as I feel it: the rapid rhythm of his heart. "It's so fast," I murmur. Then I look up at him, meeting his eyes. "Because of me?"

His throat bobs as he swallows. "Because of you," he says hoarsely.

"Because we're close?"

"Yes. And—" He breaks off, clearing his throat. "And you're pretty."

I blink up at him, my eyes still wide, and he gives me a gentle smile.

"I'm attracted to you," he clarifies. "I find you very attractive."

"Right," I say. Of course. That's something that makes people's hearts beat faster.

"Any more questions?" he says.

"No," I say in a strangled whisper, letting my hand fall back to my side. "None for now."

"Then shall we call Mr. Riggs?" he prompts.

"Yes," I say quickly. "Yes. Pull up his number. I screenshotted it. What should we say to him?"

"Any thoughts?" he says.

"I think we should explain who we are and then tell him what Elsie said and ask if he received many complaints from Carmina—or about her," I say.

"Sounds good to me."

He swipes around on his phone a few times, and I pull my own phone from my pocket. "Read it to me when you've got it," I say.

He reads me the number a second later, and I dial. I listen as it rings once, twice, and then three times before someone answers.

"Hello?"

It's a curt voice, deep, with an air of irritation. Like we've inconvenienced him by daring to call.

"Hi," I say, ignoring the bad vibes this guy is sending down the line. "Is this Mr. Riggs?"

"This is he," Stanley Riggs says. "May I ask who's calling?"

"Of course," I say quickly. "My name is Heidi. Several days ago a woman named Carmina Hildegarde died in my bookshop."

There's silence for a second, and then Stanley says, "I heard about that, yes."

I nod. "I spoke to the family of the deceased, and they indicated that she had some problems with her neighbor, or maybe others in the neighborhood. I thought since you're the head of the homeowner's association, you might be aware of any conflicts that were going on."

"Her family said she was struggling with a neighbor?"

"They did, yes."

"That's correct," Stanley says. His voice is still clipped, still impatient, but that's not going to stop me.

"Would you be willing to elaborate on that?" I say, praying he doesn't ask me why I want to know. I'm not sure how I would answer.

Thankfully, he doesn't mention it. He just says, "Not much to elaborate on, really. Carmina Hildegarde reported someone for having a dog off leash. I think there was something about the dog going to the bathroom in undesignated areas as well, and maybe some noise complaints. The walls are thinner than some of our residents prefer. But I can't remember all the details, and frankly I don't have time to look it up right now."

"And the person she reported was her neighbor?" I say.

"I'm not at liberty to disclose that information," Stanley says.

"All right," I say, thinking hard. "One last question, then. What are the consequences if someone is found to be guilty of things like having a dog off the leash or letting a dog do its business in undesignated areas?"

"Depending on the severity, perpetrators will be fined up to five hundred dollars per offense."

"Wow," I say faintly. "Uh, okay. I understand. Thank you so much for your time—"

But he hangs up before I've even finished speaking.

"Well," Soren says from in front of me as I lower the phone from my ear, staring at it. "He seems like a pleasant fellow."

I snort. "He acted like I was the single obstacle to all his earthly desires. Good grief."

"I heard," Soren says. "Your phone is pretty loud. But he confirmed it, right?"

"More or less," I say, biting my lip. "He said Carmina filed several complaints against someone in the neighborhood about their dog. He wouldn't say who, but coupled with what Elsie said, I think we can safely assume it's Mr. Foster. Did you hear him mentioning the noise complaints?"

Soren nods, the harsh overhead light playing with his hair. "Yes."

"That would only be relevant for the people who share walls. That especially makes me think it's him."

"I agree."

Even though I know it makes me look highly suspect, I fan my face; it's getting warm in here. This space is small at the best of times, much less when two grown adults are crammed inside. The stale air is slowly taking on Soren's sharp, spicy scent, and I'm not sure I can handle much more of that.

"Let's go," I say, opening the door to the pantry. I step out and shove my phone in my pocket, welcoming the fresh flow of air once more—and, even better, the scent of just-out-of-the-oven muffins.

"Wait," Soren says from behind me. "You dropped something."

I move to the counter, picking up one of the muffins. "What?" I say over my shoulder, peeling off the wrapping and taking a bite.

"Here. It's—" But he breaks off, and I turn around to see why he's fallen into silence.

Only the second I turn around, I wish I hadn't.

Because there he is, his stupid man bun still perfectly golden, his brow furrowed, his lips parted as he frowns down at the piece of paper he's holding—a piece of paper with neat fold creases and handwriting I recognize as my own.

My list.

Soren is reading my list.

15

FROM THE LIFE OF CARMINA HILDEGARDE

OCTOBER 16

Carmina Hildegarde stared out her bedroom window through the slit in her blinds. She held the slats just far enough apart that she could see without being seen in return, a practice she'd perfected after years of spying and nosing. A woman didn't always have all the advantages she needed, and when that was the case, it fell to her to pave her own way, no matter the cost.

Her eyes narrowed as she watched horrid Mr. Foster and his horrid, giant dog. The beast was on its leash this time, so there was nothing there she could report; the neighbor had denied that it was his dog who'd knocked her down, and despite the bruises and the sore wrist, she didn't really have any proof. Maybe if she caught it relieving itself in an undesignated area, she could turn that in instead? So she kept her eyes on man and pet as they meandered, the dog sniffing here and there, its tail wagging merrily.

Horrible animal. Horrible *man*.

He was a snoop, her neighbor, his beady little eyes always hunting for who knows what. That, combined with the beast...

It wasn't that she disliked dogs; quite the contrary, actually. When she was younger, back in her heyday, when she was the height of fashion and the envy of every young woman, she'd kept a little Bichon Frisé named Millicent. Millie had gone everywhere with her, tucked into her purse, her fluffy head sticking out, her tiny tongue lapping up the air.

But if one keeps a pet, one must maintain the pet properly. And while Millie was perfectly trained and perfectly behaved, Mr. Foster's dog was not.

"Ah-ha," Carmina said as she spotted the dog lifting one leg and relieving itself on a bush. She grabbed her camera from next to her and fumbled with it for a second with age-worn fingers, only barely managing to snap the shot in time. Proof. Proof that that dog was a menace.

She smiled with satisfaction.

16

IN WHICH SOREN KNOWS NOTHING ABOUT HAIR SALONS

O h, Heidi. My Heidi. That precious, headstrong, infuriating woman. The piece of paper in my hands is, without a doubt, a list she made—about *me*.

She's relegated me to words on a notepad.

It's so like her that I have to fight my laugh.

"Give me that," she mutters now, abandoning her muffin. She sets it hastily on the counter, where it rolls a few times and then falls still. Then she lurches toward me, her eyes on the paper, her hands outstretched.

"I don't think so, Miss Lucy," I murmur, holding the note high above my head. "Did you really make a pros and cons list about me?"

She jumps, her body bumping into mine, but I don't move.

"Soren," she says, stomping her foot.

"Answer the question," I say. Then, seeing the panic on her upturned face, I smile slightly. "Relax," I say. "I won't read any more of it, okay?" It kills me to say; I don't think I've ever wanted to look at something more. "Just tell me if you really made a list about me."

Her body sags, her shoulders slumping. Then, to my surprise—and complete delight—she lets her head drop forward, resting on my chest.

"Yes," she says with a sigh. "I made a list about you." She hesitates and then looks up at me, her eyes beseeching. "I know it's a crummy thing to do, okay? But I'm really not good at this kind of thing, and it helps me to organize my thoughts on paper—"

"I'm not mad, honey," I say as my smile grows. The endearment slips out almost too naturally, but I don't take it back. "I'd be lying if I said I'm not going to die of curiosity, but I'm not upset. I just wanted to know."

And the look on her face is so hopeful, so unsure, that I find myself reaching up, tucking her hair behind her ear, my thumb brushing against her skin for one electric second. "Here," I say, passing her the little piece of paper. "Take it."

To my surprise, though, she doesn't. She looks at me instead, her eyes wide, her cheeks flushed. I watch as she swallows, holding myself back with an iron grip as I'm struck with the urge to kiss that spot on her neck. When she speaks, her voice is raspy in a way I've only heard in my dreams.

"You can read it," she says.

I blink at her, surprised. "What?"

"You can read it." She pushes my hand away gently, until it and the list are pressed against my abs. "Here. Read it. Just this side."

"I—are you sure?" I say. I make myself wait, make myself be patient.

Slowly, her eyes never leaving mine, she nods. "I'm sure."

That's good enough for me. I let my eyes drop to the piece of paper in my hands, scanning it hungrily. I'm well aware that there might be things here I don't want to know, but somehow I can't stop myself. Besides...she wouldn't let me read it if there was anything truly insulting, would she?

I don't care. I read the whole thing anyway, noting that apparently she has a love-hate relationship with my hair and that she thinks I'm obnoxious; that last one makes me smile a bit.

I raise an eyebrow at her, and she bites her lip.

I want to bite her lip, too.

Cut it out, I tell myself firmly.

"Are you done?" she says, her voice anxious.

"Done," I say.

She breathes a quick sigh and pulls the paper away from me.

To give myself something to do, I move over to the counter and pick up her discarded muffin. I take a bite, chewing slowly, and then hand it to her. "Here," I say. "If we're done talking about how you secretly love my hair or how you think I smell good and that my books are incredible—"

"I also said obnoxious," she cuts in, rolling her eyes at me. She takes another bite of her muffin. Then, covering her mouth so that I don't get a glimpse of her food as she speaks, she goes on, "Did you miss that part? Because I'm happy to show you again."

"You also said it's annoying that I'm so attractive," I go on as though she hasn't said anything. "And I have to agree; it is a burden—"

"Good grief," she says, rolling her eyes, and I smile.

I continue smiling, hoping it remains natural even as my mind jumps to the one item on her list that actually troubles me: *I don't know what kind of future we would have.*

I don't know what that means, and I'm afraid to ask.

Feelings are interesting, aren't they? The same emotions that propel you to put your heart on the line are the ones that recoil at the slightest chance of rejection. I've never been particularly free with my affections; I don't date a lot, and I never have. I'm the kind of guy who has a short string of serious relationships rather than dozens of casual encounters.

Casual holds no appeal for me.

"All right," I say, trying to focus on the here and now rather than on nebulous futures that may or may not come to pass. "Let's make a plan, shall we?"

Heidi's brow furrows as she looks at me. "A plan?"

"You wanted to go to the hair place," I remind her. "And ask them about the day you can't remember."

"Oh, right," she says as her expression clears. She refolds her little piece of paper and then shoves it back in her pocket. "Yes. I do want to do that." When she reaches up to touch her hair, I say,

"How is your forehead feeling?"

"Not bad at all," she says, letting her fingers drift over the bandage. "I barely notice it."

"Good," I say. "Well, when do you want to go to the hair place?" What is that called, anyway? A hair salon? A hair stylist? A barber shop? Are those all different things?

"Let's go this afternoon," she says. She leans back against the counter just as Mel bustles around the corner from the main kitchen. "Hi," she says.

"Hi," Mel says, looking frazzled. "I lost track of time, and I left the last batch of scones in for too long. They came out dry and brown."

Heidi frowns. "Do we still have some in the front?"

"Yes," Mel says. "We have enough for now. We won't run out probably until the afternoon rush. I'm just annoyed at myself."

Heidi waves this away. "Don't stress about it, then. Just do another batch. Do you need another set of hands?"

Mel's shoulders relax slightly, some of the tension leaking out of her. "No, I don't think so," she says.

"All right," Heidi says with a shrug. "Well, let me know."

"Thanks," Mel says, and then she's off again, bustling back around the corner to the kitchen proper.

Then Heidi turns to me. "Okay. Let's do this."

I nod. "Where?"

"I have a special list-making haven that I'm willing to share with you," she says, and something in her hazel eyes sparkles as she speaks. "Just this once. You've shown yourself to be worthy."

"I'm flattered," I say with a little smile. "Lead the way, then."

I follow her out of the kitchen, through the café, back through the bookshelves, and then through the storage room door where I found her not too long ago. When we step inside, she spreads her arms wide. "This is where I make all my lists. It's one of my favorite places in the shop. I know you've been in here before, obviously, but now you can appreciate it in a different light."

"Of course," I say, amused. I glance at the humming lights overhead, the stacks of boxes, the ugly brown carpet. "It's...lovely."

She snorts and begins weaving through the boxes. "No, it's not. But I don't come here for the beauty." She inhales deeply. "You smell that?"

I sniff, too. "What—that musty smell?"

She nods. "That's the scent of books and ideas and paper. Come over here." She beckons with one hand, and I obey, following her trail.

I watch as she sits down right on the floor, in a little clearing she's obviously made herself. There's just enough room for me to squeeze in, so I sit too, crossing my legs and ignoring the warmth of my knee as it overlaps hers. I'm wearing jeans, but she has on denim shorts; her legs are mostly bare, her skin golden from the sun. I notice briefly that she hasn't shaved them in a couple days; she's getting stubble, a few light bristles that would probably feel like the skin of a kiwi if I touched it.

Interestingly enough, I really don't care what her leg hair situation is like. It's just hair, and they're just legs. Gorgeous legs, yes, but I'm more interested in the way she smiles when she's feeling mischievous, the way she chases after what she wants, the way her cheeks turn pink when she's embarrassed.

"Paper," she says once I've settled, pulling a pad of paper from out of nowhere, "and a writing utensil. Let's get to work. I need to get my thoughts down on paper," she says. "I can't keep everything straight otherwise."

I nod, forcing myself to pay attention to something other than her legs. "All right. What kind of list are you thinking?"

"We need to write down all the people who seem suspicious and all the people who had grudges against Carmina," Heidi says. She tucks some of her hair behind her ear. "Starting with the obvious."

"Whoever she was blackmailing," I say with a nod.

"Exactly." She scribbles that down on the pad of paper. "I'm putting the son too."

"Probably a good idea," I say, remembering how unaffected he seemed.

"And what about Mr. Foster?" She looks up from the pad of paper, her eyes landing on me. She traces the pen around her lips, her eyes narrowed in concentration. "I feel like murder is a little extreme as retribution for someone reporting your dog."

"Maybe," I say slowly, "but we don't know exactly how much he got fined. Stanley Riggs said it could be up to five hundred per offense, right?"

She nods.

"So that could add up to quite a lot. I'd put him down, even if it seems unlikely." I hesitate, and then add, "Write it down. Now." If I have to keep watching her trace that pen over her lips...well.

You told her you wouldn't kiss her again, I remind myself.

She raises her brow at me but writes it down. "How do we figure out who she was blackmailing?" she says then, looking back at me.

"I'm sure the police are already doing their own thing on that front," I point out.

"I know," she says. She bites her lip and then goes on, "I'm just anxious to figure this out. I keep thinking—I keep thinking —" She sighs. "I can't shake the feeling that I knew something was going to happen to her. And I *really* think that if I can figure out what happened, I might remember what I've forgotten."

I nod. "I understand. We can only do so much, though," I say gently. "Do you know when the police will return the security footage?"

"No," she says, sounding frustrated. She runs one hand through her hair. "I don't know. I guess I could ask them."

Rushing them doesn't seem like it would make a very good impression, and we really don't want to get on their bad side. Not when they're already looking sideways at us. "Tell you what," I say. "Let's wait and see what happens over the next few days, okay? If we need to in the future, we can try to visit Carmina's house again. Maybe see if they'd let us look in her room." Normally I would worry about bothering the grieving family, but...they don't really seem to be grieving.

"For now, let's go to the hair place," I go on. "We might get some insight on your missing day."

"Yeah," she says with a sigh. "All right."

My phone buzzes in my pocket as she stands up, and I pull

it out. One message from *Juniper Writing Group*. I don't think I'll forget her name or mix her up with any of the other Junipers I know—none—but it's how I entered her contact information anyway. My heart picks up speed as my thumb hovers over the message; this might be her feedback. She said she was going to read the rest of the stuff I shared when she got home and then tell me what she thought.

But do I want to know? Do I really want to know if my work in progress is a flaming pile of crap?

No—and yes. I don't want to know, but I need to know. So I take a deep breath and then open the text.

Hi Soren, this is Juniper Bean from our critique group, it begins. *I finished reading your chapters. I don't know what you're worried about; it's looking great. I left comments in the doc!*

My heart flutters with relief—I exhale loudly and then take a few more breaths before getting to my feet.

"What's that all about?" Heidi says.

"It's Juniper," I say. "In my writing group. She likes what I'm working on."

Heidi rolls her eyes and rests her hand on my arm. "I'm not surprised," she says. "I think you're the only person who thinks it's bad."

I stare down at that hand, where it's in contact with my skin.

She's touching me. I am being touched. By Heidi. Heidi is touching me.

Snap out of it.

"Up until today, I was the only person who'd read it," I point out, my eyes still stuck on the slender fingers, the little silver ring. This is so stupid. I'm being so stupid. My heart should not be racing. It's her hand on my arm. That's it. Completely benign.

She shrugs, blissfully unaware of my internal debate. "Well, now it's fifty-fifty. You think it sucks, and she thinks it's good."

"Fifty-fifty isn't anything to write home about," I say, and I finally force my gaze back to Heidi's face.

"Come on," she says. She gives my arm a squeeze and then lets go. "To the salon."

I nod. "To the salon."

***

Betty's Cuts and Dyes is a little hole in the wall off of Fifth, which is part of the historic downtown area. I guess technically Sunshine Springs does have a Center Street, but it's residential; Fifth is the most commercial road in town. It's the road that feeds into the town square, and it's lined with eateries, shops, and everything else the tourists might need. Heidi's brother's shop is there, an equipment rental service, and they do a booming business, especially in the summer.

The thing that makes Sunshine Springs so great is that we're close to so many great places. Yellowstone and the Tetons aren't far, and there are natural hot springs nearby too. There's even an old ghost town within a days' drive. There's always something to do here, or somewhere to go.

Which I suppose makes it ironic that I spend most of my time doing nothing and going nowhere except for Paper Patisserie, but what can I say? I'm a man who knows what he wants.

The breeze alleviates the warmth of the spring day, and I'm grateful that my hair is pulled off my neck so I can feel the cool air. When we step into Betty's, though, the temperature drops some fifteen degrees, and I shiver, rubbing my arms at the sudden chill.

"Hi, kids," Betty herself calls from where she's standing

behind a salon chair, painting what I think is some sort of dye onto a customer's foil-layered hair. Betty is more energetic than you'd expect from someone her age; her hair is silver and spiky, and her purple cat eye glasses reflect the overhead light as she nods at us. "Got my hands full or I'd come shake yours. What brings you back so soon?" She directs this question at Heidi. "Do you want more off?"

"No," Heidi says quickly. "It's perfect how it is."

"Oh, good," Betty says as she continues to work on the lady's hair. "And what happened to your head, sweetie?"

"That's what I wanted to talk to you about, actually," Heidi says, approaching Betty. Her eyes jump to the lady in the chair and then back to the hair stylist. "Could we wait over here until you've got a free second?"

"Sure thing," Betty says, nodding at the chairs off to the side. They have those helmet things over them, but they look comfortable, so I head on over and settle down in one of them. "I'll be with you in a bit."

Heidi joins me a second later, sitting in the chair next to mine. I look around, examining the place.

"What's that smell?" I say, sniffing.

"That's any number of hair products," she says. "All salons smell like this." Then she looks up at my hair. "But I don't suppose you have to use anything on your hair for it to be perfect like that."

I shrug, trying to hide my smile. "I use shampoo and conditioner."

"Just regular shampoo and conditioner?"

"I grab whatever's cheapest or on sale," I say.

She shakes her head. "Unbelievable," she mutters. "I don't know what you did to deserve all that golden perfection when so many women would kill for that color and softness and thickness."

"Not a dang thing," I say as my smile finally slips free. "But if it makes you feel any better, my hair was a frizzy mess when I was younger."

"It does make me feel a little better," she says, still eyeing my hair. "Thanks."

We wait for probably twenty more minutes, talking aimlessly about whatever comes up, until Betty puts her foil-headed client in the seat next to ours and turns on the helmet thingy. Then she gestures to Heidi and me, and we stand, following her.

"What can I help you with?" Betty says once we've rounded the corner into the back hallway. "I got the sense you wanted a bit of privacy."

"Thank you," Heidi says. "I wanted to ask you about the day I came in to have you cut my hair." She touches her forehead. "I'm currently suffering from some memory loss, thanks to this. I wondered if you could tell me how I was acting, or how I seemed to be doing, or if I talked about anything odd."

"Oh, dear," Betty says, her silver eyebrows flying to her hairline. "That's no good. But you really seemed fine. You said you'd had a good day, and we talked about books."

Heidi's not much of an actress; she can't hide her disappointment as she says, "That's all?"

"I'm afraid so," Betty says with a nod. "Is something the matter? Did something happen?"

Heidi sighs and folds her arms. "I don't know. It's just that the next day, Carmina Hildegarde died in my café. And so I'm a little shaken, not remembering the day before or if Carmina had been there or if anything had happened."

"I heard about that," Betty says, lowering her voice. "That's just awful." She hesitates, and some of the wrinkles around her mouth and eyes deepen as she frowns. "But you didn't mention anything about her."

And once again, I can tell Heidi is disappointed by the way her face falls.

Betty doesn't seem to notice, though; she just keeps talking. "You know she had beef with that fancy restaurant at the edge of town, don't you?"

"What beef?" I say, just as Heidi says, "What restaurant?" Her question is better.

"Chateau Marche," Betty says. She lowers her voice even further. "Word on the street was, she was gonna sue them."

Heidi stares at her, looking stunned. "I—you're sure?" she says.

"Listen, sweetie," Betty says with a wave of her hand. "You would not believe the things people tell their hairdresser. I heard about it from Patrice Riggs and from Carmina herself. She told me all about it while I was trimming her hair. She says she found a bug in her food. Of course..." She trails off. "I'm not sure if she *actually* found a bug in her food, or if she wanted to complain about something. You know how she was."

Heidi and I nod.

"But either way," Betty finishes with a sigh, "she said she was going to sue them and try to put them out of business."

I look at Heidi; she looks at me. We're comical mirrors of each other, eyes wide, jaws dropped.

We thank Betty for the information, and then we return to the car, neither of us speaking. My mind keeps replaying Carmina's last words: *Murdered.* And my guess is that running through Heidi's head is the same thing, and the same questions: How much trouble did this old woman stir up? Exactly how many people did Carmina Hildegarde have problems with?

And which one of them killed her because of it?

❧ 17 ❧

IN WHICH HEIDI REFUSES TO PAY SEVENTEEN DOLLARS FOR A SALAD

Chateau Marche is not the kind of restaurant you decide to visit one afternoon and then walk right in, but that doesn't stop us from showing up.

I don't know why I was so surprised to hear that Carmina was planning to sue this place; nothing should surprise me anymore. Not anything that woman did, not my missing memories, not the way my stomach flipped when I rested my hand on Soren's arm earlier. This is my life now—a bombshell-uncovering, memory-missing, stomach-flipping existence.

I flex my hand as we enter the restaurant, recalling the feeling of Soren's muscled forearm. I haven't touched another man's arm yet—it feels invasive, somehow—but I'll try it later when we go back to Paper Patisserie, or maybe tomorrow. Calvin should be a safe choice for that part of the experiment; our relationship is strictly platonic, and while he might have harbored a little crush on me at some point, he knows as well as I do that nothing will ever happen.

Even though I haven't touched his arm yet, though, I think I know what will happen. There will be no stomach flips, no trip-ping pulse, no shortness of breath.

"All right," Soren says, pulling me out of my thoughts. I startle, my cheeks heating as though he can see what's going on in my head right now. Which is stupid. Of course he can't.

"All right," I repeat.

"What's the plan here?" He gestures around at the little antechamber we've stepped into, an elegant, dimly lit room with large double doors that lead to the restaurant proper. "We're not dressed for dinner here, and they're probably booked tonight anyway."

"I know," I say, biting my lip.

Chateau Marche is basically a lodge. I've never eaten here, but I've looked it up before. It plays into the nearness of the Tetons and Yellowstone, with a log exterior and a rustic inte-rior. There are chandeliers that look like they're made of antlers and the heads of various animals mounted on wall plaques, and they charge seventeen dollars for a house salad. I know this because one of my hobbies is looking up the menus of restau-rants and deciding what I would order if I ever ate there.

But in no universe or plane of existence will I be buying a seventeen dollar salad. Maybe the lettuce is secretly a bunch of soggy dollar bills? I don't know. And I'm not going to find out.

"I don't think we can waltz in and ask about someone suing them," Soren says. "That doesn't seem like it would go over very well, does it?"

"No," I admit. "Probably not. It might not even be the kind of thing the wait staff is aware of."

"So what do we do, then? Just...go in and ask to speak to the chef? Or the owner? Are they the same person?"

"No," I say. "I don't think so. But either of them would probably know about Carmina's claim if there's anything to it." I look at Soren. "Because Betty was right; Carmina could have been complaining without actually planning to sue. That's the kind of thing she'd do."

"I keep thinking about the things she said before she died," Soren says now, his voice hollow, his eyes far away. "*Pick* and *lock* and *murder*."

"I know," I say quietly. "Me too." However horrible she might have been...no one deserves to die like that, slumped over, surrounded by people, seeking justice with her last breath.

I know we can't control when we die, for the most part. But it seems cruel that she didn't even get to finish saying what she wanted to say.

"Soren," I say with a sigh, suddenly feeling painfully tired. "This was a bad idea. Let's go home." I glance over at him, and my voice is beseeching even though I try to keep it steady and calm. "Let's not do this today. Let's wait until tomorrow. We're not going to be able to get a seat anyway, and we don't really have a plan, and—"

But I break off when he pulls me into a swift hug, gentle and warm, one hand buried in my hair, the other smoothing up and down my back. It's an assault on my senses, the sudden warmth of him, his peppery scent, the faint tug of his scruff on my hair and the top of my head.

"Relax," he murmurs, sounding amused, and I realize with a start that my body has stiffened. So I take a deep breath and then let the tension drain out of me, until I'm little more than a limp Heidi noodle being anchored by this gentle giant. I give myself permission to press my face further into his chest, too, breathing him in.

If we become romantically involved, this is the kind of thing that we'll do. We'll hug and touch each other and I'll smell him. Maybe it would be good to try taking those liberties, to see if I like it, to see if it's something I want to continue doing.

"You always smell good," I say, my eyes fluttering closed as I relax further into his hug.

"Yeah?" he says.

"Mm-hmm." I find myself wanting to hug him in return, so I do; I wrap my arms loosely around his waist, interlacing my fingers over his spine.

"You always smell like something tropical."

I smile. "Coconut," I say. "It's my body wash and my shampoo. I like that scent."

"It's become a favorite of mine, too," he says, and I listen in fascination as his voice rumbles through his chest. "For... obvious reasons."

My cheeks heat. "You make me feel warm," I say without thinking. "And safe. When we're standing like this"—I give him a little squeeze—"I feel safe."

He hums. "Safe is good. I want you to feel safe. With me, but also without me." He swallows; I hear it, and his voice is hoarse as he goes on, "I want you to be comfortable with me, but I don't want to be the only place you feel comfortable. I want that for you in all aspects of your life."

That's...strangely sweet. I turn my head so that I'm looking up at him, my chin resting on his chest. "I want to hug another man and see if I feel the same way," I tell him. "I was thinking Calvin."

For the briefest second, his hand tightens in my hair, a muscle jumping in his jaw. But then he nods. "If you think it will help."

I stare at him, fascinated. "You don't like that."

"Not at all," he says, a wry smile playing at the corners of his lips. "But you're in charge, honey."

"How would I feel if I saw you hugging someone else? Another woman?" I say. I don't know why I'm asking him; he's not going to have the answer. I guess I'm letting my thoughts free as they flit through my brain.

"I don't know," he says, like I expected him to. He looks down at me, his gaze curious. "How would you feel? How would you feel if you saw me hugging or kissing another woman?"

Kissing another woman? That's not the same thing as hugging. Not at all.

But I try to picture it. I try to imagine Soren, his arms tight around some faceless woman, kissing her the way he kissed me, devouring her—

"No," I blurt out, shoving the image away. "No."

Soren raises an eyebrow. "No?"

I swallow. "No," I repeat, my voice firmer. "Don't—" I break off and clear my throat. "Don't kiss anyone else. Not right now."

He nods slowly, and the hand that's in my hair tightens, pulling slightly. "All right." His eyes flick to my lips, then away again. "I'll only kiss you. Good?"

"Good," I say in a stupidly breathless voice. "And I'll—I'll only kiss you." Not yet. But...

"Whenever you're ready," he says, as though he's reading my mind. His arm tightens around me, holding me more firmly against him. "Whenever and wherever." Then he says, "Let's go home."

❧

When we get back to Paper Patisserie, Eric is engaged in a lively debate with Calvin and Gemma somewhere back by the bookshop counter. I can't tell what the debate is about yet, but I can hear their voices the second I walk in, all trying to talk over each other.

The little bell jingles overhead upon our entrance, a cheerful sound I've always loved, and it cuts through the sound of my brother and my friends. I inhale deeply, enjoying the smell of the baked goods from the café.

Is there a better smell than books and scones and fresh spring air? I don't think so. So I take one more whiff, letting my eyes flutter closed, savoring the peaceful moment before I have to launch myself into whatever's going on back there.

"It smells great, Mel," I call, and behind the bakery counter, around the corner that leads to the kitchen proper, I see her hand waving her thanks.

From behind me I feel Soren's hands come to rest on my shoulders, and my mind jumps back to when he did the same thing the day Carmina passed. I shiver at his touch; maybe because his hands are warm and the air conditioning has chilly teeth against my skin, or maybe simply because it's him.

"Sounds like they're having fun," he says, his words hovering somewhere over my left ear.

"Mmm," I manage to get out. I'm not sure he's entirely right; whatever's going on back there is bordering on heated. "Better go see what's going on."

His hands tighten on my shoulders for a brief second, and I can't help but notice how far they span; almost the full width of that space, from my neck to the slope of my shoulders. He could spread his fingers and reach my upper arms. His thumb could caress my neck in gentle, sweeping motions—

I shake my head abruptly, surprised by the turn my thoughts have taken. "Whew," I say, shaking it again. Then I give my cheeks a few firm pats and step away from Soren. "Okay, let's see what they're going on about," I say.

The voices grow louder as I make my way through the bookshelves and back to the checkout counter. When I emerge, I find my brother and my employees almost exactly as I imagined I would: Calvin and Gemma behind the counter, Eric in front, all of them leaning on it.

"No," Gemma is saying as she shakes her head. "No. If it doesn't have a happily ever after at the end, it's not a romance."

"It doesn't have to have a happily ever after," Eric argues. "As long as there's romance in it, it's romance. What else would you call it?" he says, incredulous. "It's right there in the name. *Romance.*"

"Yes," Gemma says, and I can tell she's growing increasingly more irritated, "but for a book to be called a *romance book,* it has to end with the couple being happy."

"She's right," Calvin says to Eric, looking embarrassed. He always looks at my brother with hero worship eyes, despite Eric having done nothing to earn it. "Sorry, man."

Eric throws his hands up in the air. "Take a book that's completely about a romance, where the couple doesn't end up together, and tell me what else you're supposed to call that. The romance is the only thing in the book."

"Literary fiction," Soren says, just as I chime in, "Women's fiction."

We look at each other, surprised, and then both of us nod— I think acknowledging that either of us could be correct.

"This is not as simple as you're making it out to be," Soren says, leaning back against the counter next to Eric and then looking over at him. "You're not dealing with generic descriptions; you're dealing with genre expectations and publishing labels. If a reader picks up a book labeled *romance,* they're expecting a happily ever after, and they probably won't be happy if they don't get one. That doesn't mean that what's happening in other books isn't romance; it means that the *primary genre* is not romance."

"But what if the book isn't about anything else?" Eric says, still frustrated.

"Then it's either literary fiction or women's fiction," I say. "If it focuses on a woman's inner journey, it's women's fiction. Usually romance isn't the only thing going on, though. Even if a book is mostly character driven, there's still stuff going on. It just might not be heavy on external plot." Then I frown at my brother. "Why are you here?"

He sighs, running his hand through his hair. "I came to tell you that I'm going out to the hot springs tomorrow. We got some new men's hiking boots in last week that I want to try. Invitation is open to anyone who wants to come"—he points at us—"as long as no one mentions romance novels."

"What time?" I say. I haven't gone yet this year, but I'd like to.

He shrugs. "I was thinking of leaving around ten. We can drive out, make the hike, spend the afternoon there, and then come back before dark."

I bite my lip, looking at Gemma. "We'd lose a day of sales," I say.

"Your call," Gemma says—like the amazing friend she is. But I can see how hopeful she is, her eyes shining, her perfect brows raised expectantly.

I sigh. "Yeah, all right. It won't hurt too much. We'll come." I look at the men. "You guys want to join?" I'm talking mainly to Soren, if we're being honest, although I don't mind Calvin at all. In fact...

"Hey," I say to my twenty-three-year-old employee. "Calvin." I turn my body toward him and open my arms wide. "Want to give me a hug?"

"Of course," he says immediately, a giant smile breaking over his face.

The corners of my lips twitch. He's such a little ray of sunshine. The sunshine bounds around the counter and all but flies to me, engulfing me in a warm hug with lanky arms. "Why are we hugging?" he says into my ear, and I can hear that he's still smiling. "Are we making someone jealous?"

My twitching lips pull into a real smile. "Not quite," I say, returning his hug. "Let's just stand like this for a second. I'm testing something."

"You got it," Calvin says. His arms tighten around me. "We can stay here all day."

"Another minute should be fine," I say, still smiling. I poke around at my insides while I speak, connecting to my heartbeat, examining my breaths. They're even, my pulse steady, and—perhaps most tellingly—the only emotion I really feel is a generic contentedness. I like Calvin; he's a sweetheart, and a great employee, and a good friend. But I don't feel warm or flushed from his touch; I don't want to burrow into his chest and stay like this forever.

It's as I suspected. I think I actually have romantic feelings for Soren Mackenzie, my favorite author. And what's more...I think I might have feelings for him even if he'd never written a single book.

I rotate Calvin and me so that I can see Soren over Calvin's shoulder. His blue eyes are on us, watchful, and although he doesn't look annoyed, he does look antsy; his fingers are drumming on the countertop, and his entire body seems alert. Under the lights of the bookshop, his tanned skin and perfect hair seem to glow. Like he's some sun god from ancient times, beautiful and golden and unattainable.

Only...he might be attainable after all. If I can make myself take those steps.

If I can move past this fear I have. Because my worry isn't doing me any favors. I know that. I really do.

But knowing and changing are two very different things.

"Uh, Heidi," Gemma's voice says from behind me, and I start.

"Yeah," I say from where my arms are still around Calvin— who, by the way, is grinning like a fool. I laugh, shaking my head and then letting go of him. "Thanks," I say to him as my arms fall back to my sides.

Calvin makes a little pouty face before breaking into his smile once more, scrubbing his hand over his untidy hair. His freckles seem to dance as he says, "It was my absolute pleasure."

"Okay, you guys are being weird today," Gemma says.

I glance at Soren; he's relaxed slightly, his fingers no longer beating incessantly on the countertop, his frame at ease rather than tense. The look he gives me now is curious, full of questions.

I'm not sure I have answers for him yet. I have some, I suppose—I think I can confidently say I like him—but what to do about it isn't as simple.

It's only complicated because you're making it complicated, a little voice in my brain says. That voice sounds an awful lot like Gemma, and I scowl mentally.

"Right," Eric says loudly, and I look at him.

"I'm gonna be honest," I say. "I forgot you were still here."

"Mmm," he says, his eyes narrowing on Calvin. "You were caught up in your little moment." Then he pats the counter. "We're leaving at ten tomorrow. Meet me in the parking lot of Manderley's. I'm not waiting around for anyone. We'll figure out rides then."

He leans over and gives Gemma a quick peck on the lips; then he turns and walks away, disappearing into the bookshelves without waiting for a response. A few seconds later I hear the bell over the entrance jingling, and he's gone.

"*Her heaving bosom!*" Jojo squawks from the corner,

making all of us jump. His words slice through the space around us, loud and awkward and wildly inappropriate. *"Her heaving bosom!"*

I just shake my head.

⊛

THAT NIGHT, ONCE THE SHOP IS CLOSED AND EVERYONE has gone home and I've successfully evaded answering questions I don't want to answer, I call my mother.

"Hi, Mama," I say quietly when she answers. I snuggle further under the covers, half of my body pressed into the massive, fluffy, faux fur pillow I keep on my bed.

"Hi, baby," she says, her voice cheerful. "What's up?"

"Mmm," I hum, playing with the furry pillow. "Just the normal stuff, mostly. How are you?"

I don't know why, exactly, I wanted to call her. I have no plans to tell her someone died at my shop; it would completely freak her out. I also won't be mentioning my head injury or my missing memories.

Even with all I'm keeping from her, though...I guess I want to hear her voice.

"Oh, I'm fine," she says. "The movers are coming tomorrow to get the rest of this stuff out of here, and by tomorrow night I should be in the new place."

She sounds happy, excited, so I try to make myself sound that way too. "That's great," I say. I push a smile onto my face, in case she can hear that kind of thing in my voice. "How much is left to take over?"

"Not much," she says. "A few random pieces of furniture. Some dining room chairs, and that vanity from your room. I think the mirror detaches."

"I think so," I say, a strange lump forming in my throat. A

197

lot of my most painful memories took place sitting at that vanity —staring at myself in the mirror, trying to make sense of myself and my mind and my body. Trying to see what other people might see when they looked at me; trying to see who I might become.

I don't think we look into crystal balls to see our future. We look into mirrors. We turn our heads right and left, examine the little bits of our souls we can see leaking from the eyes of our reflections. We hold those reflections up to the light, searching for familiar patterns, for our mother's curly hair or our father's Cupid's bow.

You can't see who you're going to become if you don't know who you already are, and you can't find where you're going to end up if you don't know where you're already located.

"Mama," I say, "I'm sad you're selling the house. And"—I take a deep breath—"I met a guy I think I like."

Those two admissions are completely unrelated, and I didn't plan to say either of them. But they're out there now, slipped away when I wasn't watching them closely enough, so I wait for my mother's response.

"Oh, sweetie," she says softly after a second of surprised silence. "Does it bother you that I'm selling the house?" I can picture exactly how she looks right now, her soft, kind face pulled into a concerned expression, her curly blonde hair tumbling around her.

"Kind of," I admit. I fiddle with the fuzzy pillow. "It feels a little bit like my childhood is being sold."

"Oh, I'm so sorry, sweetheart," she says in a heartbreaking voice—it's devastated, full of regret. "I'm so sorry. I didn't realize. I should have asked you—"

"No," I say quickly. "I'm glad you're doing it. I am. I know you need a smaller place, and it makes sense. Plus I really like the pictures of your new place. It's a me thing," I finish, my voice stilted. "I'll be okay. I truly will."

"Will you?" she says.

"Yes," I say, more firmly. "I'll be okay."

"But you know, sweetheart," she says, "that house was just a house." She's quiet for a second, and then she goes on, "You loved it because you love your family, and we were there with you."

"Maybe," I say. I don't know. What makes a house a home? What turns four walls and a roof into a place where laughter springs forth spontaneously and the children know they're nothing short of adored? "Is it just love?" I say, more to myself than to my mother.

Luckily, she doesn't seem to hear me. She moves on to my other confession.

"Now," she says. "Tell me about the guy."

And it's ridiculous, absolutely ridiculous, how my heart starts to beat faster just because my mother has asked about him.

"He's great," I say quietly. "He's gentle and kind and he's giving me so much time and space to figure out what I want."

"I like him already," my mother says, her voice teasing. "Is he cute?"

I smile in spite of myself. "Very," I admit.

"What does he do for work?" she says.

"He writes books," I say. "Really great books."

"Does your brother like him?"

I roll my eyes. "It doesn't matter if Eric likes him."

Except, truth be told, Eric has an uncanny knack for being able to tell the true character of a man; I've never seen him get it wrong. If Eric says a man is no good, I listen.

"Does he?" my mother persists, because she knows this about him, too.

"Yes," I say grudgingly. "He likes him. He told him to take care of me."

"Oh, good," she says, and I can hear the relief in her voice. "He sounds lovely, Heidi. I'd love to meet him someday."

I swallow. "Do you think it's—you know." My voice cracks as I go on, "Do you think I could be in a relationship with someone?"

"Of course," she says, sounding shocked. "Of course you could."

"Even though I'm a wimp about feelings and stuff? And even though…" I trail off, unable to finish.

She sighs. "I think if you want to be in a relationship with a man who cares about you, you absolutely can." Her words are softer as she continues. "You had that bad surgery, sweetheart, and I know that was hard on your body, but you're fine now. You've been fine for a long time." She pauses. "Is it the kids?"

"Kind of," I say, rubbing my stomach absently—my lower stomach, beneath which are the scarred, surgically altered remains of my ovaries. "Yes. What if he wants kids? Not necessarily Soren," I add quickly, because we're nowhere near ready for that kind of thing. "Just…in general. If I meet a man I want to marry…he might want children. And I can't give him that."

"There are other ways to have children," my mother says firmly. "And children are not the only part of a woman's future. We carry that role, yes, but we do so many other things."

"That's true," I say, and a tear slips down my cheek at her words. "We do."

"You bring people joy every day when you sell them books, Heidi," she goes on. "You feed them wonderful food and give them a place to imagine and learn and grow as they read. What is that if not your calling?"

I clamp my hand over my mouth so that she can't hear me crying—so that she doesn't hear my hungry breath and my broken voice, the tears coursing over my skin as something deeply broken in my soul begins to feel warm at her words.

Jagged pieces of myself, parts of me that no longer work, scarred tissue and a scarred heart. That incredible function of a woman's body, the ability to bear children—something I always dreamed of, and something I will probably never achieve.

"You are fiercely loyal, sweetheart," my mother continues, "and loving and kind and *good*. I cannot change your body," she says, her voice breaking, "but I can absolutely, unequivocally promise you that *who you are* has never changed. You were always meant to be Heidi. Before a woman is ever meant to be someone's wife or someone's mother or anything else, she is meant to be *herself*. That is where we anchor ourselves. We can add the rest on, but they're not where we begin. You are yourself first and foremost."

I hold the phone away from my face, pulling in deep, gasping breaths, swiping at my cheeks, feeling little bits of fuzz that the tears have cemented to my skin. I keep breathing, in and out, in and out, until I've regained control. Then I bring the phone back to my ear.

"Thanks, Mama," I say, trying to keep my voice normal.

"I wish I could give you a hug, baby," she says.

"Me too," I say. "But I'm okay." I take another shuddering breath.

"If you'd really like children in the future," she says, "I would be willing to let you adopt Eric."

And maybe it's my shaky emotions, but I burst out laughing.

"He's fully potty trained," she goes on, and I continue to laugh.

"I'll let you know," I say, wiping a few stray tears of laughter from my eyes. "I love you, Mama."

"I love you too, sweetie. Get some sleep, okay?"

I nod, tell her I love her one more time, and then hang up. I'm drifting off to sleep when there's a knock at my door.

"Hey," Eric says when I answer, his eyes soft as he looks at me. "I came to deliver a hug."

I open the door a bit wider, and he steps inside, gathering me into his arms.

We fall asleep curled up next to each other on my bed, the way we used to when we were kids.

18

IN WHICH SOREN LETS HEIDI
EXPLORE

I 've been to the hot springs out here before, but they never cease to amaze me.

Which is a strange thing to say, maybe. They give off that infamous rotten egg smell from the sulfur, and they're not much to look at, either. Lots of rocks with little pockets of water here and there. It's beautiful in its own way, I suppose, but it probably won't win any awards for most photogenic.

What amazes me is the heat.

I'm a bath guy. I usually keep this on the downlow, because people don't expect a man who looks like me to take baths, and my bathing habits are nobody else's business anyway. But I love taking baths. You sit in a vat of steaming water with sweet-smelling bubbles and relax. What's not to like?

When I was in college, though, rooming with three other guys in a dorm that offered very little in the way of luxuries, there was no bathtub. We had a cramped shower, and that was it. On top of that, the water heater was spotty, so there were several times that we took nothing but cold showers for days.

And while a group of college guys will always have ample need of cold showers...it was pretty miserable.

I don't consider myself pampered. I don't think I'm snobbish or finicky about demanding a luxurious life. But I can promise you that I will never, ever, *ever* be without a bathtub again, and I will take cold showers only when I actively choose to.

Like probably tonight.

Because look. I'm a respectful guy in general. But Heidi Lucy in a swimsuit is causing my mind to short circuit. And the crazy thing is, it's not even a fancy swimsuit. It's a black athletic one-piece. No frills, nothing unnecessary—much like Heidi herself. It's simple, straightforward, and somehow sexy as all get out.

Heidi is beautiful in her own way. She's not an in-your-face curvaceous bombshell like Gemma; she's not immediately stunning like Gemma, either. Her beauty is more subtle than that. She's leaner, with delicate facial features and a smile that reveals itself little by little. And yet as I watch the two of them holding hands and stepping down into the smaller of the natural hot springs, it's Heidi I can't tear my eyes away from.

Gemma's great. She's fun and, yes, objectively gorgeous.

But she's no Heidi Lucy.

I run my hand over my beard, taking several deep breaths as I pull my gaze away from Heidi. I'm staring, and I need to cut it out. Just because I'm crazy about her doesn't mean I can be rude about it. So I drift over to the back of Eric's SUV, where he's digging around in the trunk. It's the only car we brought, because it ended up being the four of us. And Eric seemed fine when we started out, but now he's muttering to himself under his breath and looking grumpy, glancing over his shoulder at the women periodically.

"What's up with you?" I say, making myself comfortable on

the edge of the trunk next to where he's rifling through his pile of supplies.

"Nothing's up with me," he says, but he stops to look over his shoulder again, and his rifling movements become more forceful. He moves aside what looks like several camping chairs in their bags, followed by a few sleeping bags, and then a toolbox.

"Uh-huh," I say slowly, glancing at Heidi and Gemma. Heidi has a small smile on her face, while Gemma laughs outright, her head flung back. Then I look back to Eric again. "So why are you wearing that facial expression?"

He rolls his eyes and then turns to sit next to me, perching on the edge of the trunk. He nods to Gemma and Heidi. "It's just—what the heck is she *wearing?*" He scoffs. "It's ridiculous. I'm annoyed. That's all."

I can only assume he's not talking about his twin sister and her plain black one-piece, so I turn my gaze to Gemma, taking a better look at her vivid red suit. It's one piece as well, but the front plunges into a deep vee that ends somewhere around her solar plexus. I notice too, as she and Heidi walk around in the spring, that it's almost completely backless. Other than a tie at the back of her neck, there's not a scrap of fabric until it hits the base of her spine.

A slow grin spreads over my face.

"Ah," I say, nodding. "I see."

"What do you—I don't—you don't *see* anything," he splutters, looking indignant. "There's nothing to see. Stop looking at my girlfriend."

"Sorry, sorry," I say with a shrug.

He sighs. "Sorry," he says. "She says I'm too *caveman*, whatever that means. I'm not allowed to express opinions on her clothing. But..." His jaw clenches shut, and it looks almost comically like he's forcing himself not to speak. I watch his struggle for a few seconds, his face turning redder and redder until finally the words burst out of him.

"But *look* at her! She looks like that, and I look like this, and someday soon she's going to realize how completely out of my league she is."

I shrug again, trying to hide what's left of my smile. I know how to spot a man who's head over heels but completely insecure. "You need to chill, man."

"I know," Eric says with another roll of his eyes. "I don't need you to tell me. Go flirt with my sister or something."

"You know," I say, turning to face him more fully. "Most brothers are all sensitive about men with their sisters, aren't they? Don't they get huffy and overprotective?" Not that Heidi would stand for that kind of behavior; she'd put her foot down *real* quick.

Eric snorts as he pivots and begins rifling through the trunk once more. "I'm gonna let you in on a little secret, Man Bun."

"Hey," I say, frowning at him as I reach up to touch my hair. "Only Heidi gets to call me that—"

"Nope," Eric says. His movements are aimless as he continues to dig around in the cluttered trunk, and I get the feeling he needs something to do, something else to concentrate on besides Gemma. "Here's the secret: I'm an impeccable judge of character. And you?" He looks me over. "You're harmless, and you're whipped."

My cheeks flush, but I don't deny it.

"It would do Heidi some good to socialize," he goes on. "She's terrified of relationships, and half the time she doesn't even realize it. Why would I get huffy and overprotective when I think you'd be good for her?"

Well. When he puts it like that...

"Don't get me wrong," he adds, throwing me another look. "I'd intervene if I thought you were a problem, but I don't.

Besides"—he glances over his shoulder at his sister—"Heidi doesn't appreciate being told what to do. You know that. And she might be emotionally stunted in some ways, but she's smart. She can take care of herself."

I clap him on the shoulder. "You're a good brother," I say. "So I'll let you in on a secret *I've* observed." I lean in the tiniest bit. "Heidi isn't the only woman here who can take care of herself." I clap him on the back. "So stop worrying about Gemma. She's right where she wants to be. She wouldn't put up with you otherwise."

Eric doesn't even look away from the stuff he's pushing around in the back of the car; he just raises one hand and swats me away. I laugh, standing up and then heading toward Heidi and Gemma.

"Ladies," I say with a little nod as I slip out of my shoes at the edge of their pool. I pull my shirt off over my head and then fold it neatly, setting it down by the stack of towels.

"Ooh," Gemma says, her eyes roving over me. "Not to reduce your multifaceted existence to one mere trait, but... you've got quite the body, Man Bun."

"I don't know how to respond to that," I say awkwardly.

Gemma laughs. "That's fine. No response is necessary. I'm just a girl who appreciates a view." Then her gaze shifts to her best friend. "And so is Heidi, apparently."

She's not wrong; Heidi is staring at me with interest.

The feeling is mutual, babe.

I glance down at my bare chest, where Heidi's eyes are still fixed. "You want to touch?" I say, pointing at myself. "You can." I half cringe at the words, because they sound like something a complete tool would say, but I don't mean them the same way. It's just...she looks curious. I want her to know it's okay to touch me, that she's safe.

Heidi's eyes dart up to mine, guarded, hesitant, but

somehow vulnerable too. I nod patiently, feeling a little bit like someone trying to feed a cat from their open palm. "You can," I repeat.

"I—" she says, breaking off. "Can I?"

I nod once more.

"Ugh," a grossed-out voice says from beside me, and I jump; Heidi does too. We both turn to look at Gemma, whose nose is wrinkled, her mouth twisted into an approximation of disgust.

"Oh," Heidi says blankly, staring at her best friend. "I forgot you were there."

"*Clearly*," Gemma says. "I feel like I just walked in on you two doing the dirty, and you're not even touching yet." She gestures back and forth between Heidi and me, her face still screwed up. "This is way too much. I'm out."

I blink as Gemma turns and wades to the edge of the little pool, stepping out and shaking her feet before slipping her flip flops back on. Then I look back to Heidi, frowning.

"What was that all about?" I say.

"I don't know," she says, her gaze on me once more. "But I'm gonna touch your chest."

"Go for it."

Her hand reaches out slowly at first, haltingly, until I see her steel herself, a determined look entering her eyes.

It's just the tips of her fingers that touch me at first, trailing lightly down the middle of my chest, but it feels like they're burning me, branding me as hers. She stops just short of my belly button and then moves back up to my pecs, poking one and then the other.

"They're muscular," she says vaguely.

"Mm-hmm."

"And these..." She trails off as her fingers move lower to my abs—which are maybe not as defined as Eric's but still respectable. "Muscular."

She's exploring. That's what's happening right now. She's not being coy or seductive; she's charting new paths, examining, investigating.

"You have goosebumps," she says, looking up at me for the first time since she started. Her hand falls away from my skin.

"It feels good," I say in a hoarse voice. My own hands are clenched into fists at my side, but I keep them firmly where they are.

"I can see how that would be the case," she says slowly. "You know, it's not like I'm completely inexperienced." She swallows, her eyes still on me. "I've dated before."

I nod, torn between wanting to know more and wanting to never again think about her with other men.

"But...it's been a long time," she admits. She tucks a few errant strands of hair behind her ear. "Like, since high school."

Crap. Was that her first kiss, what I did to her the other day?

"No," she says, and I blink at her.

"What?"

A little smile tugs at her lips. "You're worrying that when you kissed me, it was my first time," she says. "Right? But it wasn't. I'd already kissed a guy or two."

I sigh with relief, though I have no idea how she knew what I was thinking. "Good," I say. "Good." I glance around. "Let's sit, if you're done...?"

"I am," she says quickly. "For now."

For now.

The two of us wade to the edge of the spring, the warm water lapping at my shins as we move. We sit carefully and settle with our backs against the rim of the pool. It's not the most comfortable thing in the world, because the rocks are jutting and grooved and sharp, but it's not bad, either—especially since Heidi is next to me.

"Hey." She leans sideways after we've been sitting quietly for a few minutes, nudging me with her shoulder.

"Yeah?" I say, smiling over at her.

And I swear, she's the most beautiful thing I've ever seen in my life. Exactly like this—I wish I had a photographic memory, because I want to remember every tiny detail of this moment. Her hazel eyes, vulnerable but sparkling, her dusty lashes, her skin flushed pink; her bare shoulders, delicate and smooth, her graceful neck—so many places for my lips to land.

"I like it when you look at me like that," she says, her soft voice barely audible over the sounds of the spring around us.

I swallow, pulling my eyes away from the intoxicating sight of her bare skin. My gaze meets hers once more. "Like what?" I say hoarsely.

"Like that." She nods at me, her ponytail swinging. "Like you're thinking about all the ways you want to kiss me."

I lean over, and my lips brush her ear as I whisper one of the truest things I've said today: "I have a list of ways I want to kiss you, honey."

She shivers, though I don't know if it's because of my words or the brush of my lips. "Oh," she whispers, sounding surprised. She leans away and looks over at me, her eyes wide. "More goosebumps. That gave *me* goosebumps."

Good.

She stares at me for a second longer. When she opens her mouth and speaks, the words fall out as though she's barely thinking about them.

"I think I like you," she says.

My heart stutters, but I try to keep my face neutral. "Interesting. Tell me more."

She rolls her eyes, nudging me with her elbow. Her cheeks

are still pink, and it's absurd how curious I am about whether that's because of the sun or because she's embarrassed. "There's not a lot more to tell," she says. "I just think I have feelings for you."

Part of me wants to cheer; the other part of me is shuffling its feet nervously, second guessing every word.

"Heidi," I say, my voice low. I look at her. I want to be gentle, but I also need to say this. "Please don't tell me that if you're not sure. Okay?" I look away again, letting my gaze rove aimlessly over the scenery around us—the springs, the trees, the dirt path. Then I swallow. "I—I want this. I want to be with you. It's okay if you're still unsure, but please don't say something you might not mean—"

But I break off, abruptly, as her lips land in a light kiss against my cheek.

"I mean it," she says while I try to process what's happening. Her voice is calm, serious. "I like you."

"I—you're sure?" I say stupidly.

A little smile flits over her lips. "I'm pretty sure, yes. I feel things with you that I don't feel with anyone else." The smile fades slightly. "I'm not ready to jump into anything crazy or heavy yet. There's some stuff I'm working through and some conversations we'll need to have, but..."

And I swear I'm not even breathing right now. My mind, my body, this day, the world around us—they're all suspended, frozen in place, waiting for her.

She takes a deep breath. "But I like you. And I think I'd like to explore that."

"Explore," I say immediately. My pulse is jumping out of my skin, my muscles twitching with the desire to move, but I hold myself still, an iron grip on my self-control. "Explore however you want. I'm here." I swallow. "I'm yours."

"Hey, Heidi!"

Heidi and I both turn around to look behind us at Eric, who's now shirtless and wet but back by the car once more. He waves something in the air, and after a second of squinting I realize it's Heidi's phone.

"Your phone is ringing," he calls to her.

"Answer it," she says. She shifts where she's seated, easing herself up and then standing. "I'm coming."

"Hello?" It's a crisp, professional voice Eric answers with. "Yes, she is. Hang on a moment."

Heidi grabs her folded towel from where it's been sitting by us on the ground, and then she hurries over to him, her feet only halfway into her sandals. She takes the phone as he holds it out to her.

"Hello," she says, slightly out of breath. "This is Heidi Lucy."

I let my hands skim over the top of the water like I used to do in the swimming pool as a child—like I *still* do as a full-grown adult in the bathtub—as I watch the ripples and the way the sun glints off the surface. Heidi's voice on the phone in the background is a soothing presence, perfect amid the sounds of chirping birds and cheerfully bubbling water.

My body stills, though, when I hear Heidi's voice grow concerned and even panicked.

"What do you mean?" she's saying when I tune in.

And then I'm standing up before I even realize it. I grab the last towel and my t-shirt before stepping out of the water.

"No," she says after another minute of silence. "I—of course I understand, but—" She breaks off, and by the time I reach her side, her lips have pulled into a miserable little frown, and there are actual tears welling in her eyes.

Nope. I'm not okay with that. It hurts. It physically *hurts* to see this woman cry.

"I'll let you know when I'm back," she finally says, her voice just above a whisper. "Okay. Thank you." Then she nods and hangs up.

"Heidi," Gemma says immediately, her arms folded tightly over her chest, her towel slung low around her hips. "Who was it?"

"It was the policeman who came to the shop the other day," she says, her eyes wide and unseeing, her voice faint. She looks like she might keel over at any second, and Eric seems to think so too, because he holds out one steadying hand.

But when Heidi finally makes eye contact with someone, it's me. "Carmina had rat poison in her system," she says. Then she looks at Eric and Gemma. "They're shutting down Paper Patisserie."

And into my head pops one word, echoing loudly as it bounces around my thoughts: *Murder*.

✿ 19 ✿

IN WHICH HEIDI GOES TO A
FANCY RESTAURANT

I 'm not a rule-breaker or law-breaker by nature, but
when Eric puts in a solid fifteen miles per hour faster
than the speed limit on the way home, I don't
complain. It's unfortunate that we were only at the hot
springs for all of thirty minutes, but none of us would be able
to have fun if we stayed anyway. Not after that call from the
policeman.

My shop. My shop. My shop.

I keep craning my head anxiously to look out the window
of the car as we drive, like I'm expecting a police car to be
tailing us. I'm twitchy and nervous and probably look wildly
suspicious; it's a good thing it's just the four of us in here.

Soren reaches over and rests one hand on my bare knee; it's
only then that I realize I've been bouncing my legs rapidly. I
still them, but he doesn't move his hand. He meets my gaze and
raises his eyebrows the tiniest bit—asking if it's okay to be
touching me like this. I nod in return, letting my hand rest on
top of his. He flips his hand over then and threads his fingers
through mine with an ease that leaves me feeling strangely

breathless, his grip somehow firm and gentle at the same time, his thumb stroking softly against my skin.

I have to stop myself from kicking the back of Gemma's seat and screaming at her with my eyes alone that *I like a man and he likes me and he's holding my hand right now, this very second.*

Then I have to stop myself from kicking the back of Eric's seat and screaming at him with my very loud voice to *please for the love hurry up and drive faster.*

My shop. My beloved child, maybe the only one I'll ever have, and the officer has asked me to *shut her down.*

Not permanently—at least, if they come to their senses and realize I had nothing to do with poisoning Carmina Hildegarde. But they said that since she was at Paper Patisserie when she died, and since the toxicology report showed rat poison in her system, they needed to check the premises. They're there now, waiting for me; I think they only called when they found the place closed and locked.

Crap. That might have looked suspicious too, right? And what if they find rat poison in the shop? Do I have rat poison? I would know if I had rat poison, right?

Of course you would, I tell myself firmly. *If you haven't bought any and no one has given you any, there's no rat poison at the shop. Calm down.*

"Okay," I say, forcing myself to take deep, steadying breaths. "Okay. Eric, you drop Gemma and I at the shop, and then you and Soren—"

"Will stay with you at the shop while the police are there," Eric cuts me off, giving me an incredulous look in the rearview mirror. "And if you think we would do anything else, you don't know us at all."

I don't even argue. I suspected as much, and frankly, a large part of me is grateful. "Fine," I say. "That's fine." Then I turn to

Soren. "And tonight you and I will go to Chateau Marche. Good?"

He nods. "Good." He continues to hold my hand, his thumb still playing distractingly against my skin. "Let's do it."

My knee starts to bounce again; Soren doesn't stop it this time. The four of us drive in tense, fidgeting silence until we reach Sunshine Springs, and several moments later Eric pulls into the back lot of Paper Patisserie.

Part of me wants to storm out of the car and demand to know what these officers think they're doing, shutting down my shop when I've done nothing wrong. The other, larger part of me knows that would be shooting myself in the foot.

I know I've done nothing wrong, but they don't know that. So it's good that they're looking around and asking questions. It's good that they're poking around. That way my name—and Soren's—will be cleared.

I take a few deep breaths before opening the door and climbing out of the car. My gait feels stilted as I cross the parking lot and round the building, and I'm suddenly questioning very basic things about myself, like if I know how to walk properly and what I'm supposed to say when people ask me normal questions like *What is your name?*

"Breathe," Soren's low voice says from over my shoulder. "You're fine. Just breathe."

I inhale automatically, letting the air out again a couple seconds later. It doesn't do much for my nerves, so I try again, pulling the fresh spring breeze deeper into my lungs this time. I hold it there as I walk, keeping it close until my vision begins to fade and bright black stars start to flash around me. Then I release it in one loud burst of breath.

Eric and Gemma both turn around and give me questioning looks from up ahead, but I jerk my chin, trying to tell them not to worry about me. They glance at each other, shrug, and then face forward again.

By the time we reach the front of the building, emerging into the town square, the policemen waiting for us—or for me, I guess—have grown impatient. They don't say anything as we approach, but the tall one is tapping his foot rhythmically, his arms folded, while the short one looks surly. They don't look any more friendly than they did when they came to the shop the other day.

"Hi," I say after one awkward moment where all of us stare at each other. "Uh, I'm so sorry to keep you waiting. We closed for the day to go to the hot springs." I step forward, and then two men step aside wordlessly, allowing me access to the door. I unlock it with shaking hands. "Please, come in."

"We need to search the premises," the short officer says. He holds out a folded piece of paper, and I take it automatically.

"Of course," I say, my voice faint. I pull the door open and gesture inside. "Whatever you need."

The officers look at each other, and some of their gruffness seems to fade when they look back to me. With simultaneous nods, they go through the doorway and then disappear into the shop.

Maybe my cooperation is helping to smooth things over a bit. I certainly don't have anything to hide.

Right? Is there anything in there I want to keep hidden? I don't have any weapons, do I?

Knives! I have knives in my kitchen.

"What if I get in trouble for having knives in my kitchen?" I hiss at Soren as I turn to him, shielding my eyes from the sun.

He frowns at me. "Everyone has knives in their kitchen."

I pause as his words register. "That's true," I say, blinking at him.

217

"Plus she was poisoned," he points out. "They won't care about knives."

"Yeah," Eric says. "You'd be better off worrying about having rat poison."

"Shut up," Gemma says, elbowing Eric in the ribs. "Do you honestly think that's a helpful thing to say?" Then she looks at me. "We don't have rat poison," she says, her voice soothing. "We've never had rats. Or any rodents, for that matter. We might have some insect repellent somewhere. That's it. So just be calm, okay?"

I stop myself from asking if insect repellent is toxic to humans, because I can tell I'm spiraling, and I don't need to feed the beast. I look instead at Soren, then at Gemma, and finally at my brother.

And it's Eric who speaks, his voice grim: "All we can do now is wait."

❦

I'M NOT ACTUALLY VERY GOOD AT WAITING.

I do go inside to hover around the officers for a while, but something about watching them is upsetting on a visceral level. It's not personal, I know, but the way they move dispassionately through my shop is hard to see. They dig through cupboards and boxes and shelves with a stoicism that hurts, their unfeeling hands pushing aside the possessions I lovingly scrimped and saved to buy. When they finish their search an hour and a half later, they don't put my belongings back in their proper places. They just head toward the front door with curt nods and tell me they'll be in touch.

They scuff my checkered floor with their shiny black shoes on the way out, and I want to cry all over again.

I don't. I don't have time to cry. I listen to Jojo squawk

something about *supple skin* as I feed him a scoop of his food, and nearby Gemma calls Mel and then puts a record on. Mel shows up in no time flat, sweaty and out of breath. Then the five of us put the shop back together, none of us speaking, our faces tight.

My mind spins as I work. The police didn't find anything, of course, because there's nothing for them to find. I didn't do anything to Carmina.

But someone did.

And—my hand drifts to the healing wound on my head—I think someone did something to me, too.

The words of the frantic voicemail I left on Soren's phone ring through my memory once more, and I shake my head. What secret did I learn? Retracing my steps so far has been less than helpful; all I've discovered is that I got my hair trimmed, and that I seemed like I was in a good mood.

I rub my chest absently as I experience a now-familiar twinge of vague panic—another reminder that something in my locked memories is trapped and wants out. Then I inhale deeply and force the breath back out in a slow, steady stream as I restack the boxes in the store room.

Once the five of us get the shop back to the way it was before the officers came, Gemma, Eric, and Mel all go home. Soren watches them leave, his eyes pensive, and then he turns to me.

"Should we go, or do you want to wait?" he says.

"It's a little early for dinner," I say, "but I think we could go ahead."

He nods. "Whatever you want. I'm in no rush."

I look at him for a moment. It's the first time we've been alone since the hot springs earlier, when I let myself touch his chest and kiss his cheek and tell him I like him. And I shouldn't be thinking about those things right now, because this is *so* not the time, but the awareness settles over me before I can will it away.

There are so many new things happening in my life right now. I've never been in a mature romantic relationship. I've never lost my memory. I've never investigated a death. But somehow all those things are taking up space in my brain at the same time, bleeding into each others' territories, and it's confusing. It feels wrong to have feelings for someone while simultaneously worrying about a murdered woman, because how could those two things possibly coexist?

And yet, as I steal another glance at Soren, that little stomach flip happens again.

I clear my throat, which of course does nothing for all the flip-flopping my stomach is doing. "Let's go."

Our drive to the restaurant is mostly silent, which is good, because it gives me time to dissect all the crazy feelings rolling around behind my sternum. There's excitement and happiness and anticipation but also wariness and hesitation and fear, and I don't know what to do with all of that. I really don't. I'm not a *feelings* girl. I never have been. I've always experienced and then dealt with things quietly and in my own time.

I ghost my fingers over the bandage on my forehead; there's barely even a twinge of pain, but I take comfort in it all the same, soaking it up, tasting it. That twinge is sharp and sweet now, rather than hot and angry—like the opening notes of a song being played on the guitar.

I survived a blow to the head. I've faced down pain sharp and sweet, hot and angry, dull and throbbing—I can certainly survive a few unruly emotions and whatever hurts they twist up.

"Heidi," Soren says quietly, and I jump.

"Yeah," I say, looking at him.

He nods out the windshield. "We're here."

He's right, I realize with a start. We've arrived at Chateau Marche, and I didn't even notice.

"All right," I say, sitting up straighter and peering out the window. The parking lot is about half full; not too much of an audience, then.

The girl at the hostess stand is probably in her twenties, and she's wearing a crisp black and white uniform. She gives us a smile and doesn't comment on our casual clothing, which is very nice of her, considering this place wants seventeen dollars for a freaking salad.

"Table for two?" she says, still smiling, but I shake my head.

"We actually would love to speak to the owner for a moment, if that's all right? Or maybe the chef?" I say. I keep my voice friendly and cheerful so that she doesn't think I'm about to lodge a complaint. "It will only take a minute."

The hostess's smile slips slightly, but after a few seconds of looking back and forth between Soren and me, she nods. "Of course," she says. "This way, please."

"Thank you so much," I say.

She nods again, and we follow her as she weaves through the restaurant, past the elegantly laid tables and the dead-eyed animal heads on wall plaques. She slows as we pass through a doorway and into a hall, approaching a man and a woman standing outside what looks like the kitchen.

"Mr. Manniford," she says, gesturing back at us. "You have visitors."

The man looks at us impassively, and then he nods to the hostess. "Thank you," he says stiffly. She turns and heads back in the direction we came, leaving us.

Mr. Manniford then looks at the woman he's been talking to; a waitress, I think, short and mousy. "Tell table seven we can do the substitution, but since our meat is fresh instead of frozen, it will take a few more moments."

She nods and then bustles off.

When she's out of sight, I look at the man.

"Hi," I say, giving him the most genuine smile I'm capable of. "My name is Heidi. I was wondering if I could talk to you for a moment. It won't be long," I add.

Manniford looks me over appraisingly, assessing. Then he nods, one short, quick jerk of his head.

I hesitate, glancing quickly at Soren. The man nodded, but he didn't say anything—does that mean yes?

But Soren shrugs his broad shoulders. He clearly doesn't know either.

All right. I'm diving in.

"Uh," I say. "So. I wanted to ask you about a woman named Carmina Hildegarde. I heard she was threatening to sue Chateau Marche."

Manniford raises one brow at me, but other than that, his face doesn't change. "What about her?" he says.

"Well," I say, tucking a few strands of hair behind my ear. "I guess I wanted to know if that information was accurate. Was she threatening to sue? Was there some sort of incident?"

And I feel ridiculous. I feel absolutely ridiculous, asking this man these questions that I have no right to be asking. He would be perfectly within his rights to shut me down hard, to tell me it's none of my business and to kick me out.

Maybe he's considering it. His face is oddly blank as he looks at Soren and me, a mask of careful indifference I can't quite read.

I look him over more thoroughly, trying to pick up on any nonverbal cues he might be giving off. He's not at all what I expected, honestly. I guess I was picturing your stereotypical hot-tempered restaurateur, large and grumpy and loud and maybe European. But this guy is nothing like that. He's petite, small-framed, with thinning gray hair and glasses that perch precariously on the end of his crooked nose.

There's nothing imposing about him. Nothing that screams *I'm a murderer.*

I shiver in his presence all the same. Don't ask me why; I really don't know. It's something about his eyes. They're a pale, pale blue that looks strangely sapped; lifeless.

He might be a mild-mannered chef, or he might be a psychopath. There's really no way of knowing yet. I take a tiny step closer to Soren and try to make it look as natural as possible. The heat of his body next to mine is comforting, even though we're barely touching.

My cheeks heat as I remember how it felt to touch his chest earlier, to trail my fingers over his skin. Then I clear my throat.

Focus.

Manniford's silence stretches just slightly too long. His face remains expressionless—that eyebrow isn't even raised anymore —and he stares at us for another moment. I resist the urge to fidget, but it's difficult.

After one eternally long minute, he speaks.

"You were misinformed," he says, and a hint of a facial expression finally breaks through: a dismissive twist of his lips. "Ms. Hildegarde did express some concerns, but we were able to work through things amicably."

I blink at him, surprised. "So—she *wasn't* going to sue?" I turn my head when I notice a flicker of motion out of the corner of my eye, but when I examine the open doorway, no one is there, so I turn back to the man in front of me.

Manniford's shoulders twitch in what I believe is a shrug. "That may have been her initial intention, but like I said, we resolved her issues."

I nod slowly, my mind turning this information over. "All right," I say, still thinking. Try as I might, though, I can't come up with anything else to ask him. I have no idea if he's telling the truth or not. I should have googled how to spot a liar before I came here. Do I have time to run to the restroom and do that?

"Thank you for your time," Soren says, and I jump as his hand lands on my shoulder. I startle further when I see that same flicker in the corner of my vision again, but once again, no one is there.

Manniford clearly hasn't seen anything; he just sniffs, and he's already turning his back on us when he replies, "Of course. Enjoy your meal."

He disappears into the kitchen so quickly that it's like he was never here at all.

"Well," I say, turning to Soren, whose hand falls away from my shoulder. "I guess he didn't feel like sticking around to chat."

"I get weird vibes from him," Soren says in a low voice.

"Me too," I admit.

"But I don't think we can cite *vibes* when making an accusation."

I sigh. "No. I don't think so either." Then, chasing a nagging suspicion, I drift toward the open doorway. "Let me see..."

I stick my head out suddenly, looking left and right, and I'm hit with a rush of satisfaction when I see the same waitress from earlier huddled there—clearly eavesdropping.

"I wasn't imagining things," I say. "You're out here." I step out and look at her more closely; she's picking at the nails of her left hand, and her teeth are digging into her bottom lip. I'm hardly a detective or a body language expert, but even I can read these signs.

"Do you have something you want to talk to us about?" I say, keeping my voice gentle. "Or did you need to get in here?"

She clears her throat, her eyes darting nervously around

and then lingering on the entrance to the kitchen. Manniford is really gone, though, and she breathes a noticeable sigh of relief when she sees he's absent.

She clears her throat once more. "He didn't settle things with that woman," she says quietly, her eyes still shifting around us. "The old lady who was going to sue?"

I nod quickly, trying not to look too eager so I don't scare her away. "Carmina, yes."

The mousy little waitress takes a deep breath, and her expression grows more determined. "He didn't settle things amicably. Manniford doesn't do anything amicably. He was lawyering up. The lady came in here making all sorts of threats after she said she found a bug in her food. Manniford said she put it there herself so she could get a free meal. He never solved anything with her."

"When was this?" Soren says, stepping up from behind me once more. I lean back into him after the briefest of hesitations; I want to practice being close to him. So I let myself revel in his warmth at my back, at the comfort I feel from knowing he's here with me.

"It was...I don't know. Sometime in April? Here, I have a picture," the waitress says. She's still speaking quietly and quickly, and when she pulls her phone out of her pocket, her hands tremble. "I noticed it later, but..." She taps on her screen a few times and then holds it up to show us.

At first glance, it just appears to be a selfie—the mousy waitress and another girl, smiling at the camera. But a second later my attention jumps to the background, and my gaze sharpens on the woman there: Carmina. It's her, undeniably. She's at a table right behind the waitresses, about to take a bite of her food, and her head is ducked slightly, but I still recognize her. She's wearing a familiar heavy locket around her neck and looking down at it, and I've seen her wear the red jacket she has on, too.

"That's her," Soren murmurs, his voice close to my ear as he leans over my shoulder to see the phone.

"It is," I say.

"She said she was on a date," the waitress says.

I frown, turning around and glancing at Soren. He looks as shocked as I do.

"A date?" I say, looking back at the waitress. "Like...a romantic date?"

She shrugs, but it's a tight movement. "I guess. That's what she said. She said she had a date."

My frown deepens. "Did anyone show up?"

"No," the girl says, sounding sad, and something uncomfortably like pity twinges in my gut when I look back at the photo of Carmina by herself. "She ate alone the whole evening." She hesitates and then adds, "She looked lonely."

"A date."

"I know. A *date*."

Soren and I look at each other before his eyes jump back to the road.

I keep my gaze on him, though, as my mind works double time trying to make sense of everything.

Up until now, no one has mentioned that Carmina had a man in her life. Her son certainly didn't say anything. And I guess we can't make assumptions; for all we know, she was stood up on what was supposed to be a first date or a blind date. Maybe for all intents and purposes, she really didn't have anyone in her life romantically. I just don't know.

There's one thing I do know, though: Soren would never stand me up if we were supposed to have dinner together.

I can't believe I told him I like him. I don't know whether to be proud of myself or scared of my own daring.

It's fine, I remind myself. *Telling him you like him is totally fine. Dating him would be totally fine too.*

"I guess we should ask someone about her romantic life," I say. "There are a few other things I want to ask her son about anyway."

"All right," Soren says, nodding grimly. "I think if anyone would know about Carmina dating, it would be him." He drums his fingers on the steering wheel and then looks at me. "Let's do it."

IN WHICH SOREN AND HEIDI
DO SOME SNOOPING

Heidi is in the *zone*, and I can barely keep up.

"Now?" I say incredulously to her when she tells me she's ready to go back to Phildegarde's place.

She blinks at me. "Of course," she says, like it's the most obvious thing in the world. Then she points at the sign we're passing. "Take the next exit, I think."

I keep my eyes on her long enough to watch her tuck some hair behind her ear, and then I sigh.

"I promised I would help you, and I will," I say, flicking the turn signal on. "But I feel like I should just remind you that we have no authority to speak of, and Phil and Elsie might not be so receptive if we show up a second time."

"I know," she says, her voice quieter now. "I know they might slam the door in our faces."

"Or file a harassment claim," I say, and I try not to let the strain show in my words. "We're walking a potentially thin line here."

What we're *actually* doing is running around like chickens

with our heads cut off; it's disorganized, chaotic, and stressful. I'm a plotter; I like to know what's going to happen. But I guess you can't plot real life, and you can't predict human beings. I didn't know that the police were going to shut down Paper Patisserie; I didn't know that Heidi and I would fall under suspicion. I definitely didn't know that Carmina Hildegarde would die right in front of us, leaving us with the haunting memory of her last words.

"I know we're walking a fine line," she says. "But I don't know what else to do. I can't sit around and wait."

I can understand Heidi's frantic desire to figure out what happened to the woman. I really can.

Which is why instead of arguing, I just nod.

We fall back into silence, but it's uneasy now. Heidi's fingers are drumming on her thigh, and when I glance over at her, her face is tense.

It's tempting to succumb to the chaos and stress that keep growing inside me as we delve further and further into this mystery, but I do my best to keep a level head. I distract myself from the swirling thoughts and emotions by paying extra attention to the road in front of me, to the cars and the trees and the stoplights.

When my mind drifts to my current work in progress, I reluctantly allow it. Juniper's feedback was surprisingly enthusiastic, but my worries still haven't eased. I can't seem to get out of my own head about this book or my writing or the expectations people have for me.

Sometimes I think writing was the most fun and the most rewarding when nobody was reading my work but me. There were no expectations, no advances to earn out, no publishers to keep happy. It was just me and my characters and the worlds in my mind.

I wonder what it would be like to go back and read my

earlier work now that I've got several books under my belt. Would I be impressed with myself, or would I cringe? Would I be able to feel the passion bleeding through on the page, the passion I felt when I was writing only for myself?

I make a mental note to dig out that first manuscript tonight, the one no one wanted. What could it hurt?

I'm jerked back to the present when I almost miss our turn; Heidi taps on my arm in time for me to make it.

"Sorry," I mutter as I silently apologize to the traffic gods for not using the turn signal. I follow the now-familiar path to Carmina's townhome, once again reminding myself that I need to look for a different place to live.

When we reach the duplex, I pull up in front and park on the street. Parking in the driveway feels too invasive, considering we're uninvited.

"I want you to know," I say, "that it goes against every fiber of my being to show up here unannounced."

"Mine too," Heidi says with a little shiver. "Unannounced guests are my worst nightmare. And it does feel a little underhanded," she admits, "but I think it will be easier for them to shut us down over the phone than it will be in person."

She's probably right. I climb out of the car, and she does the same, the slamming of the car doors echoing down the strangely quiet street. A shiver runs down my spine as I look at the rows of townhomes, though I couldn't tell you why.

"This neighborhood gives me the creeps," I say.

"Me too," she says, craning her neck to glance around. "It feels like there's no one here. I don't even hear any animals."

I take a deep breath. "Let's get this over with," I say, "so we can get out of here." Because Maplewood somehow feels like it's part of a different world than our little town square, and I'm eager to return to the checkered floor and well-loved bookshelves of Paper Patisserie.

The walk up the driveway feels too long, and I feel strangely exposed, like a deer in a clearing might fear a hunter. It's a ridiculous thought, because I'm not a forest creature, and I'm certainly not being hunted. But I hurry all the same, and I can't help but notice that Heidi matches my footsteps without question. We approach the front door without speaking.

"Wait," I say at the last minute, reaching out and grabbing her arm. My fingers wrap around her wrist easily, like they're meant to be there, like touching her is what I was made to do. "Hang on."

Heidi lets her hand fall, but I don't let go of her wrist. I just keep holding onto her as she looks at me. "What is it?" she says, her eyebrows raised.

I clear my throat. "We're barging in here without asking and without authority. His mom just died. So just like last time we came...if it seems like he's grieving or having a hard time, we should leave."

Heidi nods slowly, her eyes narrowing as she thinks, her gaze drifting toward the front door she was about to knock on. "That's fair," she finally says, looking back to me. "Definitely." Then she sighs. "I don't want to make any of them feel worse, and I don't want to disturb them when they're grieving. I won't push if they clearly seem upset."

I nod too, relief trickling in.

"Anything else?" she says, cocking her brow at me.

"One more thing." I look vaguely at the front door, remembering Phil and Elsie's odd behavior the first time we were here. "Statistically, they're the most likely suspects for this murder. You know that, right?"

"Yeah," she says, her voice heavy. "I know. I just..." She bites her lip and looks at me. "I don't want to jump to conclusions."

"Well," I say, shrugging, "I guess we'll find out." Then I nod at the door, letting go of her wrist. "Go ahead and knock."

She delivers three sharp raps to the door, and we wait for only about thirty seconds before it lurches open.

"Oh," Phil says, looking surprised. I guess he's working from home again. "It's you. Good to see you."

And look. I don't like the way his eyes linger on Heidi.

I'm not one of those overly jealous guys. I'm really not. As far as I'm concerned, a man should feel confident enough in his relationships not to be jealous, and he should recognize that his partner is not a possession to be hoarded or to be shared.

That being said...Phil is married, and he might be a murderer, and so I don't care how great Heidi manages to look in a simple t-shirt—he needs to keep his eyes to himself.

"Hi," Heidi says. She either doesn't notice his interest, or she's suddenly an excellent actress. "How are you doing?"

"We're great," Phil says, smiling at her. "What brings you two to this neck of the woods?"

People grieve in different ways, I remind myself. *Maybe he's desperately sad on the inside.*

Regardless...I think Phil and I grieve in very, *very* different ways.

"Well..." Heidi says, looking quickly over at me and then back to Phil. "There's no easy way to ask this, I suppose. We were wondering if we could take a look around your mother's room."

The absolute audacity of this woman, asking to look around a dead woman's space.

"Here's the thing," she goes on, speaking more quickly now. "When your mother—uh, passed—she had time to say a few last words."

Phil straightens a bit at this, his eyes growing more alert, his expression more interested. "Did she?"

Heidi nods. "Yes. She—I'm sorry." She breaks off suddenly. "Will this upset you to hear?"

I think it's safe to say that nothing about Carmina's death seems to be upsetting Phil, but it's nice of her to ask.

"Not at all," he says—proving me right—and the gestures for Heidi to go on.

She nods, a determined mask settling over her features. "She looked me right in the eye and said *pick* and *lock*. It was very startling."

"I can imagine," Phil says, rubbing one hand over his mouth, his brow furrowed. "But I'm not sure what she would have been talking about. She didn't keep any sort of safe, that I can recall..." He trails off, his eyes distant.

"We'd be happy to help you look," Heidi says, and I have to force myself not to smile at how stealthily she's working back around to the idea of seeing Carmina's room.

"Uh," Phil says, and...wow. I honestly think he's considering it. "Well..."

It's because Heidi showed up here with perfect confidence and asked to do something ridiculous—barging into a deceased woman's home—like it was no big deal. This is how conmen work. They go about their business so confidently that everyone else goes along with it too.

"Come on in, then," he says a few seconds later, and he doesn't even look annoyed. He looks like this is something that happens every day. "Let's see if we can figure out what she was talking about."

"If you're sure?" Heidi says.

"Come on, come on," he says, stepping back and waving us in.

I follow Heidi in, feeling very strange, mostly because Phil is acting so bizarre. He leads us up the stairs without comment, and we keep following him—down the hallway, past a cloudy fish tank and an uncomfortable looking chair, before stopping at a closed door at the very end.

"This was her room," he says. And even though the past tense rings jarringly in my ears, he doesn't seem to notice; he still appears totally unaffected. He opens the door and steps inside without hesitation. "We haven't touched anything yet."

"I'm sure that would be very difficult," Heidi murmurs, her gaze already darting around the room. The bed is neat, the floor bare, and the large photos on the wall are lined up neatly. It takes me a second to realize that they're photos of Carmina herself, though undoubtedly when she was younger—in her twenties, maybe. She's glamorous and beautiful, and despite the many different styles I see in all the pictures, they all capture a sparkle in her eyes that I never saw in real life.

"I guess," Phil says, pulling me out of my perusal. He's looking at his phone, which has started buzzing in his hand. "And the police warrant was only for rat poison," he goes on distractedly. "They didn't come in here. Listen, I've got to take this."

"Of course," I say quickly. "Take your time."

Go on in, Phil mouths as he brings the phone to his ear and steps back out of the room.

Heidi and I take a few hesitant steps further into the room.

"Wow," I mutter, looking around with interest. "This place is pristine." I guess I'm not too surprised; Carmina seemed like the kind of woman who liked things to be a certain way, so there's no reason her living space would be any different.

Heidi glances over her shoulder at Phildegarde's retreating form, and then she turns to me. "I don't think we have very long before he comes back," she whispers when he's out of sight. "Let's see what we can find."

"What are we looking for?" I say.

"Honestly, I have no idea," she says. "Something that locks, or maybe a file folder that says *Look here if I'm murdered.*"

"Right," I say slowly. "Anything suspicious. Got it."

"Specifically," Heidi says, raising her pointer finger, "anything that might be worth killing over." She wanders over to the large vanity, beginning to rifle through the jars and bottles and trays on top.

I move with less certainty. I'm not sure where to start, mostly because I'm not the kind of guy who hides things or keeps secrets. I'm not sneaky or subtle. Not to mention...

"This feels so wrong," I say, wincing as I crouch down and begin opening drawers.

"It doesn't to me," Heidi says.

I look at her, my eyebrows hitching.

"She looked me right in the eye, Soren," she says with a frustrated sigh. "She looked me dead in the eye and said that stuff. It felt like she was *asking* me to do this. And maybe it's harsh, or cruel, but...she's gone." Heidi swallows. "She's dead. She's not coming back. But whoever killed her, they're still here. So I'm going to try to find out what happened to her. Even if it means digging around in her life."

I nod slowly. "Let's just make sure we don't hurt other people who are still here with our digging."

"I'm trying not to," she says, her voice softer now. "I really am."

"I know," I say.

"Just keep helping me."

"I will," I promise. "Always." Then, with another glance around, I say, "Let's keep moving."

I return my attention to the drawers I've been opening, and I can hear Heidi continue to shuffle around too. I feel around in each drawer rather than looking and digging, because it feels less invasive, but I still come up with nothing. After taking stock of the rest of the room, I decide to try the bed next.

The mattress is heavy—some memory foam contraption, I think—but I manage to lift it by one corner, holding it as high as I can to see if anything has been tucked underneath. That's where kids always hide their diaries and stuff, right? Under the mattress?

But there's no diary hidden under Carmina Hildegarde's mattress. There's nothing there at all, and I let the mattress back down gently, grateful to be releasing the weight.

"Anything?" Heidi says from the other side of the room, where she's now running her fingers over the spines of the books on the little bookshelf.

"Not yet," I say, nudging the mattress back into place. Then I stare at it.

The covers are pulled up, the comforter tucked neatly around the pillows; Carmina made her bed the morning she died.

It's a weird feeling, seeing that. Someone who makes their bed is someone who intends to *return* to that bed. And Carmina...well, she never did. She made her bed that morning never realizing she wouldn't get under these covers again.

Did she feel a difference? Could something in her tell that she'd never lay her head on these pillows again?

And good grief—why am I so morbid?

I shake my head a few times, trying to quiet the thoughts rattling around in there, before moving to check the pillows. They're way too firm for my liking—again, some kind of foam —but under the one on the right, I do find something interesting.

"Hey," I say to Heidi, not bothering to turn around. I inspect the little photo more closely.

It's a picture of a young man, the photo about the size of my open hand, the frame brassy-looking. The man looks familiar, but it takes me a minute to realize why.

"Her husband," I say as Heidi appears by my side. "I think this is her husband. He's younger here, but this is the guy from the family photo downstairs."

"Are you sure?" Heidi says, and I catch a faint whiff of her tropical scent.

"Pretty sure, yeah," I say, flipping it over to see if there's anything written on the back of the frame. There's nothing. "I'll double check on our way out."

"He looks a little like Phil," she says, pointing at the man in the picture. "Doesn't he?"

"Yeah," I say. "He does. It's the eyes."

She nods, and I get more of that coconut scent. "Yes. And the forehead."

"This guy looks less sleazy than Phil, though."

Heidi laughs softly. "I agree." She touches the photo with light fingers and then nods. "I don't think this is anything. We should probably put it back."

I think she's right. It doesn't seem like anything suspicious, so I tuck it back under the pillow. It sort of seems like that's where it should stay.

Heidi moves back to the bookshelf, her steps purposeful. She's looking closely for something, it appears, though I don't know what, while meanwhile I drift over to the trash can, crouching down next to it.

"Here's a delivery box," I say, plucking it out. "A small one. From..." I search the package until I find the shipping label. "From the pharmacy."

"She must have gotten her medicine delivered," Heidi murmurs, looking over at me.

I nod. "There's another box in here."

"Another package?"

"No," I say, frowning as I pull the little box out. I look at it. Then I hold the box up to show her. "These are pads, right? Like for your underwear?"

"Hmm?" Heidi says vaguely, her attention still on the bookshelf. When she looks at me, she frowns. "Yes," she says. "Basically. They're panty liners. But..."

"But what?" I say.

"Carmina is well past her menstruating years," Heidi says, her brow still furrowed as she looks at the box.

"Maybe it's Elsie's."

She shrugs. "Maybe." Then she looks back to the books.

"What are you doing?" I say, because she's been at that bookshelf for several minutes now.

"Look on top of the vanity," she says, pointing vaguely.

I glance over; there are several dainty glass jars and bottles, some jewelry, and...

"A camera," I say, blinking in surprise.

"Yep," Heidi says. "I took a look, and there's nothing stored on it. So whatever pictures she was taking must have been printed out. I don't know quite what her blackmailing situation looked like, but photos seem possible."

"Thus the bookshelf," I say with a nod. "Got it."

I cross the room and open the closet, moving the hanging clothes as I search vaguely for anything of note. There's nothing but folded blankets on the top shelf, though, and a neat row of shoes on the floor. Except...

"Hey," I say, bending down and picking up the lens. "I found another part of the camera. A long lens. It was back behind the shoes."

"Ah-ha!" Heidi says, and for a second I think she's reacting to my camera discovery. But when I turn around, she's not even looking at me; her gaze is instead on the large book she has open in her arms.

It's a Bible, I realize. And Heidi is looking at it like she's just been reborn.

"Look at this," she breathes, reaching into the open pages and pulling something out. "This is something," she says. "It has to be, right? Look at that." She holds up what looks to be a standard four-by-six photo.

I abandon the closet and move quickly to Heidi, my eyes focused on the picture. "Whoa," I say when I realize what it is I'm looking at. "Warn a guy, please."

It's a man and a woman in an intimate embrace, minimally clothed. The man's face is tilted toward the camera, so he's easy enough to see, but the woman is only visible in profile. She looks younger than him, but it's hard to tell by how much.

"Clearly taken through a window," I say, peering more closely at the photo, "and definitely...explicit enough."

"I don't know who this is, though," Heidi says with a frown. She flips the photo over, but there's nothing written on the back. "It looks recent-ish, right? Like, it's not decades old or anything."

"No," I say, shaking my head. "It looks modern."

"Hey, sorry," comes a voice from behind us, and Heidi and I both jump. We turn around at the same time, just as Phil walks back into the room. "That took longer than I thought it would." He stands there with his hands on his hips, looking around. "Find anything good?"

Like we're on a treasure hunt. So bizarre.

"Uh, maybe," Heidi says, shooting me a hesitant look.

I shrug. I don't think we can hide the photo from Phil, and I don't know that there's any reason to try. The man in the picture isn't him.

Heidi holds the photo out to Phil, and he steps forward, taking it. He flinches as he looks at it, but then his eyes widen.

Somewhere down in my chest, my heart picks up speed.

"This..." he says slowly, trailing off. He looks up at us, and then back down at the photo. "This is Stanley Riggs."

Next to me, Heidi's jaw drops, as I hunt around for why that name sounds familiar—until it hits me.

"The HOA guy?" I say incredulously.

"He's the head of the HOA in Maplewood, yeah," Phil says, his attention back on the picture.

"And...is that Mrs. Riggs?" Heidi says, her voice hoarse.

Phil grimaces once more, running one hand through his slicked-back hair. "Considering Mrs. Riggs is brunette and rather large...it most definitely is *not*."

FROM THE LIFE OF CARMINA HILDEGARDE

JANUARY 19

C armina practically cackled as she peered through the viewfinder of her camera. It was an unladylike sound, but since she so rarely had cause to laugh these days, she allowed it. She zoomed in further, letting the scene before her come into focus.

That dirty old man.

She hadn't meant to stumble across this particular show. But a woman had to have hobbies or she'd go mad, and although mundanity bored her, she often found entertainment peeking into other peoples' lives. Stanley Riggs had the nerve to chastise Carmina for not keeping the peace, when he was off cavorting with some wanton hussy—with her in the very bed he shared with his wife. Patrice Riggs was elegant and dignified and on the board of several respectable charities, including one that helped house battered women and children. This was the respect Stanley gave her? This was what Patrice got for raising their three children and cooking him dinner every night?

No. Carmina simply couldn't allow that to go unpunished.

She began snapping photos, a slew of them, and her laughter only grew louder as she imagined all the fun she could have with them.

She would see justice done. Stanley Riggs would pay. She'd just have to be very, very careful...

❧ 22 ❧

IN WHICH HEIDI MAKES AN
UNFORTUNATE DISCOVER

"I can't believe this."

"I know."

Soren's car is slightly too warm when we get back in; I roll down my window immediately, breathing in the fresh air as the stagnant heat radiates up and settles over my skin.

"I'll get some air going in just a sec," Soren says from next to me, and I nod, my mind still elsewhere. I watch the neighborhood roll past us as he begins to drive, winding through the perfectly kept streets.

"There was another little book on that bookshelf that I wanted to get a closer look at, thin and green with no title on the spine," I say. "But then I found the Bible, and I forgot to look." I glance at Soren. "It looked a little like a journal, one of those leather-bound ones. I should have checked."

Soren hums. "At least we saw the picture, though." He shudders, and I understand the sentiment.

That photograph from Carmina's room is still burned into my mind's eye, and I might need to sterilize my retinas somehow. There are some things a woman just doesn't want to see, and Stanley Riggs in the midst of a passionate affair is way up there.

"So she was blackmailing Stanley, and he killed her for it. Right? That envelope of money I found in the café had to be from him. It said she wouldn't get another penny out of him, basically. So she was blackmailing him with that picture, and he killed her." I look over at Soren, whose hands are fixed tightly on the steering wheel as he drives. "I mean, we don't have proof, but that seems realistic, right? And logical?"

"Very logical," he says grimly, his eyes never leaving the road. "Especially since he was hiding something that would probably destroy his marriage and his reputation in the community."

I nod, my fingers tapping against my thigh as I think. "I hope Phil takes those photos to the police."

"I'm sure he will," Soren says, but...he doesn't sound sure.

I'm not sure either, to be honest, and I'm torn. I still don't trust Phil. There's something about him that just...rubs me the wrong way. And although it's true that we shouldn't jump to conclusions, Soren is right—Phil is a strong suspect, especially when we consider statistics.

"How would Stanley have poisoned her, though?" Soren says, yanking me out of my thoughts.

I blink at him, frowning. "I don't know."

"Because he would run the risk of other victims if it was just food he brought to her house or something. Phil and Elsie could have shared anything there."

An image flashes through my mind, the snapshot the waitress at Chateau Marche showed us—Carmina, all alone, eating her meal.

It would have been easy to poison her there. But as far as I know, she hadn't returned to the restaurant since allegedly finding the bug in her food.

For that matter, it would be easy for Phil and Elsie to poison her too. Even Mr. Foster could have done it; he was her neighbor, after all. And he does seem familiar, somehow...

Ugh. I have both too much information and not enough information, and it all feels like a mess in my head. I'm starting to get a headache.

"Well," Soren says with a sigh, "I'll drop you off and then head home. I've reached maximum capacity for the day." He pauses, and then goes on, "I think..."

I look over at him, my eyebrows raised, grateful for something else to focus on. "Yeah?"

And I don't know why, but something about his expression has me reaching for his hand. Soren always projects this air of calm and reassurance, but right now he looks...I don't know. Vulnerable, I guess. He looks hesitant, like he's worried about how I'll react to whatever he's about to say.

"What?" I say, trying to keep my voice gentle. I thread my fingers through his, letting his warm hand engulf mine. "What is it?"

"Uh," he says, his eyes darting down to our hands. "Wow, that completely distracted me. I forgot what I was going to say for a second."

I turn my head so he doesn't see my smile.

"I think I'm going to dig out my old manuscript," he says, "and read some of it."

"Yeah?" I say. "Which one? The one you never published?"

"Yeah. The very first one I ever finished." He takes a deep breath, letting it out slowly. "I think I might feel better about my writing if I can see how far I've come."

I nod. "That makes sense." When he doesn't say anything else, though, I give his hand a little squeeze. "So what's making you hesitate?"

"It's just—what if I read my old stuff and it's exactly like what I'm writing now?" he says. The words rush out of him all at once, but they have a well-worn air about them—like it's something he's been repeating to himself over and over again. "Or what if it's even better than what I'm writing now? What if I've actually gotten *worse*?"

"I don't think that will happen," I say, letting my thumb stroke the back of his hand. I think for a second. "But maybe you shouldn't do that one. Maybe you should go back and read the first draft of your bestseller."

"Why the bestseller?" he says, glancing at me. A few tendrils of his hair have fallen out of his stupid man bun, blonde whispers over his forehead, his eyelashes, his cheekbones.

I force myself not to stare, answering his question instead.

"Because that's the one you're scared of," I say. When he doesn't respond, I go on. "That's the one you're worried about people comparing you against, right? You're worried you've peaked. So if you read the first draft of that one, you'll be able to see how...*first-drafty* it is—"

"Not a word," he murmurs.

"Shut up, Man Bun," I say, and he gives a low, husky laugh that does funny things to my insides. "But maybe that will help you feel better. To see that something everyone loved also started out as a simple first draft." I wrinkle my nose as something occurs to me. "Unless you're one of those people whose first drafts are super clean."

He snorts. "I'm definitely not."

"Do you see what I mean, though?"

"I do," he says slowly. "Maybe I'll try that."

We're quiet for the rest of the drive, and even though I thoroughly enjoy talking to Soren, I'm glad for the time to think. By the time he drops me off in the parking lot behind Paper Patisserie, I'm ready to collapse into bed and call it an early night.

When I round the front of the building, though, someone is waiting for me. I don't recognize the man; he's small by all accounts, petite with thinning blond hair and bifocals.

He stands up when he sees me, which is how I know he's been waiting for me rather than just resting on the bench that faces the town square.

"Hello," he says with an awkward little wave. "Miss Lucy?"

I nod at him, shifting absently through the keys on my keyring. "Can I help you with something?" I say as I unlock the door to the shop. "Are you waiting to come in?"

"No," he says quickly. He holds up his briefcase. "I'm here to deliver your security footage, if I could see some ID? I've got the disc in here. We're done with it over at the station."

"Oh," I say, blinking with surprise. "I didn't realize it's an actual *disc*. Isn't that stuff all completely virtual by now?"

The man shrugs and gives a little laugh.

I pull my wallet out of my back pocket and show him my ID—which is not cute, by the way—and when he's inspected it closely, he nods. Then he shuffles over to the bench he was sitting on when I arrived, setting the briefcase down and opening it. He pulls out a disc case from among a stack of papers, one of those clear ones I used to put burned CDs in back in the day. He hands it over, wishes me a pleasant day, and then shuffles off again, rounding the building and disappearing out of sight.

I stare down at the disc for a second, my heart beating loudly in my ears. Why didn't the little man say anything about what was on here?

I debate calling Soren, but something stops me; I'm not sure I want him or anyone else to see what's on here. Not until I've seen it and processed it, at least. Besides, I don't want to come off as clingy or obnoxious.

I think for now I'll keep this a viewing party of one.

I hurry inside, not even bothering to check if Gemma and Mel closed properly; I know they did. I rush upstairs to grab my laptop, and five minutes later I'm seated at one of the café tables, my hand shaking slightly as I hunt down the timeframe I need and then press *Play*.

The section of video I watch is short. I'm only in it for a minute or two. I rush in through the front door, and it's clear even in the grainy shot that I'm panicking; my head whips this way and that, like I'm looking for something. I disappear further into the shop and out of the camera's view; one moment later, I'm back. I sit up straighter in my seat, my knuckles white as I grip the edge of the table.

This is it. This is where I finally see how I got this gash on my forehead.

Except...the whole incident lasts all of three seconds.

"That's...what happened?" I say into the silence. My eyes are bulging out of my head, and I'm sure it's not cute, but I don't have the presence of mind to stop. My attention is too fixed on the screen.

I quickly rewind, because I can't quite believe what I've just seen. I watch in horror as I see my grainy, pixelated self rush across the screen, phone pressed to my ear—and then I see myself trip headfirst over something small and circular on the floor.

"I tripped?" I say, my jaw hanging, and when I speak again, it comes out as more of a shriek: "Over the *Roomba?*"

"*Roomba!*" Jojo squawks from the other side of the shop. "*Roomba! Roomba!*"

❦

"You tripped," my brother says, his voice flat. "Over a Roomba."

"Yes," I say as my head thuds down on the table in front of me. "Ouch." I lift it immediately, wincing as I rub my forehead.

It's been twenty-four hours since I watched the security tapes, and my humiliation has not died down one bit. Eric, Gemma, and I are seated in the café, and I'm glad the day is over; I couldn't bring myself to tell Soren what the security footage showed, so I was weird and awkward while he was here earlier.

"Don't worry," Gemma says in a soothing voice, her hand rubbing gentle circles over my upper back. "When I was in eighth grade, I burned myself with my straightening iron on accident and told everyone it was a hickey."

Both Eric and I snort.

"Or one time I tripped over my dog," she goes on. "He wasn't even running around or anything; I just wasn't paying attention."

"Stop talking, Gem," Eric says, grinning. "You're not doing yourself any favors."

"I'm telling her so she doesn't feel like she's the only one who's had embarrassing falls," she says, sticking her tongue out at my brother. She tucks her dark hair behind her ear and then looks back to me.

"Isn't eighth grade a little young to have a hickey, though?" Eric goes on before she can speak again. His voice is musing, his eyes full of laughter. "You would have been...what, thirteen? Fourteen?"

"Something like that," she says dismissively. "I've always been beautiful, and the boys have always noticed." She sniffs as she smooths her hands over her hair. "But like I said—it wasn't really a hickey."

"Mm-hmm," Eric says, and his eyes are sharper on her now, like he's thinking about giving this no-longer-in-eight-grade version of Gemma a hickey.

"Anyway," she says, waving her hand, "the point is, we've all done embarrassing things."

"Yes," Eric drawls, "but none of us have done anything quite as embarrassing as losing our memories after tripping over a Roomba—ouch!"

Gemma has just walloped Eric on the back of the head, and although it wasn't a proper beating, it wasn't a little love pat, either.

"You deserved that," I say, narrowing my eyes at him. "I feel dumb enough already."

"Fine," he says as he rubs the back of his head. "In all seriousness—Gemma's right. Don't worry about it. We all do stupid stuff—"

"Hang on, hang on," Gemma says, fumbling with her phone. "I want to record that. Here. Say it again—"

"Shut up," Eric mutters, but he can't quite hide his smile.

I sigh, smiling slightly too. Then I stand up. "All right," I say. "Be gone, gentle maidens."

"Gentle—what?" Eric says, while Gemma cackles.

"Jojo said it today," she says, wiping tears of laughter out of her eyes. "Out of nowhere. He just squawked *gentle maidens* twice and then went quiet again."

Eric shakes his head. "That bird is a weirdo. He's going to kill you in your sleep one of these days, mark my words."

The joke falls just this side of flat, and Eric can tell; he rubs the back of his neck in an uncharacteristic display of discomfort before giving a forced chuckle.

"That...wasn't great," he says after a second. "Sorry."

And then, as though we're all reliving the same thing, all three of us turn our eyes to the table next to where we're seated —the table that has since been replaced but looks exactly the same as the one Carmina died at.

Gemma sighs, a sad sound, before standing up and looking back at me. "You okay?"

"Yeah," I say around the inexplicable lump in my throat. I can't seem to get the image of her tablecloth-covered body out of my head, light blue and strangely lumpy. "I'm fine."

My best friend nods and sighs again. "All right," she says. "I'm heading out. You should go home too," she says to Eric, patting his shoulder. "You start really early, don't you?"

"Yeah," he says, looking bad-tempered. "At four. For all those early birds who do day trips and stuff and need outdoor equipment."

"That's what I thought," Gemma says, cringing. "That sounds horrible. Go home and go to bed."

"You could come with me," he murmurs, and she rolls her eyes even as a faint flush rises in her cheeks.

"Go," she says, pointing. "Now."

He grins, lands a kiss on her forehead before she can pull away, and then heads to the door. "Later," he calls to me without turning around.

I wave and then say to Gemma, "I'll see you tomorrow."

They filter out the front door, and the jingling of the bell over the door sounds strangely melancholy as I watch them disappear.

Sometimes I feel lonely. I expect everybody does at times; I'm not unique. It's something about people being here during the day and then leaving at night, so that I'm the only one left.

My eyes linger on the floor in front of the door, where I landed after tripping over the Roomba and hitting my head. Then I sigh.

I should probably tell Soren. He'll want to know, and he's been helping me this whole time. Plus—I allow myself to acknowledge —he shrinks that loneliness inside down to a less intimidating size.

So I sit back down, and then I call him. The phone rings three times, and then he answers, his deep voice saying only one word: my name.

"I'm staring at the table where Carmina died," I say, the words spilling out of me, "and Gemma and Eric were here but they just left, and I feel sad, and I don't know why."

"Mmm," he says, his hum igniting something deep in my bones. "You're allowed to feel sad. And you're allowed to not understand why. You've had a lot of heavy things going on."

I sigh. "I've always been the kind of person whose first instinct is to drown my negative feelings in productivity." My old therapist said it was because I was likely infertile, and somehow I had internalized that I needed to make up for what I perceived as that defect. She said I felt the need to be hyper-competent because I felt like it would give me worth. I think she was probably right in her assessment, but knowing what the problem is, knowing where the flawed logic is...it doesn't make it any easier to correct.

"It's taken me a long time to be able to sit with my pains and just let them be," I say. "But strangely, I almost enjoy it now. Not that I enjoy hurting or being sad," I say quickly, "but I find it comforting to let myself experience those things." I swallow, cringing. "Does that sound crazy?"

"Not at all," Soren says with a little laugh. "It sounds healthy."

"Speaking of pain," I say, my hand drifting to my forehead. "I got the security tapes back."

"You did?" he says immediately, and in my mind's eye I imagine him sitting up straighter, his eyes sharpening. "Did you see what happened to your head?"

"Yes," I say with a sigh. I can already feel my cheeks turning red. "I tripped."

"You *tripped*?"

"Yes," I say dully. "Over my Roomba."

There's silence for a second, and then Soren speaks, his voice filtering oddly through the phone. "Permission to laugh?" he says.

"Granted," I say.

His laugh is infectious; it's a light, free sound, not raucous or out of control but pleasant and full of sunshine. By the time he's calmed down, I'm smiling too.

"I'm so embarrassed," I say, pressing my hand to my cheek, trying to cool my skin. "I really thought someone had hurt me on purpose. Because that's the thing," I say as something occurs to me. I sit up straighter, thinking hard. "Even knowing what happened...I still feel that weird feeling about my missing memories."

"What feeling?"

"I don't know how to explain it," I say. My fingers drum on the table as I consider. "It sort of feels like there's something I was supposed to do, or there's somewhere I need to be. It feels like—well, like I've forgotten something important," I say. "And in the video, I was behaving sort of oddly. I was rushing around with my phone pressed to my ear. According to the timestamp, I was calling you when the video captured me. But I rushed into my shop, disappeared for a minute, and then reappeared. So maybe..."

"Maybe something happened outside," Soren concludes, and I nod.

"Yes. Maybe." I scoot my chair back and stand, hurrying over to the door. I open it and stick my head out, trying to see the town square in a new light, trying to force myself to remember anything that might have happened out here. But other than the evening breeze playing with my hair, nothing stirs.

I sigh. "Anyway," I say. "I—oh, hang on." My phone has

buzzed, and I pull it away from my ear, looking at the text. It's from an unknown number. *Heidi, this is Phil Hildegarde,* it says. *Just wanted to let you know we gave the police those photos.*

"Oh, good," I say. "Hang on, Soren." Then I quickly text Phil back. *Did it go okay?*

His response comes several seconds later. *A little awkward since my neighbor was on his way out while we were heading in, but otherwise fine. They said they'd look into it.*

"I just got a text from Phil," I say, returning to Soren. "They gave the photos to the police."

"Is it bad that I feel relieved and kind of surprised?" Soren says, and I smile.

"No. I sort of feel the same way," I admit. "I just don't quite know what to expect from them yet. He said Mr. Foster was at the station when he took the photos over, though."

"Huh," Soren says. "Phil and Elsie must have told the police about the issues he and Carmina were having." He's quiet for a second, and I can tell he's thinking hard. "Statistically speaking," he finally says, "Phil and Elsie are still the most likely suspects. But..."

"Yeah," I say with a nod. "*But.* I'm so torn with them. There's something off there, definitely, but I don't know if it's *murdery* levels of 'off.' They let us in. They let us snoop. They told us themselves that she was a difficult woman. And those pictures of Stanley..."

"I know," Soren says, his voice grim. "And we're not even taking into account any other problems she had with people that we just don't know about. We're not the police. We don't have any of their resources or authority to ask questions or anything like that."

We toss halfhearted theories around for a few more minutes, until I break off in the middle of a sentence to yawn.

Soren chuckles. "Go to bed, honey," he says, his voice soft with affection. It still blows my mind to hear him speaking to me like that—calling me *honey*. And yet...I can't deny that I like it. "We'll talk tomorrow.

"Goodnight," I say. And not for the first time, I imagine asking him to kiss me—I imagine what he might do, how he might hold me, what his lips would feel like.

How he would taste.

I shiver, tamping down on the sudden spike of heat that rises in me. Then I hang up.

TWO DAYS LATER, STANLEY RIGGS IS DEAD.

IN WHICH SOREN AND HEIDI HAVE AN IMPORTANT CONVERSATION

"All right," I say, rubbing my hand absently over my beard as I think. "Let's lay out what we know so far."

"Yes," Heidi says with a nod. "Good. Let's do that."

We're seated in her living room, me on the couch, her on the floor with her back against the sofa. I could touch her hair if I wanted; I could probably smell her faint tropical scent if I leaned forward. I resist the urge.

I hung around at the shop all day today, and then I helped Heidi and Gemma and Mel close, watching and laughing as they danced to the music coming from the record player. My smile felt strained, though, and I could tell Heidi felt the same way; she almost seemed to be desperately seeking distraction. The mask fell away as soon as Gemma and Mel left; her shoulders slumped, and her expression turned weary.

"Want to come up?" she said, and I agreed without hesitation.

"So here's the thing," I say now, leaning back on the couch and folding my arms across my chest. I would be lying if I said this wasn't to help me resist the temptation to touch Heidi. "I keep coming back to Maplewood."

"Me too," Heidi says grimly, nodding as she turns sideways so that I can see her face. "Carmina"—she ticks off one finger— "and now Stanley Riggs. There's no way it's coincidence that he was—" She breaks off, swallows, and then goes on. "That he was killed so shortly after she was. It only makes sense that the killer is in Maplewood too."

Stanley Riggs was found dead in his home by his wife, who —by all accounts—went into a fit of hysterics that could be heard by most of the neighborhood. I wasn't aware people actually did that kind of thing; I thought people acting hysterical when they were sad was something that happened more in books and movies. But maybe I'm a suffer-in-silence type. Either way, she called the police, and then she seems to have called everyone she knew. It was therefore on the local news that Mr. Riggs, beloved husband and cherished neighbor, had died from what looked like a blow to the head. The news didn't mention anything about Carmina.

Not that they'd have any reason to, of course. They don't know about the blackmail. But it still seemed sad, somehow, that while Stanley's death made the news, Carmina's didn't. I didn't even like the woman, but it feels unfair.

"Do we think the restaurant guy is out, then?" I say, forcing myself not to dwell on it.

Her eyes narrow as she chews on her lip. "I'm going to tentatively say yes," she says after a moment. "I don't think it was him."

"But he was so sketchy," I say. "Wasn't he? He was creepy."

"Yes," Heidi admits. "Ugh. I don't know."

"And what about the date that never showed?" I say.

"Weird," she says slowly, "and not something I have an explanation for, but unrelated, I think."

It's a bizarre game of Clue we're playing here, but I agree with her.

"So that leaves us with Phil and Elsie or Mr. Foster, right? And maybe Manniford at the restaurant?" I say.

"Maybe? Yes? I don't know." She makes a frustrated sound, letting her head tilt back and closing her eyes.

"And are we assuming that the same person who killed Carmina is the one who killed Stanley Riggs?"

She doesn't move as she answers. "Yes," she says. "Although..." Her eyes pop open, and she looks at me. "I guess if someone in Stanley's house found out about the affair—"

"Someone like his wife, you mean," I say.

"Yeah." She nods. "She might have been angry and just... you know." She mimes bashing someone over the head, a motion that looks half hearted at best coming from her.

I laugh softly, even though there's nothing funny about death. "You're cute," I say without thinking, my gaze tracing the line of her neck, the set of her mouth, the furrow in her brow that tells me she's thinking hard.

That furrow disappears, though, as her eyes widen and her brows shoot up. She turns more fully in my direction and looks at me for a second, her lips parted in surprise.

"What?" I say, still smiling. "Is it bad taste to tell you that while we're discussing murder?"

"No," she says, her eyes flitting over my face. Then she swallows. "I've been thinking about kissing you."

Crap.

"Yeah?" I manage to get out. The word is only slightly strangled, which I'm going to call a major success.

"Mm-hmm," she says, her gaze dipping to my lips. "Just... wondering what it would be like."

It would be amazing. That's what it would be like. It would be freaking incredible.

I close my eyes, reminding myself of the promise I made: that I won't kiss her unless she asks me to. So I take a deep breath, release it slowly, and then look back at her. "You tell me where and when, honey, and I'll be there."

She continues to stare up at me, and for a moment I think she's actually going to come sit on the couch next to me; there's a tension in her body, like she's about to move.

But then her shoulders fall, and she turns away, fanning her face with her hand.

"I need some fresh air," she says. "Let's go outside."

I nod, rubbing my hand over my mouth so she won't see my smile.

She feels it. She feels this pull between us. And though she's clearly not ready to move forward yet—and maybe she won't be for a long time—I can't deny that it makes me happy to hear the things she's been thinking about.

"Where to?" I say as we both stand.

"I need to water my plants," she says, brushing her hands over her shirt. Her cheeks are faintly pink, an exquisite color. "Let's do that."

"Lead the way."

We trail down the narrow staircase and through the book-shelves, and I follow her all the way back to the kitchen, where she pulls a large watering can out of the storage closet. She fills it in the giant stainless steel sink, and I wait silently, moving only when she walks back out of the kitchen, through the café, and out the front doors.

It's a perfect spring evening; slightly chilly now that the sun has started to set, a floral-scented breeze playing with our hair. Heidi begins watering her plants in silence, so I follow her lead, not saying anything. She waters flowers and shrubs, various plants I don't know the names of, and I watch, wondering over and over again how it's possible for her to be so incredibly beautiful.

Her steps falter after she's moved from a bunch of pink flowers to a more unruly bunch of purple ones. She blinks, that little furrow appearing in her brow again as her lips tug into a frown. "This..." she begins, trailing off. She looks at the watering can in her hand; she looks at the flowers in the flower bed. Then she lifts the watering can, holding it outward at an odd angle but not actually watering any plants. "This feels..."

"Heidi?" I say, stepping closer. "What's wrong?" She's being weird. Is she having a stroke or something?

"I think..." she says. Then she turns to look at me, her eyes so wide I can see a clear ring of white around the hazel. "I think I *remember*."

"You remember...what?" I say, still frowning at her.

"Watering my plants." Her gaze pulls away from me and darts over the front of the shop. Then she nods. "Soren, I really think I watered my plants that evening!"

My jaw drops. "Are your memories coming back?"

"Maybe?" she says. Then she shakes her head. Still, her excitement shines through as she goes on, "Not completely—I don't remember calling you still, or why I would have, but I remember being out here watering my plants! Just flashes of it, but..."

"What else?" I say quickly. "Anything else?"

"No," she says slowly. "I watered the ones here in front, and then...the ones on the side, maybe?" She hurries past the display windows and the rest of the flower beds, rounding the building, and I follow close behind. "I can't quite remember that part," she says, looking at me. That little frown is back. "But I definitely think I watered my plants that night!"

"That's amazing," I say. I step closer to her, resting my hands on her shoulders. "The rest will come back."

"I worried it wouldn't," she says, her voice cracking, and I'm startled to see tears brimming in her eyes. "I worried I would never remember."

I smile softly at her. "You will, honey. I really think you will."

She sniffles. "You can hug me," she says. "If you want—"

But she breaks off as I pull her close, as close as I can get her, wrapping my arms tightly around her. Her arms wind slowly around my waist, and the heat of her body pressed against mine makes me shiver pleasantly.

"You'll remember," I say again, pressing a light kiss to the top of her head. "You'll remember."

ॐ

"I love the shop at night," Heidi says, her voice wistful as we trail back through the bookshop twenty minutes later. "Isn't it pretty, all the dark in here and the light coming in through the window?"

I can see what she means. There's something peaceful about the bookshop like this, when everyone is gone and the shadows blanket the tables and shelves.

"It's nice," I admit.

She sighs, stopping in her tracks at the edge of the café and looking around. Then she crosses the checkered floor to the comfortable chair Carmina and I always fought over, settling herself lightly in the seat.

It's such a practiced motion, done so easily, that I have to assume she comes down here regularly at night. And since I'm taking my cues from her right now, I do likewise, sitting in the matching chair that's next to the display windows. I let my gaze and my thoughts wander as I listen to the sounds of the evening; the hum of the fridge coming from the kitchen,

261

the gentle shuffle of noise from Jojo's cage, Heidi's soft breathing.

It's impossible not to think about Carmina when I'm sitting here, the table where she died right in my line of sight. Somehow I can remember everything about that morning, and yet the whole thing still feels like a dream, too. The gasping, rattling sounds she made, the chaos of the people around us, the clatter as everything fell out of her purse—

But my thoughts still as I remember something else, something I hadn't thought about before. I didn't see anything suspicious about an elderly woman having medication in her purse, but now, knowing she was poisoned...

"Warfarin," I say quietly, my eyes narrowed as I think back. "I think that's what it was called."

"What's warfarin?" Heidi says.

"I don't know." But I've already got my phone out to check. It takes me a few spelling variations before I get it right, and my eyes skim the information with increasing speed. "Here. It's an anticoagulant. A blood thinner," I clarify. "It helps prevent blood clots. And..." I scroll more fervently, sensing in my bones that we're teetering on the edge of something important. "And it's also the main component of most rat poisons," I finish, my voice deadly soft. "It stops their blood from clotting, and they bleed internally."

In the darkness, I can make out Heidi's widening eyes, her dropped jaw. She snaps her mouth shut. "What does that even mean?"

"Maybe nothing," I say grudgingly. "But...maybe something. All we have is baseless speculation."

"Let's speculate, then," she says, a bit louder now.

"It would be a stretch—"

"Then let's stretch," she insists. "Think about it. Carmina got her medication delivered—I saw the box in her trash can—

and didn't Mr. Foster say he sometimes got her packages by mistake?"

"Yes," I say slowly.

"So it might be a stretch, but it's possible—it's possible," she repeats when I show signs of cutting in. "It's maybe not probable, but it's at least *possible* that her neighbor knew what medicine she took. He could have been trying to make it look like an overdose of her medicine."

"Phil and Elsie knew about her medications too, I'm sure," I point out.

"That's true." Then she sighs. "Would anyone else have known?"

"Not that I can think of?" I say, but it comes out like a question. "I don't think so. Manniford at the restaurant, Stanley Riggs—that doesn't seem like something they would have known."

We sit in silence for a second, and I can tell Heidi is thinking as hard as I am. But then she sighs.

"So much for speculating; my brain is all jumbled and fuzzy."

I grimace. "I know. Mine too."

"Should we put a pin in this?" she finally says. "Just for a little bit? Talk about something else to clear our heads?"

I nod, but I don't say anything. My mind is still turning over this new realization—a realization that might mean something or nothing.

We lapse into silence for several more minutes until Heidi speaks again.

"Sometimes I think of my books as my babies," she says abruptly. Her voice is quiet, but I hear every word. "And putting them on their shelves is like tucking them into bed, until they grow up and they're ready to go out in the world."

"Mmm," I say, smiling at that. She was right; it feels good to think about something besides murder. "Funnily enough, I feel the same way about my books."

"The ones you write?" she says, looking at me. I can hear the surprise in her voice.

"Yeah," I say, nodding. "I conceive them, nourish them, care for them—and then send them out into the world to be at the mercy of everyone else."

"Huh," she says faintly. "I hadn't thought of it like that." She's silent for a moment, and then she speaks again. "Soren."

Something about her voice has me tensing. "Yeah," I say.

"Am I correct in assuming you want to date me?"

I blink, startled. My heart stumbles over itself, but I take a deep breath and do my best not to let her hear my sudden nerves. "Yes," I say truthfully. "I want to date you."

In the shadows I can see her nodding slowly. "And are you someone who views dating as the first step toward marriage, or toward starting a family or whatever?"

"If you're asking if I could see a future with you..." I say, pressing my palm over my chest as though it can calm my thundering heart. "Yes. I'm not interested in anything superficial."

Another slow nod, and she reaches up to tuck some hair behind her ear. "Then you should know—" Her voice cracks, and she cuts off before resuming. "You should know that I likely can't have children."

Silence—in the room and in my mind. Just a blank emptiness as my brain scrambles to process and keep up and understand.

And I ask myself some very serious questions then. Questions that I owe it to myself to ask: Do I want to be with Heidi if she's unable to have children? Could I live a life with her if expanding our family wasn't possible?

The answer is on the tip of my tongue before I can stop it. "Yes," I hear myself saying.

The word hovers in the air for a moment.

"Um," Heidi says. "Sorry?"

Aaaand I'm an idiot. She didn't ask a question. I asked myself those questions, in my head, and then answered out loud.

Great. Really great, I think, rolling my eyes at myself.

"What I mean," I say, "is that whether you can or will have children doesn't change how I feel about you." I swallow as my vulnerable words queue up behind my lips, dancing on my tongue, pushing my pulse faster through my veins. "I would rather have you and just you than someone else and a brood of children."

She clears her throat. "And that's sweet, but—"

"No," I say, cutting her off. I'm on my feet before I realize it, crossing the distance between our chairs in several long strides. She looks up at me in shock as I tower over her; I kneel in front of her quickly. "No," I say again. "If you don't want to be with me for other reasons, that's okay." I force myself to smile. "If you decide I'm not the man for you, I'll respect your decision. But you're going to have to tell me that to my face to get rid of me, honey." I reach up hesitantly, tucking some of her hair behind her ear. "You can't use this as an excuse. If you're scared, that's fine; I'll hold your hand. If you're hesitant, that's fine too; I'll give you space and time until you're sure. But you won't be able to chase me off with this."

"I don't want to chase you off," she says in a broken whisper; a lone tear trickles down her cheek, visible only because it reflects the light of the street lamps in the square outside. "I just don't want you to regret being with me later because I can't give you—that."

This time my smile is genuine. "Leaving you because you can't have children is something I would regret probably for the rest of my life," I tell her, and I mean every word.

She looks at me with an expression I can't quite place; a mixture of surprise and hope and something else that breaks my heart—shatters it into tiny pieces.

"Aren't you going to ask why I can't have kids?" she says finally, her voice hoarse.

"Do you want to tell me?" I counter. Of course I want to know; I want to know if she's okay, if she's healthy, if this knowledge is something she struggles with. But I'm not going to push her.

"I had a surgery when I was younger," she says. Her eyes are trained carefully on me, and I can tell she's watching every microexpression on my face, trying to discern the truth of how I feel and what I think. "I had ovarian cysts when I was in high school. The doctor was worried they might be cancerous." She inhales deeply and then lets the breath out again. "They weren't, but they were large, and there were several of them. The surgery and the scarring afterward did some damage to the tissue. I'm fine now, but it's unlikely that I'm able to get pregnant."

My body has stilled. "You're okay now, though?"

She nods, and I let out a shaky breath as my head drops to her knee. "Good," I whisper, trying to ease the panic in my chest that flared when I heard the word *cancerous*. "Good." Then, before I can stop myself, I press a kiss to her skin, a smooth patch above her knee, where my forehead has been resting. "You're okay. You're healthy. Yes?"

I want to hear her say it one more time.

"Yes," she says softly, and I look up at her.

I need her to be healthy and happy always and forever. I need those things regardless of whether I'm part of her life or not.

"Soren," she whispers.

"Mmm."

"I think—" She breaks off before continuing. "I think—"

I wait, but all she says is a quiet "Never mind."

I shrug. I'm tired, and my brain is overloaded. It's full of Heidi and our future, but it's also full of Carmina and the future she'll never have.

"How would we be able to find out if Mr. Foster bought rat poison?" I say, my voice musing. I get the sense Heidi wants to change the subject. So I settle more comfortably on the floor next to where she's still sitting in her chair. "We'd need to see a receipt or search his garage or something, and neither of those are realistic."

"A receipt," she murmurs, clearly lost in thought. "You know, there *was* a receipt..."

I turn my head sharply to look at her. "Where? When?"

"In Carmina's purse," she says slowly. "With the envelope of cash. I found them under the chair after all the stuff fell out of her purse, remember?"

"Yes," I say, my pulse picking up once more. "You don't still have it, do you?"

"No," she says. "I threw it away."

"Ah." I nod. "It was probably nothing, anyway."

"Probably." Then she gestures to the door. "You should get going. Let's pick this up tomorrow."

But later that night, probably thirty minutes after I've gotten home, my vibrating phone jolts me from my half-asleep thoughts. I feel around for it on my nightstand, sitting up in bed.

"Hello?"

"Soren," Heidi says. There's something about her voice that wakes me up fully and immediately; not just because it's her but because of the buzzing, crackling energy that seems to be coming down the line. "I found a picture of the receipt," she says breathlessly.

I blink. "Wait—what?"

"I took a few photos of the envelope of cash," she says, the words falling quickly and piling on top of each other, "and the receipt is off to the side, and Soren—it was Phil. *It was Phil.* He bought rat poison one week before Carmina Hildegarde died."

✥ 24 ✥

FROM THE LIFE OF CARMINA HILDEGARDE

APRIL 7

Carmina Hildegarde had never been thusly treated in her entire life, and she could feel the rage radiating from the roots of her perfectly coiffed hair down to the tips of her perfectly manicured toes.

Her date had been going beautifully. The food smelled delicious, the company was exquisite, and—she wouldn't hesitate to admit—she'd looked positively stunning. Yes, she'd received some odd looks, sitting there and seemingly talking to herself, but she'd never minded that. Who were these people that she should care what they thought? They weren't her family. They weren't her lovers. Their opinions did not matter.

Her date had taken a turn for the worse, though, when she had begun to assemble a bite of vegetables and had discovered, to her disgust, one tiny, wriggling bug—tucked right between a carrot and a potato, coated in sauce but somehow still alive.

She'd demanded to see the chef, of course, and the manager —she'd demanded to see anyone and everyone she could.

And she'd been scorned.

She'd been accused of placing the bug there herself so that

she could get a free meal—as if she would ever cart around any sort of insect for any purpose at all.

She sniffled now, hours later lying in bed, her aching body covered in a thin quilt. She inhaled deeply and then let her breath out again.

Their opinions did not matter. She would not cry. Such behavior was not worth her tears. She would not cry.

She would not.

But as she pulled the portrait of her darling husband out from under her pillow, she thought perhaps that she had never missed him more.

❧ 25 ❧

IN WHICH HEIDI ATTENDS A
FUNERAL

I attend the funeral of Carmina Hildegarde with Gemma, Eric, Mel, and Soren.

I'm a little plus-minus on being here. Now that I know Phil and Elsie bought rat poison a week before Carmina died, I'm hesitant to be in their vicinity. Soren's right; they've always been the most likely suspects, and the receipt I saw is pretty damning.

It's not a signed confession, but it's not nothing, either. It runs around in my mind, playing games with the rest of my thoughts and questions.

Because there are parts of this that still don't fit to me. It seemed so obvious the other night; Phil *purchased* the rat poison right before Carmina died, so Phil probably *used* the rat poison. But the more I've thought about it, the more questions have popped up. Why would Phil and Elsie have allowed us to snoop around if they were hiding something? Why did they kill her now? Can we really discount all the other people Carmina had issues with?

And good grief—what about Stanley Riggs? How does he come into all of this?

I shake my head, taking a deep breath and trying to clear my head. Now's probably not the time to be asking these questions. So I force myself onward, my footsteps firm despite my reluctance.

I'm not the only one of our group that's hesitant today. Eric doesn't want to be here at all; he came for me and Gemma, I can tell. He's not callous or unfeeling, but he does shy away from emotionally intense situations. And he doesn't even know about the receipt yet; Soren and I decided not to tell anyone until we could think it through more.

How will Phil Hildegarde behave at the funeral for the mother he doesn't seem to miss—the mother I suspect he murdered? Is he going to be visibly grieving? Will he cry?

It's a morbid train of thought, maybe, but I can't stop the curious questions from nudging the corners of my mind as we make the walk from the car to the graveside.

It's a rainy spring day, one of those where the world has turned muted gray and Technicolor green. Why is it that the grass always seems greener when it rains?

There are droplets of water dripping from the tree leaves overhead, and the ground is soft under our feet. I wince as I look over at Gemma, whose black heels are sinking several inches into the lawn we're crossing. I'm glad I wore flats; Mel was smart too.

Soren is a steady presence behind me, never letting me get too far ahead before he hurries to catch up again.

"You walk so fast," he says as we're passing a large head-stone with an angel on top. "Like you always have somewhere you need to be."

"I *do* have somewhere I need to be," I say, looking blankly at him.

He rolls his eyes, which makes me smile.

"Come on, Man Bun," I say. I'm struck with the sudden impulse to reach out and take his hand, and for a second my instinct is to suppress that—but I take a deep breath and then follow the desire. "Let's go," I say, holding my hand out to him.

He stares at it for a second before he takes it, his fingers weaving through mine. "I want to keep you close," he admits, his voice a low murmur in my ear. "It makes me nervous now, being around Phil. Especially since he knows we've been digging around."

I sigh. "I know," I say as we walk. "It makes me nervous too."

"We need to give those photos you took to the police."

"I will," I say. "I'll send them over later this afternoon."

We continue to walk, hand in hand, until we reach the graveside ceremony. There aren't many people here, but a few; I spot Phil and Elsie, dressed in black, and maybe ten more people.

None of them look very sad at first glance.

Although...

My gaze jumps back to Phil, and I blink in surprise.

He doesn't look sad, necessarily, but he doesn't look well, either. There are dark circles under his eyes, and his hair, normally slicked back, falls limply around his face. It's greasy, and that combined with the scruffy shadow on his face makes me think he probably hasn't showered in several days.

Interesting. And...strange.

I don't let myself dwell on it right now. I drift instead to the row of easels next to the casket, leaning in to look at them more closely. They each display a different photo; the first is a black and white glamor shot of Carmina as a young woman, beautiful and poised. The next is a wedding portrait, and she's even love-lier in that one; her smile is stunning, her eyes sparkling. Then comes a family photo, the same one that hangs in Phil and Elsie's house; seeing it now, though, I can't stop the little voice in my mind that wonders if that little boy grew up to be a murderer.

When I move on to the last photo, I'm expecting to see Carmina looking the way I always knew her—older, elegant, haughty. But I'm shocked to discover how wrong I am.

It is Carmina, and she is older. But that's the only part I got right. She's standing by a graveside in this very cemetery, looking worse than I ever saw her look in life. She's dressed in elegant black, but her hair is distinctly disheveled, and her face is swollen and puffy. A heavy locket hangs around her neck—one I've seen before, I think. I peer at it more closely, noting too the stiff portion of her sweater at the base of her throat, the unusually high neckline—

"Oh," I say as something unexpectedly painful twinges behind my belly button. It's backward. Her shirt is backward in this photo.

Why did they display this? It's cruel.

I swallow the sudden lump in my throat, blinking my eyes rapidly. Then I look at Soren. "She was so lonely."

He frowns, leaning over to look at the picture. "What do you mean?"

I inhale shakily. And it's stupid, maybe, that this one photo has me holding back tears, but...

"Her sweater is backward," I say, pointing at the portion of her shirt that's right at the base of her throat. "Look. You can see the patch right here where the tag is inside."

"Okay..." Soren says slowly, his eyes narrowing. "I see it. So what?"

"So," I say, taking another deep breath. "No one told her, Soren." I look at him, blinking more rapidly still. "There are people all around her. Someone took this photo. But...no one bothered to tell her that her sweater was backward. No one cared enough to tell her. Not even her family." And it's horribly, desperately *sad*, pulling painfully in a way I don't even understand.

Phil walks past me then, and instead of shying away, I hold out one hand to stop him. "Phil," I say.

"Hmm?" he says, looking at me. He still looks awful.

"This necklace," I say, pointing at the heavy oval locket. "Did she wear this a lot?"

"Yes," Phil says shortly. "It has a picture of my father inside."

"Ah," I say, and understanding clicks into place. "Thank you."

I wait until he's moved past us before turning to Soren. Then I pull out my phone and hunt around my photos until I find the photo the waitress at the restaurant sent me. I peer at it more closely until I see it.

"Her date," I whisper to Soren. "The date at Chateau Marche where no one turned up. It was with her husband."

Soren frowns. "Her...*dead* husband?"

"Yes," I say.

His frown deepens, and I fight the urge to smooth those lines out of his forehead. "What?" he finally says.

"Her husband," I repeat, pointing at the photo on my phone. Carmina is wearing the locket, clearly looking down at it. "His picture was in this locket, and she had the photo of him under her pillow. That was who her date was with. She wore the necklace with his picture, and she had dinner with him."

"I...don't think I get it," Soren says.

I swallow the lump in my throat. "That's okay," I whisper as my eyes return to the photo of Carmina in the cemetery. "I know I'm right."

I stare at the picture some more. There's a nagging little

voice in my mind as I look at Carmina's swollen, grief-stricken image, a voice I can't quite make out; it's like when you've met someone before and you learned their name but now you've forgotten it. It's insistent, a memory so close I can almost reach out and touch it, but try as I might, I can't pull any details to the front of my mind.

I sigh.

Sad. This is all so sad. And I'm feeling something oddly like pity blooming in my gut, a swelling that rises past my belly button up to my sternum until it's in the back of my throat—maybe tears, maybe vomit, I don't know, but *something*. Something strange and uncomfortable, something that makes me wish I had been kinder to Carmina Hildegarde, or at least snuck her an extra blueberry muffin every now and then.

I glance over at Soren; the way he's grimacing and rubbing his chest tells me he's feeling a similar sense of regret.

"Why did they put this picture up?" he mutters, his eyes narrowed on the photo. "Isn't that kind of like kicking a woman when she's down?" His face flushes when he says these words, and I think he's realizing how odd it sounds to describe a dead woman as simply being *down*.

"Maybe they wanted to show how important her husband was to her," I say, but it's a halfhearted suggestion, one I don't really believe.

We stay there, looking on in silence, until someone announces that the service is about to start. Then we go take our seats next to where Eric, Gemma, and Mel have already sat down. Some sort of pastor begins to talk, a droning, monotonous blur of background noise that I should pay attention to but don't. I'm too fixated on Phil instead, and how honestly horrible he looks.

Why does he look so bad now? Why is this the first time we're seeing him like this? Because his current appearance isn't something you'd want to fake. No one would ever purposefully make themselves look that bad. So if he feels so awful at his mother's funeral, why has he been so normal before today?

I glance at Elsie, who's dabbing at her eyes with a white hankie. Her nose is a little red, maybe, but other than that, she looks the same as last time we saw her.

And what about Carmina's last words—*pick* and *lock?* What was that all about?

I'm startled out of my swirling thoughts when I realize the pastor has finished speaking; Phil is now the one standing in front, talking about his mother.

"It means a great deal to us that you all came out today," he says in a subdued voice. "My mother would have loved that you took time out of your busy schedules." He swallows, his gaze darting to the coffin and then to the large, rectangular hole in the ground. "We will always remember your kindness, and as we move forward with this new chapter of our lives, we'll remember the good people of Sunshine Springs, too."

I sit up straighter at this, although it takes me a second to realize why I feel suddenly on edge.

What *new chapter of their lives?* What does that mean?

But my heart sinks as Phil answers my question, going on, "We've decided that this town holds too many painful memories." He scrubs one hand over his mouth and then says, "So we'll be moving forward someplace else when all of this wraps up. I know my mother would have understood and supported us in this decision." He nods at the little crowd of us. "Thank you again for everything."

I look over at Soren, just as he's looking at me. His expression is as troubled as I expect mine is.

My gaze jumps back to the pictures of Carmina, skating past those of her earlier life and landing on the one of her in the cemetery. And abruptly, so jarringly sudden that I almost gasp out loud, comes an echo of a voice—tired, quiet, and yet also unyielding.

"*I know what you did.*"

Those five words are faint, but they ring through my mind with such persistence that I know I *must* be remembering.

I saw Carmina that night. I'm almost positive. I might have known she was going to die.

And I think...she might have known she was dying, too.

It's only when I feel something coming to rest on my knee that I realize I've begun tapping my foot. I look down to see Soren's large, gentle hand there, his skin golden against my black pants, the pressure firm and comforting. On the other side of him, Eric, Gemma, and Mel are both looking over at us, all of them wearing identical smirks.

I shake my head, fighting an inexplicable and highly inappropriate smile, given where we are and what I've just remembered.

Soren can clearly tell something's up with me; he keeps glancing over, and he doesn't take his hand off my knee. It stays there while Phil wraps up his comments; it stays there while Carmina's casket is lowered into the ground. And when the service is over, he leans sideways immediately, whispering in my ear.

"What is it?" he says, and I shiver at the feeling of his warm breath against my skin.

"You can't do that in public," I whisper back, rubbing my neck and my ear. "That whole ear-skimming thing."

"I could do *so* many things in public," he murmurs, "if you'd let me."

My jaw drops, and I gape at him like a fish. But he just smirks and touches my bottom lip with one finger.

"Soren," I whisper-hiss as the people around us begin vacating their seats. "We're at a *funeral!*"

"I know," he says ruefully, that little smile still pulling at his lips. "I know. But somehow I just...can't stop thinking about you." He shrugs, and his cockiness fades into something more vulnerable. "Pathetic, huh?"

Something surges in my chest, something warm and all-enveloping—like I've just had hot chocolate and it's heating me from the inside, except there's not a drop of hot chocolate in sight.

"No," I say, more gently now. "Not pathetic." I can't stand the thought of Soren Mackenzie ever thinking he's pathetic —ever. So I'll put that to rest right now. "Never pathetic."

He gives my knee a squeeze, and then he smiles once more. "Let's get going, shall we? I think everyone else is at the car by now."

We stand, and then I reluctantly turn toward Phil and Elsie.

I think they—or at least Phil—killed Carmina. I don't know everything yet, but I think it happened.

And yet...in case I'm wrong...

I approach them with hesitant steps, smiling when I reach them.

"I'm so sorry for your loss," I say quietly.

They nod at me and murmur their thanks; Phil doesn't even make eye contact. I step aside so other people can get through; as I'm turning away, I hear a woman offering to bring dinner to them.

"I'm sure you don't feel like whipping anything up," she says.

"That's kind," I hear Phil say. I turn to look just in time to see him patting Elsie's knee. "But my wife does most of the cooking."

And another piece of the puzzle presents itself before slipping neatly into place.

☙❧

"WHAT IF IT WAS ELSIE?" I SAY LATER THAT AFTERNOON, when Gemma, Eric, and Mel have left. It's just Soren and I in the empty shop; I like closing the store on Sundays. The two of us sit side by side on the checkout counter, surrounded by bookshelves, our legs swinging gently.

"Elsie?" Soren says, looking sharply at me. He's still in his funeral clothes, a tan suit that fits him stupidly well. I've changed, though; I don't like dress clothes.

"Yes," I say with a nod. "*Just* Elsie. I overheard Phil mention that Elsie's the one who does most of the cooking. And it made me think..."

"She could have poisoned Carmina if she was doing the cooking," he finishes for me.

"Plus she could have used Phil's card. Couples share stuff like that all the time."

"That's true," Soren says, his eyes narrowing as he thinks. His gaze grows faraway, and I can tell he's putting things together in his head. "That would explain why Phil let us look around without seeming bothered." He looks back to me. "If he didn't know what his wife had done, he wouldn't mind anyone poking around."

"Exactly," I say, nodding again. "More of the story fits when you look at it this way."

"How would we figure out if that's what happened?" Soren says, his voice musing.

"Mmm," I say. I tilt my head, thinking. "Didn't someone say the walls in those places were really thin? I think it was Stanley Riggs. He said the walls were thinner than some of the residents liked." I look at Soren. "If there was fighting going on, Mr. Foster might have heard."

"Maybe," Soren agrees. "Do you want to talk to him?"

"Yes," I say. "Just...not today." I'm tired. I'm so, so tired. Emotionally, physically, mentally. "Let's hang out here for now. Unless you need to go," I add quickly.

"Nope," he says, his voice relaxed. "There's nowhere I need to be."

"Good," I say. "Stay with me." My heart beats a little faster at this, because it feels like such an overt declaration of my feelings, but Soren just nods.

"I'll stay with you," he says simply.

Except the way he looks at me isn't simple. It doesn't feel like an offhand comment; it feels like a promise.

We sit in silence for a while, our legs still swinging, the atmosphere comfortable and relaxed rather than awkward or full of tension.

"I keep on thinking about Carmina," I say finally. "I keep on thinking that I should have been nicer to her."

Soren sighs. "I know," he says heavily. "I've been thinking the same thing." Then he looks over at me. "You were always kind to her, though."

"I was," I say, "but only to her face." I swallow, staring absently at a spot on the floor. "I should have talked to her. I should have asked her about herself. I should have made her feel less lonely. Even small talk—little questions about herself. I should have asked her those things."

When only silence greets me, I look at Soren. His blue eyes are fixed on me, full of something I can't name.

He slides off the counter and then turns to me, stepping closer, closer, closer—until his hands are resting on either side of me, caging me in, and he's so close I can see each individual eyelash. My breath stills in my chest, my pulse moving straight from normal to rapid.

"Let me ask you something, Miss Lucy," he says, his voice hoarse. "Has anyone ever taken the time to ask *you* the little questions? Your favorite food, your favorite color, your favorite thing to do?" His hands leave the counter and come up to cradle my face instead; his thumbs stroke my cheekbones, warm trails over my skin that crackle with invisible sparks. "Has anyone ever asked you those things simply because they couldn't stand not knowing everything about you?"

I swallow thickly. There's something obstructing my throat, holding my voice hostage, so all I'm able to do is shake my head.

"Mmm," he says with a slow nod. "I thought so. Tell me, then. What's your favorite color?"

I can't believe he's asking me these things, and I can't believe I *want* him to. There's nothing deep or intimate about colors and foods. And yet...

"Green," I say, except it's more of a croak. "My favorite color is green."

Another nod. "What kind of green?"

"Like the grass after it rains," I say. I feel like I'm in a trance —I can't look away from him, can't even move. All I can do is sit here on this counter, my hands gripping the edge, my knuckles white as an electric buzzing sensation fills my body.

"Like the grass after it rains. Noted," he says softly, his thumbs continuing their mesmerizing trails over my cheekbones. "And what about your favorite food?"

"Uh," I say, trying not to get distracted by how close he is or how good he smells. That buzzing feeling is zipping through my limbs, up and down my spine, a current beneath my skin that's tugging me toward him. "Ice cream, maybe. Or stir fry."

"I'll learn how to cook stir fry," he murmurs, and one hand moves to my hair—stroking gently, tucking it behind my ear. "What else should I learn how to cook?"

The words I'm thinking do *not* match the words that come out of my mouth.

"Kiss me," I breathe.

It's truly not what I meant to say, but I don't take it back. I just move my hands to his sides, tangling my fingers in the fabric of his shirt.

"What?" he says, his eyes sharpening, his hands going still.

Learn how to cook egg-fried rice, my brain says.

"I want you to kiss me," my mouth says.

"I—are you sure?" he says hoarsely. But his gaze has already dropped to my lips, burning and hungry, and his hands have moved to my jaw. "I can wait, honey. I can always wait."

"I don't want you to wait," I say as that buzzing sensation settles deep in my stomach. Then, as something occurs to me, I add, "Not unless you want to."

"No," he says, and his voice breaks. "I don't want to wait." He still seems conflicted; his eyes dart over my face, as though he's searching for any sign that I don't mean what I'm saying.

And I find, quite suddenly, that I don't have the patience for that. So I lean in, close my eyes, and press my lips to his.

He freezes in surprise for several long seconds, but I don't pull away. I stay exactly where I am, my amateur kiss frozen in place.

Until, finally, he gives in.

He tilts his head with a groan, his lips taking charge, slanting over mine. They're hot, insistent, demanding—and yet somehow he keeps them from becoming overwhelming. He pushes just enough, and when I slide my hands up his chest and then wrap my arms around his neck, he moves his grip from my face to my hips. He pulls me closer, to the very edge of the counter, and I can feel the heat of his hands through the fabric of my shirt.

So I wrap my legs around his waist, tighten my arms around his neck, and kiss him with everything I have.

❧ 26 ❧

IN WHICH SOREN'S DREAMS
COME TRUE

This woman. She will be the death of me—the sweet, beautiful death. She's fire and ice, open and closed off, playful and serious—and she's kissing me with a fervor that makes my head spin. Her touch, always so hesitant before, is growing more sure.

My grip on her tightens as her legs wrap around me, and I fight the impulse to pick her up and move her somewhere more comfortable. This is one fire that will burn dangerously if we let it, so I think it's best to stay where we are.

I let my lips play with Heidi's, trying to monitor my grip on her so that I don't leave bruises. I don't want to scare her or hurt her or give her a negative experience in any way—especially because if I have my way, I'll be kissing her like this for the rest of our lives. Her body is warm pressed against mine, and soft —*so* soft—and I would like to live here, like this, forever.

I force myself to slow down, to loosen my grip, to move things in a calmer direction; she matches the change, her hands playing lazily in my hair as the kiss morphs into something slow, languid, delicious. Her head drops back as I press my lips up and down her jaw, her neck, savoring every inch of skin, inhaling her, breathing her in—her ragged breaths send electricity through my veins until there's nothing I want more than to carry her off to the nearest bed.

Which is how I know it's time to pull back.

I give her one last kiss, deep and lingering, before removing my arms from around her and placing them firmly on the counter again.

"I'm so—" I gasp, trying to catch my breath. "I'm—"

In love with you. I'm so in love with you.

But I don't think I can say that, as much as the words keep trying to burst free. Not yet. She's not ready.

"I'm a really big fan of yours," I finally say instead, letting my head rest against hers. "Do you know that?"

"Mmm," she murmurs, a little smile curling her red, freshly kissed lips. "I think so." She hesitates and then says, "I'm a pretty big fan of yours too, Man Bun." The words are hoarse, tinged with vulnerability, so I let go of the counter and cradle her face in my hands.

I press a feather-light kiss to her nose, to her cheeks, to each of her eyelids.

Let's get married. Let's live together forever.

"Let's get you some rest," I say instead. "And let's figure out our next move."

"What next move?" she says, pulling back slightly so she can look me in the eye. "With the two of us?"

"No," I say, smiling. "I think *that* next move is clear, isn't it? Can I date you? Can I take care of you? Can I kiss you whenever I want?"

Her already pink face blooms in color once more, and I watch as she tries and fails to fight her smile. "I suppose," she says. "But I'm not sleeping with you yet," she adds quickly.

"I can't even think about sleeping with you right now or I'll lose my mind," I admit, my voice dry. "I'm a commitment guy anyway. We'll take things very slow. As slow as we need."

She nods, that little smile tugging further on her lips. "I can't—" she begins, pressing her palms to her cheeks and then burying her face in her hands. "I can't stop smiling!"

I laugh, wrapping my arms around her and pulling her close. She's precious. Adorable. I want to kiss her again.

But there's a time and a place, and my self-control is not perfect, so I let go of her and step back. "All right," I say, holding out my hand.

She takes it and then hops down from off the counter—the counter that I will never look at the same way again—before looking up at me.

"*Velvety tongue!*" Jojo squawks from behind us, and we both jump. "*Velvety tongue!*"

We turn to the bird, our eyes wide.

"Does your psycho bird know we were making out in front of him?" I whisper.

"That's not possible," Heidi says, her eyes narrowing as she looks at Jojo. Then she glances at me. "Is it?"

"Hmm," I say, my gaze still on the parakeet. "What kind of nonsense did you guys listen to with him in the room?"

Her cheeks somehow turn even pinker. "None of your business," she says, and then she tugs me away, heading for the café.

⚜

"So you remembered her voice saying...what was it?" I ask the next day. We're in my car, the windows rolled down as we head over to Maplewood. Heidi's left Gemma in charge, and when we left Eric was hanging around too, trying to sneak muffins from the display case.

"I think I remembered her saying *I know what you did.* She sounded...odd," Heidi says. "Sort of broken, I guess. Sad."

"That is sad," I say, and I rub my chest, trying to ward off the little tug of regret that's pulling somewhere behind my sternum.

It was just a stupid chair. I could have found somewhere else to sit. Why was I so petty?

I reach over and take Heidi's hand, weaving my fingers through hers. It's a simple action, but the way she accepts it almost eagerly makes my heart feel like it's going to explode out of my chest.

My girlfriend. I'm holding my *girlfriend's* hand.

I wish I could take the scenic route to Maplewood so that I could hold that hand for even longer.

I can't, though. And more to the point, I don't even know if there *is* a scenic route to Maplewood. It doesn't matter, anyway; we're on a bit of a time crunch. Phil and Elsie said they were moving.

When I pull up in front of their duplex, I spot the *For Sale* sign in their yard immediately. "They're running," I say quietly.

"I think so too," Heidi says, her voice grim. "I've been thinking about Phil, and how he looked at the funeral. I think he found out what Elsie had done. That's the only explanation I can come up with, based on what we know or suspect. Or... maybe something happened between them and Stanley Riggs, and that's what caused his spiral."

"He looked pretty bad," I admit, picturing Phil's appearance at the funeral.

"He did—much worse than we've seen him so far."

I nod. "But Elsie looked fine."

"She did." Heidi sighs and then looks out the window at the

duplex. "Well, let's go see what Mr. Foster has to say, or if he'll even talk to us at all."

We get out of the car, and maybe I'm being paranoid, but I close my door as quietly as possible. You can hear a car door slamming out on the street from inside a house, right? I think you can. The last thing we want is to alert Phil and Elsie to our presence.

Heidi's clearly on the same page, because she closes her door quietly too. I round the car, and together we head down the sidewalk and then up Mr. Foster's driveway. And because I am a respectful boyfriend, I spend no longer than two seconds with my eyes on Heidi's legs, long and tan in her cut-off shorts. My mind flashes back to the way those legs wrapped around me yesterday, and I shake my head.

Focus, I tell myself firmly. *This is not the time or the place.*

I hurry my pace so that I can walk next to Heidi instead of behind her as we approach the front door, and when we reach it, I knock firmly.

No one answers.

We wait for probably thirty seconds, Heidi's toes tapping impatiently, until I decide to try again. I knock harder this time, not violently but loud enough to be heard. This time the door swings open after a few seconds.

"Hello," the man at the door says, looking at us like he can't quite remember where we're from. He looks pretty much the same as he did last time we spoke; thin and reedy, with dull eyes and glasses.

"Hi," Heidi says, giving him a smile. It's friendly but not entirely genuine; somehow it only makes me appreciate her real smile more. "We spoke not too long ago about Carmina Hildegarde. I was wondering if we could ask you a few more questions about your neighbors. Do you have a moment?"

Mr. Foster's eyes jump back and forth between us. "I don't

really—I mean, I haven't—" But his voice falters as he searches blatantly for an excuse.

"It will really be only a moment," I say. "And then we'll be out of your hair."

He lifts his hand absently to touch the top of his head, and I wince when I remember he's very bald.

Oops.

"Would that be all right?" Heidi says, steering firmly past my blunder. I shoot her a grateful look, but her eyes are trained on Mr. Foster.

"Oh, all right," the man says with a sigh. "Come in, I suppose."

I watch, amused, as Heidi steps promptly into the town-home, following after him.

This woman. She goes for what she wants, and she's not afraid to be insistent.

"How are the walls in these places?" she says as I close the door behind us. "Pretty thin?"

"Uh, yes," Mr. Foster says, his voice wobbly as he runs one hand over his bald head again. "I'd say so."

A large dog bounds around the corner, and I barely have a moment to react before he's jumping on me, his paws on my chest, his tongue wagging.

"Whoa, boy," I say, even though I'm not sure if the dog is male or female.

"Get down," the man snaps at the dog, and it drops to all fours before padding over to Heidi and sniffing at her legs.

"Did you hear a lot of arguing from the unit next door, or not so much?" Heidi says, ignoring the dog. She keeps her voice casual, as though she's not too interested in the answer, but I see the tension in her shoulders.

"Oh, yeah," the man says, sitting down at his table. He doesn't invite either of us to sit, so we remain standing, hovering awkwardly around the kitchen table. He relaxes further, maybe put at ease by the direction the conversation has taken. "They were loud."

"Mmm," Heidi says with a nod. "How so? It must have been irritating."

Mr. Foster shrugs his narrow shoulders, his fingers drumming on the table. "There was a lot of yelling, but I'm used to it." The dog comes and sits next to him, and he scratches it behind the ears absently, his eyes still on Heidi.

"Who did all the yelling, do you know?" she says.

The man snorts. "All three of them. The son and the daughter-in-law ganged up on the old lady a lot, but she did her fair share of yelling too. I heard them through open windows, too, while I was working out in the garden in the back."

"Oh, did you?" I say, surprised. I hadn't considered that.

"Oh, yeah," the man says with a vigorous nod. "The old woman's window faces the back. She sat there and stared outside a lot. And she yelled at the son a lot about his wife. She wanted her son to leave the wife. Said the fish didn't like her."

Heidi frowns. "The fish..."

"Didn't like her, yeah," the man says. "I didn't ask. Sounded batty to me." He pauses and then rubs the back of the neck. "Truth be told," he says, his voice more reluctant now, "I feel kind of bad about what happened to that woman. Carmina, I mean. Bruce is pretty enthusiastic, and he likes to meet new people." He pats the dog's head. "He—uh, he sort of knocked the lady down one time."

Heidi shoots me a glance before looking back at the man. "He knocked her down?"

"He didn't mean to," Mr. Foster says quickly. "But I—uh, well. I feel kind of bad about it. I said he didn't do it."

It's easy to feel bad now that Carmina is dead, I find myself thinking. *It's easy for me to feel bad about fighting over that stupid chair now that she's dead. Shouldn't we have regretted these things while she was still alive?*

My discomfort and regret are bitter on my tongue, but I don't try to banish them. I swallow them instead, and when they hit my stomach, I commit them to memory—the faint nausea, the piercing sorrow, and the knowledge that things could have been different, and it's partially my fault that they aren't.

"You..." Heidi says, and I'm surprised to see her eyes narrow as she looks at Mr. Foster. She points at him. "You were there that day. When Carmina died. *That's* why you looked familiar." She straightens. "You were at Paper Patisserie, weren't you?"

"I—well—" he stutters, his face flushing a dull, mottled pink. "Yes, but only because—well—"

"What?" Heidi says, and some of her politeness from earlier disappears. "Why were you there when she died?"

Mr. Foster finally throws his hands up in the air. "I was following her, all right? I was following her. Just a little. Just—to see if she—if she was okay," he finishes, his words turning sulky. "I'd noticed she seemed unsteady on her feet, and I was worried it might be my fault. Even though Bruce jumped on her months ago..." He shrugs. "She seemed very wobbly and slow when I saw her out on the sidewalk. So I followed her, just to see if I was imagining it. She might have sued me or something if there were long-lasting effects."

Ah. So he wasn't even really worried about Carmina; he just wanted to make sure he was in the clear.

This woman was surrounded by a lot of really lousy people.

Heidi continues to do the talking, for which I'm supremely grateful, because there's a sudden lump in my throat that's making it hard to breathe, much less speak. So I listen as she wraps things up with Mr. Foster and his dog, exchanging curt pleasantries that betray her disapproval and her desire to get out of there.

The polite smile drops off her face the second the door closes behind us, the fresh spring air a calming draught.

"Wow," Heidi says, looking over at me. She plays with the ends of her hair as she looks back over her shoulder at the front door.

I reach out and take her hand, and she twines her fingers through mine without hesitation, without even looking down.

"Yeah," I say, my voice heavy.

So many implications to everything that man said. And yet to me, the most striking things we learned are that Carmina may actually have been justified in reporting her neighbor to the HOA, and that Mr. Foster was there the day she died.

"He's pretty horrible."

"He is," Heidi says. "I wondered if I'd been imagining things, thinking he seemed familiar. I must be remembering him from the shop that day. And the dog thing—"

"She was old," I say, my mind whirling as I try to imagine it. "Think about how thin and rickety she was. A dog that size jumping up on her would absolutely have thrown her off balance."

"It would have," Heidi agrees, and she sounds as grim as I do. Her hand tightens in mine as we trail down the driveway and then down the sidewalk.

I open the passenger door for her when we reach my car, and she slides into the seat silently.

"What about the fish thing?" I say when I've gotten in the driver's side and closed the door. "'The fish don't like her,' or whatever she said."

"There were fish," she says, her voice musing, her eyes far away—searching her memory, maybe. "In the hallway upstairs. Right?"

"Yes," I say with a nod. "It was a gross fish tank."

"Yeah," she says. "And I wonder..." She falls silent, but a second later, she turns to me. "If a fish tank is gross like that, all murky, it means no one is taking care of it. No one is cleaning it or whatever. And Elsie said that Carmina didn't like animals, but...I don't know if that's true. I kind of wonder if the fish tank was gross because Carmina had died, and she was the only one who'd been taking care of the fish."

I sigh, leaning forward so that I can see Elsie and Phil's townhome through the windshield. "I think that's possible."

"I do too," she says. She squeezes my hand. "Let's head over to the police station. They need to see these photos of the receipt."

❦ 27 ❦

IN WHICH HEIDI MAKES A
MIDNIGHT PHONE CALL

"All right," I whisper to Soren, crouching in front of his chair. "Let's think about this."

He looks at me, startled, and then sighs, his shoulders slumping. "Oh, good," he says. "It's you. Distract me, please."

Paper Patisserie is lively with customers today; the weather is getting warmer, and spring is morphing into summer, which means that Sunshine Springs is getting more and more tourists.

Soren has taken to sitting at the chair by the window rather than the chair he and Carmina always fought over. I haven't asked, but I know it's because he feels guilty. I wish I could absolve him of those emotions, but that's not my place. So I try to keep an eye on him instead, to stop by his seat whenever I spot a frown pulling at the corners of his lips.

Right now, though, I'm not crouching next to him because he's frowning. It's because my mind is speeding in twenty directions at once, and talking to Soren always seems to help me figure out my thoughts.

"Why do you need distracting?" I say, glancing at the laptop open in front of him. "Bad writing day?"

"Not exactly," he says, grimacing at the computer. "I'm reading the rough draft of my bestseller."

I raise one eyebrow. "I see," I say. "I'm proud of you. That's probably scary." I hesitate and then ask, "What's the verdict?"

He rubs one hand over his face. "It's...not good," he says.

"I think *not good* means something different to you than it does to me," I admit, "but that's good, right? It's good that the rough draft is not good?"

"In theory, yeah," he says, "because hopefully that means I've grown as a writer. But it's still not fun to read."

"Huh," I say, thinking about that. Then, curious, I ask, "What is it like, reading your own writing? Do you read your own books?"

"No way," he says with a snort. "Never. Not ever. I mean, I like seeing the characters again, but after the book is published, I can't really make changes, and that's what my brain always tries to do. If I went through and read my books, I'd constantly be finding things I wanted to change or fix. So I steer clear."

I nod. "That makes sense."

"Anyway," he says, shaking his head a little. "What's up?"

"Just thinking about Carmina," I say with a sigh. "And trying to figure out what she meant, *pick* and *lock*."

"Mmm," he hums. "I still don't know about that one. All I know is..." He trails off, looking out the window with an almost wistful expression.

"What?" I say.

"All I know is that I'd like to go to the farmer's market with you this weekend, and I'd like to not have to think about murder while we're there," he says quietly. Then he turns his eyes back to me. "It's taking over my life and my thoughts, and I don't like it." He tilts his head. "Want to go to the farmer's market with me this weekend?"

I smile faintly. "Yeah," I say. "I do."

"Can we try not to worry about all this while we're there?" he goes on. "Even just for a little bit?"

I nod, swallowing down the sudden knot in my throat.

Because I know what he means. These days Carmina is most of what I think about. Which is to be expected, of course —she died recently, right in front of us. But it does become draining, living in those shadows.

And I find myself wondering if this wave of tiredness that washes over me will ever really go away.

"Go ahead and get some work done," I tell him, standing up and patting his leg. Now doesn't seem like the time to brainstorm what Carmina's last words meant. I think we both need some normalcy.

So I spend the rest of my day as normally as I can; I help out in the kitchen, I shelve books, I chat mindlessly with Gemma, Mel, and Calvin. I sneak peeks at Soren—my *boyfriend*—and I soak up the sun that's spilling through the display windows.

It's nice. Refreshing.

But it also feels insincere. Like I'm pretending everything is okay when it isn't. And maybe I would feel okay about putting Carmina's murder on the back burner if there were other people mourning her passing.

But...I'm not sure there are. And it feels wrong, somehow, to set aside her death just because it's not convenient for what I'm feeling.

I don't know that I owe Carmina Hildegarde anything. But I started this journey; I need to see it through to the end. So even though I spend the day doing normal, mundane things...when I go to bed that night, I let myself return to

Carmina. I stare at the ceiling and try to lasso my racing thoughts, all of which are jumbled and confused and oddly emotional.

I squeeze my eyes shut, blinking a few times, but it doesn't stop the sting of tears.

And I can't believe this. I can't believe there are tears in my eyes because I feel bad for Carmina Hildegarde—the woman who was so insufferable in life.

But...it's so *sad*. And really, shouldn't someone mourn her? Shouldn't *someone* care that she's gone?

Maybe I can be that person.

So I let myself cry for the old woman I barely knew. I let myself remember everything I know about her, about the life she was living before she died. The shirt inside out in the photo at her funeral; the callous son and daughter-in-law; the picture of her husband under her pillow and his picture in her locket.

She was so lonely.

And I freeze, then, in the process of wiping my eyes, my hands hovering over my cheeks. There's something nagging at my mind, something I can't place—those last thoughts play eerily in my thoughts, sending up flags.

But why?

His picture in her locket.

His picture in her locket.

I sit up in bed, my teary eyes widening. "Picture," I breathe into my quiet, dark bedroom. "Locket. Pick. Lock." I feel around blindly in the dark for the switch to my lamp and then turn it on; the light floods the room, and I wince.

But I don't wait for my eyes to adjust. I grab my phone and then, disregarding the time stamp that tells me it's the middle of the night, I call Soren.

It takes him four rings to answer, which feels like way too long when I'm practically dancing out of my skin.

"Soren," I say when I hear his groggy, half-audible *hello*. "Wake up."

"Already awake," he grumbles. "Thanks to you."

"Sorry, Man Bun," I say, smiling. "But I think I figured it out."

"Figured what out? And is this really a middle-of-the-night conversation—"

"Yes," I say. "It is. *Pick* and *lock*—I think I figured them out."

There's a second of silence, and when Soren speaks again, he sounds much more alert. "You did?"

"I think so," I say. "I can't guarantee it. But I don't think she was talking about picking a lock, Soren—I think she was talking about the *picture* in her *locket*."

"Oh," he says—and then, with understanding, "*Oh*."

"Yeah," I say, nodding. "That could be it, right?"

"Yes," he says.

"So how do we get in that room again to look at what's in her locket?"

He sighs, a gusting sound that sends static down the line. "I don't know, Heidi; I don't think we should be going in that house anymore. Phil and Elsie are wild cards. The police know now that they bought rat poison a week before Carmina died; they'll definitely keep looking around."

"Yes," I say, "but who knows how long that will take? What if we went in with an excuse?" I bite my lip, thinking. "Like I could say that I lost my earring and that I think it came out when we were over there."

"I don't know," he says again. "I'm worried about your lack of fear, though."

"It's not that I'm not scared," I say, although truly, I feel very little fear right now. "I'm aware of the dangers. And I want to be careful. I just also think some things are worth the risk." I swallow as my eyes prickle once more. "It's hard to explain."

I hear him sigh again, and then he says, "If we did this—*if*— I would want to bring a weapon or something with us."

"Deal," I say quickly, although I have no idea what kind of weapon he's going to be able to sneak in. "Whatever you think you can get away with."

"And I reserve the right to pull the plug at any time," he goes on. "If we get in there and something feels off, we leave immediately."

I hesitate this time, but then I nod. "All right," I say grudgingly. "That's probably smart."

"Fine," he says. "We'll go tomorrow. Now get some sleep, honey."

"Mmm," I say, smiling a little. "I think I really like it when you call me that, Man Bun."

He laughs softly. "I'll deny it tomorrow, but I think I like it when you call me *Man Bun,* too."

"You should leave your hair down," I say. "I want to run my fingers through it. I've always wanted to do that."

Soren groans. "I can't have this conversation with you in the middle of the night. Go to sleep. I'll come by in the morning."

"Goodnight," I say.

And when I finally drift off to sleep, there are still tears in my eyes, but there's a smile on my lips, too.

I'll check the locket, Carmina. I'll check it tomorrow.

❧ 28 ❧

IN WHICH SOREN HAS A VERY BAD FEELING ABOUT THIS

I don't wait until my usual time to come in the next morning. By the time Gemma flips the sign on the door from *Closed* to *Open,* I'm there, standing outside. She opens the door when she sees me, her eyebrows raised.

"You're early," she says, a knowing look in her eyes. "She's in the storage room."

"Thanks," I say, slipping past her and into the shop.

Heidi's comments about running her fingers through my hair made their way into my dreams, but not in an enjoyable way. I dreamed that she was playing with my hair, braiding it, putting it in pigtails, until a vaguely shadowy figure came and captured her from behind. I spent the rest of the dream looking for her, panicked and desperate, always running through molasses and never able to get enough oxygen. I woke up sweating and anxious.

So when I reach the storeroom and step inside, I lock the door behind me.

"Hi," Heidi says, looking up at me from where she's crouched next to a large box. "You're here early." She shoots me a smile, small but genuine, before turning her attention back to the box in front of her.

Her hair is long and loose today, and she's got on a plain white t-shirt that makes her golden skin glow. She's beautiful.

I maneuver my way over to her, my heart racing, my chest heaving as I look down at her. "I desperately want to kiss you," I say hoarsely.

She glances back up at me, surprise flashing in her eyes, and then she stands up. "I think that can be arranged." She rounds the box and steps up in front of me, tilting her head. "Are you okay?"

"Yes," I say, moving closer to her, sliding one hand into her hair. "I had a bad dream, and I wanted to see you."

"I'm sorry," she says softly. Then, hesitantly, that precious woman goes up on her tiptoes and presses her lips to mine.

I breathe her in, my fingers curling around the back of her neck, one hand at her waist. Her lips are impossibly soft, tentative and sweet, and I let her take her time, moving at her pace.

I want to scoop her up and carry her away, somewhere safe, somewhere beautiful, where she can be protected and happy forever.

It's only when her arms slide around my waist, her fingers tightening on the fabric of my shirt, that I let myself deepen the kiss. I tilt my head and slant my lips over hers, tasting her, listening to her little sigh of contentment as my heart soars and my body comes alive.

She is perfection.

I don't know how long I lose myself in her lips, but by the time I hear a knock at the storeroom door, my pulse is pounding through my veins like I've just run ten miles. I press one last kiss to her lips before pulling back slightly, smiling down at her.

She removes her arms from around my waist and holds her

hands up to her cheeks for a few seconds before fanning herself.

I can't help my smirk at the sight of her flushed skin; I did that to her. I'm the one who has that effect on her, and my stupid male ego likes it.

"Let's go back out there," I say, taking her hand in mine. "Or I'm going to kiss you again, and then we'll never leave."

She doesn't reply, but her cheeks maintain their pink flush, and my smile grows.

It feels weird, to be this happy when I know we're about to go nudge our way into a killer's home, but that's what Heidi does to me. She makes me feel light and free and like anything is possible.

When we open the door to the storage room, Gemma is on the other side, one eyebrow raised, a knowing smirk on her lips. I ignore this completely and move past her. I hear her hissing something to Heidi, her voice giddy, but I just return to the front of the store and wait. I watch as they linger in the bookshelves, whispering together, with Heidi looking embarrassed and Gemma looking triumphant, and I smile.

"You ready?" I say when she finally makes her way to me.

"Yes," she says after a second's hesitation.

"We don't have to go," I add. "In fact, I'd really prefer not to."

"I need to," she says, looking apologetically at me. "I don't necessarily want to, but I need to. You don't have to come if you don't want, but I really—"

"Stop it," I say, my voice gruff. "If you're going, I'm going. I've got a pocket knife too." I had to dig around for it at my place, because I'm not the kind of guy who keeps a weapon on him at all times. I found it on the top shelf of my closet, covered in dust.

"All right," Heidi says with a nod. "Let's get this over with, then."

We drive over to Maplewood in silence, the radio playing softly in the background, our hands linked together. I can't help but hold tightly to her; there's a lead weight in my gut, an underlying feeling that something might go wrong, and it's making me anxious.

I let go of her hand when we get out of the car, but the second we're next to each other walking up the driveway, I take hold again.

In fact, I might like to hold her hand for the rest of our lives. That could work, right? We could make that work?

When we reach the front door, Heidi takes several deep breaths. I watch her inhale and exhale, the gentle rise and fall of her chest and shoulders, as something inside me eases the tiniest bit.

She's nervous. Good. I was half-wondering if she would forever be barging forward without fear. Knowing that she understands how risky this is helps me feel better.

Still, when she finally knocks on the door, she does it with confidence. The sound seems to echo throughout the empty street, but she stands tall, not fidgeting, not shirking.

Phil opens the door after about a minute.

"Hi," Heidi says, her voice gentle. "Um, how are you all doing?"

It's an unnecessary question, because Phil looks horrible. He's clearly not doing well. There are dark circles under his eyes, his skin is pale, and there's a stain on the collar of his wrinkled dress shirt. He looks like a man who's been wearing the same clothes for a week and who hasn't showered in just as long.

I take a step closer to Heidi from behind, my body pressed against her back, and I'm not even trying not to look like the bouncer at some big city nightclub. I don't know all the details of what Phil and Elsie have been getting up to, but I don't want them to think for even a minute that they can harm Heidi.

Phil grunts his greeting rather than saying anything; he shoots a look behind him and then looks back to us. "It's not really a good time," he says shortly. "You should probably go."

He looks...nervous. Scared, even. It's in the darting of his eyes and the almost compulsive twitch of his head as he keeps checking over his shoulder.

And I wonder, then, how much Phil really had to do with his mother's death.

If he knew anything about it at all—or if it was all Elsie.

"Absolutely," Heidi says, her voice sympathetic. "I'm so sorry to barge in. I really just was wondering if you'd found an earring, by chance—I lost one, a little gold stud, and I've searched everywhere. I first noticed it missing the evening after we were here last time. Have you found anything like that in your mother's room?"

Phil's eyes narrow slightly, his gaze darting over Heidi's face as though he's searching for lies.

"Here," she says after a second of silence. She reaches into her pocket and pulls out a little gold earring. "It looks like this."

This seems to reassure Phil; his shoulders slump, and his expression clears.

"I haven't seen anything like that," he says, shooting another glance over his shoulder, "but I haven't been in my mother's room since you were here last. It's a bit uncomfortable for me to go in there, you know."

"Of course," Heidi says. "I understand completely." She oozes sincerity and innocence, and I can tell she's going out of her way to hide that she's suspicious of Phil and Elsie. She wants him to think she's clueless about what really happened. And, to be fair, we don't have any concrete proof that it was

Phil—or Elsie. "If it would be easier for you, we could come up and try to find it. I wouldn't bother, you know, except that my father gave me these before he passed. I'd like to find the other one if I can."

I glance down at her, startled. But she doesn't look at me, doesn't give any indication about whether those earrings are actually from her dad.

Phil darts a glance over his shoulder once more and then mutters, "Just...hurry."

Heidi nods, and Phil steps aside, ushering us in. We bustle our way up the stairs as quickly and quietly as possible, and a chill runs down my spine when I hear the faint sounds of Elsie speaking in the kitchen, I think on a phone call.

Hurry. It's a flicker of a thought, one that tugs on the dark corners of my mind. *We need to hurry.*

And then another thought, louder: *We shouldn't be here.*

I swallow thickly and keep moving.

Last time we were here, I didn't pay much attention to the fish tank in the hall; now, though, I look more closely as we pass. The water is cloudy, and there's a faint smell emanating from it.

I think Carmina was the one who took care of those fish, and now that she's gone, they've been left to die.

Gross. Just...gross. And wrong. So wrong.

I walk faster, resting my hand at the small of Heidi's back and nudging her to speed up too.

When we reach Carmina's room at the end of the hallway, the first thing I do is close the door.

The second thing I do is lock it.

"Hurry," I say to her in a low voice. The word comes out breathless, slightly frantic. "Hurry. Come on."

The knife in my pocket feels ten times heavier than it is; I'm aware of it with every step I take as I move around the room. We both go to the vanity first, but the locket that once rested on top is no longer there. Heidi begins looking through the handsome wood jewelry box that sits in front of the mirror, and I start opening drawers.

And it's stupid, but in the back of my mind I swear I can hear music playing, the kind that's low and hurried and suspenseful, like the *Jaws* theme. It drives me further, faster, until I'm digging wildly through the drawers, clothing flying as I pull things out by the handful.

"Here," Heidi whispers, and my head jerks up.

"Where?" I say, standing in time to see her holding up a necklace. "Is that—"

But I break off as, just outside, someone knocks on the bedroom door.

IN WHICH HEIDI
CONTEMPLATES A KNIFE
FIGHT

The knock at the door brings my words to a halt, and something unpleasant prickles over my skin—fear like icy fingers caressing the back of my neck. My grip tightens on the locket in my hand.

It's larger than your standard locket; an egg-shaped oval not quite the size of my palm, but close. It's heavy, too. I shove it in my pocket and then look at Soren, whose eyes have followed the disappearance of the locket and are now back on my face.

"Yes?" he calls once I nod at him. "Hang on." He hurries over to the door and unlocks it, pulling it open. "Sorry," he says, and he makes a show of looking at the door handle with confusion. "Not sure why that locked. Did I lock it on accident?" he says, glancing at me.

"Maybe," I say with a shrug. My voice is casual, but my heart is pounding as I take in Elsie and Phil standing there, looking suspiciously at us.

Actually, Phil isn't looking suspicious. He just looks miserable. His eyes dart back and forth between his wife and Soren and me, and somehow the dark circles under his eyes seem to have grown in the last ten minutes.

Elsie, though—Elsie looks very strange. She has a hostess-perfect smile on her face, a friendly expression like she's about to ask if we'd like anything to drink, but her eyes are glacial.

"Anyway, sorry about that," Soren says, and even though his voice is just as casual as mine, there's tension in his shoulders, and his knuckles are white where he grips the door handle. "We weren't able to find the earring."

"Why don't we all look for it together," Elsie says, and her smile grows.

"Uh, that's okay," I say, forcing a smile of my own. "We can just—"

"I insist," she cuts me off. She steps into the room, followed by Phil—poor, cowardly Phil, who looks like he would rather be anywhere else than here.

Me too, Phil. Me too.

The blood pumps more wildly through my veins as Elsie's smile grows more brittle, like it's ready to shatter, like the whole thing will crumble and fall right off her face. She moves further into the room, her eyes never leaving Soren and me.

When she yanks the door out of Soren's hand and pushes it closed, I throw up in my mouth a little—a nervous response I've never experienced before and never want to experience again.

"Elsie," Phil says, only it's kind of a miserable groan. And I realize belatedly why he's said this: Elsie's hands have just closed around the heavy gold clock on Carmina's nightstand.

"Uh," I say, scooting backward. My body bumps into Soren's, and his hand wraps firmly around my wrist.

What even is happening right now?

What's happening right now is that Soren was right, and we shouldn't have come here, a scathing voice of reason pipes up from the back of my mind.

"Elsie," Phil says again, scrubbing his hands down his face. "Put that down. You can't just—you can't just *attack* people, Elsie!"

"Don't talk to me like that," she snaps at him, any last hints of pleasantness falling away. "Like I'm crazy. Like I'm going around attacking everyone I meet." Her lip peels back in clear disgust. "Am I crazy for wanting my mother-in-law to stay out of my marriage? Am I crazy to want to stay out of prison? No! No one wants their mother-in-law to interfere. No one wants to go to prison."

Phil says what we're all thinking. "Yes," he says, "but those other people don't kill their mother-in-laws or their neighbors, Elsie. Put the clock d—geez!" He yelps as she takes a swipe at him, and I fumble in my pocket for my phone.

"Elsie!" Phil shouts, his misery replaced by rage. "What do you think you're—stop it—stop!" He catches her arm as she's trying to bring the clock down on his head again, and I watch, frozen, my eyes wide.

"Don't act like you weren't there," she screams at him. "Besides," she breathes, "it's too late now. Help is coming."

What. Is. Happening.

Time is somehow moving too quickly and moving not at all; every new moment lingers before speeding away, and I'm helpless to do anything but take it all in with wide eyes and utter bewilderment.

Soren tugs on my arm from behind and pulls me backward, stepping in front of me. I watch as he digs a pocket knife out of his pocket, my brain trying to play catch-up.

"Do you know how to use that thing?" I say, tapping his arm. My voice is hoarse and shaky.

"Not really," he mutters. I keep my hand on his arm as he lifts it, trying to pry the blade out of the knife.

"Like, at all?"

"Not really," he says again. "I didn't think I'd actually *need* it. Here." He passes me the knife. "Your nails are longer—"

"No they aren't!" I hiss, shoving his hand away. "I don't know how to use one of those things—"

"I'm not asking you to stab anyone," he says, rolling his eyes. "Just pry the blade out—"

"*You* pry the blade out, Man Bun—"

"Shut up!" Elsie shrieks, a shrill sound that causes all of us to freeze. "Just—shut up!"

We shut up.

And it's interesting, the way your brain begins to cope when it realizes its primary function—to *exist*—is being threatened. There's an endless stream of half-baked thoughts flying through my head, none of them good—*we could dive out the window* is one, *we should engage in a close-quarters knife fight despite having no close-quarters-knife-fight skills* is another—as I take in the room, fashioning everything I see into an escape mechanism of some kind.

But I was not made for life-or-death situations. I was not made for this.

I was made to sell books. I was made to curl up in sunny patches and bask.

This is too much, and I am *not* interested. I have things left to do in this life of mine. I have books to sell and scones to bake, and nowhere in my plans is *Get murdered by a psycho*.

So on my phone, which is already in my white-knuckled grip, I dial 9-1-1.

Elsie sees me, of course. Everyone sees me, because we're all standing frozen, staring at each other, our chests heaving, the room totally silent.

But as the operator asks what my emergency is, I drop the phone. Because from downstairs comes the distant sound of the front door opening and closing, followed by the heavy trundle of footsteps up the stairs, and my heart stops as I realize that we're about to be very outnumbered. Unless—is this someone who will help us?

But the footsteps come closer, heavier, down the hall, unpleasant thuds, until finally someone appears—a large, dark-haired woman, out of breath, pearls askew, eyes blazing.

"I'm here," she says to Elsie, gasping for breath. "What's—"

"The *wife?*" Soren blurts out, echoing my thoughts as he cuts her off.

But it's the wrong thing to say. In fact, I think it's the *worst* thing he could have said. Because Patrice Riggs is all but spitting fire when she turns her eyes on him.

"That's all I ever am," she snaps, her jowls wobbling. "The *wife.* The clueless, vapid, well-behaved wife. And yet everyone knows that if you want to get something done, you ask the woman."

She's not completely wrong there, I have to admit.

"I'm so confused," Soren says, and I nod.

"Me too," I mutter back.

For some reason both of us turn our eyes to Phil, but he just shrinks more miserably into the background.

"Elsie didn't kill Carmina Hildegarde," Patrice snaps, and wow, does she command a room; her voice is booming, her presence giant. "Not technically. *I* did."

She drops those words into the utter silence like a stone in water, rings and rings and rings of disturbance as confusion and horror lap over my skin.

"So don't rob me of that achievement," Patrice goes on, positively radiating fury. "I killed the self-righteous old bat, and Elsie killed my cheating scum of a husband, and you two have been poking around for far too long."

"*What?*" I say, looking at Soren.

His eyes are bugging out of his head as he says, "I have no idea—"

"Shut up!" Elsie screams again.

Except this time I really can't. "But—how did you kill Carmina?" I say faintly, pointing at Patrice.

"Poison, obviously," she says with a sniff. "I tried to get her a few months ago at that restaurant, but after she found a bug in her meal and people started looking at the kitchen too closely, Manniford wasn't willing to try again. Coward," she scoffs.

"I knew he was sketchy," Soren says under his breath.

And it occurs to me then that the only reason Patrice is telling us this must be that we're going to die. That's how these things happen; if the villain monologues, it's because the good guys are going to die.

Why don't I read any detective novels? Why do I only read romances and literary fiction? Nothing in Soren's books have prepared me for this moment. Nothing in my Regency romances have told me what to do when two insane women are screaming at me.

But then I think of all the scary movies I've tried to watch with Eric, and I shiver. No way. I couldn't even handle Soren wearing a face mask all those years ago when we met; why would I ever read scary books?

"Okay. But—you—" I say, looking now at Elsie. "I thought you were trying to kill Carmina."

Elsie shrugs. "I was. My weapon was Patrice."

"And vice versa," Patrice says, her voice suddenly even and calm. "I'd hoped to eke a bit more blackmail money out of Stanley, but..." She shrugs. "Eventually he just needed to go."

"All right," Soren says slowly, and when I look over at him, I can tell he's just as confused as I am. "So let me get this straight. Carmina was blackmailing Stanley...but then she died."

Patrice's brow furrows with her irritation, but she just nods.

"Right," Soren says. "Okay. So then we found the photos of Stanley and his—uh—his mistress," he says, "and we gave the photos to Phil and Elsie."

Patrice and Elsie nod.

"And then we thought, why not try to get some money out of him ourselves?" Elsie says with a shrug. "But Stanley'd had enough, I guess. So Phil and I had to kill him."

"Ah," Soren says, and I nod. That timing actually does make sense; it was after Stanley's death that Phil started looking rough.

"Maybe that's when he realized he was married to a lunatic," I say to Soren, and he nods.

And then, before I even register what's happening, Elsie is lunging at me.

She's utterly unhinged, madness sparkling in her eyes, the heavy clock raised over her head.

Slow motion.

Soren turns around, pulling me close, shielding me in a matter of milliseconds. The clock comes down on the back of his head, and I scream—though what I say is beyond me. I don't think there are words; it's just a stream of terror.

I feel his body shudder; my arms tighten around him as my heart stops completely. But when he remains standing, when he remains cocooned around me, I look up at him, surprised. Then I peer around him at Elsie, who's holding the clock in her hand, looking peeved and glaring at the back of Soren's head.

"It hit your man bun," I say, my eyes wide, my voice faint. "Your man bun cushioned the blow—"

But Elsie lunges again, and I flinch away. And Soren's

arms, which had gone temporarily lax, are too slow to stop me from losing my footing.

I tumble backward, the world spinning around me before I feel a sharp crack of pain on the side of my skull—

And everything goes black.

I WAKE UP IN A DIMLY LIT ROOM.

I jacknife straight up, my eyes flying open as my racing heart threatens to jump right out of my gaping mouth. My gaze darts here and there, taking in everything I can see, until I realize I'm in a hospital bed.

Again.

I'm in a hospital bed...again.

And there's a hulking giant of a blond man sitting beside me in a chair that isn't quite big enough for him, fast asleep, his jaw hanging open, a little snore escaping his parted lips.

A sigh of relief escapes me, and my galloping heart begins to slow—like even in sleep my body was worried that something had happened to Soren.

"Soren," I say quickly, reaching over and tapping his knee. "Soren!"

He stirs, his eyes opening. It only takes a second for that gaze to sharpen on me; he sits up straighter, leaning toward me.

"Heidi?" he says, his voice low and anxious. His hair is anxious, too, strands of it escaping his man bun and falling haphazardly around his face. "You're awake. How do you feel?"

"What happened?" I say instead of answering. "What's going on? What happened?"

Except...even as the words leave my mouth, I'm assaulted with a set of memories—Carmina Hildegarde's bedroom, Elsie's bizarre smile, Patrice, the confrontation that turned violent.

"Your man bun," I gasp, my eyes wide, and my gaze moves to Soren's hair. "You've saved us all." It's maybe an odd thing to say to my boyfriend's hair in the wake of a very real trauma, but I'm not sure I'm all there right now.

I do know one thing: I'll never complain about that man bun again.

"How did we get out of there?" I say. "You don't look hurt. Are you all right?"

Soren grimaces. "I'm fine. The police were already on their way, thanks to your phone call. But after you collapsed, I sort of —uh—" He rubs the back of his neck, looking sheepish. "I sort of lost it."

"What do you mean?" I say with a little frown that sends a little twinge of pain through my throbbing head.

You feel pain, I remind myself as I take inventory of my body for the first time. My head is sore, pulsating with a dull ache, but the rest of me seems okay. *You feel pain. You are alive.*

"I don't even know," Soren says, looking weary. He slumps in his chair. "I watched you falling to the ground like it was happening in slow motion, and then I just—went berserk, honestly. I think I was screaming? Phil actually tackled Patrice—"

"Good job, Phil," I say, surprised.

Soren nods. "And I basically attacked Elsie and lifted her entire body up and just *held* her there until help arrived."

"Wow," I say, stunned. "Like a caveman."

"Yes," Soren says. "I'm not proud of it, but it got the job done, so..."

"And the locket," I say when I remember. I feel around in my clothes, my gaze darting around the room when I realize I'm dressed in a hospital gown. "Where's the locket?"

"The police have it," Soren says, and for the first time since I awoke, I notice a spark in his eyes. "Guess what was inside?"

I shake my head and then regret it as it gives a few dull throbs. "Tell me."

Soren leans closer, threading his fingers through mine. "*The receipt.*"

My jaw drops as my hand closes around his. "No."

He nods. "The receipt. It was folded in there—not the whole thing, because maybe it wouldn't have fit, so it looked like Carmina had specifically cut the top and bottom to make it take up less space. But it was the receipt that showed Phil's card purchasing rat poison."

"She knew," I say faintly. I relax back into the hospital bed. "Carmina knew—" But I break off as my head continues to clear, as memories continue to offer themselves up—and I hear, as though from a great distance, the foggy echo of a voice.

I close my eyes, squeezing them shut, as I try desperately to cling to the tendrils of memory floating closer and closer.

More snippets of that voice, old and weary. A warm breeze. A sense of panic and the need to act. And—and—

My eyes pop open.

I remember.

I remember.

I HEAD OUTSIDE TO WATER MY PLANTS, WATERING CAN IN hand. I smile at the feel of the spring breeze, let it play with my hair; I listen to the sounds of the warm night. Then I get started on my flower beds.

I work silently, enjoying the faint wafts of floral that drift up toward me until a sound makes its way to my ears.

"I know what you did."

I freeze, standing up straight. At first I wonder if I'm hearing things, but then I hear the voice again.

"I know what you put in the cookies I ate," it says, "and I'll make sure you burn for it."

My eyes widen and my hands clench tighter around the handle of my watering can. I walk silently down my row of flowers and toward the side of the shop, where the voice seems to be coming from.

I don't round the corner; I just stand there and listen.

I'm not normally an eavesdropper. I'm really not. What you talk about is your business. But there's something about this conversation that sends icy fingers down my spine, even though I've barely heard anything.

"Don't lie," the voice snaps—it's familiar, somehow, female and decidedly aged. "Those cookies weren't from her. She would never. They were from you. But I want you to know..." There's a shuddering breath, and then the voice continues. "That I don't have anything left to live for. So I'm letting myself die—and I will haunt you for the rest of your miserable life, you little brat." The woman's voice breaks, a vulnerable, heart-wrenching sound. She's quiet for long enough that I can tell the person on the other end must be speaking, but then her voice talks again.

"I know that." Her voice cracks once more, and she pauses. "I know no one will miss me." She sniffles. "They used to love me, you know. They used to beg for my photo. But it's a fickle world out there, you fool, and if you think they won't forget you just as swiftly as they forgot me...you're delusional." And these words are spoken with such coldness, such bitterness, that I shiver.

It's only when I feel my nails digging into my palms that I realize I'm holding onto the watering can so tightly it might break. My heart is thundering as my mind races, trying to make contextual sense of what I'm hearing.

Because it sounds like this old woman is speaking to someone who's trying to kill her.

But there's no way. There's just...no way.

Right?

This is Sunshine Springs. Things like murder don't happen here.

But what if they do? *a little voice whispers in my mind.* What if this woman is going to die?

I bite my lip as I listen. She said she would let herself die. She said no one would miss her. So I crane my neck, listening harder—

And my blood freezes in my veins at the next thing she says.

I reel back, stunned. How can this be?

And how can I help?

I have to help. I need to help.

Inside, *I think.* I can invite her inside and make her something to eat. Maybe she'll talk to me.

But panic wells up in my chest as I turn on my heel and hurry back to the shop's door. I can't handle this alone. I don't know the first thing about talking someone down from death. I need help.

I go inside and set the watering can haphazardly to the side, rushing back through the shelves. I think my phone is on the book desk—yes. There it is.

I grab it, and before I can even question why, I'm pulling up Soren Mackenzie's contact information.

Soren knows things. He's smart and calm and steady and I need that. I need that right now—so why isn't he answering his stupid phone?

I begin speaking as soon as I hear the beep, only barely paying attention to the words as they rush out of me. "Soren, I think I just learned a really scary secret, and now I don't know what to do, and I'm freaking out, so come to the bookshop as soon as possible. Please hurry." *I rush back through the bookshelves as I talk, that frantic feeling growing.*

I need to get to that woman. I need to talk to her.

Only I'm not looking where I'm going. I'm not paying atten-
tion. I don't see what's on the floor in front of me. I only feel it,
the disruption in my hurried steps. I pitch forward, and every-
thing goes black.

❧

I DON'T REALIZE I'M CRYING UNTIL I HEAR SOREN'S
muttered curse from next to me.

"What is it?" he says, standing up. He grabs a box of tissues
from the corner table and yanks a few of them out, passing
them to me.

"I remember," I say, swiping furiously at my eyes. "I
remember what happened. I remember everything."

And it hits me then, the enormity of what has happened,
and my tears fall faster.

I cry, and I cry, and I cry.

I cry into the night, offering Soren limited, blubbered
explanations—that Carmina Hildegarde knew she had been
poisoned, that she had no desire to live any longer, that she *let*
herself die. I cry in the minutes and then hours and then days
that follow my return home.

I cry because while I never grew up believing in the
concept of *too late*...I was wrong.

I was too late to help Carmina. I was already too late when
I overheard her phone call. And I think...I think I'll spend the
rest of my life wondering what might have happened if I had
talked to her before I tried to call Soren.

If I had talked to her before she was ever poisoned.

If only leaves a bitter aftertaste, one that lingers and leaves
you feeling queasy, one that makes you want to cry and curse
and wish for ignorance.

I know that what happened to Carmina wasn't my fault. I didn't poison her.

But I think I'll always wonder anyway.

One thing I do know?

I will never tell anyone the final thing I heard Carmina say, the one that sent me reeling and sent ice down my spine.

Carmina Hildegarde had poisoned Elsie, too.

She had tried to retaliate against her daughter-in-law, but she'd failed, succeeding only in making Elsie violently ill; and when I overheard her on the phone, she'd known she wouldn't get another chance. She'd sounded sad, defeated.

I will take that knowledge to my grave. I don't see any point in revealing it now.

So it's something I'll have to live with.

◈

Soren keeps me updated on the case, but I don't really need him to. It's all over the news. Sunshine Springs isn't large, and this kind of scandal is something we don't see every day. A double murder shakes things up nicely.

The symptoms of rat poisoning, it turns out, may not appear until several days after the poisoning—a fact I find online in the days following. And judging by what I heard Carmina say on the phone, Elsie gave Carmina cookies that Patrice had baked and brought over—only Carmina didn't believe what Elsie said. She didn't believe Patrice Riggs baked those cookies.

She was woefully mistaken.

"I wonder what the restaurant guy used when he tried to poison her at the restaurant," I say one morning while Soren and I sit eating scones from the bakery.

"I don't know," he says. "But she didn't eat any of it, anyway, remember? The bug."

"Yeah," I say with a sigh. Everything is still fresh and raw and painful.

"Why do you think it was Elsie who bought the rat poison and not Patrice, if Patrice was the one who poisoned Carmina?"

I narrow my eyes, thinking. "My guess? She wanted to keep her hands as clean as possible." It fits with what we know of the woman who worked with charities and played the doting wife.

"I think," Soren says now, "I could go the rest of my life without hearing the word *murder* and be very happy."

"Agreed. Let's talk about something else for a while," I say, shoving the last bite of scone in my mouth.

"Just—one last thing," he says.

I nod, raising one brow at him.

He takes a deep breath. "Remember the little green book that was on Carmina's bookshelf?"

It takes me a second to place what he's talking about. "Oh," I say when it clicks. "Yes. I remember."

"Well..." he says, rubbing the back of his neck. "I kind of...took it."

"You what?" I say.

"Yeah," he says. "I took it. I probably shouldn't have," he goes on, "but you were right; it was a journal. I guess I just... wanted to know more about her life and her thoughts. I grabbed it in all the commotion of the police and the ambulance." He watches me for a second, and I can tell he's feeling me out, seeing how I'll react to this news. When I don't say anything, he speaks again. "I was going to read through it soon. This weekend, probably. If you want to join me."

I don't have to think about it for very long. "Yeah," I say. "I do." Because I feel the same pull—to learn more about

Carmina. To remember her—and then to put this whole thing to rest. "This weekend sounds good."

"Great," he says. "Also. Want to date me?"

"I'm already dating you," I say with a little smile as I chew.

"Want to date me some more?"

"Yes," I say as my smile grows. "What did you have in mind?"

"Hot springs," he murmurs, weaving his fingers through mine. His eyes sparkle. "Just you and me this time."

I nod, ducking my head to hide the blush blooming in my cheeks. "Let's do that this weekend, too." Then I stand up, pulling my hand away from his. "I need to get back to work," I say. "Wait for me?"

"Always," he says.

I think I might just take him up on that.

🎇 30 🎇

FROM THE DIARY OF CARMINA HILDEGARDE

ugust 5

A   I don't understand how I could have birthed such an idiot.

I've certainly never been as gormless as my offspring, and my darling Errol was nothing short of perfect in every way. But we did something wrong with that boy.

He's forgotten my birthday again.

It's days like this that I miss Errol more than ever. He would know just what to say if he were still here; he would know just how to make this day special.

I did buy myself a muffin this morning from the little café in the town square, though I do that most days. That horrid blond man was there, the one with the unseemly hair, and he took the seat closest to the restroom again. My bladder isn't quite what it used to be. I like to stay close to the ladies' room when I go out. Perhaps I'll try to go earlier next time.

I suppose it doesn't matter how this day turns out; not really. I don't imagine I'll live much longer anyway—not with the way I'm getting on in years. But I did make a lovely birthday meal for Philip and Elsie and I to eat together, and they forgot that they'd promised. So I ate by myself and left the dishes for them.

I'm not sorry.

I think I'll take a bit of a birthday nap.

OCTOBER 16

I've finally done it—I've finally gotten a photo of that menace dog next door breaking the rules. My horrid neighbor eschews common decency, taking more care of his pet than he does the people around him, but I won't stand for it a moment longer. My body is still sore from being knocked over; my wrist is still stiff. If that horrid man thinks he can get away with lying about toppling me over, he has another thing coming.

JANUARY 19

Dirty old Stanley Riggs has taken a mistress, and I've got photos. I'm going to take him for every penny he's worth, and then I'm going to donate all of that money to the charity his wife works with. What a horrific, conniving scoundrel.

I certainly never would have put up with such behavior. My sweetheart would never have looked twice at another woman. And he was always so handsome, even when his hair began thinning, even when his hands began to shake.

I miss my Errol.

APRIL 7

Sometimes I feel sad.

I went on a date with my darling Errol this evening. I looked stunning, if I do say so myself. But dates with my husband's photo, I've found, are providing less and less comfort as time wears on.

I miss him. I miss having someone who smiled when they saw me. I miss the time when people knew who I was, when they valued me, when they found me beautiful and charming and worthy of their attention.

What a fickle world we live in.

I miss my darling.

I hope I'll be by his side again soon.

EPILOGUE
SIX MONTHS LATER

My mom's new house isn't actually that bad.

I knew it wouldn't be. I knew I was weirdly attached to the old house because it's where I grew up. But it's nice to actually come see her new place, to get a feel for it, so I can imagine her living her best life here.

There's a cute neighbor, too, a single dad in his sixties whose daughter and grandchildren come over every weekend and play in the backyard together. My mom hasn't said anything about being interested, but I'd bet money it will happen.

I knock on the front door, which is painted a cheery blue, and wait for her to answer. Soren is next to me, stupid man bun in place, his hand wrapped tightly around mine.

Too tightly, in fact.

"You're cutting off my circulation, Man Bun," I tell him with a little smile.

"Sorry," he says quickly, loosening his grip with a guilty look. "I'm just nervous."

"She'll love you," I say as my smile grows. "She already loves you."

"Yeah," he says, "but this is the first time meeting her in person. I want to make a good impression."

"You've already made a good impression. This is the longest I've ever dated anyone in my life. It's the first time I've ever felt this way about a man. She's a big fan of yours for making that happen."

He looks slightly mollified at this.

The front door swings open, and there's my mom, her hair curly and wild, her smile stretching as wide as I've ever seen it.

"You don't need to *knock*, baby," she says, standing aside. "Come in, come in!"

"It felt like I should, since it's a new place," I say, stepping in and pulling Soren behind me. "Mom, this is Soren Mackenzie."

Soren holds his hand out for my mom to shake, but she ignores it entirely, throwing her arms around him instead. "Hi, sweetie," she says, hugging him tightly. "It's so wonderful to finally meet you."

He looks briefly startled, but then he smiles and returns her hug. And I know, as I watch the tension drain out of his shoulders and his expression relax, that my mother has worked her magic once again. She's put him instantly at ease.

I want to be like her when I grow up, but I've got a long way to go.

I am trying, though. In fact, I've been doing something new at the shop. I've been striking up conversations with the people that come in, learning about them and their lives and the things that make them happy. And I've found something remarkable, something so simple but so profound: most people love to talk about themselves. Most people love to share little pieces of their lives with the ones who invite themselves in. Most people crave some sort of connection, whether big or small.

And another thing I've discovered? It is incredibly easy to make someone smile. What an amazing power that is. There's something deep in my bones, in my soul, that recognizes that part of my purpose in life is to provide comfort, to provide a safe place, to help people smile more. I think that's why I was drawn to the idea of a bookshop and a café in the first place, so that's what I'm going to keep doing.

I think maybe it's what I could have been doing all along.

Patrice Riggs and Elsie and Phil Hildegarde are paying for what they did. Elsie's and Patrice's sentences will undoubtedly be longer than Phil's, and Phil and Elsie will be separated for years to come, but I'm not sure their marriage would have survived this anyway. Soren and I have promised each other that if we end up married, we won't kill each other's parents. We've also promised that no matter how successful or unsuccessful his writing career happens to be, we will not resort to blackmailing our neighbors. I'm personally not too worried about that one, because I've read his current manuscript and it's amazing, but it's possible I'm biased.

My mom leads Soren and I to the kitchen, where he sits down at the small table. I wander around, though, checking things out, opening cupboards, inspecting shelves and nooks and crannies.

"Well?" my mom says from behind me, and even though I'm not looking at her, I can hear the smile in her voice. "Does it get your seal of approval?"

"So far," I say as I emerge from the pantry. "But I need to see the whole place before making that call." I'm going to approve wholeheartedly, of course, regardless of what the rest looks like—how can I not, when my mom is so obviously happy here?—but I do want to see everything.

My mom waves her hand. "You want the tour?"

I nod, smiling a little. "Yes, please."

She leads us through the little house, and it's clear with every room we poke our heads into that my mother has already begun putting her own personal touches into this place. And I find myself thinking as we move from room to room about what kind of home I might want with Soren one day—a house in the suburbs? An apartment in the city?

I don't know. What I do know is that whatever my future holds, I want him to be in it.

My phone rings just as we're circling back to the kitchen. I pull it out of my pocket but don't answer; instead I look at my mom. "I love it," I say honestly. "It's perfect for you."

She beams at me, and something warms in my chest. Then I answer my phone.

"Hi."

"Hey," Juniper says, her voice bright and cheerful. "Let's hang out this weekend. Aiden says he can't play with me because he has a billion papers to grade, so I'm gonna be bored."

I can't stop the little smile that pulls at my lips. "What did you have in mind?"

"Let's carve pumpkins," Juniper says. "I found a stencil to carve Shakespeare's face, and I want to see how mad it makes Aiden."

"Halloween has already passed," I say.

"Yes," Juniper says, "but the pumpkins don't know that. They're still out here thriving."

I shrug; it's sound logic. "Okay. Let's do pumpkins."

"Invite Gemma. I want to see the engagement ring," Juniper says. "And Mel too, if you want. We'll have a party." She pauses, and then she adds, "Look at you, being all social. I'm so proud."

Over the last few months, I've gotten to know Juniper as she's come to Paper Patisserie for writing group with Soren. She's easy to be around and completely friendly; Gemma and I adopted her immediately. Or maybe she adopted us—either way, we've gotten close. Mel loves her too, supplying her with motherly hugs whenever she's around, and even though Juniper doesn't say much about that, I can tell she loves it.

"Thank you," I say. "Your place or mine?"

"Mine," she says. "More room, I think."

"I agree. Do you have pumpkins?"

"Yep," she says. "They're on the porch, looking all cheerful and happy. I haven't had the heart to tell them Halloween is over."

"Mmm," I say, and my smile grows. "Considerate of you. Let's do Friday. I'm visiting my mom right now, but I'll be back by then."

"Sounds good," she says. "Come over Friday evening. Bring snacks," she adds. "And I'll make some too."

I nod. "See you then."

"Bye!" she says, and with that she hangs up.

We spend the next two days at my mom's house, Soren sleeping on the family room couch and me in the guest room. He insisted on those arrangements, by the way—I tried to get him to take the bedroom and let me take the couch, but he wouldn't do it.

Such a gentleman.

We help my mom get organized while we're there, rearranging a few closets and the pantry so that she can easily reach the things she uses the most. When it's time for us to head back to Sunshine Springs, I'm tired, but my heart is full.

It's several hours past closing when we arrive at Paper Patisserie, but Gemma has left the main light on for me. I unlock the front door and step inside, smiling at the jingle of the little bell.

"Want something to drink?" I say to Soren, who nods.

"Water's fine, thanks."

I go back to the kitchen and grab two glasses, filling them with water. Then I return to the other side of the counter and set them down.

"It's good to be home," I say with a sigh.

"It is," Soren agrees, leaning against the counter.

My gaze wanders around my little café—my happy place—until finally it lands, as it so often does, on the table where Carmina passed. We've replaced the actual table, but I still think of her every time I see it.

"Is it bad," Soren begins, and when I glance at him, I see his eyes are on that spot too, "that lately I've been thinking I'm sort of glad she passed away? Not because I wanted her to die," he says quickly. "It's not that. It's just...falling in love with you has made me realize how horribly she must have missed her husband. It's sad that she was murdered, but at the same time—"

"You're glad she gets to be with him again," I say with a nod. "Me too."

We read Carmina's diary, and it broke my heart. Most of what she wrote about was how much she missed her husband; it could not have been clearer that she was unhappy and desperately lonely, increasingly suspicious of her son and daughter-in-law, left behind by a world that had once cherished her.

We sit there in silence for a few minutes, long enough that when Jojo squawks from the other end of the shop, we both jump.

"*Hold your hand! Hold your hand!*"

"That stupid bird," Soren mutters, even as his hand

tightens around mine. Then he looks at me. "Are you ever going to tell me what he's been quoting?"

"Well, there were two books in there," I admit. I guess it can't hurt to tell him now. "One that Gemma chose and one that I chose."

"And one of those was a romance," he guesses. "It has to have been, right?"

"Yes," I say with a grin. "The romance was a historical Gemma wanted to try, and it got spicier than either of us expected."

He nods, and it's kind of cute how satisfied he looks, like he's proud of himself for figuring it out. "And what about the one you chose?"

"Ah," I say. "I'm actually a little surprised you haven't gotten that one too."

He raises his eyebrow at me, and I laugh.

"It's your book," I say, shaking my head. "*Everything Between.*"

Soren's jaw drops. "But that's—" he says, breaking off. Then he tries again. "That's the one that flopped."

I shrug. "It's my favorite of yours. Even before we got together, it was my favorite. Haven't you heard?" I tug him closer, smiling. "I'm your biggest fan."

"I'm your biggest fan, too," he says as his eyes sparkle. He leans closer and presses a kiss to my lips, soft and gentle.

"*The longest of times!*" Jojo squawks. "*The longest of times!*"

"Ah," Soren says softly, his lips brushing against mine as he speaks. "That one does sound familiar."

"Mm-hmm," I say with a smile. "Question: Do you forget the stuff you write?"

He kisses me again. "On a regular basis," he says. "But only some of it. And I want the longest of times with you, so...I think I'll remember that one."

And I can almost swear that I see the ghost of Carmina Hildegarde then, in her seat at the table, raising a glass and toasting the two of us. There's the image of a man there, too, his arm wrapped around her. Her husband, I assume, though I'm very aware that I'm just seeing things.

"To a long and happy life," I see her ghostly shape mouth, and I wrap one arm around Soren. Then I watch as she fades, the man at her side, until the tables of Paper Patisserie are vacant once more, expectant, waiting, ready for whatever tomorrow will bring.

❧

IF YOU ENJOYED HEIDI LUCY LOSES HER MIND, please consider leaving a review! And if you'd like to stay up to date on what's next for Gracie, sign up for her newsletter here.

ACKNOWLEDGMENTS

I don't know what to write here anymore. There are too many people I love, too many people who've helped me, to list them all. So thank you to everyone, all of you, for everything you've done. Thank you to my friends and my family, who've held me up and supported me and answered my weird questions. Thank you to the bookstagram community, without which I am very sure I would have no readership. And as always, forever—to my God. I have no words, but You need none.

ALSO BY
GRACIE RUTH MITCHELL

Maid of Dishonor (Love Mishaps #1)

Say Yes to the Hot Mess (Love Mishaps #2)

Move It or Lose It (Love Mishaps #3)

Juniper Bean Resorts to Murder (Happily Ever Homicide #1)

Heidi Lucy Loses Her Mind (Happily Ever Homicide #2)

A Not-So Holiday Paradise (Christmas Escape)

Eye of the Beholder (Stone Springs #1)

City of Love (Stone Springs #2)

No Room in the Inn

Made in the USA
Middletown, DE
01 October 2023